NUMB

JOHN W. OTTE

FORT WORTH PUBLIC LIBRARY

W9-ART-108

MARCHER
LORD
PRESS

Numb by John W. Otte
Published by Marcher Lord Press
3846 Constitution Avenue
Colorado Springs, CO 80909
www.marcherlordpress.com

This book or parts thereof may not be reproduced in any form, stored in a retrieval system, or transmitted in any form by any means—electronic, mechanical, photocopy, recording, or otherwise—without prior written permission of the publisher, except as provided by United States of America copyright law.

MARCHER LORD PRESS and the MARCHER LORD PRESS logo are trademarks of Marcher Lord Press. Absence of ^{TM} in connection with marks of Marcher Lord Press or other parties does not indicate an absence of trademark protection of those marks.

This is a work of fiction. Names, characters, places, and incidents are products of the author's imagination or are used fictitiously. Any similarity to actual people, organizations, and/or events is purely coincidental.

Cover Designer: Alexander "Portugal" Rito, rito@designproject.pt
Creative Team: Jeff Gerke, Kate Dunn

Copyright © 2013 by John W. Otte
All rights reserved

The author is represented by MacGregor Literary, Inc.

Library of Congress Cataloging-in-Publication Data
An application to register this book for cataloging has been filed with the Library of Congress.
International Standard Book Number: 978-1-935929-99-4

Printed in the United States of America

For Jill

"Many women do noble things,
but you surpass them all."

1

CRUSADER PERCHED LIKE A GARGOYLE on a second floor ledge across from the safe house's entrance. He ignored the rain pouring down his face even though it blurred his vision. The weather didn't matter. Neither did his posture. God created him to execute the Ministrix's justice. Soon he would fulfill his ordained purpose.

The building across the street from him consumed his attention. It was unremarkable in its construction, a four story box made of standard terracrete. Its dull beige exterior matched that of its neighbors, making the entire block look like a row of rotten teeth. Low bushes lined the front of the building. To the untrained eye, the building would appear to be a simple apartment building or maybe an office complex. But Crusader knew better. He could see the subtle way the front entrance had been reinforced, and the forcefield emitters tucked into the windows in case of siege. No, this was no ordinary building. It was a Praesidium safe house and his prey was inside.

He fought the urge to shift. His legs could have cramped but he couldn't test them now. Numbness wrapped him in a hazy cocoon. He breathed a silent prayer, thanking the Almighty for this divine gift. Why God had made Crusader numb, he didn't know, but he had been this way for as long as he could remember. He didn't know pain. He wasn't hindered by emotions. Normally, this helped on his missions. But if he rested in one position for too long, he could stiffen up without realizing it. He needed to shift his weight, keep the blood flowing. But that wasn't an option, not now. Better to remain focused on the task.

Crusader blew water from the tip of his nose. A guard wandered by a window, not even bothering to look outside. This was the third time Crusader had seen that one. He had counted twelve guards so far. Difficult but not impossible.

Conversation drifted up from the street. A young couple strode toward the safe house, apparently unconcerned about the rain. The man nuzzled the woman's neck. She giggled, wrapping her arms around him. Her red hair was bobbed in keeping with local fashions, but her strong stride marked her as a nonnative, most likely from the Praesidium's Orion Stations.

The man's goatee, tightly trimmed, framed a wide grin that split his hawkish features. His eyes, bright and green, flashed as he laughed. If Crusader didn't know better, he'd peg him as a native. But that was why Balaam was one of the Ministrix's best agents. He could blend into any culture. Even though

Balaam knew Crusader was in the area, he didn't show any sign. His focus remained on the girl. They walked up the steps and through the front door.

Crusader leaned back. He hated working with a partner but hadn't been given a choice. Sub-Deacon Siseal, his superior, had insisted. And with a mission this important, Crusader couldn't blame him. Killing a Ministrix Deacon was unheard of and yet they had no choice.

Deacon Palti had been in charge of Ministrix Intelligence, second only to the Revered Hand himself. To rise through the ranks of the One True Church, to be examined at every ascension, and to end like this. Crusader closed down that train of thought. Distracting. Didn't need that.

The gnawing void within him grew sharper. Didn't need that either, but he couldn't avoid it. That chasm went everywhere with him, devouring him from inside his mind. If he focused on it, it raged. If he ignored it, it growled beneath his thoughts. Guilt over what he had done. Guilt that could only be stilled through obedience to the Ministrix. So the Revered Hand taught. So Sub-Deacon Siseal assured him. So Crusader believed. Killing Palti would be another step toward removing the void from his life.

An hour dripped by. His "parrot," a device perched on his shoulder, chirped. He barely heard it over the patter of raindrops, but it was enough. Without a sound, Crusader dropped from his perch and drew his blaster. He whispered to the parrot to start recording. Sub-Deacon Siseal would want proof that the job was done correctly.

There. A green flash from a second story window. Crusader slunk from the shadows to the main door. He fished a lockpicker from his pocket and pressed it to the keypad. The machine whirred. While it worked, Crusader pressed explosives on either side of the doorframe. By the time he finished, the doors hissed open.

After counting to three, Crusader dove through the opening. A pair of Praesidium guards shouted in surprise. Crusader fired and burned holes through their chests. Then he rolled across the floor and popped to his feet. Two down and they wouldn't be the last.

The safe house's foyer was deceptively empty. It appeared little more than a two meter by two meter room with an arch opposite the door. The plaster coating the walls was dingy and cracked. Crusader suspected that the arch had numerous security sensors embedded in its metal, placed to detect unauthorized entries. He strode through anyway.

A hallway stretched to his left and right. The floor was stained and pitted, the walls likewise showing a great deal of wear. He glanced to either side. Looked like a dining room to his left, a living space to his right. In front of him was a closet. He pressed himself into it as half a dozen people thundered down the hall, their voices a riot of confusion. Crusader waited. Let them gather around the bodies, close to the door. He then whispered a command to the parrot and turned his head away.

The world dissolved into a roar. He counted to three and emerged from his shelter. The door had been blown apart. Crusader surveyed the damage. Six more Praesidium agents, dead from shrapnel wounds. No survivors. Acceptable. He kicked a chunk of terracrete out of his way. His target still waited within.

He cleared the kitchen first, then proceeded to the living area. No hostiles there either. The room looked run down and decrepit, like the rest of the safe house. An open door revealed a flight of stairs. He crept up the stairs. No one opposed him. If the guards had overcome their initial panic, they had likely clustered around Deacon Palti. Crusader peeked around the corner into a deserted corridor. If Balaam's reconnaissance was right, the heretic Palti would be in a central room on that floor. He slunk out of the landing and down the hall, his arms relaxed but ready.

The cold metal of a blaster bored into the back of his neck.

"Hello, Crusader."

He knew that voice. "Hello, Kolya."

He turned, bringing the Praesidium spymaster into view. Krestyanov didn't appear to be much of a threat. He had a thick waist, with thinning raven hair and beady blue eyes. But Crusader was still impressed. A lesser man would have panicked at the sound of Crusader's entrance. Kolya Krestyanov, however, looked like he had simply rolled out of bed for a drink. The smaller man's raven hair was a bit unkempt and his beady blue eyes flashed. But he stood tall, his breathing even.

"So what brings you to Lanadon? This charming world has no Ministrix post."

"You know. Palti. He's ours."

"I don't think you're in a position to claim ownership of him, my friend. You may have made a mess downstairs, but I was ready for you, yes? This game between us ends tonight."

Kolya's eyes squinched and he held his breath. About to fire.

Crusader lashed out and swept Kolya off his feet.

The Praesidium agent fired anyway.

A tingle snaked across Crusader's cheek. He grunted. A graze. He'd have to be more careful.

Kolya rolled to the right but Crusader pounced on him and smashed his head against the floor, knocking him unconscious. A door opened behind him and Crusader spun.

Balaam raised his hands, a crooked smirk tugging at his lips.

Crusader lowered the blaster. "The girl?"

"Taken care of. She answers to the Supreme Judge now, not only for her heathen ways but also for her promiscuity." Balaam pointed to Kolya's fallen form. "What about him? Undeserved mercy does not become us."

"Could've killed me. Talked instead. That kind of stupid's good for us, bad for them. Better cover for you too."

Balaam closed his eyes. "Get on with it then."

Crusader cracked a fist across Balaam's temple. The other agent crumpled to the floor.

Standard operating procedure. If Balaam simply disappeared after an attack, the false identity he had assumed for his mission on Lanadon would be worthless. But if he appeared to be another victim, he could feed the Praesidium false information when the heathens investigated the attack, and then disappear with his cover intact.

Crusader catalogued the sounds around him: the crackle of the fire below, the hiss of communicators, the plaintive bleating of a fire alarm. Nothing to indicate he would be intercepted. He set out through a dull hallway, gaze flicking to the doors he passed. Empty rooms slid past him. He poked his head in one bedroom. The sheets had been kicked off the simple cot, as if the sleeper had been rushed. He grunted. Probably the occupant was guarding Palti.

He came to a large set of doors. Unlike the rest of the safe house, this was new construction, recently added. Crusader tapped experimentally at the lock. Sealed tight. No matter.

More charges, placed in key structural positions. Crusader ducked behind a half wall and tripped the fuse. The world dissolved in smoke and thunder. After a count of two, Crusader dove through the gaping hole.

He grunted as another tingle wormed through his shoulder. He dropped behind a counter and pressed his palm to the wound. Not too much blood, but the fight could make the injury worse. Better to finish his enemies quickly.

He leapt to his feet and tracked the first and closest target with his gun. The Praesidium guard's eyes widened as he looked at the burned hole in his chest. Crusader's arm jerked to the next. Then the third. He coolly counted through his six opponents. The lasers cut through the last just as the first collapsed to the floor.

Crusader paused, again drawing measured breaths and listening. Nothing. He rechecked the power pack. It would be enough. He stepped over one of the bodies and opened the door they had been guarding.

Palti pressed up against the far wall behind a table. Crusader stared down at the diminutive man. He looked so different without his vestments. Ensconced in his rectory within New Jerusalem Station, Palti commanded fear and respect in all who entered his lair. Now, dressed in the simple clothing of a Lanadon, he appeared frail. His wispy grey hair barely disguised the fact that he was balding. A pockmarked face surrounded rheumy eyes that squinted at him.

"Crusader?" Palti shuffled forward. "For the sake of grace, please, don't do this!"

"Have to."

"You don't. Look, they were getting ready to move me tomorrow. You can tell Siseal that you raided the house and I was already gone. Please. You and I have history together."

"Doesn't matter."

"But I can help you! I know about the guilt, don't I? We spoke of it often. I can tell you how to get rid of it, once and for all! Just spare my life and I'll tell you what I know."

Crusader regarded the sniveling man. Then he pointed to the parrot. "Recording. They know you're here. And I have to do this."

"Why?" Palti's groveling disappeared in newfound defiance. "What have I been charged with?"

"Heresy. Treason. More than enough."

"How can you be sure of any of that?"

Crusader shrugged. "You're here."

"And what if I hadn't been? You would have killed all those people for nothing."

"Not nothing. They're sinners before God and deserve what they got."

"Aren't we all?"

Crusader didn't answer. He didn't have to. They both knew the truth. A truly loyal member of the Ministrix had nothing to fear, an assurance Palti could no longer claim.

Palti sighed and stood up straighter. "I suppose there is nothing I can say to convince you, is there?"

Crusader shook his head. "No."

Palti's eyes closed and a smile tugged at his lips.

Crusader hesitated. Why would he grin at a time like this? It made no sense. But then, in the past Crusader had witnessed odd behavior from those who could feel. Irrelevant distraction.

He still wished he could know.

"Better a good Turk . . ." Palti whispered, then opened his eyes, the smile broadening a bit. "May God have mercy on you for what you're—"

Crusader snapped his arm up and fired, catching the former Deacon between the eyes. The elderly man crumpled. Crusader stared down at his dead body, making sure that the parrot got a good image to prove he had succeeded. He turned and walked back through the carnage. A brief check on Balaam. Still out. Crusader grunted. Hadn't meant to hit him so hard.

Then it was down the stairs to the ruined front door. He touched his shoulder, his cheek, dabbing at the blood. The flow had stopped. He rubbed his fingers together, spreading the fluid evenly over their tips, and stared at the crimson stain.

He paused in the ruined doorway. Taking a deep breath, he reached out and drew his palm across a jagged piece of metal. The skin tickled. He pulled his hand away, turned it over. Blood welled up in the new cut. But that was it. The tingle, the blood. Nothing more.

Crusader stared at his palm for a few seconds more before releasing his held breath. He'd known nothing would happen. He'd still had to try. He rubbed the blood onto his pant leg and stepped over the threshold, leaving the mission behind.

2

"And will you, Horatio Siseal, perform the duties of Deacon of Ministrix Intelligence to the best of your God-given abilities? Will you continue to comport your life with the same purity, chastity, and devotion that have marked you as an instrument of the Almighty's Divine Will?"

Crusader glanced up from his sketch. The hologram of Siseal's investiture filled the center of the pub. Although Siseal was only an illusion here, Crusader still got a good read on his new supervisor. Siseal wasn't as old as Palti. Tall, straight backed, almost regal in his features, he exuded steely confidence.

In the hologram, Siseal met the Revered Hand's gaze with his own cold eyes. "I shall with the help of God."

The Revered Hand stepped back. He looked somewhat frail and withered, but fire still burned in his eyes. Several Intelligence sub-deacons darted forward. Crusader recognized a few of them: abd al Sami, in charge of Research and Development; Cuvier, who headed Information Control; Ramirez, overseer of Counterintelligence. They draped Siseal with the raiments of his office: the straight iron staff, the deep blue stole, the gilded cross with ruby starburst. The transformation was complete. Siseal was now Deacon of Ministrix Intelligence and Crusader's superior.

More than that. Although it wasn't directly stated, Siseal was also the heir apparent for the Revered Hand himself. Statistics didn't lie. In the past two centuries, the Deacon of Ministrix Intelligence had taken up the mantle when a Revered Hand had died, every time but twice.

"Someone turn that junk off."

Crusader examined the crowd in the bar, locating the offending individual. An asteroid miner by the looks of him, dingy from hours in a cramped drill-suit. He and his friends crowded around a table and sneered at the holographic well in the middle of the room.

"This ain't no Ministrix post." The miner's voice was slurred from too much drink. "Who cares what Lord High Fancy-Pants there is now? Don't make a quantum's cuss worth of difference to any of us here. 'Sides, that mess happened a month ago."

Crusader rose from his booth and started for the miners' table. With each step, he prioritized his targets. Four men. An easy fight if it came to it. The one with his back to the wall would be the most dangerous. His thick arms crossed over a barrel-like chest. But he noticed Crusader's approach and averted his gaze. He wouldn't interfere.

Neither would the others. They spotted Crusader coming and nudged the complainer. The miner finally turned and looked up.

Crusader leaned in close. "I'm watching that."

Sweat erupted across the man's brow. "Then enjoy yourself, sir, as will we." With a trembling hand, he raised his glass in a salute.

Crusader fixed his gaze on each of the man's companions to ensure that none of them would attack when he turned away. Doubtful they would.

He plodded back to his seat and watched as the rest of the ceremony played out. The Revered Hand placed his hands on Siseal's bowed head and muttered inaudible words, then loudly declared him invested in his office. No one in the Cathedral of Light applauded. The occasion was too serious for that.

Crusader glanced at his waitress and signaled for a refill. She brought him the water just as Siseal began his homily, a glowing endorsement of the Ministrix's efforts to expand the reign of Christ to all civilized worlds. "The universe is His, for He made it. And it is He who founded His True Church, the Ministrix, and given us His authority. He has given us a mandate to bring all into our ranks and it is a duty we dare not shirk. While we face many obstacles within and without, we shall prevail. We must prevail. For His sharp sickle is almost in His hand and He waits for us to begin the harvest."

Siseal continued his speech but Crusader tuned him out. What Siseal said was nothing new. Crusader had heard it all before. Instead, he turned his attention to the bar. He had no mission here. But he could earn extra favor if he brought justice to a truly unrepentant sinner. The miners? No, they ignored him. The bartender? He was surely a sinner, but in no obvious ways.

Crusader's gaze fell on a young woman who entered the bar, a basket tucked under her arm. His eyes narrowed. Her clothing was just baggy enough to conceal her figure. And her hair, black as space, was barely restrained by a simple tie. A prostitute perhaps, dressed modestly to avoid detection? Crusader's fingers flexed. That wouldn't be much, but every bit helped.

No, wait. She sat at the bar, setting the basket on a stool next to her. She reached inside and fiddled with something, the edge of a rich blue blanket peeking over the edge. Tiny hands darted up toward her and she smiled, her tired expression melting to one of happiness. She turned to the bartender and spoke a few words. The man's sour face wavered. Then he sighed and stepped away. When he came back, he set a tray in front of her, a steaming bowl with two pale white biscuits. The woman said something else, her posture relaxing. Then she dove into the food, pausing occasionally to check on her child.

Crusader's fingers relaxed. Not a viable target. Yet he couldn't stop watching her. The image pricked his mind. His hand darted into his pack and pulled out his charcoal pencils and a blank sheet of paper. He drank in the way the neon illuminated her hair, creating a halo that danced as she tore off hunks of bread.

Crusader roughed out her face and her hair. He then added some gentle strokes, trying to reproduce the halo effect on the paper. He smudged one of the lines and grunted. Almost. Not quite perfect. He glanced at his subject again, letting his gaze drift across her lips, down her graceful neck. His fingers skimmed the paper, leaving delicate trails that slowly converged into the woman. Crusader leaned back, comparing his recreation with the woman.

He frowned. It was a reasonable resemblance. Yet, there was something wrong. The face was off. Something didn't fit. The nose? The shape of her eyes? What was wrong?

Needles danced down the back of his head and across his spine. He froze, focusing on the sensation. Would he finally . . . ?

No. The sensation was gone. He sighed, stashing the pencils back in his pack.

The parrot chirruped on his shoulder, indicating an incoming call. He waved his hand over the booth's privacy controls. A screen slid out of the wall and surrounded the table. The noise died and the crowd disappeared.

Crusader tapped the parrot and a hologram appeared above the table, depicting an inverted steel triangle imposed on a starfield, the symbol of the Ministrix. It took a moment for the parrot to decrypt the data stream. When it did, the logo dissolved into a severe looking man, the same one he had seen in the holographic pit a few minutes earlier.

Crusader stiffened to attention. "Deacon Siseal."

"Be at ease, Crusader. How has your leave suited you?"

"I am ready to serve, sir."

Siseal's narrow face pinched into a smirk. "As I thought. Know that the Revered Hand appreciates your aid in dealing with my predecessor. Palti surely faces a more stern Judge than any he would have in this life."

"Yes, sir."

"There are yet more who must answer for their sins in this case. You know that Palti succumbed to the most odious heresy, correct?"

It wasn't really a question, but Crusader nodded anyway. Some dared question the Ministrix's rightful role as God's chosen people, not in the way the atheistic Praesidium did. Instead, a heretical belief had spread through the lower ranks of the Ministrix. Crusader hadn't studied those beliefs in depth. That was outside his duties. But he had heard his colleagues whisper about it.

"Our analysts sifted every iota of data in Palti's files and have discovered his link to the heretics. That they dared to pollute someone so close to the Hand with their lies is an affront to us all. You must track down the one who corrupted him and eliminate her."

A woman? No problem. Crusader had carried out similar assignments in the past. A target was a target. There was no longer Jew nor Gentile, slave nor free, male nor female. All would meet justice by His hand. Crusader was merely the instrument of His wrath.

"Very good, sir. Orders?"

"You are to leave immediately for Tower Station. Inquisitor will meet you there with the mission parameters. Questions?"

Crusader hesitated. The Ministrix always provided him with sufficient information but there was one detail he wished to know immediately.

"Will I be working with a partner again?"

Siseal laughed, a hard chuckle. "No, this mission will be yours alone."

"Very good, sir."

"Do your best. Stick to the mission parameters, and you shall earn more favor."

The image blurred and vanished.

Crusader retracted the privacy screen, gathered up his belongings, and walked to the bar. He fished a credit chit out of his pocket, pressing it to the access slot to pay for his drinks. He turned to his left, meeting the gaze of the woman. She dipped her head almost immediately to avoid his gaze.

Crusader considered leaving, but hesitated. He fingered the sketch's edges. Incomplete as it was, he knew it was wrong and always would be. No reason to keep it. He walked down the length of the bar and set it before the woman.

She looked at it, and then him, with wide eyes.

"Thank you," she murmured.

Crusader waited for some sort of response within. Perhaps his heart rate would increase. Perhaps his cheeks would warm. Something. Anything.

He found only the numbness.

He turned and walked out of the bar. As he worked his way through the space port, he did the math. It would take five days to reach Tower Station by public transport. If only the Ministrix had provided a private ship for him this time. It would make his job that much easier. But surely Deacon Siseal knew how long he'd need to make it to Tower. Inquisitor would wait for his arrival. Or since Siseal arranged this, Inquisitor and Crusader would likely arrive within an hour of each other.

Didn't matter. In five days, Crusader would have his target. He hoped she would spend her last days well. Once he was on her trail, she wouldn't last long.

3

Isolda Westin slammed her wrench against the master drive intake valve and wondered if cursing it out would somehow change its mind about working. But then, this component was originally installed over fifty years ago, which made it the newest component on a ship twice as old. None of the systems were optimal. Yet she kept this antique running or suffered the captain's wrath.

She leaned against the console and caught a marred reflection of herself in the metal surface. Grime covered most of her face and her blond hair was starting to worm free of her ponytail. She leaned in closer. She looked like a green-eyed raccoon. At least, she looked like the pictures of raccoons she had seen. If she could fix the tunneler drive, maybe she'd be able to indulge in a long shower. But right now, that looked like a mighty big "if."

She tucked a stray lock of hair behind her ear and ran through the maintenance check-list again, turning to face the rest of the engineering bay, a room ten meters by five meters that was supposed to be painted a bright orange, but had long ago faded to a mottled mixture of browns and rust. Her gaze settled on the main valve access hatch. The valve was free of debris. She had cleaned it herself two weeks earlier. Her gaze skipped over the curtain that led to her berth. The problem wouldn't be there. Next up, the fuel feed display. Could it be the fuel? Their last stop had been at Loquacious Outpost. The techs at LoqOut weren't entirely honest on the purity of their deuterium. A few stray ions could trip up a tunneler drive and create a distortion. But no, the sensors indicated the mix was well within tolerances. It couldn't be that.

"Big surprise. The wobble's getting worse, Westin. What are you going to do about it?"

Isolda groaned and closed her eyes. Of course Veronica would happen through the engine room when something malfunctioned. The captain's daughter took special delight in mocking her.

A tremor rattled the deckplates and Isolda froze. Was the situation getting worse? She swallowed the butterflies flittering up her throat. Was this what happened before . . . ? She tightened her grip on the wrench. She couldn't lose it now, especially not in front of Veronica.

The skinny moron flounced down the stairs and leaned against a console, accidentally resetting three different systems.

The ship's shimmy became more pronounced. Isolda gritted her teeth. As if she didn't have enough work as it was.

She glanced at Veronica then immediately looked away. The teenager wore a tight jumpsuit that appeared painted on. Slashes of clear material showed off generous portions of her skin. Isolda had seen a lot of girls wear similar outfits at her last Praesidium port of call. That didn't surprise her. No one in the Praesidium seemed to care. She wondered why she stayed within Praesidium space. Loose morals, shady ethics, and the so-called Toleration Act kept her life in constant danger.

But even the Praesidium was better than living in the Ministrix.

"You know, Daddy says he's gonna ditch you at Tower when we get there. He says he's never seen a more incompetent engineer."

Isolda popped open a hatch and ducked her head inside. No broken connections in the inertial subsystems. The warble wasn't coming from there. Another intense tremor rumbled through the ship. Isolda froze and held her breath. The vibration faded but her heart kept racing. She had to find the cause soon before . . . No. She wouldn't think about that. Not now.

"And I have to agree."

Isolda jumped, banging the back of her head on the hatch cover.

Veronica giggled and twirled away. "At least the last three were interesting. Or cute. You, though, you're nothing but nebular trash. Have been since the day you were born. Why else would your parents have abandoned you?"

Isolda bit her cheek. Warmth dotted her eyes. As if she needed another reminder of her mother. Her grip tightened on the wrench. Maybe she could jostle the feed a bit, make the shimmy worse. Then she could "trip" and smack Veronica with the tool. Sure, she might get in trouble, but she could claim it was an accident.

No, she couldn't. More than that, she shouldn't. She knew better. Revenge didn't belong to her. She shut the hatch.

"You might as well call Daddy now and tell him the truth." Veronica inspected the back of her fingernails. "You don't have any idea what's wrong with the tunneler aperture, so why not just toss in the towel and call it a day? You could spend the time packing."

Isolda frowned. The aperture? What did that have to do with anything? A sneaking suspicion sent Isolda over to the display panels. Veronica went still, confirming Isolda's hunch. Sure enough, the tunneler aperture was misaligned. Not by much, only a few microns. But that could easily set up a harmonic feedback through the other systems, like the master drive intake valve.

A few keystrokes realigned the magnetic inducers to optimal and the shimmy died. Isolda turned to Veronica and fixed her with an angry glare.

Veronica wilted, then stuck out her chin. "I'm still telling Daddy you took too long to fix it."

Isolda clenched her fists and swallowed the retort that bubbled up her throat. She should verbally eviscerate the little brat, threaten to tell her mother or something. While Captain Tisdal pretended like he was in charge, everyone knew that his wife held the real power. If she heard what Veronica had done, there was a good chance she'd come down on her daughter like a comet impacting a planet.

But no, Isolda couldn't do that. Not really. There was some truth to what Veronica said. She *had* taken too long to diagnose the problem. If Veronica hadn't let slip what she did, Isolda might never have fixed it. It was her fault for not spotting the issue and correcting it right away. Besides, if she said anything, there was a good chance Veronica would keep arguing, and that was the last thing Isolda wanted. She bowed her head and hoped she looked sufficiently defeated.

Veronica smirked and flounced out of the engine room.

Isolda sighed and went to work resetting the rest of the systems. It didn't take long. A tweak there, a minor adjustment there and soon, the engines were running at peak efficiency. Or at least what passed for peak efficiency. She sighed. Crisis averted. The panic drained out of her.

She plopped down in her chair and called up her personal messages. She hadn't had a chance to check them since they left Beniz Prime three days earlier. Most were routine: a newsletter from the engineering guild, a few low paying job offers.

She smiled when she saw the name on one. Gavin Odell. She called it up and her friend's pudgy face appeared over the holo-emitter.

"Hey, Isolda! You would not believe the week I've had. If I had known that accepting that promotion would lead to this many headaches, I probably wouldn't have taken it." He laughed, a reedy snicker. "Who am I kidding? I still would have. The money's not bad and I'm getting a bit more respect." His features darkened. "Not as much as when . . . well, I suppose I'm not supposed to talk about that, am I?" He brightened and smiled. "Sorry. Where was I?"

And so it went, ten minutes of random stories about people she didn't know. She closed her eyes and let her friend's voice wash over her.

". . . and naturally, the jerk blamed me even though I warned him that zero-g basketball wasn't for someone with vertigo problems. Look, I gotta wrap this up. Uh . . . remember that voucher I sent you for the free cabin? The offer's still good. Just let me know you're coming and I'll make sure to roll out the red carpet. I mean, Pearson Lines isn't the greatest of the luxury liner companies, but the *Sybaritic* really isn't all that bad. Hope to hear from you soon."

The image faded. Isolda almost closed down the system but stopped when she noticed the subject line of one particular job offer: "Beyond Tunnel Space." Could it be . . . ? Opening the message revealed what appeared to be a corrupted image file.

Isolda glanced around the engineering bay. Even if Veronica didn't come back, someone else might wander through. But it looked like she was going to be left alone for a little while longer.

Isolda called up the raw data. She quickly found the pattern of incorrect numbers about two-thirds of the way in. She set to work, substituting a few integers here and there until the hologram resolved into an older gentleman with white bushy eyebrows that seemed to have scared the rest of his hair away from them.

"Uh, is this on? Confounded contraption, can never tell when it's recording." He squinted up at her. "Hello, Isolda? Oh, dear. I wish you were here. The research is going well enough. I've made a few breakthroughs but I'm sure you remember those studies released by . . . what was his name again? Well, no matter. But the lab is a mess and I haven't had a decent meal in months. I know Elata's people do their best but they're not as good as you.

"I do wish you would come back. No one blames you for what happened. At least, could you maybe send me a message and let me know you're okay?"

The image disappeared. Isolda leaned back in her chair and swiped at her eyes. She missed Dr. Keleman, even if he had never been satisfied with her cooking. At least there was one person in the universe who cared whether she lived or died.

4

"**Thank you for traveling** with Dasras Lines." The steward flashed a smile that was all teeth. "Please remember us for your next journey."

Crusader's fingers clenched into a claw, perfect to fit around the man's neck. First the liner had been delayed leaving Matrika because some moron failed to submit the proper departure permits. Then the tunneler drive failed two days into the journey, stranding them for hours while the engineers made repairs. And finally, the liner had been put on low priority status when they arrived at Tower Station. While most of the passengers had enjoyed watching the various ships coming and going from the massive deep space station, each second had weighed heavier and heavier on Crusader. All told, the blunders added up to a full day's delay.

But it wasn't the steward's fault. Crusader nodded to the young man and stepped out of the docking port and lined up for the customs queue, a line that snaked through an octagonal corridor made of brightly burnished metal. He paused as the various sensors probed him for hidden weapons. They wouldn't find any, but he tensed anyway, ready to fight if something went wrong.

Next, it was a cursory questioning by a bored-looking woman wearing a Tower Security uniform, a blue and white jumpsuit with a chess rook over her heart. He kept his answers short and simple, making sure he made eye contact with her.

She let him through to a larger room, a wide circle with eight different elevators cut into the walls. In the center of the room was a pillar with public data terminals. He shouldered his way past other passengers to the nearest terminal. Crusader called up a resident search queue. He scanned the recent arrivals list until he spotted a name. Bernard Gui. A few more keystrokes brought up Gui's private comm channel. Crusader tapped out a brief message: "Arrived." Within a second, a return reply appeared on the screen, naming an art gallery in the entertainment district.

Crusader shoved his way to a lift and rode it deeper into Tower Station. When the doors parted, he was met by a garish barrage of lights and colors, accompanied by too much noise. He strode out into the District. To his left and right were four stories of storefronts, all of them facing the open air. A cursory examination revealed half a dozen shops for consumer electronics, along with the usual holovid dispensaries and restaurants. Crusader wove through the traffic on the main floor, which snaked around kiosks where local merchants hawked their wares. Like most trans-tunneler stations, Tower did its best to entice travelers to stay and waste money they didn't have on things they didn't need. Most of Tower's permanent residents were trapped here by their debt. It was a diabolical system, for they could never be truly free. Even as they worked to pay off their accounts, the amount only went up.

Sadly, Tower Station did not have a Ministrix mission. Crusader knew that the administration made hefty donations both to the True Church and their opposites in the Praesidium to remain neutral in the on-going conflict. The Revered Hand allowed them to maintain their illusion. Eventually, though, the Ministrix would bring Tower under its control as it would the rest of humanity.

Crusader walked through the milling crowd, ignoring the hawkers who tried to bring him into their establishments, especially the women who flaunted themselves in a vain attempt to seduce him. The rainbow lights of the marquees almost drowned out the gallery toward the back. Crusader sidled into the room.

Garish holographic art hovered in-between knots of patrons. A few physical sculptures but not many. Even some paintings. Crusader wished he could examine the art. Maybe after the mission. He looked over the crowd again. No one seemed overtly interested in him.

All except for the man in the back. He stood before a two-dimensional image, a data reader tucked under his left arm. The man scratched his head with his right hand while looking to his left at another display. He coughed twice and thrust his hips to the right. All clear. Crusader crossed the room to his side. He stared at the horrible holographic art that hung in the air before them, a badly rendered image of two women sharing a cup of tea. This was art?

"Bernard," he said.

"Henry," the man replied. "The flight was not enjoyable?"

"No."

"A pity." Inquisitor stepped back. "I'm afraid I must go. But please, use my room. Habitation Sector C, number 204. Best hurry, my friend. There isn't much time."

With that, his fellow agent disappeared. Inquisitor would no doubt be on the next transport away from Tower. While he was skillful in setting up missions and ferreting out valuable information, Inquisitor never got his hands dirty.

Crusader waited fifteen minutes and then left. He did his best to remain unhurried, but if things were as tight as Inquisitor made it sound, it would be best to learn about the target and prep himself for the mission.

C-204 lay deep within the station, close enough to the main power plant to pick up a severe vibration in its floor plates. The room was little more than a bed, a bathroom, and a data terminal that flickered with advertisements for the station's amenities. He set his parrot on the bed and activated its scan mode. Lights blinked across its perimeter and then an arrow appeared, indicating a corner of the terminal. Crusader ran his hand along the bottom edge. He pulled away a data chip.

He rolled the device, smaller than a pea, between thumb and forefinger. No irregularities he could detect, meaning it hadn't been touched since Inquisitor left it. He set it on top of the parrot. The lights twinkled around the rim and a hologram sprang to life over the bed, a generic computer construct of a human face wearing a blank expression.

"Greetings, Agent Crusader. Your mission parameters are as follows:

"Target is currently working on board the *Regent's Light*, a Class 4V-JOL ore freighter en route to your position. At present time, she will arrive in eight hours. Confirm: Target acquisition in eight hours."

"Confirmed. Eight hours." Crusader once again considered going back to kill the liner captain but that would cut too much away from his already limited prep time. And the death would only stir up the locals. That wouldn't help.

"With the departure of Inquisitor, you will be the only Ministrix agent on board Tower. Confirm: You will be without backup."

"Confirmed," Crusader said. "No backup."

The construct squinted its monochrome eyes. "Deacon Siseal has mandated the sinner know justice is upon her. So must those around her. To that end, you must conduct this mission at close range and in a public place. Confirm: You must reveal yourself prior to the kill."

What was this? Given the neutrality of Tower station, it would be better to conduct any sort of operation at long range. He was a proficient sniper. Or maybe a bomb. The target would be just as dead. Why risk exposure?

"Confirm: You must reveal yourself prior to the kill."

Worse, with only eight hours to prep, his exit would be all the more difficult. He'd barely have enough time to scout the area and plan the kill. A subtle assassination would allow him to blend into the crowd and leave later. But if he was seen, the authorities would be after him. He might have to fight his way free. Not that the prospect of killing more people worried him;

all fell short of the glory of God and deserved whatever they received. But it was a logistical nightmare.

The parrot blatted at him and the construct's serene face flushed purple. "Possible compromise. Due to failure to confirm, Agent Crusader marked as noncompliant and will be reported to Deacon—"

"Confirm: I must reveal myself."

The construct faded to blue. "Mission briefing complete. Dossier unlocked. God's blessings upon your day."

With that, the face spun apart, dissolving into a cascade of text. The *Regent's Light* would dock at Upper Pylon Seven in eight hours.

Crusader frowned. Would the target leave the ship? Hard to say. He called up the station's docking schedule on his room's terminal. The *Regent's Light* was scheduled to depart again eighteen hours later. If the ship needed repairs, the target might not disembark. Had to get her somewhere he could finish her.

A whispered command sent the data scurrying away. The parrot pulled up the target's biographical data. Isolda Westin, age 24. Engineer aboard the *Light*. Not much by way of history but then, Crusader didn't need to know her life's story to kill her. He shuffled past all of it and called up her image.

When he saw her blonde hair and pale green eyes, his chest tightened. Strange tingles danced across his arms and the back of his legs. He wondered if there had been a power conduit rupture in the room. It would take a plasma burn to evoke that much feeling across his skin.

But no, the room was fine, simply bathed in the light of Isolda Westin's image. His legs couldn't hold his weight. Crusader fell to his knees. He stared into her eyes as a shudder ran up his spine. What was going on? Was he sick?

Maybe the room had been compromised. Could be a neurological agent of some kind. He fumbled for the parrot and called up a security sweep. The device chittered and bathed the room in a green light, deep scanning the surroundings for any sort of weapon, field, gas, toxin, anything that could explain his odd reaction.

While it worked, Crusader took several deep breaths and closed his eyes. The strange symptoms faded, swallowed up by the numb. The parrot reported the room was secure and safe. No problem. Probably just a burst of adrenaline. Happened sometimes. Back to work.

He called up Westin's biography again and set the parrot on the bed. Best to start planning. Envision the process and let God be glorified through the results. He would lie in wait outside the lifts to the Entertainment District. When Westin emerged, he would follow her into the flow of human traffic, eventually overtake her on a parallel course. Make sure she saw him coming. Then . . . what? A gun? No. A knife. He had one in his pack he preferred using. Well balanced, sharp, it had served him well in the past. He would draw it, let it catch the light, and then . . . and then . . .

The void exploded in his mind. He tumbled out of his vision. Just as he pictured Westin's eyes widening with horror, he couldn't go on. The thought of touching her with the blade, marring her perfect skin . . . The guilt shredded his mind, conjuring up images of smoke and sound of distant sirens.

His stomach bubbled and his hands shook. He fell back, scuttling away from the image until he hit the opposite wall. What was happening to him? Was he sick? Perhaps, but his numbness usually mitigated the symptoms. Heat crawled from his scalp to his soles, followed quickly by icy needles.

Crusader tried to focus again. The mission. Ignore the rest. Visualize the . . . the result. He had to do this. Failure meant adding to his guilt. He had to do this or he would never be free.

No.

He couldn't do it. He couldn't force himself past the mental block. He couldn't still the confusing storm that raged within him. He only knew two things for certain: first, he knew he couldn't kill Isolda Westin.

And if he didn't, he was as good as damned.

5

Crusader spent half an hour lying in his room before he regained control of himself. Try as he might, he couldn't picture the killing blow. That in and of itself wasn't a problem. He had learned long ago that a mission never went exactly according to plan. There had to be room for improvisation. But he had a job to do. He couldn't remain paralyzed forever.

Steps. That was the best course. His instructors had taught him any task could be broken down. A complex mission would overwhelm a lesser agent because he only saw the sheer size of it. But the same mission could be dealt with in smaller pieces.

First step: He hacked the database for the corporation that owned the freighter and planted orders for Isolda Westin to report to their sector headquarters upon arrival. That would bring her through the Entertainment District where he could make the kill according to the Deacon's wishes.

Second step: He walked the route, scouting it for an initial observation post, the approach local authorities might take, and for an escape vector.

Third: He booked passage on three different transports leaving from docking bays on opposite ends of the station. If the mission didn't go smoothly, he'd be able to make it to at least one of them.

Fourth: he tried a dry run through the mission. He hid in his perch. He shadowed an unsuspecting tourist. But when he reached the point of the kill, he froze again. Cold sweat sluiced across his body and he retreated down an exit vector, fighting the urge to actually leave Tower.

He returned to his quarters and called up the target's dossier again. According to the data collected by Siseal's subordinates, Westin was responsible for Palti's collapse into heresy. Ministrix analysts hypothesized she'd worked aboard a Praesidium vessel eighteen months earlier, one that had hosted a summit between the Ministrix and their rivals. Palti's personal shuttle had broken down. Westin had been assigned to fix it. She must have corrupted him then.

A heinous crime, an affront to both the Almighty Lord and His Ministrix. Isolda Westin deserved punishment.

Crusader called up the holographic image of Westin and once again slammed into the same mental block. As Crusader looked into her image's eyes, he felt lighter. His heart threatened to leap up his throat, followed by his breakfast.

He had to kill her. He couldn't murder her. Torn between two impossibilities, he finally went to his observation point and waited. She would be there soon enough.

The lockdown signal warbled through the *Regent's Light* corridors. Isolda sighed. In spite of Veronica's "tweaks," they had made it to Tower on time. Predictably, Captain Tisdal still blustered about Isolda's stupidity. He even threatened to deduct any damage to their cargo from her pay. It was a hollow threat. The shipping guild wouldn't stand for it, but Tisdal would still try. And if he didn't succeed, he'd take it out on her on the next trip.

Isolda went to her quarters, such as they were. Little more than a small closet separated from the rest of the engine bay by a curtain. Tisdal claimed the arrangement allowed his engineer to be close to her work. In reality, the crew could paw through her meager belongings whenever her back was turned.

She stuffed her belongings into a rucksack. Even if she didn't request a new post, there was no way she'd leave any of this for the station techs to steal. There wasn't much. Personal data reader. Two grease-stained jumpsuits. That was it.

She took the passageway from the engineering bay to the main crew deck. She waved to a few of her crewmates and then headed for the exit port.

Captain Tisdal glared at all of the outgoing crew, nodding to some, intensifying his scowl for others. When he saw Isolda, his features became particularly twisted.

Isolda resisted the urge to stick out her tongue at him. Although it would be gratifying, it would also guarantee her the need for a new post.

"Westin, stop," he said.

She halted in her tracks then turned to face him.

"Orders for you. You're to report to sector headquarters immediately."

"Why?"

"I'm sure I can't tell you." Tisdal sneered at her. "Believe me, I haven't yet had the opportunity to submit an incident report regarding your incredible incompetence. But if you've performed just as poorly in your other postings, I suspect your ineptitude has caught up with you."

Isolda bristled at his harsh words. She should really stand up for herself, say something. Reveal how it was all Veronica's fault. But no, the Captain was right: She should have caught the sabotage earlier. She was lucky they hadn't been late. Then the entire crew would have been penalized and it would have all been her fault. Just like last time.

The captain flicked his gaze over her, then sniffed. "Best be on your way."

Isolda mechanically marched out through the ship's airlock, a rectangular room painted a garish shade of orange with black lines bordering the walls and ceilings.

Then it was through to Tower's main commercial dock. It was little more than a long corridor, fifteen feet high. The walls had probably been shiny silver at one point, but now patches of corrosion tarnished the effect. The floor was little more than grating that kept people from walking on the power conduits below. Every thirty meters was a door that led to another ship. Thankfully, there weren't many people in the dock itself, just the *Regent Light*'s crew and a half dozen others from a smaller vessel.

As she headed for the door that led to the rest of Tower Station, Isolda wracked her brain. So far as she knew, none of her former employers had cause for complaint. Maybe it was routine. Her gut tightened. Of course it wasn't. Who was she kidding? Something else was about to go horribly wrong.

"Can't You give me a break for once?" she muttered under her breath. Of course, no answer came. Why would it? She reslung her pack over her shoulder and trudged through the dock. Might as well get it over with.

She crossed the threshold. Bold signs warned her she was now in the station's jurisdiction. Petty station managers always flaunted their authority. She made her way through customs and then found a Station schematic. According to the diagram, she had to go through the Entertainment District to reach sector headquarters. She waited for a free lift and then rode it down.

The doors opened and a musty odor washed over her, stale sweat mixed with burning meat. The warbling buzz of hundreds of voices scratched her ears. She winced. The Station's air filters obviously weren't working. She would have to wade through the human sea after all. Squaring her shoulders, she dove in and fought the current, trying not to be swept from her feet.

If she hadn't been so annoyed, she might have taken the time to gawk at the people around her. While she had traveled throughout the Praesidium and even skirted the fringes of the Ministrix, she had never seen so many different people. A family from the Erstwhile Cluster scampered past her, their colorful clothing setting off a riot behind her eyes. Three silky Positon matriarchs haggled with a local merchant, clearly trying to overwhelm him with their combined pheremones. She even thought she saw a glimpse of a cyborg, although why one of them would have left the Hive was beyond her. So much diversity on display, and this was just a deep space station. She could barely imagine what a planetary city would contain. Humanity had changed so much since they'd spread out through the galaxy. It was sometimes hard to remember that they were all the same at the core.

Her gaze fell on one man in particular. He stood out of the crowd like a nova at night. Bright green eyes, auburn hair. He had been staring at her. Now, though, he studied a merchant's wares on a freestanding kiosk. She tugged her sack close. Probably just a thief looking for an easy mark. Nothing to be worried about.

There she was.

Crusader took a moment to study her. He had memorized her features from the hologram but there was always a disconnect between a recording and reality. Sure enough, there were subtle differences. Her hair was longer, her face leaner. Westin adjusted the strap of her pack, squared her shoulders, and stepped into the crowd.

He slipped from his post. Instead of walking into the crowd, she had taken a moment to assess it. But she didn't pause for too long before heading through the District. She was cautious. Observant. But not hesitant. Bad. She might spot his approach. He would have to be careful.

Crusader stepped behind a lumbering Benizan merchant headed in the same direction. She wasn't enough to truly hide behind, but Crusader only wanted her to screen his approach.

Sure enough, the merchant moved on a parallel course with Westin. Only a matter of time now.

"Watch it."

Isolda backed up, allowing the cyborg man to brush past her, his implants whirring and clicking with every step. A sharp corner of the man's battle armor caught her pack, tearing the fabric. Her reader clattered to the deck, spilling data chits across the metal. Isolda groaned and dropped to her knees, scooping them up.

She was able to snare the close ones quickly enough. But a passerby kicked one and sent it skittering across the floor. Isolda glanced around for an open pathway and then crawled after it.

Then her gaze fell on the man she had spotted before. He looked away quickly but she was sure he had been staring at her again. Ice pooled in her stomach and she scooped up the stray chit and rushed back to her belongings. The faster she could get to the sector headquarters, the better.

Had she spotted him? Crusader hunkered down behind the merchant. He counted to ten then peeked over the merchant's shoulder. Westin shoved her data reader back into her pack. Then she started through the crowd again, only this time at a much faster pace.

He abandoned his cover, stepping around the merchant and moving into the crowd. There was no longer a reason to hide.

Her time had come. Judgment was upon her. He slid his right hand into his sleeve. His fingers brushed the knife's hilt . . .

His heart slammed into his ribs and the breath exploded from his lungs. No! Not now. His knees weakened and he stumbled, jostling an Erstwhile man. The Erstwhiler spun, his fists coming up and his jaw jutting out, but Crusader scowled at him. Thankfully, that was enough to dissuade the man.

Crusader wiped away sweat from his brow and forced his legs to keep moving. He couldn't stop. Not when Westin was so close.

The prey stumbled into a small crowd clumped around a merchant hawking supposedly legal wares. When she tried to step left, two people blocked her path as they joined the growing audience. She turned right, only to stop short as a few peeled away from the knot of bodies.

Trembling fingers pulled his knife free. Crusader shut his eyes. Deep breath. Her scent drifted through him, citrus chased by cinnamon.

No! Ignore the distraction. Eyes open. Ready for the kill.

Crusader raised the knife over his shoulder. Someone, a woman, shouted behind him. Good. That should get the target's attention. Another breath. Release. Bring the knife down into her chest as she turned.

As he expected, Westin turned to face him. Her gaze darted to the knife in his hand and her eyes widened. Her mouth started to open, maybe to scream or beg for mercy. Crusader tensed his arm, ready to drive the blade home and . . .

Can't.

His arm dropped to his side. He gasped, his eyes burning. "Look out!"

Who shouted? Crusader whirled to his right in time to see the blaster leveled on him. His mind snapped into focus. He dropped. Heat singed the top of his head, a spike of pain that dissolved into the familiar tingle. The numbness was back.

A scream. A shriek. Now the whole crowd roared. Burnt flesh assaulted his nostrils. Someone had been hit. Bystander. Crusader dove away. Where was Westin? No sign of her. Same with his attacker. They had both vanished into the retreating crowd.

His face settled into a stony mask. Had Siseal really called this a simple assignment? Should have known. That usually meant complications. No matter. He would find Westin and her savior. And once the latter was dead, he would . . .

His mind hitched and he winced. Why had he hesitated? No, couldn't stop now. Just one more complication. He would deal with it. And then Westin would be dead. This time, for sure.

6

Isolda's rescuer pulled her out of the fleeing crowd and into a small alcove near an entrance to the District. He pushed her in as far as she could go, holding her in place with his free hand while he peeked around the corner. Dozens of people stampeded past their little safe haven, each of them shrieking or babbling in fright.

She struggled to catch her breath. What had happened? That man had been going to stab her! But the shout, the shot, then chaos as everyone fled the District. She had almost been trampled, only to have this man snare her hand and pull her to safety.

He turned back to her, favoring her with a warm but tense smile. "I think we're okay for now."

She gaped at him. He was handsome, that was the first thing she noticed, with sparkling green eyes and wavy auburn hair. He stood at least a foot taller than her and had broad shoulders. Wait. He was the man she had spotted earlier, the one she'd thought had been following her! "Who are you? What are you—"

He held up a hand. "No time for that now. We have to get you to safety."

His words slammed into her stomach like a fist. "Me? What do you mean?"

"Do you know who that man was?"

She shook her head. The man laughed, a rueful bark.

"You're lucky. He's called Crusader. He's one of the Ministrix's top assassins and, from what I understand, he's after you."

Another blow, this one made of ice. The cold crept from her stomach, up her spine and down the back of her legs. "Me? But why?"

He shook his head. "I don't know."

She collapsed against the wall, staring at her rescuer's chest. His broad chest. Her pack fell from her shoulder into a heap on the floor. He chuckled, warmth radiating from his green eyes.

"Don't worry, Isolda. I'm here to protect you."

"You are?" She could barely hear her own whisper.

He nodded. "Clark Hollister, Praesidium Intelligence, at your service. Now, come on. We've got to get you out of here."

He held out his hand. She hesitated but then took it. He smiled and a jolt shot through her chest. He led her from their hiding place and back into the crowd. This time, though, the riotous noise seemed miles away. All she had to do was focus on the man holding her hand.

Steps. Crusader didn't know where Westin or his attacker went. He didn't even know if they were together. He could search for them but that would waste valuable time. They could slip away all too easily. He had to limit their options, box them in.

He stepped over the corpse of the shot man and headed to the nearest security station. Six officers emerged from their den, dressed in armor and clutching laser rifles. No threat. Half held their weapons too tightly, close to their chests. Their eyes practically leapt free from their faces. Only one showed any resolve. He would have to be dealt with first.

"Sir, are you all right?"

Crusader back-handed him, dropping him to the deck. He stepped over his groaning body and scooped up the rifle. The guards' leader turned, giving Crusader an easy shot at his exposed jaw. He took it, the laser blast obliterating the bottom half of the guard's face.

The rest of the guards were easy prey, thrown into a near panic at the loss of their commanding officer. He fired two quick shots at the nearest guards. The laser sliced through a knee and a hip, sending the men down to the deck. He tried to fire at the next, but the weapon refused to work. Crusader glanced at the power readout. Spent already? He frowned. Sloppy work. He flipped the rifle around and cracked it across the third guard's head and he crumpled. The last died as Crusader slipped his knife through an exposed joint in his armor. The blade pulled free with a wet sound and the young man collapsed. He dropped the rifle next to their bodies and kept moving.

Crusader strode into the station. He looked over the displays and nodded. The fools had left the system unencrypted. He sat behind a console and called up the security protocols. The internal scanners revealed that most of the fleeing crowd hadn't made it out of the District. Good.

A few quick commands ordered the District's containment system activated. With a distant grind, the metal slabs slid into place, sealing off the District from the rest of the station.

Somehow, Clark managed to worm his way through the cluster of people around the District exit. Isolda clung to his hand tightly as he dragged her along. Why weren't these people leaving? Sure, the doors weren't wide enough to let them all out at once, but they should have—

Then she understood. The exit had been sealed by a wall of metal, one bordered by yellow and black stripes. Someone had tripped the emergency blast doors.

Clark's shoulders fell. "Not good. This is not good."

He tugged at her arm and led her back through the crowd, no easy task. But somehow, Clark cajoled his way to the back.

"What's going on?" Isolda asked.

"One of two things. First, there could be an atmospheric breach somewhere in the District. But since we're not suffocating, I think it's more likely that Crusader's tripped the containment system. Come on, we have to get to a security station."

He pulled her through the crowd. She buffeted past far too many panicked individuals. A hot spike of guilt stabbed at her chest. This was her fault. None of them would be in this situation if it wasn't for her. Now more people would be injured thanks to her. Just like last time.

"Why me?" she asked.

Clark glanced over his shoulder at her. "It's hard to say. The Ministrix's logic is inscrutable at times. You must know something they don't want getting out. Why else would they send Crusader after you? Why else would they alert all their operatives in this sector to watch for you?"

Now the hot spike flared into full-blown terror. "You mean there are more of them?"

"Not here, no. Just Crusader. But he's the worst of the bunch." He squeezed her hand tight. "Never fear, Isolda. Once we deal with him, we'll get you out. And then we'll figure out what they're after."

Crusader set his parrot on the console, whispering a command to the device. It accessed the security system and uploaded an encryption algorithm into the containment program. Once it was done, only he would be able to open the doors.

While it worked, Crusader busied himself with some minor clean up. He deleted the surveillance footage of the botched attack and inserted a block so his next steps would go unrecorded as well.

He checked the parrot. Still working. Next he pulled up the scanners. Six hundred people clustered around the exits. No problem. He had recognized Westin's data reader as a Nimotech Omega Array. Nimotech was subsidized by Ministrix

Intelligence. Every Nimotech device had backdoor codes that allowed Ministrix agents the ability to access and track them.

Not only that, but Crusader also had recognized his attacker's weapon: an Immerson-950 limited series with a flash-damper cone. While there were probably a lot of Immerson weapons on Tower, the cone wasn't standard issue and had surely cost him extra. The rare materials used in its manufacture would stand out like a beacon on the security scanners.

He fed in the parameters for the search. A moment later, he had them. Someone carrying a Nimotech data reader was with another person armed with the Immerson flash-damper cone. The scanners put them within six meters of a security substation. He nodded. His trap could work.

"Parrot, scramble security protocols for every door except—" His gaze flicked to the nearby terminal. "—U-7. Create a breachable encryption with a three minute delay. Execute."

The parrot chirruped. Crusader scooped up the device and affixed it to his shoulder. There was a weapons locker next to the entrance, stocked with half a dozen laser rifles. He pulled one from its charger and slung it over his shoulder. Time to finish the hunt.

Isolda glanced down the corridor, unsure of what or who she was looking for exactly. Clark had told her to "keep watch" while he worked with the security interface, but she wasn't sure what he expected her to do. He had the gun. She was armed with a limp travel bag. She doubted that it would make an effective weapon against this Crusader.

She glanced at Clark. He was bent over the terminal, his brow furrowed. He mouthed silent curses as he tapped away. He looked up at her and then froze. But the tension in his face quickly dissolved and he winked at her. She turned quickly away, a tiny thrill slinking up her spine.

"We may have a problem," Clark said. "Crusader's good. A little too good. He's got us locked out of every door and his encryption is . . . well, it's unbeatable."

"Then we're trapped?" She winced at the squeak in her voice. Smooth. Really smooth.

"Did I say that? The encryption wasn't completely set on door U-7. It took me a while, but the door's open. That's our way out."

Isolda looked back at the still sealed door. A broad stripe of crimson labeled it J-5. She groaned. "That's on the other end of the District!"

Firm yet gentle hands turned her around. She found herself face to face with Clark, so close she could feel his breath on her cheek. "Listen to me. We're going to make it, okay? I won't let anything bad happen to you."

He leaned forward. His sheer proximity set off a riot of sparks that jangled up her spine and exploded in her mind.

"Do you trust me?" he whispered.

She closed her eyes as warmth trickled down her scalp and pooled in her feet. "I do."

He squeezed her hand. "Then come on. Let's get out of here."

Crusader waited. He had found a new perch, a thick ventilation pipe that ran along one wall, and observed the now deserted District. Rotating red lights painted the walls and an alarm klaxon signaled the doors had been sealed. He shifted to one side, glancing up toward the J-sector doors. No sign of his quarry yet. No matter. He could wait.

A Positon matriarch poked her head out of a shop's door and looked around. After a few seconds, she darted out into the empty corridor, running for the nearest exit. He let her go. A distraction. He couldn't let it ruin his mission.

Breathe. In through the nose. Out through the mouth. Focus on the steps. Ignore the tremble that rattled his skull. Ignore the curdling in his stomach and the way it bled through his chest. Ignore the void as it clawed at his back and roared in his ears. He had to finish the mission.

There. Westin and her rescuer emerged from one of the corridors that should have led out of the District. He hefted the rifle, sighted down the barrel on Westin, and placed his finger on the trigger. A little pressure and the mission would be over.

But no. Not like this. He had his orders. *You must conduct this mission at close range and in a public place.* The words thrummed in his mind. In some ways, he had already failed. While many had witnessed his first attempt, no one would be around to see him succeed. He shouldn't compound his failure.

He slung the rifle over his shoulder and drew his knife. With one more deep breath, he dropped from his perch.

An immense figure dropped down halfway across the District. Isolda stifled a shriek. Clark quickly stepped between her and Crusader. She peeked over her rescuer's shoulder to study the assassin.

In many ways, he was unremarkable. Tall and well-toned but not too muscular. Dead blue eyes straddled a pug nose in the middle of a square face. His closely cropped black hair barely covered his scalp. She realized that in any other circumstance, she probably would have walked by him without a second look.

But now he held her attention all too well. Especially the six inch knife in his hand. He started forward in a slow, even stride.

Clark pushed her back a step. "Keep behind me," he whispered. "I'll take care of him."

"Hands where I can see them." Crusader's voice was little more than a growl, but it sent a wave of chills across Isolda's arms.

Clark did as he was told, holding his arms out to his side, his palms open and facing Crusader. In a motion so quick it barely registered, Clark pulled his gun from his waistband and fired. The laser sliced through Crusader's chest. The man stood, his face the same inscrutable mask, but he dropped to his knees. His hand touched to his chest. Then he collapsed to the deck.

Clark motioned for her to stay put. "Let me go make sure he's dead. Stay here."

With that, he started toward Crusader's prone body. She clasped her hands together. *Let this be over with, Lord. Let it be over.*

The strength leaked out of Crusader. Poured, more like. He couldn't breathe. Punctured lung? Hard to say. Bleeding . . . more problematic. The sticky wetness spread beneath him. Not enough to cause death, but he doubted the one who shot him would let him recover.

How had he not seen the shot coming? Westin's rescuer had moved so fast, as if he had somehow willed the weapon into existence. Drawing a weapon that quickly indicated extensive training. He had assumed the rescuer had been just another bystander. Stupid assumption, stupid mistake. A fatal one.

He tried to push himself up but his arms didn't cooperate. He sucked in a tight breath, ignoring the tingling storm in his chest. He had to move. He had to finish the mission.

A foot nudged his body. He tried to grab it but his arm swung wildly, missing his target. Someone laughed. Crusader frowned. He knew that voice.

"So sorry, my friend."

The foot shoved him onto his back. The glaring lights blinded him, but his vision cleared. And he found himself staring into the face of Balaam, his fellow agent.

7

Crusader's mind locked. Balaam? Here? Trying to kill him? Protecting the target?

"We all have our orders," Balaam whispered. "It is nothing personal."

Of course it wasn't. Crusader understood that. But he had his orders, as well. He tightened his grip on the knife. Balaam's gaze flicked in Westin's direction. Crusader slammed the blade down into the other agent's foot.

Balaam howled. Crusader rolled and bowled into Balaam's shins, tripping the other agent. Crusader lunged for the gun but came up short, his blood-slicked fingers staining Balaam's coat.

Isolda knelt behind an overturned kiosk. The two men wrestled for Clark's gun. He had told her to stay back, but should she? Even though this Crusader person was badly injured, he apparently still had a lot of strength. How could she cower when Clark needed her help?

Clark lurched to his knees. Before he could raise his gun, Crusader exploded from the floor and tackled him. The gun spun out of Clark's hand and clattered down the deck. He couldn't escape Crusader's grasp. He'd have to out-fight him, and it didn't look like he could.

Isolda clenched her jaw. She'd have to tip the scales back in Clark's favor. Then they'd get away from Tower. She'd nurse him back to health, but that wouldn't be so bad—

She shook her head. Focus! First she had to get the gun.

She crept out from behind her sanctuary and edged around the fighting men. Crusader glanced in her direction. Clark tackled Crusader and they rolled mere centimeters in front of her. She skidded away. Clark nailed him in the gut with his knee and then dove for the gun. Crusader snared his leg and dragged him away.

Isolda blinked away tears. *C'mon, God, this is ridiculous. Get me out of here in one piece!*

Crusader had to end this. He couldn't fight much longer. Two minutes, max.

Balaam punched Crusader's chest wound. Needles exploded deep within. Crusader grunted but didn't let go. He rolled Balaam over, twisting the other agent's arm behind his back.

"Who ordered this?" Crusader demanded.

Balaam laughed, barely a wheeze. "Sorry, my friend. I—"

Balaam's voice dissolved into a gasp as Crusader wrenched harder.

Crusader leaned in, his mouth close to Balaam's ear. "Tell me."

Heat slashed his shoulder and Crusader looked up. Westin had recovered the gun and shot him. Not good. He released Balaam, rolled to his right. Westin's second shot missed. He leapt up but his legs tangled and he spun out into a nearby kiosk cart. The wheeled cart tipped and spilled its contents, cheap data readers the size of a small book, across the deck. Crusader snatched one of the devices and pitched it with a snap of his arm. The reader hit Westin in the hand and she dropped the gun. She cried out and clutched her hand.

Problem solved for now. Focus on Balaam.

Balaam dragged himself a meter closer to the knife. Crusader lurched forward, diving toward the knife before Balaam could retrieve it. The other Ministrix agent tackled him, fingers clawing at his throat, closing the windpipe. Crusader pried at Balaam's hands but it was no use. Greyness crept into the edges of his vision and the world began to fall away.

No choice. He drew his arm back, flattened his palm, and struck Balaam hard at the bridge of his nose. Balaam's head snapped back fatally with a wet crack and his grip loosened.

Crusader rested before pushing the corpse off of him. Killing him had been necessary, but it was still a wasted opportunity. Now Balaam couldn't answer his questions. Who had ordered his mission? Why had he targeted Crusader? And why was he protecting Westin?

Westin! Crusader looked to where she had last stood. Gone. Of course.

He paused, a sensation building in the pit of his stomach, a leaden weight that drilled cold tendrils through his chest, their bands wrapping around his heart. He staggered. From the wound? Hard to say.

Steps. Break it down into steps. First priority: clean up. No telling how long before security would regroup. The less evidence he left for them, the better his chances. Crusader retrieved his knife. A quick search revealed the gun was missing. He grunted. Westin had taken it. A complication, but one he'd deal with later.

Second priority: escape. Good thing he had inserted the block in the security mainframe. Tower Security would have trouble identifying him without surveillance footage. There were eyewitnesses, but their panic would blur their memories.

He started for one of the sealed exits. Within moments, he could hear the sea of people trying to push through the doors. Westin might be one of them, but he didn't have time to check. Tower Security could bypass his coding at any moment.

Crusader paused, just around the corner. He took a deep breath, noting the flurry of needles that danced through his chest. Step three: healing. He had a full med kit waiting for him in his room. He could assess the damage, patch himself up. But he had to make it there first.

He counted to four and ordered the parrot to unseal the doors. The barrier retracted and the crowd surged forward. Crusader pressed into the mob. He kept his head low as they stampeded past the waiting security personnel. As soon as he was sure they had made it, he ducked into a side corridor.

He nodded to himself. Good. On to his quarters.

And then the last step: information. With Balaam dead, there was only one person on Tower who might have the answers he was looking for. He'd have to find Isolda Westin again.

8

Isolda bit the inside of her cheek and whimpered. She clutched her aching hand. Were the bones broken? She had to ignore the pain as she flowed with the crowd out of the District. Tower Security, dressed in black armor with large assault rifles at the ready, waved them on. Should she stop and talk to them? Warn them what they faced? Probably not a good idea. Every officer she saw wore the same expression, radiating barely restrained panic. They probably wouldn't want to talk to a civilian, especially not one with a gun in her waistband. Maybe she should have left it back at the fight scene, but having it helped keep her calm.

No. Her best course of action was to make it to safety. Unfortunately, she had no idea where "safe" was on Tower. There had to be somewhere she could go. For now, she'd keep moving with the crowd. Regroup. And then, once things were a bit more settled, she'd approach Tower Security and tell them what happened.

Warmth coursed through Crusader's veins, chasing away the shivering storm raging through his chest and radiating out through his limbs. He closed his eyes and savored the sensation. The fast-acting healing gel would soothe the aches and mend his injuries.

He opened his eyes. His room had been undisturbed in his absence. A good sign. It meant Tower Security hadn't breached his cover yet. He could operate a little while longer.

Harsh red lights drew his attention to the room's monitor. A message from Tower Command assured the Station's citizens that the violence was over and that Security was on the scene. They also apologized to any visitors, for Security had issued a lockdown order. No ships could dock or depart. No communication with the outside world either.

He frowned. That was a mixed blessing. Westin wasn't going anywhere for the time being. But at the same time, he couldn't seek additional orders.

Did he even want to? Balaam had claimed he'd been acting on orders, but that could have been a lie. As near as Crusader could figure, one of three things was true: First, Balaam had told the truth and had been sent to kill Crusader; second,

Balaam had lied about his orders; or third, someone had sent Balaam but had intended for Crusader to kill his fellow agent.

Complicating matters was the fact that Westin still lived. Deacon Siseal had ordered Westin's death. Balaam's interference didn't negate Crusader's orders. Crusader had to—

His mind struck a wall. His frown deepened. Still the block. That made his situation even more complex.

He sat up straighter. Perhaps Balaam had acted too early. Maybe Deacon Siseal had ordered two executions. Crusader was to kill Westin, but then Balaam was supposed to kill him. That scenario was possible. But why?

The Deacon had said that Westin was responsible for Palti's corruption. Was Deacon Siseal worried that Crusader had succumbed to heresy as well?

It was a ludicrous thought. His mission on Lanadon had been recorded. Deacon Siseal should know that Palti hadn't corrupted him, even though he'd tried. But perhaps Crusader had done something to create doubt about his faithfulness.

There was only one way to know for sure. He plucked the parrot from his shoulder and set it on the table. "Holographic interface: activate."

The parrot warbled. It projected a series of reports: its status, a mission clock, data feeds from the tap into Tower Security. Security hadn't discovered that breach yet. Good. He could use their own systems to help him.

He could track Westin. If she still had Balaam's weapon or her data reader, he could find her easily. But Westin wasn't the priority, not right now. Unraveling Balaam's involvement was. Besides, the medical gel hadn't completed its work yet. He wasn't ready for another confrontation. And with Tower in lockdown, she wasn't going anywhere.

One of his instructors with Ministrix Intelligence used to say, "There's always a trail," as an encouragement and a warning. Everyone left information without realizing it. If Crusader could gather enough scraps, perhaps he could piece together some answers.

He had to reconstruct Balaam's activity. How he had arrived on Tower. Where he'd stayed. He started the parrot's biometric recognition program. He called up an image of Balaam from their mission on Lanadon and fed it into the program. The parrot shut down its interface as it scoured Tower Security records for Balaam's image.

He turned to his bags and pulled out a clean sheet of paper and his pencils. The parrot needed time. And so he set to work, allowing his fingers to move almost of their own accord, light lines emerging across the paper as he worked on a sketch.

Within minutes, the parrot warbled. Crusader stared at his half-finished drawing. It was a woman again, always a woman. This time she sat on the edge of a bed, her knees tucked up under her chin. As much as he wanted to finish it, he had to see what the parrot had found.

The device called up a security hologram, showing Balaam arriving at Tower Station shortly before Crusader. He called up customs records for the hour after Balaam's arrival. He could eliminate most of them. Wrong gender. Wrong physical descriptions. Soon he was left with four individuals, any of which could be Balaam's cover.

He tried to access the customs surveillance tapes, only to find that the data had been corrupted. He grunted. Balaam was good. He must have disrupted security to protect his identity. Clever, but not insurmountable.

The first identity, that of a merchant from the Kioro Cluster, was easily dismissed. Balaam would have had to have started traveling a year earlier just to reach Kioro in time before coming here. A good cover but terribly inefficient.

The second identity was a Lodekkian troubadour. Possible, but unlikely, especially since the customs records indicated that the Lodekkian had filed a touring schedule with the Tower Entertainment Consortium. Too elaborate for a cover.

The third caught Crusader's attention. Another merchant, this one supposedly from Oligran 9. The customs official had noted nothing overtly suspicious about the merchant, but he'd added that the merchant had arrived on a ship called the *Purim*, a vessel the official thought too small to carry much cargo. Why would a merchant travel without merchandise?

Crusader checked the fourth identity. An out-of-work engineer, but a quick inquiry to the Tower mainframe revealed that the engineer had spent the last three days in the medical bay after contracting a case of Wayfarer's Flu.

So Balaam had arrived on a personal ship, posing as a merchant. Good. Another inquiry into the system revealed that the *Purim* was still docked. Even better, someone had been entering and exiting the ship at regular intervals. That likely meant Balaam had used the *Purim* as a base of operations.

Any answers Crusader might find would be on board the *Purim*. He scooped up the parrot and affixed it to his shoulder and turned to leave. As he did, his gaze fell on the half-finished sketch. The woman's face remained mostly blank, but her shoulder-length hair framed a thin face . . .

Crusader's heart hammered in his chest and a spark trickled down his spine. With trembling hands, he snatched up one of the pencils and roughed in the face, once again allowing his fingers to move on their own. Could it be?

It was.

Isolda Westin stared back at him from the page, her eyes warm and her lips curled in an alluring grin. He lurched forward, his chest cramped around his heart. Sweat burst from his skin and he wheezed. What did it mean? Why did she have such an effect on him?

Eventually the strange sensation faded and his heart resumed a normal cadence. He looked at the drawing a moment more before sliding it back in his bag. Westin would wait. First he needed to figure out what Balaam had been up to.

9

Isolda peeked around the corner back into the Entertainment District to see if things had gotten back to normal yet. Almost. Security had cordoned off the area where Clark had . . .

Her throat constricted and she screwed her eyes shut.

She took a few deep breaths to calm the tremors that shook her body. She glanced at a nearby display panel, and a sour taste rose in her throat. The Station was still in lockdown. Not good. She couldn't run. Tower was big but it was finite. Crusader would find her. If she was going to survive, she had to leave.

No, first she had to hide. A nearby kiosk, one that sold bolts of cloth, had been knocked over in the chaos. She darted to it. Isolda hunkered up against it and pulled a broad cloth over her.

Could she do something about the lockdown? Probably not. That was imposed by Tower Security. She could try to crack the system, but that didn't strike her as a wise idea. The last time she had tampered with a computer system, she had tripped a dozen failsafes and been banished from ever setting foot in Gateway Station again. Besides, she doubted Security would stand by while an outsider overrode their control.

Someone stomped past her hiding place. She pushed deeper into her makeshift tent. The person kept going.

If lifting the lockdown wasn't an option, maybe she could focus on finding transportation. There had to be dozens of ships whose departures had been delayed thanks to the lockdown. If she could secure a berth on one of them, she could be gone the minute the lockdown was over.

She pulled out her data reader and logged into the public access forums of Tower's mainframe. A quick check of the dockmaster's log confirmed her suspicions: twenty ships, all of them with departure times scheduled for just before or after the lockdown had started. If she could get one on of them . . .

No, this wouldn't work. All twenty were loaded and ready to depart. Once cleared, they would leave.

Her gaze skipped down the list. A few of the waiting ships were requesting the help of a new engineer. She could submit offers through the guild, but that would take time as well. Too much paperwork, negotiations, counter-proposals. Normally good things, but not when her life depended on leaving Tower as quickly as possible.

Maybe she could get on one of the ships scheduled to depart in the next few hours. They might be delayed by the lockdown, but she might have better luck. Three quarters of the way down the list was an entry for a Pearson Lines Shuttle. A broad grin tugged at her cheeks, the first she had worn in a long time.

A few quick commands brought up information on the Pearson Lines Cruisers. A trumpet fanfare erupted from the reader's speakers. "Pearson Lines: Luxury anyone can—" The booming bass voice fell silent as she muted the audio output. She held her breath. Had someone heard that? No one approached her hiding place. She'd have to be more careful.

Pearson owned five Cruisers, basically traveling pleasure palaces. She checked Pearson's roster. Which one was closest to Tower?

Yes! The *Sybaritic*. Gavin's ship! Unbelievable that it was nearby. This could work. Maybe.

She pulled up her personal messages and skimmed through the ones Gavin had sent her six months ago. She opened Gavin's message and turned up the volume again, just a little. He smiled up at her from the screen, his bleached blond hair practically glowing next to his too-tan skin.

"Hey, Isolda! Just got your message. Are you sure you want to leave? It doesn't sound like anyone is blaming you for what happened. If it was anyone's fault, it was Dr. Keleman—"

Isolda bit back a sudden rush of tears. She had forgotten that this message was about that. She fast forwarded until the serious look on Gavin's face melted into a warm smile.

"—just got promoted again. I know, I know, there's not much difference between 'second assistant to the Upper Deck steward' to 'senior assistant to the Upper Deck steward,' but it got me a little more in my paycheck, plus a bigger cabin I can almost stand up in. But that's not all. They gave me a guest voucher. I can invite anyone I want to spend a week on board the Sybaritic . . . uh, in the Lower Deck section, but that'd just be where you sleep. Yeah, you heard that right. I can't think of anyone I'd rather have come and spend some time with me. I know you probably won't be able to use it for a while. Just think about taking a short vacation here, okay?"

Gavin rattled off the voucher code for her. She jumped back to the Pearson Lines information and found the reservation queue. The system accepted the voucher number and promised her a spot on the Lower Decks. A recording of a smiling woman with straight white teeth promised her "peerless luxury for the frugal individual." Uh huh. Sure. She didn't expect anything extravagant. All she wanted was someplace far away from Tower.

She scrolled through the fine print, pausing at a clause: "The redeemer is responsible for transport to the *Sybaritic*." She flipped back to the dockmaster's log. The Pearson Lines shuttle was indeed slated to head out to the *Sybaritic*. The situation seemed perfect until she called up the ticket price.

Five hundred credits. Just for the shuttle.

Her throat constricted and she choked. She called up her personal account information. Just as she suspected: Captain Tisdal hadn't paid her yet. There was a marker for her salary, but it suggested the full amount was being held "pending guild review." She closed her eyes and moaned. A review could take hours, possibly even days. That left her with only two hundred credits to her name. Not enough to get on the Pearson Shuttle, not enough for a ticket on any of the other ships scheduled to leave Tower.

Now what? She couldn't stay on Tower, but she had no way to leave either.

No. Now wasn't the time to wallow. Now was the time to act. What else could she do? She squared her shoulders and finalized the transaction, reserving a room on the *Sybaritic*. She had a safe haven to reach now. All she had to do was find a way there.

10

Crusader kept his head down as he exited the elevator onto Tower Station's docking corridor. Tower Security may have pieced together enough information from witnesses to put together a partial description of him. While the medical gel had lessened the bruising and cuts from his fight with Balaam, Crusader still bore enough marks to draw attention to himself.

He wound his way past knots of chattering people, all of them discussing the lockdown. Then two Security personnel stepped in front of him. Crusader stopped, looking up long enough to evaluate them. If he acted fast, he could incapacitate the woman on the left quickly. Jab to the throat, sweeping kick to drop her. The man wasn't a concern. Crusader read fear in his eyes. Judging by his appearance, he was only twenty, maybe twenty-one tops. First assignment? Probably. The rookie would freeze, maybe even faint.

But guile before violence, especially since he hadn't cut the security feed here. "Not leaving," Crusader said. "Just need to check something in my ship. The *Purim*. Only be fifteen minutes."

The guards conferred with each other in hushed tones. Crusader waited, keeping his fingers relaxed and his stance neutral. No need to warn them of a potential attack, not yet.

The woman turned to him. "Okay, go on ahead. But we're going to alert the Command Deck of your visit. They see your engines light, they'll turn your ship into free-floating atoms, got it?"

Crusader nodded. Given what he'd done, it made sense for Tower to be on alert. He'd have to be careful on board the *Purim*. He needed the data. He nodded. "No problem."

The guards stepped aside. Crusader nodded to them and walked into a hexagonal corridor of burnished silver. The well-lit hallway hummed as Crusader strode past the hatchways dotting the walls every fifty meters. There. The *Purim*'s dock.

The station's gleaming door slid aside at his approach, revealing the brown corroded metal of Balaam's ship. Crusader examined the hatch, spotting the sensor ports embedded above the hatch's corners.

He tipped his mouth closer to the parrot. "Sensor rebound interface, active."

The parrot chittered and a pale blue light shot from the device into the sensors. A few moments later, something pinged from inside the *Purim* and the hatch ground open.

Crusader ducked as he stepped through the portal. Once inside, glow panels lining the dark grey walls sprang to life. Crusader looked both ways. To his right was a corridor that most likely led to the cargo hold and the engineering bay. To his left, another corridor with doors labeled "sleeping quarters," "med bay," and "cockpit." Balaam would probably keep his orders there. Good place to start.

He worked his way forward, ducking around a few open panels that spilled their contents into the deck. Crusader frowned at the disarray. A true Ministrix agent should keep his ship in better repair. Three steps descended into the cockpit. Crusader looked over the two brown leather seats facing a bank of holoscreens. He slid into the one on his left.

The panels before him flickered then flared, presenting Crusader with a dizzying array of information. The *Purim*'s computer, tricked by the parrot into thinking Crusader was Balaam, dutifully reported the ship's status. Crusader blinked in surprise. Sloppy or not, the *Purim* was a good ship. Decent power output, a state-of-the-art tunneler drive, even a modest array of weaponry and shields. Crusader ran a hand across the smooth steel paneling. A ship like this would be very handy in carrying out his missions. Better than what he usually had at his disposal.

He called up the communications log. When he saw the list of incoming messages, he frowned. More sloppiness. Balaam hadn't encrypted or encoded the entries. If someone else had gotten into the ship and accessed its systems, Balaam's cover would have been blown.

That worked to his advantage now, though.

One message caught Crusader's attention. Three weeks earlier, a high priority transmission from someone identified as

"Hyrcanus." According to the log, when Balaam had received that message, he'd transferred it to his quarters.

Crusader powered down the cockpit systems and headed aft. He poked his head into each room as he passed. A small kitchenette. A modest medical bay. And then Balaam's quarters.

He crossed through the door and stopped short. Unlike the rest of the ship, Balaam's quarters were immaculate. Dark wood paneling lined the walls, dotted with polished sconces that cast soft light onto a large bed covered with a rich blue comforter. A heady musk drifted through the air. He stepped into the room and looked around. Recessed into one wall was a holographic emitter.

"Access communication from subject Hyrcanus," he ordered.

Nothing happened. Crusader tensed, wondering if he had tripped a security protocol. No telling what kind of traps Balaam had worked into his ship.

But then the steel triangle sprang to life in front of him, ringed with a timecode. The logo spun apart and resolved into a featureless face, a computer construct. It stared at Crusader's chest for a few moments before speaking.

"Hello, Balaam. These orders come directly from Sub-Deacon abd al Sami. We are transmitting a dossier file to you regarding your target, Isolda Westin. She will be at Tower Station in three weeks. Once there, you are to engage her in a Connor Trap, variant two, with Crusader. Once you have completed the Trap, you may contact me via this channel." A series of letters and numbers looped around the face. Crusader recognized it as a standard Ministrix Intelligence channel. "Further instructions will be forthcoming."

The image faded. Crusader sat down on the edge of the bed and stared at the empty space. A Connor Trap? That's what this was about? He had participated in them before: two agents, one acting as the aggressor, the other as the savior. The aggressor would simulate an assassination attempt on the target, the savior would rescue the target. The apparent rescue would create trust between target and Ministrix agent. It was an effective method for extracting useful information from a target who might not normally be cooperative. In a normal Connor Trap, all violence was carefully choreographed so both agents would survive the encounter.

But in variant two, the "good guy" would really kill the "bad guy." An effective way to deal with two situations at the same time. Gain information and eliminate a problematic agent. Crusader knew of a few Ministrix agents who had been taken out with variant two Connor Traps, because of heresy, insubordination, or treason.

So that had been Balaam's plan. The other Ministrix agent was trying to kill him to foster trust between him and Westin. It would have worked too. Balaam was good at that kind of deception. He would have comforted Westin afterwards, maybe brought her back to his private ship, where the two of them would have . . .

Crusader's right hand snared the comforter of the bed and squeezed. He looked down at it, surprised.

He relaxed his fingers.

He called up Balaam's dossier on Westin and skimmed the information. Very similar to what he had received from Siseal, although there was an additional note that suggested Westin was somehow affiliated with a Dr. Fredek Keleman, a theoretical physicist who had gone missing from the Praesidium a few years back.

He stood and steadied himself against the smooth wood paneling. He had part of his answer, and he could piece the rest together. Sub-Deacon abd al Sami was the head of Ministrix Intelligence's Research and Development wing. So Westin had information abd al Sami wanted, hence the Connor Trap. And abd al Sami also wanted Crusader dead.

Had Crusader done something to upset the sub-deacon? He couldn't think of anything, but who could know the mind of another person?

So what was his next step? He was still under orders to kill Westin. That hadn't changed. While Sub-Deacon abd al Sami wanted Westin kept alive, Deacon Siseal outranked him. Until Deacon Siseal rescinded the order, Westin was still marked for death.

And yet . . . and yet Crusader wasn't sure he could do it. What should have been a simple assassination had turned complex, with the truth hovering just beyond Crusader's reach. If Westin had information that abd al Sami needed, wouldn't Siseal want that data as well?

Maybe he should contact Siseal and ask for clarification.

No, that wasn't an option. Even if he could communicate with Deacon Siseal, by the time Siseal responded to any inquiries, the lockdown would be lifted and Westin could have slipped away. Besides, Crusader had only an incomplete understanding of what was happening. It would be better if he didn't contact the Deacon until he could deliver a more complete report.

And there was still how the numbness had disappeared when he'd seen Westin . . .

Crusader started for the exit. He wouldn't contact Siseal. Not yet. Instead, he'd try to dig up more information. If he could learn why abd al Sami had ordered the Connor Trap, the information he wanted Balaam to learn, then he'd be in a better position.

He nodded to the Security officers as he walked past them.

"Find what you needed?" the woman asked.

"Yes, thank you for your patience," Crusader said.

The woman grimaced. "Look, sorry about the lockdown. I know you probably want to get out of here, but . . ." Her voice trailed off.

Crusader nodded. "No one else going anywhere. That's fine with me."

11

Going to the Pearson offices proved a waste of time. Isolda found a harried employee, one who seemed more interested in shoving his personal belongings into a duffel bag than helping a customer. She had to block the door to keep him from fleeing. When she explained she wanted to book passage to the *Sybaritic*, he told her Pearson had subcontracted the shuttle route, and he sent her to an office in the Corporate Sector.

Isolda peeked out of the elevator. No sign of Crusader. She darted down the halls, following what few signs there were, until she found the door to Erickson Shipping, Limited. She took several deep breaths. This had to work. It was her only way off the Station.

When the doors parted, Isolda froze at what she saw. The Erickson office was a complete mess. Parts from a dozen devices littered the floor. Isolda was pretty sure one of them was a tunneler drive aperture. Why anyone would take one off a ship and put it in an office was beyond her. Two-dimensional images covered the walls, depicting different planets and star clusters. None of the pictures were all that remarkable. But what caught her attention most was the woman sitting behind the desk.

She had propped her feet up on the grey metal table, her eyes closed and her jaw slack. Her brown and grey hair frizzed out, creating a nimbus that appeared to defy gravity. She wore a rumpled jumpsuit that displayed a large E over the woman's heart.

Isolda stepped over what appeared to be a broken-down computer core and leaned in close. The woman didn't stir. Isolda cleared her throat, hoping to wake her. No response. Isolda sighed and then touched the woman's booted foot, shaking it a bit.

With a snort, the woman sat up. Her eyes popped open and her gaze fixed on Isolda. She stared at Isolda before grinning. "Sorry 'bout that. Not much for me to do while the lockdown's in effect. Thought I'd catch up on my sleep, y'know?"

Isolda glanced at the mess around them. She shook her head. It was better to press on. "I hate to disturb you, but—"

"Disturb me? Missy, you ain't done nothin' of the sort yet. So what can Erickson Shipping do for you? Got a load of freight that needs to go from point A to point B?"

"Kind of," Isolda said. "I need a spot on board the shuttle going to the *Sybaritic*."

The woman frowned. "Why are you here then? That's something that Pearson should handle."

Isolda's stomach twisted. She mouthed a few words before she found her voice. "But the man in the Pearson office said—"

"Let me guess: looked like a ferret about to get smacked with a mallet? Little shorter than you?"

Isolda nodded. The woman guffawed.

"Figures. That's Stanley Oppenheimer for you. Stan's a good guy but easier to spook than a cat in Schrödinger's box. Probably figured whatever caused the lockdown was gonna come after him next."

Isolda's knees buckled and she tried to steady herself. "Does that mean you can't help me?"

"Who said that? Well, to be honest, I can't. I'm just the public liaison officer."

Isolda stifled a laugh. If this woman was considered the best candidate to interact with the public, she wondered how the company stayed solvent.

If the woman noticed Isolda's smirk, she didn't let on. "You'd need to speak to the shuttle captain. Lucky for you, he's here." She turned in her chair and bellowed, "Herb! Get out here. You gotta help someone."

The office's back door opened and a man ducked through. Isolda caught herself staring. The man was huge, towering nearly a meter over her yet so thin he appeared malnourished. That didn't seem possible, given the fact that he held a plate heaped with cut up sausage and was in the process of shoving the pieces into his stubble-encircled mouth.

"Well, if I would have known we'd have such pleasant company, I might have brought extra for you." He wiped his hand on his shirt and reached out to shake. "Name's Herb Erickson, owner and primary captain for Erickson Shipping. What can I do for you?"

"I was—"

"She wants to get on the shuttle to the *Sybaritic*," the woman interrupted.

Herb frowned, his thin eyebrows almost joining over his deep-set blue eyes. "Stan's gone missing again?"

"Lockdown."

"Ah. Of course." Herb set down his plate and pulled a data reader off of the desk. "Well, not a problem, not a problem. Shuttle was only three-quarters full anyway. All I need is your account number to deduct the ticket fare and we're good to go."

Isolda looked down at the offered data reader but didn't take it. "Well, I've got a small problem: I don't have the full funds. I was hoping that maybe we could work out some kind of a deal."

Herb frowned and he tucked the data reader under his arm. "Sorry, ma'am, but this isn't a charity. We barely broke even last quarter as it is." He turned to head back into the inner room.

"I realize that." Isolda took a step after him. "I didn't expect to get it for free. I'll give you what I can. And I'm a licensed engineer. Maybe I can work off the rest in transit?"

Herb turned and fixed her with a stern gaze. "Little lady, the trip will only last four days. How bad of a condition do you think my shuttle is in that you'd be able to work off a fare, full or otherwise, in that little time?"

"Well, the station's still under lockdown. Maybe I can help, um, clean up the office before we go?" Then she'd be hidden away and harder for Crusader to find.

The woman behind the desk sat up straighter. "What's wrong with the way I keep the office?"

Isolda swallowed a moan. What else could she offer? She looked around the office, her gaze skipping over the collected debris and pictures, hoping to find something, anything, she could offer them.

Wait.

A set of shelves sat in one corner, filled with nicknacks and trinkets. But an item on the lowest shelf caught her attention: a small brown bowl filled with white sand and dotted with black stones. At first, Isolda thought it was a Zen garden, but then she saw the pattern. Someone had drawn an oblong oval in the sand and positioned five of the stones at one end. It almost looked like a foot. And tucked behind the bowl itself was a small scrap of terrycloth.

Could it be?

She turned back to Herb and the woman. She might as well try.

She cleared her throat. "*Ou pas ho legon moi kyrie kyrie, eiseleusetai eis tayn basileain ton ouranon, all ho poion to thelayma tou patros mou tou en tois ouranois.*"

Herb's eyes grew wide. He looked at the woman, who had paled as well. Then he turned to Isolda and took a step closer. "*Kai su Baythleem gaue Iouda oudamos elaxistay ei en tois haygemosin Iouda. Ek sou gar exeleusetai haygoumenos, hostis poimanei ton laod mou ton Israal.*"

Isolda fought to keep from smiling. She knew it! But now she had to provide the right countersign. It had been a while, but after wracking her brain, she had it.

"*Ki im-asoth mispet vahabath khesed v'hazenaya leketh im-elohaka.*"

Herb tossed the data reader back onto the desk. The woman practically exploded from the desk and raced to the door, hitting the security lock.

"Why didn't you say something when you came in?" the woman demanded.

"I didn't notice the basin and towel until—" Isolda's breath burst from her lungs as the woman crushed her in a hug.

"It's been a while since anyone came through this way," Herb said, then frowned. "Why are you trying to get to the *Sybaritic*? Normally we get people to Odegon Sector Control. That's the next station on the Railroad."

Isolda blanched. "That's not where I'm trying to go."

Herb's face closed down, his disapproval evident. "So you're using the call-words to a take a vacation? That's not what they were meant for."

"I know it looks like—"

The woman snared her by the arm and spun her around, pushing her toward the door. "Shame on you, shame!"

"There's a Ministrix agent after me. He tried to kill me once already. I just need to get off Tower. I have a friend who works on the *Sybaritic*. The agent's name is Crusader," Isolda said.

"Wait!" Herb ran around her and stared into her eyes. "Crusader? He's here?"

Isolda nodded.

Herb turned to the woman. "Leslie, we need to get her out of here." He took Isolda by the hand and walked her over to a chair. He shoved the stack of data cards off the seat and helped Isolda into it. Then he started for the back room again. "Give me a few moments, let's see what I can do."

Isolda watched him disappear through the doors and turned to Leslie. "How does he know who Crusader is?"

Leslie's cheeks puckered. "We used to be Ministrix. Herb served on board a destroyer. Maybe he heard of this guy there, can't say for sure."

A few moments later, Herb came back out. "All right, we've got it all taken care of. You've got a berth on board the shuttle, no problem. And I called in a favor to the command deck. Our shuttle will be the first off when the lockdown is lifted."

Isolda gaped at Herb. "How did you manage that?"

He smiled. "I told 'em one of our passengers was royalty traveling undercover and needed a priority clearance." He winked. "And it's true. You are a daughter of the King, right? Now let's see what we can do about getting the lockdown lifted."

12

Crusader called up the parrot's tracking program. Westin's data reader and Balaam's weapon were still together, in an office in the Corporate Sector. Not a problem.

He re-entered the Entertainment District and paused to take it all in. Life had returned back to normal, or mostly so. Yes, the merchants were back at their kiosks and visitors and residents mingled through the open corridors, but now the sounds of the District were muted and the people appeared on the edge of frantic. Best to remain on his guard.

He set out through the District, sticking to the wider flows of foot traffic to blend in. He considered what he'd learned on the *Purim*. Deacon Siseal had ordered Westin's death. Abd

al Sami had ordered the Connor Trap that would have protected Westin. Westin likely had information that abd al Sami
wanted. Did Siseal know about this information? Didn't seem
likely since abd al Sami had undercut Siseal's orders.

Crusader nodded to two Tower Security officers. They
returned the gesture, their gaze flicking up and down Crusader.
He waited for any further response. One regarded him with a
narrowed gaze, then turned away. His partner followed suit.

Crusader walked over to a kiosk and ordered a cup of coffee.
If Westin had information abd al Sami needed but didn't want
Siseal to learn, Crusader's mission became more complicated.
If this information was important enough for abd al Sami
to interfere in a mission ordered by the Deacon of Ministrix
Intelligence, Deacon Siseal should know what it was. Best to
keep Westin alive long enough to learn what this information
was. But then, reinterpreting or ignoring one's orders was a
good way to be marked as rogue and killed.

Crusader collected his coffee from the barista and took a
tentative sip. Too bitter. But then, he hadn't ordered it for its
taste. He started for Tower Security headquarters.

Why would abd al Sami want Crusader dead? That part
didn't fit. Crusader hadn't said or done anything that could be
considered treasonous or heretical. The only possible connection was . . .

Crusader almost tripped over his own feet. Palti. That
had to be it. Maybe abd al Sami thought Palti had corrupted
Crusader. It was theoretically possible. The heresy that had
claimed Palti spread quickly, shared between family, friends,
coworkers.

He lifted the cup to his lips for another sip. Or maybe abd al
Sami wanted Crusader dead to hide his own indiscretions. He

choked on his mouthful of coffee. That could be it. Perhaps abd al Sami had succumbed also. That would explain why he was trying to protect Westin, maybe even why he wanted Crusader dead. Cover his tracks in case Crusader noticed something that would lead back to the sub-deacon.

No matter how he proceeded, he had to make sure Balaam didn't have any more information. And that meant he had to check the source. Crusader started walking again, this time deliberately stumbling and shuffling. He screwed his face into a wince and rubbed his head with one hand. He had to make this look believable.

The doors to Tower Security headquarters parted before him. Three guards looked up from their computer terminal. One rose to full height, his face set with what Crusader assumed was annoyance, not alarm.

"Look, buster, now's not a good time. Just turn around and—"

"But I need help." Crusader shielded his eyes against the lights, even though they weren't too bright. Had to be convincing. "Looking for a crewmate of mine. Think he might have been involved in that fight earlier."

The guards froze and exchanged uncertain glances. The one who spoke stepped around the desk, his gaze darting down to Crusader's feet and then up again. "Why do you think that?"

"Not me, my captain. See, we arrived yesterday on the *Praesidium Satyr*. Cap gave us leave today. My buddy, he got pretty drunk, started tossing insults around. He went off on his own. Then we heard about the fight and well, Cap's worried it's my crewmate. Sent me down here to find out if it was."

Once again, the guards glanced at each other. Crusader waited, keeping his face calm. If they checked his story, they'd find an entry for a slow freighter matching the name, along with a captain's report about a missing crewmate, all manufactured by the parrot and inserted into the Secuirty database.

"Look, only guy we got here is dead with no ID."

Crusader nodded. "Could be him. Moron never takes ID with him on leave. Thinks it keeps him from getting in trouble."

The guard laughed. "Didn't really help him this time, did it?"

"Don't know it's him."

The lead security man rubbed his jaw and then nodded. "All right. I'll take you down to the morgue, see if you recognize the deader. Okay?"

Crusader motioned for him to lead the way. They walked past the main desk and down a hall. Crusader kept track of what he saw. A break room to his right, no one in it. An armory, similarly abandoned.

When they reached the end of the hall, the guard waved his hand over a sensor node and dull grey doors parted. Crusader stepped into the morgue and looked around. No attendants. He scuffed his foot on the floor. Not as slippery as he would have liked but it would have to do. He set down his coffee on a nearby desk as the doors slid shut.

The guard turned to face him. "Hold on while I—"

Crusader struck. He wrapped his arm around the guard's neck, shoving his left hand over his mouth. Crusader's legs knocked the guard's out from under him and he drove the man's head onto the desk's edge. The man collapsed. Crusader checked for a pulse. Still alive. Probably a fractured skull.

He had to move fast. He stepped over the guard and looked over the sealed lockers. He found the correct one and thumbed the controls. The door irised open and a slab rolled out, carrying Balaam's corpse. Crusader stared down at his fellow agent, then gagged a bit. He frowned. His stomach roiled at the sight of the corpse. Heat stung his eyes and he dabbed at them. Tears?

The void roiled in his chest, thorns corkscrewing through his arms. Balaam was dead and it was his fault. He'd killed a fellow Ministrix agent instead of his ordered target. His guilt would only grow, become more powerful.

He took deep breaths, shook his head. "Parrot, begin scan for anomalous signals. Locate any embedded data readers." He plucked the device from his shoulder with trembling fingers and set it on the slab next to Balaam. Best to keep working, hope the internal storm would subside. What was wrong with him?

A quick search of the room found Balaam's personal effects. Not much to go on. No ID, like the guard had said. Crusader glanced at the Security officer. Still breathing.

Next was a cheap data reader, a knock-off Balaam had probably purchased once he arrived at Tower. Crusader skimmed the available data. Nothing incriminating. He pocketed the reader.

The parrot chirruped then blatted. Crusader frowned. No results. If Balaam had received any further instructions from abd al Sami, he hadn't recorded it anywhere.

Crusader picked up the parrot and affixed it to his shoulder. He retrieved his coffee cup. He spilled it at the injured officer's feet, under his body, and on the soles of his shoes

"Help me! Someone help!" he shouted.

A few moments later, the doors whooshed open and three more security personnel filed through. They stared at their comrade before turning to Crusader.

"What happened?"

"I'm sorry," Crusader said, trying to inject some regret into his voice. "I spilled my coffee and he slipped. Think he may have hit his head on the desk."

One of the guards knelt down next to the injured man and checked him. "He's still breathing. Might be a concussion."

"Commandant's gonna love that, especially with the lockdown lifting."

Crusader froze. "What?"

"Yeah, a bunch of captains got together and filed some sort of complaint to the Station Administrator. Something about 'restraint of trade,' buncha junk like that. Never mind that a murderer might be slipping away right under our noses."

Crusader's mind spun free. The lockdown was over? He had to move fast. He turned to the security officer in charge. "May I go? Checked the body. Not my crewmate."

The officer looked at him then nodded. Crusader turned and left, trying hard to walk slow, deliberate.

He stepped out of Security headquarters and ducked into a side corner. He called up the Station Commander's orders on his data reader. Sure enough, a coalition of captains had filed a formal complaint, and the Commander had given in. Crusader frowned. Looked like the ringleader was some guy named Herb Erickson.

Why did that name look familiar? Crusader's eyes widened. He called up his surveillance data. Westin had been in Erickson's office a few minutes ago. Now she wasn't. According to the parrot's data, she had left the office ten minutes ago, headed for . . .

Crusader burst from his hiding place. He shoved his way past the people filtering back into the District and ran to an elevator.

The elevator car deposited him in the docking ring, right into a long line of passengers waiting to board the now free-to-depart ships. Crusader struggled his way toward Erickson's assigned berth.

There! The doors that separated the Erickson shuttle from Tower lay just ahead. Maybe he could bluff his way on. Claim to have a ticket. Claim to have been mugged. Claim he was looking for his estranged wife. Anything. He couldn't lose her now.

Then the red light above the door blazed and he skidded to a halt. Through the thick window, he saw the boarding tube retract and, a moment later, the hull of the Erickson shuttle drop away, disappearing as the Tower doors closed.

He slammed a fist into the wall next to the door. He winced, dropping the fist into his other hand. Why had that hurt so much? And why had he punched the bulkhead in the first place? He stared at bleeding knuckles, trying to comprehend his next move.

And then the numbness descended. His hand no longer hurt. His thoughts ordered themselves. He could finish this. He had to finish this.

Steps. That's what it would take. And he knew what the first one was.

13

Deacon Horatio Siseal leaned forward so he could better enjoy the view. The surface of Earth slid past him, spinning silently below New Jerusalem Station. He felt he could reach out and rake his fingers through the clouds. He smiled, a wry quirk that lifted one side of his lips. It had taken him many years to reach this point in his career. And now here he was, in the office overlooking Earth. The power. The respect. The fear. He could have even more if he could hold things together just a little longer.

He rose from his chair and stepped away from his desk. He strode across the lush crimson carpet through the vast emptiness of his office, pausing long enough to retrieve his iron staff.

The rod clanked against the deck plates as he headed for the conference room. Charis, his assistant, fell into his wake.

"What is the latest news from the summit talks?" he asked, not breaking his stride.

Charis consulted her personal data reader. Siseal favored her out of the corner of his eye. Still young, in her late twenties, her shimmering red hair pulled back in a bun. Her bright brown eyes darted over the screen before she shook her head. "Nothing substantial, sir."

Siseal nodded. Negotiations between Ministrix and Praesidium had been constant for well over a century, producing little but noise. But occasionally, things did not go as planned. Thirty years earlier, a minor functionary within the Ministrix had set events in motion that had led to the dreadful Paulson Compromise, a binding agreement between the two powers that had placed a cap on the number of military vessels each side could construct. When it happened, the ruling Revered Hand had blamed the Deacon of Intelligence and had had him executed for damnable incompetence. Siseal didn't want to share that fate, so he kept a close eye on the talks.

"And the investigation into the Praesidium spies? Progress?"

Charis once again consulted her notes. Her mouth went taut. "Very little, sir. Karlstadt reports some evidence they might be based on Eps-Prime. Should he pursue?"

"No. There may yet be more leads for him to unearth. He should remain in place. But do task Hyrcanus to go to Eps-Prime. Make sure to emphasize the importance of this assignment. The Praesidium has come too close to discovering what we're doing. They have to be stopped."

"Understood." More notations, accompanied by chirps.

"What of the search for the Catacombs?"

Charis fell silent. Siseal checked her once again. She wasn't looking at her data reader. That did not bode well.

"I see," he said.

"They doubt any such place exists."

Siseal's grip on the staff tightened and he drove it into the floor with a loud clang. "It does. The Catacombs are real. They must find it."

"Yes, your grace."

Siseal picked up his pace. Lower acolytes stepped out of the way to let him pass, his long robes swishing along the metal deckplates. He navigated the sterile corridors until he stepped into the conference room. The sudden darkness left him blind and he paused, allowing his eyes to adjust from the bright hall.

Seated around the mahogany table were his sub-deacons, dedicated men all, dressed in the robes of their office. Siseal leaned his rod against the wall near the head of the table and took his seat. Charis stepped to his side, her data reader poised and ready.

"Gentlemen, good day and blessings. May the Almighty One crush our enemies beneath our heels."

"May His vengeance be upon them," the others replied.

Siseal scanned the edges of the table. All ready to begin. Except Sub-deacon Altair abd al Sami—he didn't meet Siseal's gaze. Instead, he toyed with his own data reader, punching in commands. Sweat trickled down his brow, stained his robes. Siseal frowned. The environmental controls had chilled the air too much today, so it couldn't be heat. Sickness? Unlikely.

"Is everything all right, abd al Sami?" he asked.

Abd al Sami jumped and met his gaze. "Uh . . . yes, your grace. My apologies."

"If there is a matter that requires my attention, I suggest you mention it now."

Abd al Sami quickly shook his head. "No, your grace. Nothing of the sort. It's merely that one of my operations seems to have hit a minor snag."

"A snag?"

The other deacons turned to face abd al Sami.

New sweat poured down the man's face.

"Forgive my imprecise speech, your grace. It is but an inconvenience. That is all."

Siseal's eyes narrowed and he glared at his subordinate. "Should this 'snag' require your full concentration, perhaps you should attend to it rather than stay here and distract us, yes?"

"Very good, your grace." Abd al Sami gathered up his belongings and started for the door. Then he stopped and turned. "A thought, Deacon Siseal. Could I make use of Phinehas's strike team? I think that could help alleviate this inconvenience."

Siseal dismissed him with a wave of his hand. "By all means, Altair. By all means."

Abd al Sami bowed low. He retreated in a blur of robes.

Siseal turned to the others. "Very well, brethren. Without any further delays, let us begin by discussing—"

Charis's data reader chirped, breaking his concentration. He turned and glared at his assistant.

She didn't blanch at the reproving look. Instead, she studied the screen before leaning in close.

"A report from Crusader, sir."

"Indeed? What does he say?"

"He too seems to have hit a minor snag. The message reads, 'Target acquired, mission incomplete. Tracking now. Will report again when successful.' He suggests the target is currently on board a cruise ship, the *Sybaritic*."

Siseal frowned. "I see."

"Orders, sir?"

Siseal leaned back in his chair, steepling his fingers before his face. Things were delicately balanced. Too much pressure could tip things in the wrong direction, and that could take him down too.

"None. Allow this to play out."

"Very good, sir." Charis took a step back, resuming her place.

Siseal turned to the gathered sub-deacons. "Again, let us start. I feel there are many matters to discuss to safeguard our beloved Ministrix. May we apply ourselves to the task with divine diligence. Sub-Deacon Marx. Your report?"

Siseal did his best to concentrate as his subordinates shared their information. And yet, try as he might, he couldn't stop himself from thinking about Isolda Westin.

14

Isolda finally relaxed when the *Sybaritic* appeared in the viewport.

The Pearson Lines ship wasn't beautiful. Far from it. A ring of boxes rotated around a central pillar, which housed the drive units. Spindly antennae and sensor rods sprouted seemingly at random from the mottled white surface. In aesthetic terms, the cruise ship was hideous. Yet Isolda loved the *Sybaritic* from the moment she saw it. A great pressure unwound from her chest.

The shuttle trip had been uneventful. Herb Erickson had given her a private room, sequestering her from the rest of the passengers. Based on the crew's near reverential treatment, Isolda suspected Herb had continued his sham that she was royalty. She didn't deserve such treatment. The only upside was the privacy.

The *Sybaritic* spun away from her viewport. Attitude thrusters thrummed through the deck as they brought the smaller ship to dock with the cruise vessel. She gathered up her things. Still not much. Herb had scrounged up a few extra outfits, most of them too tight. Everything she owned could fit in a small duffel.

A shudder followed by high pinging ran through the ship. A red light over her cabin's door turned green, signaling the docking with the *Sybaritic* was complete. Isolda scooped up her bag and headed toward the boarding tube.

A knot of people had already formed around the only exit. Herb stood by the open door, thanking each person as they shuffled through.

He caught Isolda by the arm, gave her a friendly squeeze. "Take care of yourself, Your Majesty." He winked.

Heat bled through her cheeks. She mumbled her thanks and stepped through the door.

The exiting passengers came to a halt in a small room made of gleaming black metal. The walls, floor, and ceiling appeared seamless. Someone shoved Isolda forward and she jostled the person in front of her.

Three melodic tones chimed. "Welcome to the *Sybaritic*, the pride of the Pearson Cruise Lines." The voice from the hidden speakers was feminine and warm. "Please remain calm while we conduct a scan to ensure the health and safety of our passengers."

A bright blue line appeared on the walls, ceiling, and floor. The resulting box slowly worked its way through the room. Isolda tensed. She didn't have Clark's weapon anymore. Herb had confiscated the gun. But would the sensors pick up anything unusual? She couldn't be turned away, not when she had come this far.

The light voice continued. "We're pleased you've chosen us for this journey. Next time, why not take your own ship? All Pearson cruise vessels have ample docking facilities, allowing you extra freedom in scheduling." The voice paused briefly.

"Once the scan is complete, you will be met by a Pearson Lines representative. They will give you further orientation and answer any questions you may have."

Isolda braced herself as the sensor beam passed over her. She knew she shouldn't be able to feel it. All the same, she could have sworn the hairs on her arms stood on end as the bright blue light bathed her body.

"Traveling with children? Be sure to check out the *Sybaritic*'s Play Deck. Zero-g sports facilities, aquaponics bay, and meteor sculpture stations, all available for reasonable prices." Another pause.

"Worried about traveling with your valuables?"

One older man clutch his bag tighter to his chest. Clearly he was.

"See the *Sybaritic*'s purser office," the disembodied voice said. "We can store whatever you have in a secure location."

The blue light flickered out as it reached the end of the room. With a soft sigh, a pair of doors opened in front of the passengers.

"Thank you for your patience and enjoy your stay."

The crowd surged forward and Isolda jogged to keep from getting run over.

A smiling young man in a crisp white jumpsuit with a bright green slash across his chest waited for them on the other side. He waved them all closer.

"I'm sorry about that, folks, but you can never be too careful. Good news, though, you all check out so we're going to get started. My name is Harold Regan. I'm the chief steward here on the *Sybaritic* and I guarantee you'll be interacting with my boys and girls all throughout your stay. So if there's anything you need, just let us know."

He led them into a transparent tube. Once Isolda stepped inside, she looked around her. The tube ran along the ceiling of an immense room, at least three hundred meters long and a hundred meters wide. The ceiling danced with blue light, making it look a little like sky. Isolda looked down. Underneath them were trees, what looked like a river, and . . . was that a castle? Isolda's eyes widened. Tucked against a far wall was an imposing three story stone fortress, complete with moat and drawbridge. Bright blue banners snapped in the breeze. It looked like they were walking over some kind of forest. Was the room filled with holograms? Maybe. It was hard to tell from a distance.

Apparently she wasn't the only one surprised at finding a forest inside a cruise vessel. Whispers rippled through the passengers.

Regan practically radiated pride as he held up his hands to stop everyone in the tube. "You like this? It's the newest feature of the *Sybaritic*. We call it the 'Fantasy Forest.' The trees, the rocks, everything is synthetic. We have a full compliment of configurable robots that can populate the woods to your specifications. Right now it's the children's hour."

A gaggle of children ran through a small clearing beneath their feet. Isolda knelt down, her eyes caught by a blur of motion in the trees. An animal of some kind bounded after the kids on all fours. Then it leapt, tackling one of the children.

She gasped. "Is that safe?"

Regan looked to where she was pointing and laughed. "Perfectly. The children are playing 'Glomp.' A pack of teddy bears are chasing them. When they're caught, the bears will just hug them."

More small creatures erupted from the woods, piling onto the tackled child. Now that they were in the open, Isolda got a better look: large glass eyes, wide grins, brown and tan fur. Adorable. The targeted child rolled, his face shining with glee, before breaking free and running after his playmates.

"Let me assure you, the 'Fantasy Forest' is not just for children. Later this evening, we have a war game scheduled. But if you're not a fan of violence, I can also promise more adult fare. Just consult the cruise itinerary in your cabin when you arrive."

The crowd moved a bit faster. Isolda's stomach curdled. She supposed she shouldn't be surprised. Pearson Lines was a Praesidium corporation, after all. She had a pretty good idea of what that "adult fare" would be. She would check her schedule, if for no other reason than to avoid the Forest.

Regan continued the tour, leading them from the forest enclosure to the pool deck, the zero-g sports facilities, and finally, a spacious lobby. The oval room had a soaring dome ceiling. Elevators dotted oak walls. Suspended overhead was a massive hologram depicting the *Sybaritic*'s current position, a dotted line through the stars depicting its intended course. Isolda giggled. Their course would take them far from the Ministrix and all its posts. Perfect.

"Thank you for joining us. Now if you'd be so kind as to present your ID, we will process your reservations and send you to your accommodations."

Other stewards appeared and organized the passengers into lines. Isolda looked the crewmen over, hoping to spot Gavin. No sign of her friend. She waited in line until she was called forward by a portly steward. He seemed friendly enough, but when Isolda presented her identification, the steward's mouth tightened. He still smiled, but condescension steamed off him as he poked a finger toward one of the elevators.

Isolda stepped into the car and was joined by a number of other passengers. Most wore rattier clothing. One man's bag was stained with grease along its bottom. Lower class passengers, all.

The ride into the depths of the *Sybaritic* took close to ten minutes. When the doors opened, Isolda practically burst onto the deck. One of the other passengers had apparently packed some overripe Nimm Cluster cheese in an improperly sealed container. About halfway through the trip, Isolda had practically choked on the burning aroma. It was good to get into some fresher air.

But not fresh enough. Whereas the docking area was light and spacious, the lower class decks were cramped and dark. Several corridors branched out from the elevator's lobby, so narrow Isolda doubted two people could walk them side by side. Instead of rich wood, the walls and floor were mottled grey metal. There was adequate lighting, but it bathed everything in a harsh glow that bleached out the colors. Isolda still smiled. As dreary as it was, at least it was safe.

"Isolda!"

She turned.

Gavin waved. Her friend stood a dozen centimeters shorter than her, his red hair cropped short. His eyes, as grey as the bulkheads, sparkled with laughter. His pudgy face split into a large grin as he stepped forward, arms wide. She raced over and hugged him.

"I'm so glad you finally decided to come and see me! I was beginning to think you had forgotten about me." He released her and took her by the hand, dragging her down one of the halls. "We're going to have so much fun! I know the lower class facilities aren't the greatest, but I think I can sneak you onto the upper decks every now and then. There's even a staff get-together in the Fantasy Forest in two days. Huh? Why the face? Oh, don't worry, nothing like that. Kind of a picnic-slash-war games thing. I know, I know, weird combo, right, but that's what Regan likes. You met him, right?"

Isolda didn't interrupt Gavin's running commentary. She felt a little guilty as he chattered about his big plans for their week. All she really wanted was to lie low and research what her next move could be.

Gavin stopped outside a dingy white door. "Well, here we are. Deck Double-Z 704, your home away from home."

Before he could open the door, Isolda wrapped him in another hug. "Thanks, Gavin, I really appreciate this."

He groaned. "How many times do I have to tell you, call me 'Gav'? And it's no problem, really."

"No, I mean it. Look, I didn't get a chance to explain why I needed this room. I'm in trouble, Gav. Big trouble. The Ministrix is after me."

His eyes widened. "Why?"

"I don't know."

Gavin studied her face. "Is there some way we can find out? Maybe we can contact Elata. She could try to reach Naaman . . ."

The mention of Elata drove a spike through Isolda's gut. She didn't need a reminder of that, not now. "You really think Naaman exists?"

Naaman was legend in their circles. Supposedly one of the higher-ups in Ministrix Intelligence was sympathetic to their cause, possibly even a true Christian. People called this individual "Naaman." But no one knew for sure if he or she even existed.

"Why not? I heard this rumor a few months back, something about some Ministrix Deacon defecting. They say they sent an entire squad after the guy, tore up a city block to get him." Gavin's eyes widened. "You don't suppose they'll send the same team after you?"

Isolda shook her head. "No, they only sent one guy after me at Tower and—" She paused to glance around. She suddenly felt like thousands of eyes stared at her. "Look, can we continue this in the room?"

"Sure. No problem."

He thumbed the switch and, with an audible screech, the door retracted into the wall. Isolda stepped through quickly. The cabin was little bigger than her closet back on the *Regent's Light*. A mattress was suspended against the ceiling. A desk with data terminal was to her right, a small porthole looking out into the void of space right in front of her. Beneath that was a sink with two glasses on it. She probably would have to share a public restroom. And to her left was a chair and . . .

She gasped. Someone was already in her room! Whoever it was lounged in a seat facing a small porthole.

"Sir?" Gavin stepped around Isolda and walked across the cramped room. "I think there must be some sort of mistake."

"No mistake."

The man rose and turned around. Cold sluiced down Isolda's back and through her arms. How was this possible?

Staring back at her, his face cold and his eyes dead, was Crusader.

15

Crusader stepped around Westin, who was now quaking, and thumbed the cabin's privacy lock. The doors slid shut and sealed themselves with a whir. Then he turned back to his quarry.

Westin still seemed paralyzed, so Crusader turned his attention to the steward. Short and thick, he didn't pose much of a threat. He blustered and tried to make himself taller, throwing out his chest.

"You can't be in here. This isn't your cabin," he said. "Security to Lower Class—"

"Communication system's disabled," Crusader said. "No one will hear you."

He glanced at Westin. Her face drained of color and she looked ready to collapse. He pulled out a chair. She tensed, took a step back. He froze. Would she fight him?

After a moment's hesitation, he pushed the chair to her. She stared at it, her eyes wide.

"Might as well sit down," Crusader said.

She didn't move. "Gav." Her voice was little more than a squeak. "This is him. This is the guy. He's the one who . . ."

Crusader turned to the steward. His eyes bulged but he didn't show any sign of attacking. Good. Crusader still had control. But Westin hadn't responded well to gentleness. Perhaps a more direct approach. "Sit down." He added a growl to his words.

The steward dropped to the floor. Westin didn't move for a second, then she sat, her eyes never leaving Crusader.

She filled his mind. He hadn't prepared himself for how she might affect him. Just the mere proximity to her was overwhelming. He wanted nothing more than to sit across from her and drink in her every feature, try to figure out why she felt so familiar to him. The room spun around Crusader. He felt strangely light, as if his head had somehow opened to the vacuum of space. The void roared in his ears. He resisted the urge to steady himself against the nearby bulkhead. He forced himself to look away from Westin.

"Are you here to kill me?" she asked.

"If I was, I would've done it thirty seconds ago."

He risked a glance at her. She frowned, her face pinched and wrinkled. He checked on the steward. Still not a threat.

"How did you get here before me?" she asked. "I left you back on Tower."

"You did," Crusader agreed. "Hard to outrun me."

The void lashed against his mind. It wasn't a lie, not really. He had stolen the *Purim*. Balaam's ship was faster than he'd originally thought, a small blessing in this mess. It had allowed him to arrive at the *Sybaritic* before Westin. He shifted his weight, trying to ignore the pinpricks raking the back of his skull and into his shoulders.

"So now what?" Westin asked.

"Need information," Crusader said. "From you."

She laughed. "Why would I give anything to you after what you did? You killed Clark!"

"No."

She stared at him, her eyes flashing with fire. "I was there, remember?"

"I know." He whispered a command to the parrot. A hologram of Balaam blazed to life between them. "Told you his name was Clark?"

She nodded, but the barest flicker of doubt passed over her expression.

"Said he was someone who could help? Maybe Praesidium Intelligence?"

"Yes . . ."

"Lied. Not Praesidium. Ministrix, like me. We called him 'Balaam.' Don't know his real name." He shrugged. He whispered to the parrot to shut down the image. "Suppose his real name could have been 'Clark.'"

"You're lying."

He knelt down, bringing himself to her eye level in her position on the chair. "No, I'm not." They stared at each other for a few moments before Westin looked down, swiping away a tear. Did she believe him? Maybe. Why did he want her to?

"He . . . he said you were going to kill me."

His chest tightened. He was no good at this, building trust with a target. No, not a target. He couldn't think like that. Not now. Not if he wanted to figure out what was happening.

"Those were my orders," he said.

She froze.

"That's it." The steward started to rise. "I'm calling security."

Crusader lashed out, sweeping the man off his feet. He was on the other man in a flash, fist raised and ready to knock him out.

Then soft hands grabbed his wrist. He looked over his shoulder at Westin, who stared at him with unmasked horror. He relaxed, released the steward's jumpsuit.

"Sorry," Crusader mumbled. He helped the steward to his feet. "Like I said, those were my orders. But I . . . disobeyed. Broke them."

"Why?"

Isolda's barest whisper sent a jolt down his spine. He closed his eyes, swallowed hard. But the numbness failed him again.

"Had to," he said. "Something didn't add up."

He explained about the difference in orders, how Deacon Siseal wanted her dead but abd al Sami wanted her alive, how the Connor Trap was supposed to work. Westin sat back down halfway through the tale, her eyes never leaving his. Her face paled as he explained the details of what Balaam would have tried.

"Abd al Sami must think you have something big, and he must believe it enough to defy Deacon Siseal's orders," Crusader said. "That's something Deacon Siseal should know."

Westin blinked a few times. "Why does this Siseal—"

"Deacon Siseal," Crusader said.

"Why does he want me killed?"

He considered pretending ignorance. But as he met her unwavering gaze, he knew he couldn't.

"Imanol Palti. He was Deacon of Ministrix Intelligence. Remember him?"

She frowned and shook her head.

"A year and a half ago, you temp-crewed on a Praesidium frigate that hosted a summit between the Ministrix and Praesidium. Palti was there."

Westin's eyes darted back and forth. "Yeah." She turned to the steward. "The *Horizon Spanner*. Remember how I told you about that?"

Crusader glanced at the other man. He hadn't realized he was Westin's friend.

She turned back to Crusader. "What does that have to do with anything?"

"Palti succumbed to heresy after the summit. Deacon Siseal believes you are responsible. That's why he sent me."

"Heresy? What kind of heresy?"

The steward's hand darted out and squeezed Westin's knee.

Crusader's eyes narrowed. "Corruption of the Ministrix's doctrine. This heresy parrots texts, twists them out of their true meaning."

Westin stared at him and then burst out laughing, a brief, mirthless bark. "I don't believe this. First of all, I never met any Ministrix mucky-muck on the *Horizon Spanner* or anywhere else. Second, it's not a heresy, it's—"

The steward squeezed again. Westin fell silent. She collapsed back in her chair, crossing her arms.

"Not here to argue theology," Crusader said. "But you asked."

"So what information is this abd al Sami looking for?" the steward asked. "Is it about this so-called 'heresy'?"

Crusader shook his head. "We have enough data on that already." A thought occurred to him. He didn't know if it would work. "Unless you know something about the Catacombs."

The steward tensed and his fingers clamped even tighter on Westin's knee. Her lips pressed into a thin, white line.

They knew. They both knew.

Crusader's fingers curled into a fist. Perfect. Better than that. If he could learn this information, find the Catacombs, it would bring him a great deal of favor. Enough to placate abd al Sami. Enough to guarantee Deacon Siseal's good graces. Enough to maybe even quiet the void that howled inside him even now.

Before he could press the issue, though, Westin shook her head. "I don't think it's that."

"What's abd al Sami in charge of?" the steward asked.

Crusader speared him with a sharp gaze and the man shrunk back. But he answered anyway. "Sub-Deacon abd al Sami is in charge of Ministrix Intelligence's research and development wing."

A frown creased Westin's forehead.

The steward shifted then glanced at her. "Maybe he's after Dr. Keleman's research?"

Westin's head snapped to the side and she fixed the steward with a wide-eyed glare. Another lead worth pursuing.

She turned back to Crusader, met his gaze with her luminous eyes. "So now what? If you think I'm going to give you anything, you're going to wind up frustrated."

"Okay."

Westin sat back in her chair, surprise painted across her face. "Okay?"

Crusader shrugged. "I'm not going anywhere. You have time to think about it."

"That's where you're wrong, buddy." The steward started to rise but hesitated. Maybe he was worried that Crusader would stop him. Then he stood. "Unless you're gonna kill us, what's to stop me from calling security and having you thrown off the ship?"

A slight shudder rose from the deck plates. Crusader glanced at the room's vanity, where a glass rattled next to the sink. He turned back to the steward, who had paled. He knew what those vibrations meant as well. The *Sybaritic's* tunneler drive had activated. The ship was under way.

"Feel free," Crusader said, then stepped past him toward the door. He turned and dropped to one knee, looking Westin in the eyes. "You don't trust me. Don't blame you. But remember two things: I could have killed you both on Tower and here. I didn't. Can help you, maybe. Other agents may come after you. If you want to live, you'll need my help."

"Why should I believe anything you say?" Westin asked.

He had expected this. He fished a data chit, a small piece of plastic the size of his thumbnail, out of his pocket and held it out to her.

She eyed it as though it were a weapon. "What's that?"

"The data I've collected so far. Balaam's personnel file. His orders. My orders." He moved his open palm toward her, urging her to take it. "See for yourself. It's all there."

The steward snorted. "You could have faked it."

Crusader shrugged. "True, I could have. I didn't."

Westin looked into his eyes. His pulse quickened and he worried that the numbness would fail again. She took the chit and tucked it into her pocket.

Good. It was a gamble, revealing classified information to Westin. But now he was committed to it. He rose and crossed the room to the door. "I'm in Upper Class, Cabin A-9. Call if you want to talk."

The doors parted and he stepped through. Now all he had to do was wait.

As soon as the doors shut behind the Ministrix assassin, the tension in Isolda's body drained through to the floor. She fell forward, her head coming to rest in her trembling hands. Gavin leapt to the door and slapped the lock. She almost laughed. Like that would stop Crusader if he wanted back in.

But Gavin didn't stop there. He scooped up Isolda's bag and grabbed her by the arm. "C'mon, we have to get you out of here. Maybe we can find you a different room, or maybe I can have you stay with a coworker of mine. She has a roommate and her cabin is kind of cramped, but I think—"

Isolda pulled her arm free. "How would that help? He's on the ship, Gav. I'm on the ship. And yeah, it's big, but I won't be able to leave for what, five days? If he wants to find me, he will."

Gavin fell silent. Isolda closed her eyes. An image of Clark—or whatever his name was—danced before her eyes. Had he really been Ministrix too? She didn't want to believe Crusader, but he had seemed so earnest, so honest. She didn't get the sense that he was lying.

"So what do we do?" Gavin asked.

She glared at him. He worked on the *Sybaritic*. He should know better than her. "I don't know. We can't give him the Catacombs. And I won't give him Dr. Keleman's research. Could you imagine what would happen if the Ministrix got their hands on it?"

"They may not be able to get it to work. I mean, look at what happened when the doc tried."

A new spike of grief stabbed her chest. She screwed her eyes shut, her memory dredging up the smell of smoke, the sound of emergency klaxons, the taste of blood. She didn't want to go there.

"So what do we do?" Gavin asked again.

She sighed. "I said I don't know." She tried to smile, but her lips barely twitched. "Let me sleep on it, okay? Maybe we'll have a better idea in the morning."

16

Isolda didn't want to look at the clock. She knew it was late. Or early, maybe. She was in that nebulous time when night slips to morning, a transition most people slept through.

Not her. Not tonight.

She looked over at the chair where Crusader had been sitting just a few hours before. She had given it a wide berth for most of the evening, as if she could ignore it out of existence. But it seemed to hover next to her, just out of the corner of her eye, mocking her.

He was here! She had been so sure she had lost him, but he had shown up anyway. Would she ever be able to shake him? He had even pursued her into her fitful sleep. Every time she had closed her eyes, he had been there, his dead, blue eyes boring into her mind.

She tucked her knees up under her chin. So what could she do? Even if she informed ship security, it probably wouldn't help. Who knew what kind of precautions Crusader had taken after arriving. She had seen him in action. She knew how deadly he could be.

And yet . . .

He hadn't attacked her. He could have, but like he'd pointed out, he didn't. And he seemed genuine, or at the very least, honest.

Her gaze fell on the data chit sitting on her desk. Did it really contain what Crusader had said it did?

She shook her head. Ridiculous. Gavin was right: Crusader could have forged anything and put it on there.

But would it hurt anything just to see what it said?

Isolda climbed off the bunk and retrieved her data reader and the chit. She slipped the chit into the side of her reader and ordered the device to read whatever was on it.

The reader hummed to itself and its display lit up. The chit contained three files: "Balaam Dossier," "My Orders," "Balaam's Orders." A faint smile tugged at her lips. Not the most creative names.

She opened Balaam's Dossier first. An image appeared. Her breath caught. It was Clark, sort of. The features were all the same, but she barely recognized him. He smiled coolly up at her, his lips peeled back in an arrogant sneer. His expression sent trails of ice across her skin.

She shuddered and dismissed the image, turning to his file. Much of it had been redacted. There were blank spaces where his name, home system, and other identifying factors should have been. But what remained was enough. Mission reports, all involving the seduction of young ladies. Letters of commendation for exemplary service to the Ministrix. Lists of aliases, including . . .

A heavy weight settled in Isolda's chest. One of the aliases was "Clark Hollister."

She closed the dossier and pulled up Crusader's orders. A chill wormed through her as she listened to the passionless voice order her death in a public place, with as many witnesses as possible. When she listened to Balaam's orders, though, that chill was replaced by fire that started in her cheeks and worked its way through the rest of her. She had been so taken with this "Balaam," she very well might have fallen for it.

She read through the dossier and listened to the orders four more times before she shut down the data reader. Isolda bounced her head lightly against the bulkhead. What Crusader had said seemed to be true. At least, these files backed up his claims. While she was no expert on detecting computer forgeries, she thought they looked genuine enough.

So what did that mean? She looked at the room's intercom. Should she call Crusader, see what else he had to say?

She shook her head. What was she thinking? Even if he hadn't attacked her before, he might change his mind now. No, it was best to try to get some sleep and think about it more in the morning.

She burrowed under the covers and screwed her eyes shut. Maybe sleep would claim her quickly.

Instead, Isolda's mind was filled with images of Crusader. Only this time, his eyes didn't seem dead. They looked sad.

The alarm grated against his mind. Already? No, that wasn't the clock.

He stirred, the rough blanket scratching at his bare arms and legs. A groan rumbled up his throat.

"Stay asleep, baby." The husky voice cooed near his ear. "I've got this one. Probably just a tripped circuit."

He rolled over, the covers twining around him. He wanted to sleep, but the void overwhelmed him, pried at his eyes, tore at his ears. Wake up! Stop her!

He settled on his back, his eyes drifting open. Westin stood at the foot of the bed, zipping up a simple uniform, the steel triangle on her shoulders, over her heart. She smirked, leaned over, rubbed his foot.

"I told you, go back to sleep. I'll take care of it."

She stepped back, the door behind her hissed open.

Hell raged behind her.

Flames shot up the walls, clawing into the bedroom. He reached out to stop her as she blew a kiss to him, took a step back into the burning embrace . . .

Crusader bolted up in his bed, knife in hand. His gaze jumped through the darkened state room, assessing the shadows. No threats.

He struggled to calm his breathing. His pulse thundered in his ears. Within moments, the numb reasserted itself, and he stilled. A dream? It had been years since he had one . . . He had never had one that vivid, he knew that much.

What did it mean? Could it be prophecy? Unlikely—few had such gifts. The Revered Hand, surely. Other Deacons within the Ministrix, probably. Not Crusader.

He threw his legs over the edge of the bed, scattering a sheaf of papers. He looked over his work. Multiple sketches of

Westin, different poses, same sad eyes in each. He traced his fingers over the lips of one. Something familiar there.

A shudder worked its way up his spine, a delicious tremor that caused him to suck in a breath and hold it. And then it was gone, vanishing into the numbness again.

He released the breath and stood. The cabin's lights rose in response, illuminating a plush room in muted burgundy and blues. He strode to the window overlooking the *Sybaritic*'s leisure deck. Mostly deserted, thanks to the late hour, but Crusader spotted a few couples stealing through the shadows, clinging to each other.

Crusader walked to the intercom. He punched in Westin's cabin number but his finger hovered over the "Send" button. Why call her now? He didn't know. He knew only that he wanted to.

He forced his hand to his side. No. Let her wait. Soon enough she'd realize that she needed him.

Isolda's door chimed far too early for her liking. She groaned, rolled off the uncomfortable bunk, and plodded to the door.

The door hissed open, revealing Gavin. He smiled up at her, an apology darting through his eyes. She grumped at him and hit the button that raised the mattress back to the ceiling. She collapsed in the big chair, the same one Crusader had sat in just the night before.

"Bad night?"

"Bad bunk," she said.

"Oh." Gavin set some breakfast on her lap: croissants, orange juice, a slice of melon and a hunk of pineapple. He set his own tray on the desk opposite her and ate his meal without waiting.

"So today," he said between bites, "I have to lead a group through the bridge at 1430. I figured we could stay here until then. I know it's a little cramped, especially with two of us in here, but I think we can make do. I know you're supposed to eat in the lower class dining room, but I've got some connections down in the kitchen. We can probably have a good lunch and dinner snuck down here. I've also got a call in to security to make sure a patrol goes by here every half hour or so. They're not promising anything, but I figure it will be enough to keep that guy away from you—"

"What are you talking about? Do you think I should hide?"

Gavin's eyes widened at Isolda's question. "Um, yeah."

"I am not going to hide! I didn't do anything wrong."

"I know that."

"Besides, there are three good reasons for me to enjoy myself while I'm here. First of all, it'll make me harder to find, harder than just sitting right here where he knows he can find me. Second, I'll be in public. And third, I think he's telling the truth. If he wanted me dead, he would have done it yesterday."

"How can you trust him? He's Ministrix!"

A sarcastic reply died in her throat. Anything she could say would sound ridiculous. Her initial fright from the night before had given way to . . . well, not trust. Not sympathy either. But as Isolda laid awake, replaying the conversation with the Ministrix assassin, considering the data he had given her, nothing she remembered had seemed threatening. Maybe she was just fooling herself.

"I am not saying that I do," she finally said. "So is that bridge tour open to anyone?"

17

The doors to the lift opened. Before Isolda could step out, Gavin put an arm across the doorway.

"Are you sure about this?" he asked.

Isolda lifted his arm out of the way. "Stow it, steward. I'm going on the tour." She ignored Gavin's heavy sigh and walked out in the elevator lobby.

He stepped around her, waving to the gathered crowd. "Good afternoon, everyone! My name is Gav. I'll be your tour guide this afternoon."

Isolda tuned out Gavin's banter. He had practiced his spiel all the way from the lower class decks, mumbling it under his breath. Isolda could have recited it with him. Probably improve it too. *Thanks for paying an exorbitant amount to lounge around in a spaceship with amenities found in your nearest amusement parks...*

"I miss anything?"

Isolda froze, steel slamming around her mind. Her head whipped to one side. Crusader looked down at her. She spun forward, her lips clenched shut. She glared at Gavin, willing him to notice.

"What are you doing here?" The words, a bare hiss, finally escaped her mouth.

"Taking the tour. Thought that'd be obvious."

"No, I mean . . . are you stalking me?"

"Yes."

The quiet declaration sent further chills down from her skull and into her boots.

"And I've never seen a cruise liner's bridge before," Crusader went on. "May be useful someday."

Gavin wrapped up his introductory remarks and motioned for people to follow him. He glanced at Isolda with a broad smile. But his expression turned brittle, his grin frozen and his eyes wide. He must have spotted Crusader.

"Let's go then." Gavin's voice cracked. He winced and scurried away.

Isolda fell into step with the rest of the crowd, keenly aware that Crusader was only a meter behind her.

The crowd crossed through an archway into the Fantasy Forest. A wall of warm air cascaded over her, carrying with it a mossy, wet smell. The nearest walls were painted beige and they curved down into the ground. The crowd pressed into a small, grassy clearing shaped like a half-oval. Colorful wildflowers bordered the edges of the forest. A few even had butterflies perched on the petals.

Once they were all inside, Gavin led them along a stone pathway through gnarled trees. The ground was uneven, as were most of the stones that made up the path. As near as Isolda could tell, they really were walking through a dense forest, even though she knew that wasn't true. She peeked up toward the sky. Through the branches of the trees, she thought she spotted the tube they had walked through the day before, high overhead.

Then she spotted movement. She froze, as did many of the passengers. Gavin kept walking, chattering on about the state-of-the-art engineering that kept the Forest working.

Something exploded from within the trees. A massive creature sprinted from the fringe, something metal flashing in its hands. Isolda leapt back as the thing screamed in fury. She slammed into Crusader.

"Unit override! Stand down!" Gavin ran over and interposed himself between Isolda and the robot, a large centaur with a drawn sword. The creature's face, a rictus of rage, slackened and became impassive. Its arms relaxed and the sword clattered to the ground.

Gavin turned to the crowd and smiled sheepishly. "Sorry for the scare, ladies and gentlemen. I know that looked a little frightening, but none of us were in any real danger." He stepped closer to the inert centaur and knocked on its forehead. "The denizens of Fantasy Forest have multiple failsafes to make sure no one is ever injured."

"Then why did it charge us just now?" someone shouted.

"It was an oversight. I can assure you, even if I hadn't stopped him, we would have been perfectly safe. Their weapons can't actually hurt you. The blades are all blunted and are surrounded by a safety field that lessens the impact. The worst that they can do is tag you." Gavin hefted up the sword and smacked his hand against its edge. A small burst of paint splattered across his palm. He held it up to the crowd. "See? If you were in a battle, you'd know that you were hit, but that's all. Now let's keep going."

The crowd followed, a few people grumbling. Isolda cast one last glare at the centaur before stepping away. As she did, she noticed that Crusader had a hand at his waistband. Her eyes widened.

"Are you armed?" she whispered.

Crusader nodded, his gaze still on the robot.

"Aren't you worried that ship security will notice?"

He shook his head. "Haven't so far."

"What if they do? Don't you think they'll take your weapons?"

"They can try."

A chill slithered down Isolda's spine. She hurried to catch up with the rest of the group. Gavin continued his running narrative, pointing out areas of interest in the Forest: the castle, a river, a ridge that could be easily defended from elven attack. Isolda picked up on the tension in her friend's voice and posture.

Eventually the group passed through a stone arch and up a series of ramps into a gleaming silver hallway. Lit panels lined the walls, displaying schematics of the ship. The images rotated or grew larger, highlighting different sections. Isolda stopped to examine them, thinking maybe she'd find some interesting data. Instead, she discovered only gibberish. The supposed statistics and data streams were random characters. She rolled her eyes. It was all just flash for the passengers.

Gavin led them up a ramp and onto the main bridge. The crowd clustered toward the back. Isolda had to strain to see over people's shoulders.

The bridge was large, much larger than it had to be, a semicircle with a broad window that followed the room's curve. Low panels with blinking lights and data readouts lined the window, none of them taller than Isolda's waist. The room glowed with rich colors, burgundies and royal blues from the carpet and strips along the controls. Crew in crisp white uniforms bustled about. Most orbited a man in the middle of the bridge. He turned to the tour and smiled warmly, his teeth gleaming, his beard neatly trimmed. He strode forward, his posture straight and his head tipped back ever so slightly. A captain, if Isolda had ever seen one.

"Greetings! Welcome to the bridge of the *PLC Sybaritic*. I am Captain Oswalt Norrison. From here, our entire ship is controlled, all of its systems regulated. Why, I could probably run the whole ship by myself." The captain laughed, a gregarious boom that echoed around the room.

One of the crew, a woman with an engineering logo on her arm, rolled her eyes.

Isolda stifled a giggle. The engineer would make Norrison pay for that stupid remark.

The captain, oblivious to the impending revenge, strolled toward one end of the controls, the group in tow. "Let me assure you, Pearson Lines only employs state-of-the-art technology and we spare no expense to maintain our technological standards. Six months ago, the *Sybaritic* was in dry-dock at Westward Station for a complete overhaul of her starboard engine housing . . ."

Isolda tuned out the chatter and drifted closer to the displays. Unlike the light show in the corridor, these screens had actual hard data she could examine. The first panel showed an overall schematic of the ship, labeling the crew areas, the passenger decks, the private docking berths, all of it. Next, a computer systems throughput analyzer. She wasn't an expert but as near as she could tell, it looked like the system lagged a bit.

A smile tugged at her lips when she saw the next panel. Engine systems, tunneler drive harmonics— this made sense to her. She let out a low whistle when she saw the energy output. The *Sybaritic* definitely put the *Regent's Light* to shame.

"Engineer?"

She turned at the soft voice. It was the engineer she had noticed.

Isolda nodded. "You really produce that much energy out of the engines?"

The woman smiled. "And that's with two of the generators down for inspection." The engineer looked Isolda over, her lips pursed. "Where have you served?"

"Freighters via the guild, mostly. A couple of light cruisers here and there."

"Between assignments?"

Isolda glanced over at Crusader, who seemed to be listening to whatever drivel Norrison spouted. But he checked on her out of the corner of his eye.

"You could say that."

The engineer pursed her lips again, but this time, thoughtfulness lurked in the other woman's eyes. "Do you have any experience with the Elan-X series of apertures?"

"I've served on two ships that used Elan-X7s."

"Good. Why not ditch the tour and come with me down to engineering? We could use another tech." She leaned in close. "Just between you and me, Captain Norrison *can't* exactly run the ship by himself."

"Of course not." She grinned, and a tremor shot up Isolda's spine. This was perfect! A job would mean she could stay on the *Sybaritic* longer than Crusader. He'd eventually have to leave. Sure, he'd know where she was, but she could find a way to sneak off at some future port of call, disappear again. The question of whether or not she could trust Crusader would be moot.

The woman led her away from the group but the engineering panel blatted, a low trill. The engineer froze.

Isolda could see why. A feedback loop had formed within the tunneler aperture, a harmonic resonance that would eventually overload the sensitive instruments. She had never seen nor heard of anything like it.

"Any ideas what this is?" The engineer leaned over the panel, calling up system diagnostics.

Isolda scanned the new data. Fuel injection systems were nominal but that wouldn't last, given the way the aperture was vibrating. "Software problems?"

"I doubt it. We just upgraded the monitoring programs last week and they were running well within specs when I checked them an hour ago."

"Engineer Laskin, report!"

Isolda glanced at Norrison. The gregarious nature had disappeared. A stern, disciplined face stared down at them.

"Don't know, sir. Working on it."

Norrison glared at Isolda as if he blamed her, then he turned to the group. "Ladies and gentlemen, I hate to do this, but we'll need to cut our tour short. We seem to be facing some sort of technical issue."

"Not technical issues."

The simple declaration, quiet yet rough, cut through the captain's words. Crusader stepped forward. He shoved Engineer Laskin out of the way. He ignored her protest, flipping through the data. He stopped on a graph showing the aperture output charted against energy input.

"Problem's there. Ever hear of a tunnel buster?"

Norrison shook his head. So did the engineer. Isolda had never heard of one either.

"Clever little thing," Crusader said. "Don't know all the science of it, but it's basically a bomb. You drop it in the path of a ship you want to stop. The moment it detects the ship in tunnel space, it detonates, disrupts the harmonics, and the ship drops back into normal space. Someone really wants to get on this ship right now."

The color drained from Norrison's face. "You mean . . ."

Crusader nodded. "You're about to be boarded." He fixed his gaze on Isolda. "By the Ministrix."

18

Westin paled. Subtle, but Crusader noticed. Her breathing sharpened, her carotid artery throbbed. Scared? Most likely.

Crusader frowned. Hollowness tugged at his arms. No, not his arms—a hollowness in front of his chest. He found himself wanting to pull Westin close, hold her. Really? The ache intensified, clawing at his chest. Not the void this time. Warmer. Softer. His hands twitched upward, a subtle reach for her.

He wrenched his arms to his side. Focus.

The other passengers were murmuring. One of the bridge crew had herded them into a tight knot at one end of the bridge. Hard to tell if they had heard anything, but they had to know something was happening.

The captain was talking. "They're coming here? Why?"

"No idea," Crusader said. "Could be an inspection. Maybe they want someone on board."

Westin flinched, took a step toward her friend, the steward. Crusader clenched his jaw. It was possible the Ministrix was here for some other reason. But he didn't believe in coincidences. All things worked for the Almighty's glory. Even this.

"Security!" Norrison's voice boomed through the now silent bridge.

Crusader clamped a hand on the man's shoulder. He squeezed hard enough to make sure he had Norrison's attention. "Bad idea. Anyone in their way will be collateral damage."

"So what should we do then?" The fight drained from Norrison as quickly as it appeared.

"All passengers in their cabins, all non-essential crew in their berths. No interference. Let them board and go."

Norrison nodded, then scurried away parroting Crusader's suggestions as if he had thought of them.

Crusader turned to Westin next. She shied away but didn't run. "You, go to my cabin," he said. "Upper Class, A-9. Lock yourself in. Stay there until I come back."

"And where are you going?"

He pulled the parrot from his pocket, affixed it to his shoulder. "Might help if they see a familiar face when they get here."

The steward—what was his name again?—pressed between them and jabbed a finger in Crusader's face. "No way. If anyone's going to meet them, it should be a representative of the ship."

Crusader crossed his arms. "Fine. You volunteering?"

The steward's eyes blazed, but he didn't answer.

"Didn't think so. Go with her if you're scared. I don't care."

The steward's mouth tightened and Crusader braced himself for another verbal barrage. But Westin took him by the arm and tugged him away.

"Ladies and gentlemen." Norrison's voice blared from every speaker. "Our engineers have detected a problem in our tunnel drive. We will be coming out of tunnel space in just a few moments so they can repair it. The transition might be a little rough, so I am hereby sounding general quarters. Return to your cabins immediately. We will unlock the ship's entertainment library. You may enjoy any of our entertainment features, gratis. Thank you." Norrison replaced the microphone and then herded the confused tour group toward the exits.

Westin lingered, cast a look in his direction. Crusader nodded. She left.

Once the tourists were gone, Norrison returned to Crusader's side. "Now what?"

"We find where they'll dock." Crusader leaned over the ship's schematic and scrolled through the map. They wouldn't choose a normal docking berth. Most people would expect that and position security forces accordingly. They'd look for something they could breach with minimal effort. They'd want someplace with easy access to most of the ship too. He stabbed his finger onto the schematic. "There. Secondary maintenance port."

He turned and started for the bridge's entrance. Before he could make it, though, a hand dropped onto his shoulder. He glanced back at Norrison.

"Thank you," the captain whispered. "If we make it out of this, I'll be sure to comp your room."

Crusader quirked a brow at him. "I appreciate that."

When Crusader was halfway to the secondary port, the *Sybaritic* bucked under his feet. He spilled headlong into a bulkhead. Once he was on his feet again, he picked up his pace. The tunnel buster had done its work. The *Sybaritic* was back in real space, far from its destination, far from help. The Ministrix team would board in moments.

So who would it be? Probably not an inspection team. Holiness Compliance Officers, while thorough and far-reaching, were not known for their bravery. The nearest inspection post was light years away, behind the Ministrix border.

Military raid? Also doubtful. The *Sybaritic* had no strategic value. No way the Deacon of Defense would authorize a strike on a Praesidium vessel, and a civilian one at that, outside of clear Ministrix jurisdiction.

Crusader turned a corner, the secondary maintenance port coming into view. That left Intelligence. Given the use of a tunnel buster, it was either a strike team or a botched covert insertion. A tunnel buster could easily be mistaken for a problem with the engines. The Ministrix had used that to sneak agents onto Praesidium vessels in the past. Maybe the *Sybaritic* was about to pick up another passenger. Maybe. But Crusader felt it was still more likely to be a strike team. Maybe it would be Amalric's team. Crusader had worked with him in the past. They had an understanding.

The lights in the corridor flickered and a series of low metallic thumps resounded down the corridor. The Ministrix ship had docked.

A shower of sparks erupted in the middle of the door. Crusader's face pinched into a frown. So much for the covert insertion idea. He backed around the corner, turned his face away. Any moment.

The light from the blast pierced his closed eyelids, the roar drowned out all else. The sharp smell of explosives clawed up his nostrils. He coughed, ignoring the tingle wriggling down his throat. He took a deep breath. Then he spread his arms out, parallel to the deck, palms outward. He stepped around the corner, careful to keep his movements slow.

Smoke crept along the deck from the hole in the port. Crusader didn't like it. There was too much. Had they dropped a cloaking grenade in along with the breaching charge? Why the extra precaution? Even though the haze obscured the far end of the corridor, he could still spot flickers of movement. There, the point man coming through. Now two more. Soon the entire ten-man team was through and inching down the corridor.

Crusader waited. The fog wouldn't hide them forever. Sure enough, the point man came out and snapped his rifle to point at Crusader. A storm roiled in Crusader's stomach. He clamped his jaw shut, fighting to keep the bile from his mouth. A tremor worked its way up his arm.

More of the strike team emerged, each of them aiming at Crusader in turn. The final man to appear was their commander. Crusader recognized him immediately. Phinehas. Not the best commander but competent in his own way.

"Crusader." Phinehas dipped his head in a curt nod.

Crusader returned the gesture. "Good to see you. I have a situation—"

"This will save us some time," Phinehas said. "Kill him."

19

Crusader didn't wait for the squad to obey. He dropped and rolled forward as they opened fire. Heat flashed past him, not an actual hit but close enough to worry him. He popped off the deck and slammed into the point man. The soldier tried to shake him off. Crusader smashed him face-first into the bulkhead.

The man's weapon came free as he fell to the deck. Crusader scooped it up and shot the nearest soldier's knee. He used the distraction to pull the point man's pack free. Then he fell back, peppering the corridor with shots. He knew he wouldn't hit anyone, but the random firing would discourage the team from advancing.

He made it around the corner. He ignored Phinehas's shouted orders, instead opening the pack. Not much. Spare power packs for the rifle. Field med kit. Crusader smirked as his fingers closed around the explosives. Not many—the point man must have used the rest for the breach—but enough.

His head snapped up, suddenly aware of the silence. Not good. Activate the parrot's sensors? He cursed himself for not thinking of it sooner. No time now.

"Coming after me?" he shouted.

There. The rustle of fabric, right around the corner. He had surprised someone. He dove back, firing a few more times. Someone shouted, a strangled curse. Lucky shot, couldn't count on another. Crusader sprinted away, pulling the charges from the pack and activating the parrot. He dropped the point man's pack. He wouldn't need the rest of it. Not where he was going.

Isolda paced the cabin, frustrated. Crimson light bathed the room, an emergency message scrolling by on every display. Captain Norrison appeared periodically, a pre-recorded message encouraging the passengers to remain calm while the crew worked to sort out the present situation. She laughed. The crew was cowering, not working.

Just like her. She balled her hands into fists. She shouldn't be hiding. She should be . . . well, she didn't know exactly what. Something. Anything. It was better than sharing an assassin's room with Gavin.

She turned to a bag sitting on the king size bed. Maybe there'd be something in there. Crusader was an assassin—who knew what kind of weapons he might have in his room? She strode over to the bed and ripped the bag open.

"What are you doing?" Gavin asked. "I don't think he'll be happy."

"I don't care. There's gotta be something in here we can use."

In the bag, she found only clothing and toiletries, which she pawed through and pushed aside. There wasn't much here. Certainly nothing deadly. Did he even have any extra weapons? He said he was armed and she doubted he lied—she'd seen his knife, after all. But nothing more? She dumped out the contents and shoved them around. A data reader, clothing, reams of paper covered with half-finished sketches. Had he hidden the rest of his guns under the bed? She knelt down and stuck her arm underneath. Nothing.

"Look at this."

She glanced at Gavin, who held Crusader's data reader. "I thought you didn't want to mess with his stuff."

He shrugged. "Too late for that. Check this out, though. We've got the command codes to his ship. The *Purim*." He held it up and smiled. "We could get you out of here."

Isolda frowned. "Gav, they brought the *Sybaritic* out of tunnel space. What makes you think they wouldn't be able to stop a smaller ship too? Besides, Crusader told us to stay here."

Gavin rolled his eyes. "And we're going to take advice from the man who was sent here to kill you? I've got a plan. Right now, we've got about a dozen private vessels docked in our landing bay, including the *Purim*, okay? In case of an emergency, you can set the docking bay to blow all the private vessels out of the *Sybaritic* at once. We set the timer, get on the *Purim*, and then bang, we're out. They'll think someone panicked and jettisoned the ships. Then we just hit the engines and go. It'll work. Trust me!"

Isolda chewed on her bottom lip. It sounded like it could work. Maybe.

There was no denying the excitement boiling off of Gavin. "Isolda, I can do this. You know I can."

She did. He could. "All right, let's go," she said.

Gavin used his crew code to override the lock on the doors. Emergency lights bathed the corridors a bloody crimson. They raced down the empty halls.

Isolda paused as she passed a large window overlooking the Fantasy Forest. A lone figure knelt in the transparent tube that ran from the docking port to the rest of the ship. She leaned forward, trying to get a better look at him. Was that Crusader? What was he doing? It looked like he was fiddling with something near his feet but she couldn't really tell for sure.

A pang of regret shot through her. It didn't feel right, stealing his ship and leaving him behind. She felt like she should do more for him, but what else could she do?

"Thanks for everything," she whispered, and turned to follow Gavin to the nearest elevator.

Crusader peeked around the corner. The assault team had killed the lights. Smart move. But not good enough. He still spotted them, the glint of their equipment dancing through the shadows. He snapped the rifle to his shoulder and fired. Someone cursed and hit the deck. He fired a few more random shots and then retreated down the tube. Still no time to scan his work and make sure he did it right. He'd just have to hope that providence was on his side.

Was it? He gritted his teeth at the thought. No matter how he looked at it, he was defying the Ministrix. Sub-Deacon abd al Sami had ordered his death. Deacon Siseal had ordered Westin's. Neither had happened yet because of Crusader. Now he was fighting a Ministrix strike team. The Ministrix bore God's righteous sword for the judgment of the lost and fallen. Who was he to resist? But should he really just allow himself to be killed?

He'd have to sort that out later. Time to get out of the tube.

With a ponderous groan, metallic doors closed at the other end of the tunnel, cutting him off from the rest of the ship.

He skidded to a halt. Not good. Who had done that? Had the strike team hacked the ship's security systems to try and contain him? Or maybe the *Sybaritic*'s officers were trying to box in the strike team. Either way, he was trapped.

He hung his head. Not how he wanted things to go, but nothing he could do. He turned around. The tactical team entered the tube, their weapons trained on him. They approached slowly, suspecting a trap.

Good for them.

Crusader let his weapon clatter to the floor. Arms out, palms forward. Hopefully they wouldn't notice his preparations. More of the team emerged. No one said anything. Crusader took a deep breath, held it, then released it. Ready as he'd ever be. "Detonate," he whispered.

The tube shattered in flames, throwing the tactical team into the Fantasy Forest. A crack snaked from the wreckage, traveling the length of the floor. It shot between Crusader's feet. The floor shattered beneath him and he too fell into the Forest.

Branches clawed at his face, his hands. The last thing he saw clearly was the stone banks of the river rushing up to meet him and then darkness exploded in his eyes.

150

20

They were halfway to the docking ring when the elevator bucked violently, throwing them to the floor. It came to a halt. Isolda froze, fear screaming through her. What was that? Did something rupture? Was the ship venting atmosphere? Was death coming for her the way it had . . .

No, she and Gavin seemed fine. She pushed Gavin off of her and looked around. She knelt down next to the elevator's access panel and pried it open. A few tweaks to the controls unlocked the doors and allowed her to push them open. She shimmied through the opening. A glance confirmed the corridor was deserted. The blinking lights of a Fantasy Forest control panel distracted her, but then she remembered to help pull Gavin from the elevator car.

"So where are we?" she asked.

Gavin looked around. "Looks like deck six. Nowhere near the docking bay."

"Figures."

He smiled weakly. "Sorry. But it's not all bad. We go down this hall, we can find an engineering crawlspace. It'll be a bit more round-about, but we can crawl all the way to the docking ports."

She broke into a jog. He soon puffed along next to her. She cast a reassuring smile in his direction. She'd have to find a way to make this up to him when they made it out.

If they made it out.

She shook her head, trying to dislodge the nagging thought. No ifs here. They would make it. She knew they would.

They darted past a large bank of windows that overlooked the Fantasy Forest. Isolda glanced to her left and then skidded to a halt.

"Gav, look at this."

He stopped as well. She walked up to the glass, pressed her hands against it.

The transit tube was destroyed. Small fires burned in the Fantasy Forest beneath the shattered tube. She leaned forward, trying to see through the ruined trees.

"Captain Norrison isn't going to like that," Gavin said.

She ignored her friend. There, caught in a tree, was a person wearing black armor of some kind. Near the trunk was another. And over by the river bank . . .

Isolda gasped. Crusader lay sprawled on the rocks, blood spattered across his face. He didn't move. Was he even breathing? She couldn't tell. She bit her lower lip.

"Let's go, Isolda," Gavin whispered. "We have to get out of here."

She nodded absently. She took a step but then stopped, a slight movement catching her eye. Crusader's arm had moved. Just a little. He was alive! Relief surged through her.

But it died as quickly as it appeared. Three more men in black armor appeared, looking down from the end of the destroyed tube. They turned to each other and conferred before one produced a length of rope and fed it out to the Forest floor.

She spun on Gavin. "They're going to finish Crusader off."

"Good," Gavin said. "That'll give us enough time to get to the ship." He started to move.

She snared his arm. "We have to help him."

Gavin stared at her, his eyes wide. "Are you crazy?"

She ignored the question. "Where's the nearest security locker? Maybe if we get some weapons—"

"Do you know how to use them?" He barely waited for her to answer. "And those are Ministrix commandos. You think the two of us could take them on?"

"Then we'll need reinforcements."

"From where? Thanks to your 'friend,' Captain Norrison ordered the entire ship, including the security personnel, into lockdown. By the time we could find anybody and persuade them to break orders, it'll all be over for him. Let's just get out of here."

Isolda thought for a few moments then turned and dashed down the corridor.

"Where are you going?" Gavin shouted. "The docks are the other way!"

She ignored him. She knew where she was going. She was going to save Crusader.

Light danced through Crusader's closed eyes. He coughed, setting off a storm of static in his chest. He winced. From the severity, probably broken ribs. At least two. He took a deep breath. He hadn't punctured a lung.

He propped himself up, noting the weakness in his left arm. Dislocated shoulder. He bent the arm, then wrenched it away. The shoulder reset itself. He'd need to find medical help soon. If he survived that long.

He looked around at the wreckage. One member of the strike team had landed in the upper branches of a tree. Another lay in a heap two meters to Crusader's left. Given his injuries, not an acceptable trade-off, especially since the survivors were preparing to rappel into the Forest.

He pulled himself off the rock with his good arm. Had to find a weapon. Stick, rock, didn't matter. The fight wasn't over yet and nobody was going to come and help him.

Isolda let out a triumphant squeal when she spotted the gaming substation. She ripped the access cover open and exposed the controls. Bypassing the security proved to be easier than she had expected. Whoever was running the station had left it online.

Gavin skidded to a halt next to her. "What are you doing?"

"Getting reinforcements."

"From the game robots in the Forest?"

"You have a better idea?"

How many? She hit the "All" button and waited for the computer to activate the units. Next came the targeting subroutine. She frowned. Not a lot of choices. Definitely no way to say "Ministrix commando team." She settled on "wearing black." Was Crusader wearing black? She couldn't remember. Hopefully not.

"In case you forgot, they're not going to be able to hurt the commandos. Their weapons aren't real," Gavin said.

"I know."

"Then how is this going to help?"

Isolda smiled and smacked the "Engage" button. She turned to Gavin. "This will give him a fighting chance. Now let's get out of here."

Not good. No weapons. The fallen branches, while appearing to have weight, proved useless. No mass. No loose stones either. Crusader propped himself against a tree trunk and waited. He wasn't giving up. But he'd have to face Phinehas empty-handed.

The three commandos appeared in the forest, their leader at the center. Phinehas smirked down at Crusader. "It's nothing personal, Crusader. But I have my orders."

"I'm sure." Could he kick Phinehas's legs out from under him? No. "Can you just tell me one thing?"

Phinehas's eyes narrowed. Did he recognize it as a stall? Probably. But any time Crusader could gain would be time he could potentially use.

"What?" Phinehas asked.

"What did I ever do to Sub-Deacon abd al Sami?"

Phinehas snorted. "Do you really think he shared that with me? Do the Deacons ever? They decide, we obey. That's the way it works."

The lights in the Forest blazed. A trumpet blared in the distance. The commandos whirled, ending up back to back in a defensive circle.

A high-pitched voice giggled, the sound darting through the forest. "Glomp!"

A herd of centaurs exploded from the trees. Their hooves churned the ground as they came, the leader pointing at the commandos. Phinehas fired at him, his beam lancing through the lead robot's shoulder. The centaurs didn't stop until they tackled the commandos.

The centaurs were followed by elves, dwarves, teddy bears, all manner of creatures. The game robots laughed as they piled onto the commandos. The Ministrix troops struggled to get free but they couldn't get out from under the pile.

A giant teddy bear latched onto the leg of one of the commandos and squeezed. "I wuv you!" the robot squealed.

Crusader stared at the mass of thrashing limbs. He didn't know why this had happened, but it was best not to stay here. Let the *Sybaritic*'s security deal with them. He had to find Westin.

Isolda double-checked the data reader and re-entered the security code. The *Purim*'s access panel blatted at her again. She slapped the panel. Why wasn't it working?

Getting across the *Sybaritic* and to the *Purim* had taken longer than she'd thought it would. They'd kept stumbling across sealed doors. While they'd managed to bypass each one, that took time. She hoped her diversion had worked, but she had to assume that the commandos had killed Crusader and were after them.

But they had finally arrived outside Crusader's ship. Only now the blasted thing wasn't letting them in, even though they had its access codes.

"Come on!" Gavin bounced on his heels and looked back up the corridor.

"I'm going as fast as I can." She ground her teeth, entered the code again. The same harsh buzzing. "I don't get this."

"I changed the code."

Isolda whipped around. Crusader hobbled after them. She gasped. The assassin looked half-dead. The blood caked to his face stood out against his pale skin.

He took another limping step forward. "I told you to stay in my room."

"Like we're going to listen to you," Gavin said.

Crusader fixed Gavin with a withering gaze. Her friend shrank away.

"You're going to leave me here?" Crusader asked.

"Wouldn't you?" Isolda countered.

"No. You need me."

"Like a hole in a hull."

Crusader ignored Gavin's comment this time. He stared at Isolda.

"How do you think you'll get by the Ministrix ship?" Crusader asked.

"Easy," Gavin said. "She's got me."

Crusader snorted. "There's your hole in the hull."

"Hey!" Gavin snapped.

Isolda forced herself to meet his gaze.

He nodded. "You need me," he repeated. "Not just for the codes. Need to find out what the Ministrix wants. You can't do that alone."

Isolda considered it. He certainly seemed willing to stand up to the Ministrix. And he might have resources she wouldn't in figuring all of this out.

She stepped aside. "Then let's go."

21

Weakness crept up Crusader's legs, clawed at his chest. He couldn't collapse, not yet. He glanced down the corridor toward the *Purim*'s medical bay. The equipment there could help. But they hadn't escaped yet. Phinehas's team could work free of the pile at any time.

The steward pushed his way past Crusader and headed for the cockpit. Westin followed but she paused long enough to touch his arm. His skin sizzled at the point of contact, different from the tingling in his chest. The surge of energy chased away the lethargy. Westin turned and headed down the corridor and Crusader followed, the medical bay forgotten.

He frowned when he reached the cockpit. The steward had slid into the pilot's chair and was working to call up the systems. Westin dropped into the copilot's seat and busied herself as well.

"You set the bay to eject the other ships?" Westin asked.

"Way ahead of you. Powering up main thrusters," the steward reported.

The deck plates vibrated under Crusader's feet, a rhythmic pinging accompanying the rattle from deep below.

"Powering up the weapons." The steward whistled then turned in his chair to look at Crusader. "You don't fool around, do you? You can head on back to medical if you want. We've got things under control here."

Crusader stared at the man. He had changed somehow. Crusader actually considered doing what he was told. But he shook his head. "No. My ship. I stay here."

The steward's jaw clenched but he turned back to the viewport. He pointed ahead. "You guys ready for this? In three, two, one, now."

A muffled *whump* sounded below the ship.

"There go the bay doors," Gavin's fingers danced across the controls. "Brace yourself."

The world pitched wildly in the viewport. Crusader's stomach lurched as the hulls of other ships flashed past them. What was that idiot doing? They'd be lucky if they didn't slam into another vessel.

"Relax," the steward said. "All of these ships are owned by Pearsons' wealthiest customers. There's no way Pearson would risk damaging them. It may not seem like it, but everything is fine." He touched the controls.

The spinning in the viewport stopped and the churning in Crusader's stomach stilled. He let out a long breath.

"Now all we have to do is wait here until . . ." The steward sat up in his chair and looked out the viewport. "Well, now, isn't that interesting."

"What?" Westin asked.

"There's only one Ministrix ship and it's clamped onto the hull." The steward turned in his chair, a wolfish grin on his face.

"Of course," Crusader said. "This deep in Praesidium space? Any more than that would attract too much attention."

Isolda leaned over the console. "They don't seem to have noticed us. No active scans, anyway."

"I say we take advantage of it," the steward said.

"What are you thinking?" Westin asked.

"I thought we'd swing around and try to take out the Ministrix ship, make sure they can't follow us."

"No." Crusader grabbed the back of the pilot's chair. "Don't destroy them. Just disable the engines."

The steward glared at him. Westin touched his arm and his features softened. Cold clawed at Crusader's heart before the numbness overwhelmed him again.

"Okay," the steward said. "Quick strafing run and then we're on our way."

The steward's fingers flew over the controls. Crusader checked the sensor readouts. The steward had tweaked the *Purim*'s thrusters. The ship had started a gentle tumble, not enough to attract attention, but enough to reorient it for a strafing run. Crusader's eyes narrowed. Whoever this steward was, he was good.

"There she is."

Crusader ducked low to see where he was pointing. Perched on the *Sybaritic* was a squat, sleek vessel, vaguely shaped like a grasshopper. Its black hull stood out against the gleaming surface of the cruise vessel.

The steward grunted. "They're going to notice once I fire up the weapons and engines. You sure I can't take it out?"

"Gav." Westin's voice was a mere whisper.

He sighed. "Okay, okay. You got it."

The steward mashed his hand on the controls and a whine built behind them. The ship dropped closer to the *Sybaritic's* hull. Crusader took another look at the steward. He wasn't just good. He was likely an ace. As near as Crusader could tell, the *Purim* skimmed the cruiseship's hull with only two meters' clearance. The Ministrix ship grew larger in the viewport. Crusader worried that they would collide with it. But then the commando ship leapt from the hull in a burst of flame. Westin shrieked as the *Purim* sliced through the thrust, shoved closer to the liner. Then they blasted away from the *Sybaritic*.

"We've got a problem," the steward said, his voice a bare grunt. "They're coming after us. Any ideas?"

Silence descended on the cockpit. Crusader tried to formulate a plan, but a wave of fatigue sloshed through his mind.

Westin broke the quiet. "We should run. I don't know what kind of weapons we have, but I'd be willing to bet they've got better."

"Maybe not," the steward said. "We've got some pretty high end stuff here. Two tractor beams, a full complement of missiles and laser bursters."

"No. We run. Tunnel out, random directions, at least half a dozen times. Lose them," Crusader said.

The steward sighed, his fingers flying over the controls. "As ordered. Laying in a course, firing up the tunneler drive. And we go in three . . . two . . ."

The computer blatted at them. "Incoming message, priority one."

"Hold," Crusader said. "Computer, sender ID."

"Hyrcanus."

"Time to download?"

A bank of red lights blazed on the panel, accompanied by a harsh trilling.

The steward looked over the instruments and laughed ruefully. "What does it matter? They just grazed our starboard thruster. We need to get out of here now!"

The computer, oblivious to the panic in the steward's voice, answered anyway. "Approximately two minutes."

"Evasive maneuvers," Crusader ordered, leaning over the chair. "Get me those two minutes. We need that message."

"Why? Is it really worth dying for?"

He turned to Westin. Maybe she'd be more reasonable. "Hyrcanus was Balaam's liaison. He might know what all this is about."

Westin blinked, looked down at the panel. "Gav, do it."

The steward grumbled under his breath. "As ordered."

The starfield dropped away as the *Purim* dove into a corkscrew.

Crusader's stomach lurched. He dug his fingers into the chair back. He glanced at the computer. Fifty percent downloaded.

The ship bucked under his feet and the steward cursed. "They hit one of our inertial sinks. Seventy percent, heading south fast. You know what'll happen if it gives out."

Crusader did. Total structural failure. "Keep moving. Almost there."

The starfield spun the other way and Crusader stumbled, tripping to one wall. His head slammed into the panel. The stars burst through the viewport and swam through his head. He fought to stay conscious. He knelt, closing his eyes and waiting for the confirmation signal.

The computer bleeped and the steward shouted, "Firing the tunneler!"

The engines thrummed loudly. The noise threatened to split Crusader's skull, and a series of pops ran through the hull. They were gone.

Crusader rose from his crouching position. "File received?" he asked.

Westin checked the panel. "Got it. The computer is processing it now."

Crusader nodded. Another piece to the puzzle, hopefully. But why would Hyrcanus be contacting Balaam now? "Can you check the engines? Make sure they're still working?"

Westin nodded. "No problem. Give me a half hour."

"Fine. You." He pointed to the steward. "Remember the plan. Six random tunnels. Then find some cover."

"And what are you going to be doing?" the steward asked.

Crusader turned to leave the cockpit. "Medical."

***

Isolda walked out of the *Purim*'s engine bay a half hour later. Thankfully, the engines had held up pretty well under the assault. She had been able to patch things together with what spare parts they had. She had even managed to tweak an extra twenty-five percent efficiency out of the tunneler apertures. The previous owner obviously hadn't known his way around the engines.

She froze. Crusader emerged from the medical bay, his shirt off and his chest wrapped with bandages. He looked a lot better. The color had returned to his cheeks and he seemed a bit more alert. And yet his eyes remained dead orbs set in his face.

He nodded to her. "Finished with the engines?"

"We should be good for a while. You may want to find a repair bay after you drop us off."

Crusader frowned. "What makes you think we're separating?"

Cold sluiced down Isolda's back. "I just figured that once we had escaped—"

"No. You have something Deacon Siseal needs."

"But I don't know what it is!"

"Until we figure out what abd al Sami's after, we stick together."

Crusader took her by the elbow and steered her back toward the cockpit.

Gavin turned around as they entered, worry splashed across his face.

Crusader shoved her into the copilot chair and then crossed his arms. "Status?"

Gavin glanced at Isolda, then turned to Crusader. "We're almost done with the last of the random tunnels." He frowned. "What's going on?"

"Time to be honest, 'Gavin.' Who are you really?"

Isolda froze. This wasn't good. There was no telling what Crusader might do if he learned the truth.

The color drained from Gavin's face. His mouth worked for a few moments, producing no sound. "I'm Gavin Odell, steward for Pearson Lines."

"No." Crusader leaned over Gavin. "Not a steward. You fly too well. Who are you?"

Gavin shrank back in his chair as Crusader bore down even closer. He then looked down and away. "I am . . . I was . . . Gabriel Liddel."

Crusader's head snapped back as if struck. "Helmsman for the *Second Horseman*? The traitor?"

Gavin bristled. "I'm no traitor."

"You disobeyed direct orders."

"They wanted me to sanitize an entire colony!"

"Not your place to question orders, is it?" Crusader said. "You knew that. Obedience brings salvation. So the Ministrix teaches, so we believe. By refusing your orders, you cut yourself off from the Church and thereby damned yourself for all eternity."

Gavin's face soured. "And what were your orders again?"

Crusader didn't answer. His brow furrowed. "So why be a steward? Why not a pilot? If you piloted for either the shipping line or the military, the pay would be better."

"I can't join the Praesidium Navy, thanks to the Toleration Act. And we didn't think it'd be a good idea for me to try to be a pilot for Pearson. It might lead to awkward questions."

"'We'? The people who forged your new ID?"

Gavin's eyes grew wide at Crusader's question.

The assassin leaned in closer. "So the Catacombs are real. You went through them. Started as Gabriel Liddell, came out as 'Gavin Odell.'"

Gavin stammered for a few moments. Isolda shut her eyes. This was a disaster.

"This is what abd al Sami wants. He wants the Catacombs." Crusader turned to Isolda. "And he must know you have that information."

"How do you know that abd al Sami is after the Catacombs?" Gavin sat up a little straighter. "He doesn't know for sure that it exists. *You* didn't know until just now. What if he doesn't want the Catacombs at all? If this abd al Sami is in R&D, I'm thinking he's wanting Dr. Keleman's research."

Crusader glowered at Gavin. To his credit, Gavin didn't back down.

Isolda leapt between them, planting her hands on Crusader's chest. "Why don't we listen to the message? Maybe this 'Hyrcanus' person will give us a clue."

Crusader nodded and reached past her to the controls.

She breathed in, surprised at the sudden rush of musk. Dizziness chased through her head. She closed her eyes. What was wrong with her?

Then Crusader stepped back, and her head cleared. She turned to face the holo-emitter.

A cloud of static appeared, a flickering ball that transformed into a face . . . kind of. Its features remained hazy. Several times, it expanded to almost comic proportions but never grew clear enough to where she could recognize the individual. She cast a questioning glance at Crusader.

"Security feature," he said.

"Uh, hey, bud," a male voice said from the recording. "Listen, I know you got your hands full, what with your current . . . business trip. Good luck with that. I know you always enjoy them. Anyway, I got a problem. You know that infestation

I'm dealing with on Eps-Prime? Yeah, we're having trouble tracking down the nest. If you wrap up your business early and you've got nothing else to do from the home office . . . well, stop by, okay?"

And with that, the hologram disappeared.

"We almost got killed for that?" Gavin said. "How did this help us?"

"By telling us where Hyrcanus is," Crusader said.

"Who is Hyrcanus?" Isolda asked. "And why do we want to know where he is?"

"He was Balaam's liaison officer," Crusader said. "It's possible Balaam may have shared some information with him, information we can use to figure out what's happening. And now we know where he is. Eps-Prime. Hunting for a Praesidium spy cell."

"That'd be great if we knew what he looked like!"

"I do. I can find him," Crusader said.

"And he can tell us why this abd al Sami wants me so badly?" Isolda asked.

Crusader nodded. "The Catacombs."

Gavin snorted. "You mean Keleman's research."

Isolda nodded. She looked at Crusader and a hollowness opened up inside her chest. As good as it would be to be free from this nightmare, she couldn't help but wonder if maybe it wasn't so bad after all.

22

Altair abd al Sami gripped his legs so hard he worried he would rip his kneecaps off. No word from Phinehas or his team yet. They should have intercepted the *Sybaritic* two days ago. They should have submitted some sort of report by now. Something had gone wrong.

He spun in his chair, finding himself face-to-face with a mural of the Triumphant Christ. The Revered Hand insisted every Ministrix official display the work in his or her office. It depicted the Christ stepping down from the cross, His hand outstretched with an accusing finger. He pointed to the surrounding crowd, engaged in debauchery and decadent living.

Standing next to Him in the image, raising the iron bar of the Ministrix, was the Revered Hand himself, answering the call.

The mural was supposed to inspire devotion to the Ministrix's cause. And yet Altair could see only accusation in the Christ's eyes. He was on the cusp of failure. If Phinehas didn't secure Isolda Westin, that would lead to questions he didn't want to answer. Especially not to Deacon Siseal. His grip tightened on his legs. If he had to face that ridiculous gloryhound and explain this . . .

"I take it I am intruding?"

Altair whirled, startled by the hazy voice. He groaned when he realized that the disembodied head of Kolya Krestyanov hovered over the holo-emitter.

"What do you want, Krestyanov?" he demanded.

The Praesidium spymaster smiled broadly. "Is that any way to greet a friend? No exchange of pleasantries?"

Altair groaned, his eyes grinding shut. His assistant had a habit of patching Krestyanov's calls through without asking first. He'd have to chastise him again. Maybe replace him. But that was a problem for another time.

"What do you want?" He emphasized each word, loading them with as much venom as he could muster.

Krestyanov sighed. "Such rudeness. Very well. We do have business. We have detained one of your strike teams. They attacked a civilian liner, blew a hole in its hull. Only swift action by the valiant crew stemmed the violence. We also captured their transport craft. While your agents have not spoken openly to my people, we have completed a preliminary analysis of their ship and believe the leader is codenamed 'Phinehas.'"

Altair swallowed a groan. The day just kept getting better and better.

Krestyanov laughed. "Let us arrange a trade, yes? You currently hold one of my field agents in the Tezcatlipoca Penal Colony. You must agree that Simone Weathers is too beautiful to languish in an asteroid prison, yes? You give me her, I give you Phinehas and his men. Even trade."

A trade? Altair looked down at his desk. He looked up at the image. "No deal. That's not even. Weathers worked our Jovian shipyards for the past year."

"You can hardly blame us," Krestyanov countered. "We know you are up to no good. Does the term 'Sharp Sickle' mean anything to you?"

Altair snorted. As if he would admit to it, even if it did. "No."

Krestyanov's eyes narrowed. "It does to someone in Ministrix Intelligence. I suppose it should not surprise me that a functionary like you would not know. But something is happening in your shipyards, and we would like to know what."

"Do you think it has something to do with how many ore freighters we produce per quarter at Jupiter?"

"More than that," Krestyanov said. "You think we have not seen the data and know what it means? The increased requisition orders for tunneler drives? The disappearing shipments of armor plating? The Ministrix seems to be preparing for war, yes?"

Altair stared at Krestyanov, unsure he'd heard correctly. As a bluff, this one was poorly contrived. Ever since the Paulson Compromise had taken effect, both governments had been forbidden from building enough warships to start a war, let alone win one. No, this was simply a ploy to free Simone Weathers, simple as that. "Regardless of what you hoped to find, Phinehas was in your territory for what, all of two days? No. You want Weathers back, we'll need a bigger fish than him."

Krestyanov's smile sharpened. Altair felt like cornered prey. "Bigger fish? Like Phinehas's prey? Like Crusader and his traveling companion?"

"What?"

"Do not play coy with me, my friend. I have seen the security footage myself, how Crusader was aboard the *Sybaritic*, how he fought against Phinehas's team. I know he disappeared after the fight, how he took another passenger and a steward with him. Perhaps you would like to tell me what is going on?"

Altair swallowed hard and waved a dismissive hand. "Internal squabble. Sorry it spilled over into your territory."

"I see. Well, perhaps if we capture Crusader and his friends, then maybe you would be more willing to trade. Or perhaps Crusader himself is so big a fish that we won't want to trade. I shall speak to you later, my friend."

With that, the image fuzzed and faded.

Altair spun to his computer terminal and put together a summons for Amalric and his commandos. He had to find Crusader first. There was no telling what would happen if the Praesidium got their hands on him instead. Deacon Siseal could find out what Altair had been trying to do. If that happened, Altair was as good as dead.

His fingers hovered over the console. Better safe than sorry. He tasked in Inquisitor for the hunt as well. Who better than Crusader's former liaison to track the man?

Once the orders were dispatched, Altair breathed a bit easier. He looked at the mural again. The eyes didn't seem quite so accusing now.

23

Crusader shoved his way through the human stampede, straining to find her. They said she hadn't emerged yet. He had to make sure she was safe.

A fleeing man wearing a drab white prison jumpsuit slammed into him and knocked him off balance. Crusader should have stopped the prisoner but he didn't care. Not now.

He burst free from the pack. He choked on the acrid smoke and squinted as it stabbed his eyes. Pale orange light flickered on the rocky walls.

Round the corner into the waiting arms of hell. Shouting against the flames' roar. Protecting his face as heat lashed against it.

There she was.

Westin. Dead, wreathed in flames.

He collapsed to his knees. He hadn't been fast enough. He'd failed her. Failed.

Strong hands wrapped around his shoulders, his arms, dragged him back. He struggled, flailing. Let him go. Let him go to her. He didn't want to leave. He didn't . . .

A soft pinging roused Crusader from the dreams of fire and darkness. He sat up and looked around the cargo hold of the *Purim*. Mostly empty, just a few crates tied into one corner. Med supplies, some food, shiny trinkets for Balaam's conquests.

He sat on the mat, hands pressed to his cheeks. The void roiled and twisted inside him, chewing at his stomach, clawing at his spine. He screwed his eyes shut, swallowed hard to keep the bile down. Slowly, surely, he calmed himself. He glanced at the parrot. 0530. He did the math. Six hours of sleep. Not enough, but he knew he wouldn't get any more.

"Time for the Litany," the parrot said.

Of course. He rose from the cot, stretched. No lingering pain from the fight. The medical gel had done its work well. They'd reach Eps-Prime in another two days, and he'd be back in fighting form then.

But Morning Litany came first. He turned to the parrot and knelt on the floor, palms up. The parrot projected a face above itself. Crusader tensed. It was that of Deacon Palti. The worship program selected random avatars for the leader. Crusader must have forgotten to purge this one from the queue.

He stared at the hologram. Palti had been good to him. Had given him the best assignments, protected him the few times he had failed. How could such a good man go bad? How could he have succumbed to the heresy?

He should delete the image. Yet he remained kneeling. Time to begin.

"This is the day the Lord hath made," Crusader said.

Palti's image responded. "Let us seek His justice and might in it."

A pause. Crusader focused on his breathing. In through the nose. Out through the mouth.

"With what shall I come before the Lord, and bow myself before God on high?" pseudo-Palti intoned.

"I shall give my flesh for the sin of my soul." He remembered Palti's teaching on the Litany. *We give our all, for we can give nothing else.*

"He has told you what is good. What does the Lord require of you?"

"Be justice, love rightness, walk upright for your God." *The threefold divine demand, the standard to which we all strive.*

"Draw near, you executors of divine justice, each with your weapon in hand."

"Here am I, send me."

"Your eye shall not spare and you will show no pity."

"Here am I, send me."

"Fill your hands with burning wrath and spread it upon His enemies."

"Here am I, send me." *Let us fulfill the calling the Almighty One has given us without compromise, without pity.*

"This shall be their lot in their pride, because they scoffed and boasted against the people of the Lord of hosts."

"I shall be terrible against them. They shall shrivel and bow down to Him, each in their place, all the coasts and islands, the nations and worlds." *None can stand against God's righteous wrath, nor against us, the instruments of divine vengeance.*

"You devastators! Happy shall they be who pay you back what you have done!"

"Happy shall I be when I visit justice upon your little ones, dashing them against the rock!" *We do not shrink from the tasks to which the Almighty calls.*

And so it continued for another half hour. The simulacrum of Palti led Crusader through the prescribed call and response to focus his mind on his tasks. The words came easily, but as they echoed in his mind, he realized he hadn't lived up to them. He had been ordered to kill Westin, not save her. He had failed, risking God's divine wrath. What he had said to the traitor the day before mocked him. Perhaps he could fix things. Finish the mission now. It wasn't too late.

Crusader blinked in surprise as the hologram terminated and the hold fell back into darkness. The parrot sat before him, inert. Was the Litany over already? He affixed the parrot to his shoulder. Time to act.

His knife was in its sheath inside his pack. He strapped it in place and slipped the blade out. He pulled himself up the ladder and onto the main deck. He would have to act fast, take out Westin first. If he did this right, she wouldn't make any noise to alert the traitor. Even if she did, Crusader knew he could dispatch the traitor easily. Obedience brought salvation. So the Ministrix taught, and so he—

The cabin opened and Westin came out. He froze. Her scent, warm and inviting, washed over him. His grip on the knife weakened.

Westin's gaze locked on the knife. "Crusader? What's going on?"

He should act. Do it. Hand over her mouth, draw the blade across—

No. He couldn't. The resolve he'd felt in the cargo hold evaporated.

Maybe it wouldn't hurt to let her live. Just a little while longer.

"Nothing," he said. "Thought I heard someone. Must have been you. Sorry."

A lame excuse, but Westin seemed to accept it. But she didn't take her eyes off the knife until he had slipped it back into its sheath.

Crusader looked her over. She still wore the same jumpsuit she had been wearing when they'd left the *Sybaritic*.

"I think Balaam had some women's clothing in his quarters," he said. "You might be more comfortable in them."

Westin smiled, a wry quirk of her mouth. She stepped back into the cabin and motioned for Crusader to follow. Once inside, she opened a closet door and reached inside, pulling out something made of satin and lace. A lot of lace. "I think I'd be a bit too comfortable in this," she said.

Heat flashed up Crusader's spine, lodging in his cheeks for a few moments before the numb swallowed it. She had a point.

She started for the corridor again but paused in the door. She looked over her shoulder at him, hesitation bleeding through her eyes. "I was about to get some . . . I don't suppose you'd like some breakfast?"

He nodded. A grin flashed across her lips before she slipped from the room. Crusader followed her down the corridor into the meager galley. They both reached for the same cupboard, hesitated, reached again. She laughed, a high tittering.

"Why don't you sit down?" he said. "Let me handle this."

He set to work, sorting through the galley's stores. Not much to work with. A few cartons of powdered eggs, past their expiration. Dehydrated milk, even older. He hadn't noticed how bad the supplies were on the trip to the *Sybaritic*. None of this would do for Westin.

He settled on some quick-prepare pancakes. A small bag of sausages frozen into one mass lurked in the back of the freezer. A carton of orange juice passed the sniff test. Not perfect, but the best he could do under the circumstances.

Soon, he had the sausage frying. That should kill any lingering germs. The pancakes were done in seconds. He served it all on two plates and set one before Westin.

She poked at it with her fork, her mouth pursed. But she smiled and tried a bite. Her eyes widened. "This isn't bad." Her smile grew lopsided. "An assassin who cooks?"

"We all need hobbies."

She burst out laughing. He didn't understand. He was serious. He had to find something to pass the time between missions, and sketching couldn't fill every moment.

He studied her face. He wished he had his pencils and paper at the table. He'd rather sketch than eat. But his supplies were in the cargo hold. Some other time, perhaps.

"So what other secrets are you harboring?" Westin speared a sausage and nibbled one end. "Wait, let me guess: 'You could tell me, but then you'd have to kill me.'"

"Yes."

Her gaze dropped to the plate.

He pushed his own food around before venturing a glance toward her. "How about you? What kind of secrets do you have?"

She met his gaze with narrowed eyes. "I'm not telling you about the Catacombs or Dr. Keleman's research."

He nodded. "I know."

She started eating again, a little more relaxed but still on her guard. "So what kind of secrets do you want to know? Don't you have a dossier on me or something?"

"I do, but it doesn't have much. Where did you and Liddel meet?"

"You mean Gav?" She leaned back, shrugged. "I used to serve on a ship. We met there. He was passing through but we hit it off."

He kept his face neutral even though he wanted to snarl. He had hoped the two of them had met at the Catacombs. Apparently he wouldn't make a good interrogator. But he might as well press on. At some point, she might slip and give away some information he could actually use. "How about family?" He poked a bite of pancake into his mouth.

Westin went still. Her hair formed a screen around her face. He studied her. Shuddering shoulders, small gasps. Crying?

"I'm sorry." The words slipped out of his mouth before he could consider them.

"It's okay," she whispered. She sat up, forced a smile, and took a sip of her juice. "I never knew my dad."

Crusader's stomach flipped. He glared at the food. He should have known better than to use it. "Your mother never told you anything?"

She laughed, a brittle chuckle. "Not really. She told me he took off before I was born. I've never even seen any images of him or anything like that." She sat up a bit straighter. "Mom used to say I was lucky I didn't know him."

"Where's your mom now?"

She stilled once more, staring at the tabletop.

Crusader waited a moment before comprehension dawned. "Oh."

She looked up at him. "You didn't know?"

He shook his head. "What happened?"

"Nobody really knows. She was an engineer too. When I was about five, she took this job—freighter run, supposed to be really easy—and she never came home. The ship just disappeared."

"Disappeared?" A prickling sensation washed over him. He clenched his jaw, trying to focus. It wouldn't help to get distracted.

"The guild investigated, sent a ship along its course. They found some debris. Not a whole lot, not enough to figure out exactly what happened. The guild decided it had to have been some sort of freak accident."

"I'm sorry." Crusader shifted in his chair. Westin's attitude was making him uncomfortable. He didn't like seeing Westin like this. He should have been focusing on the information she was sharing, sifting it for the data they needed to untangle this mess they were in, and yet he couldn't get past her words. She was . . . sad. That was the right word. And he wished he could pull her pain into himself. He was sure the numb could handle it.

What was wrong with him? His superiors would be furious.

She smiled across the table at him, her eyes dimmed. "It's okay."

"Where were you when this happened?"

She hesitated, then picked up her fork. "With friends." She stabbed some pancake. She was trying to act nonchalantly, but he could read the tension in her posture, the nervous fidget in her fingers.

The Catacombs? Maybe. Worth pursuing. "Why didn't she take you with her?"

Westin glanced at him, then down at her food. "She could have and almost did. The captain loved kids. We had even moved all my stuff into our cabin. But at the last minute Mom decided she didn't want me to come."

Furrows crossed her brow. "She was nervous about something even before that run. She never said anything, but I think she was scared. I think she tried to make us disappear. She pulled me out of school, left our house in the middle of the night. I remember sleeping on a lot of couches, hiding in bad parts of back-route colonies. She even considered sending me across the border into the Ministrix."

Crusader blinked in surprise. "The Ministrix? Really?"

Westin nodded. "Apparently we have family there. Mom's sister, I think. I even have a cousin about my age. Never met her, but that's what Mom told me."

"Know where they live?" Crusader asked. "I've been all over. Maybe I've met them."

Westin snorted. "I doubt it."

"Try me." This was good. He was establishing rapport with her. If he could get her to share this information, he might be able to get her to reveal more later.

"I think the planet was called Mishael." She frowned. "Where was it again?"

"Close to the Gum Nebula." The words slipped out of Crusader without any conscious thought.

"You've been there?" Westin asked.

"No, I haven't." Crusader wracked his brain. He was pretty sure he had never been to Mishael before. So how did he know where it was?

Westin leaned toward him, concern etched on her face. "Are you okay?"

A fair question. He didn't know how to answer. Maybe it would be better to just move on. "Fine. You were saying about your mother trying to find a place for you?"

"Right. Mom finally dropped me off with our friends so she could take that job." She swiped a tear from the corner of her eye. "I wish she had never heard of the *Vaettir*."

Crusader froze. "The *Vaettir*?"

"You've heard of it?"

How much could he tell her? The *Vaettir* mission was a near legend within Intelligence. He knew the details well enough. Any Ministrix agent would.

She leaned across the table, put her trembling hand on top of his. "Crusader, if you know something, please tell me."

Crusader closed his eyes. "The *Vaettir* was destroyed by Ministrix Intelligence."

When he looked again, Isolda stared at him with wide eyes. The color had drained from her face. "How do you know that?"

"They talk about it in our training. An example of dedicated service. The agent—called Coppersmith—was supposed to plant a bomb in the cargo hold, get away. Couldn't. Local customs officers tied him up in paperwork. So he snuck on board." The next sentence caught in his throat. He swallowed hard and pushed it past his lips. "Finished his mission."

"What was he after?" Isolda's voice was a bare squeak.

Crusader shook his head. "Don't know. Never told us that. Just wanted us to follow Coppersmith's example. Never give up. Complete your assignment." His mind drifted back to the Litany, and he averted his eyes. He clenched his jaw. "No matter what."

Isolda stared at him then pushed her plate away. "Please excuse me. I'm not hungry anymore." She fled from the galley, brushing past Liddel . . . Odell . . . whatever he called himself now.

Odell watched her go, then turned back to the table. His face brightened. "That food for anyone?"

Crusader gestured toward the table. Odell dove for the opposite chair and started shoveling the food down. Crusader got out of his chair. While he could pump Odell for information, he doubted he would get anything helpful. And he wouldn't enjoy the company either.

So Isolda's mother had died on the *Vaettir*, a victim of a Ministrix operation. Isolda had almost died too. Had Isolda's mother been an innocent bystander? Maybe. His instructors had never explained what Coppersmith had been after, so it was possible his intended target was a passenger, a different crewmember, someone other than Isolda's mother. Maybe even cargo.

More importantly, why couldn't he focus when he was around Westin? Even if he wasn't going to kill her, he was a member of Ministrix Intelligence—he should be focused and dedicated, not swapping stories with his target over breakfast. And yet, there was something right about what had just happened. A part of him wished she hadn't left, that they could have kept talking.

Almighty One, Lord of Hosts and Supreme Avenger, help me. Make me the instrument of Your wrath that You have always intended. Help me to serve Your True Church the way You would have me do.

Crusader waited, sure that the numbness would grow stronger. Or maybe he would finally find the resolve to do what Deacon Siseal had ordered.

Instead, he felt the distinct urge to sketch more pictures of Westin.

Crusader slid down the ladder into the cargo hold. He settled in with his sketch pad and set to work. He couldn't obsess over any of this now. Plenty of time to figure out what was going on when they found Hyrcanus.

24

Isolda hesitated outside the cockpit entrance. Gavin lounged in the pilot chair, his feet propped on the console. He held a drink in one hand and used the other to scroll through star charts, technical schematics, and seemingly whatever came up. She winced. She had ruined another life. Pearson Lines would log his desertion, and that would probably keep him from finding another job. Just what she needed on her conscience.

She forced herself to smile. "Are you okay?"

He turned in the chair and looked at her. He smiled as well, the kind she supposed he showed passengers on the *Sybaritic*. "I'm great. How about you?"

Even his voice sounded plastic. She took a step into the cockpit. "Gav . . ."

He lowered his head and sighed. "How do you think I feel? I thought I could finally stop running. I mean, sure, my job on the *Sybaritic* wasn't much. Well, it wasn't anything. But I thought things were looking up. The Ministrix had no idea where I was, I was starting to fit in with the other stewards, life seemed good. And now I'm on the run again. Only this time, I've got the Ministrix's best killer with me and he's steering us into what has to be a trap. And then there's . . ." He glanced at her and his voice trailed off.

She frowned. "What?"

He laughed, a sharp, mirthless bark. "Nothing. Forget it."

She slid into the copilot's seat and studied his profile as he scuffed at a corner of the console. His frown deepened.

"Isolda . . . have you ever wished you could go back and do things differently?"

Now she laughed. "You have to ask me?"

He reddened. "Oh, yeah. I suppose you have. Well, me too. I sometimes wonder . . . I wonder how things would have been different if I had followed my orders."

Horror rippled up her spine. She stared at him. "How can you think that?"

Gavin shrugged. "I don't know. It would have been easy, you know. Just push a button or two. Lay in an orbital path that would have taken the *Second Horseman* over the target, let the weapons system do the rest. Quick, easy. Nothing to it."

She reached out and touched his arm. "You did the right thing."

"Don't be too sure. You know why we were ordered to sanitize that colony? They claimed to be farmers but they were really a screen for a smuggling base. And we're not talking about sneaking a few forbidden luxuries into the Ministrix. No, these guys were smuggling pregnant women out of the Ministrix for use in Praesidium laboratories. Those smugglers deserved what they got."

"But not the colonists," Isolda said quietly.

"Doesn't really matter, does it?" He chuckled again. "I keep replaying it in my mind. Orders come in, the captain sets us all in motion, and there I am, at the helm, so sure of myself in my newfound faith. I stood up, crossed my arms, defied my orders. I thought I was doing the right thing, that all those innocent colonists would live because I took a stand. And what does the captain do? He has me arrested and tossed in the brig, and the orders were carried out anyway. I threw everything away—my family, my friends, my reputation—and it didn't do any good. They all died anyway."

"You did the right thing." Her repeated words sounded hollow even to her own ears.

He smiled, looked away. "Yeah, I know. 'Great is my reward in heaven,' right? But sometimes I wish I could have some of that here, y'know?" He swiped at his eyes. She squeezed his arm. He placed his hand over hers and looked up. Their eyes met.

"Interrupting?"

Isolda jerked away from Gav, breaking the contact. She turned to find Crusader standing in the door.

"Not at all." Gavin turned back to the controls. "Figured you'd be showing up soon. We're almost there."

"I know."

Crusader stepped closer to her seat. Isolda could feel his presence loom over her.

Gavin glanced at the data readout. "Reversion . . . now."

Stars blazed into existence across the viewport as the *Purim*'s tunneler drive disengaged. A pale green and brown orb hung before the cockpit.

Gavin looked over the sensors and then turned to her. "Well, we're here, but now we've got a problem. I know Eps-Prime is a neutral planet, but they've got both a Praesidium and a Ministrix embassy."

"Ministrix *mission*," Crusader commented.

Gavin glared at him. "Whatever. If the Ministrix is after us, you know they've flagged the *Purim*. They'll be watching for us. Any suggestions?"

Crusader stepped forward, pointing to a control bank. "Large selection of false transponder signals. Sort by date of use, pick one Balaam hasn't used for a while."

Gavin did as he was told. "All right, we are now the *Logankirk* hailing from Pinnacle Station. Sound good to you?"

Crusader nodded curtly. He sat down in the co-pilot chair and started to work at the console.

Gavin watched him for a second, then panic exploded across his face. "What are you doing?"

Crusader held up a hand. "Tapping into the local Ministrix network."

"What if you make a mistake and trip their security?" Gavin asked.

"Why are you doing that?" Isolda asked quietly.

Crusader faced her. "Looking for patterns. Personnel requisitions. Computer usage. That sort of thing. If Hyrcanus is here, running counter-espionage, he'll leave tracks. We follow them, find him, get our answers. Then we leave. Simple."

Isolda met Gavin's questioning gaze. "He knows what he's doing."

Gavin grumbled but turned away. Crusader returned to work, flipping through the data faster than Isolda could follow. Fear wormed up her back. He moved so quickly, he could be doing anything: warning the Ministrix, setting up an ambush. How could she know for certain? All they could do was trust him.

Then she spotted something. A picture of her flashed through the holographic interface. It was so quick she almost missed it. "What was that?"

"Nothing." Crusader's word was little more than a grunt.

"I want to see it. Go back."

Crusader looked up at her. "It'll only scare you."

"I doubt it."

Crusader studied her face. "We'll see." He stabbed the controls with his finger.

Her image reappeared, along with those of Gavin and Crusader. She leaned over Crusader's shoulder to read the text that scrolled beneath the pictures. Her eyes widened. "This has got to be a joke."

Crusader shook his head. "No joke."

The images were part of a public announcement from the Ministrix calling for information on Isolda's whereabouts. Anyone who recognized her or her companions should report to the local mission and receive a substantial reward. If it resulted in her capture, the payout was . . .

"Seven million credits?" She looked at Crusader in shock. "I don't know anything worth that much!"

"Abd al Sami would seem to disagree," Crusader said. "Good news is, this shows they don't know where we are." He pointed to a line of code. "This means the announcement isn't local. Every mission in this sector received this. If they're casting that wide a net, there's a good chance we can slip through."

"And what if we can't?" Gavin asked. "That's an awful lot of money. Everyone is going to be looking for us. If we land, we're going to get caught."

"Won't be there long enough. In and out. Easy."

Isolda looked from the Ministrix agent to Gavin. Her friend shook his head emphatically. She groaned and closed her eyes. She knew what Gavin would want to do. They could easily keep running. But Crusader seemed so sure this would work . . .

"Let's keep going," she said. "We'll just have to take our chances."

Gavin snorted and turned away. Crusader went back to work.

After ten minutes, he turned from the controls. "Got him. Hyrcanus has been working primarily from a hotel called the Rapture. I have its address. When we land, we go there right away."

"Whatever you say." Gavin mashed the controls and the ship shot forward.

Isolda sat in silence as Gavin wove them through the traffic surrounding the planet. At one point, Gavin pointed out the front viewport at two large ships. "Eps Customs Cruisers. They're hailing us."

"Problem?" Crusader asked.

Gavin looked over the controls. "Not really. They seem to have accepted the transponder signal."

"Of course. It's Ministrix."

Gavin's eyes hooded. "Okay. Well, they've cleared us for landing. We're heading in now."

"Good." Crusader rose from his chair. "Let me know when we've landed."

"Why?" Isolda asked. "What are you going to do now?"

Crusader met her gaze with his dead eyes. "Prepare for the hunt."

25

Isolda tightened her grip on the glass, sure that it would shatter. She shot a quick glance at Crusader. The Ministrix agent simply sat there, doodling on a piece of paper. How could he remain so calm? Once they'd arrived at the Rapture, he had found a quiet table in the hotel bar and parked himself. He'd ordered water for everyone. And then they'd waited. And waited. Crusader kept drinking and drawing, occasionally glancing at the main entrance. Gavin tried to talk to him several times, only to be ignored.

Isolda looked around at their surroundings. The Rapture had been patterned after some sort of Middle Eastern architecture. The walls were covered with small tiles, creating intricate rosettes and flowering vines. Lights that appeared to be made out of paper globes hung from the ceiling. Plush couches were scattered throughout the lobby. A bank of elevators lined the far wall.

After an hour, Gavin slammed down his glass. "That's it. I'm taking a walk."

"Bad idea." Crusader's voice, a bare rumble, drifted across the table. "Hyrcanus could be here at any time."

"I think you can handle him on your own." Gavin held out his hand to Isolda. "Want to come with me? I spotted some shops down the street. Maybe we could find you some fresh clothes?"

A tempting offer. She had tried cleaning her jumpsuit, but the *Purim*'s laundry processor had proved ineffective. Getting a change of clothes she could wear in public, would be nice.

She looked to Crusader. He stared back, his face blank. And yet she wasn't sure, but it seemed like there was a flicker of something in his eyes. Desire? Regret? Maybe even fear? It was enough to convince her to stay. "Buy me something nice, Gav," she said. "I trust your taste."

Disappointment flitted across Gavin's features. He glared at Crusader but got up and headed for the door. The assassin didn't seem to notice. He remained focused on the piece of paper.

Isolda examined Crusader. He almost appeared as a statue chiseled from granite, unblinking, unflinching, the only movement that of his pencil. She wasn't even sure he breathed. And yet there was a softness to him: a twitch of his lips, the way he scrutinized the paper. Isolda leaned forward. Her gaze traced his jawline, his shoulders . . .

He noticed. He looked in her direction. "Problem?"

She stammered. "No. Just curious. About you."

He shifted in his chair. "Why?"

She shrugged. "We've spent the past week and a half together and I barely know anything about you. Like your name."

"You know it."

"Crusader? That's it?"

"Only one I have."

"That's ridiculous. What name were you born with?"

"Don't know. Don't care either. 'Crusader' is who I am now."

Isolda leaned back in her chair. "But what was your name before that?"

Crusader looked at her. More specifically, he seemed to look through her, as if his answer were printed on the wall behind her. "Couldn't tell you. Doesn't really matter. This is what I do. It's what I'm good at. It's what the Almighty designed me for."

"You think God wants you to kill people?"

Crusader took a sip of his water. "Why else make me numb?"

"Wait, what are you talking about?" Isolda asked.

"I don't feel pain or emotions," Crusader said matter-of-factly, like he was describing the weather.

"No emotions? That would be . . . horrible. And you think God made you that way?"

"That is what my superiors have taught me. My numbness is a divine gift which allows me to be the perfect instrument of His wrath."

Isolda gaped at him. "That's not God. That's not what He's about."

"Are you so sure?" The barest glint of laughter shone in his eyes.

If she wasn't so frustrated with him, it would almost be charming. "Of course! How can you think that?"

Crusader leaned back in his chair and examined the table. "'Do not leave alive anything that breathes. Completely destroy them as the Lord your God has commanded you. Otherwise, they will teach you to follow all the detestable things they do and you will sin against the Lord your God.' Deuteronomy."

She was surprised at his quiet vehemence. Then she found her voice. "Maybe God wanted that from His people at one point, but that's not the way He works anymore."

"That's what you say. The Revered Hand thinks differently."

"It's not just me!" She thought frantically before latching onto something. "'Our struggle is not against flesh and blood, but against the rulers, against the authorities, against the powers of this dark world and against the spiritual forces of evil in the heavenly realms.'"

A frown creased Crusader's brow and the smoldering fire in his eyes blazed to light, threatening to melt Isolda. "You're misquoting that."

"I am not."

"But that's not what Paul wrote there."

"Are you so sure?"

Crusader's eyes narrowed, their gleam turning predatory.

A thrill shot up Isolda's back. She knew his interest was only in the debate, not in her, but still, seeing it made her heart race.

"Perhaps I am mistaken." Crusader's words were slow, measured. "I'm no theologian. But you've had advanced training."

"I wouldn't call it that," Isolda said.

"My mistake. Not all of us are fortunate enough to spend time in the Catacombs."

Isolda smiled at him. "Nice try. I'm not going to slip that easily."

Crusader mirrored her expression. "Can't blame me for trying. Still trying to figure out what abd al Sami wants. The Catacombs, Keleman's research. Who is this Keleman, anyway, and what was he researching? Or maybe you have another idea what it might be?"

"None."

Crusader's face froze and any emotion disappeared. "Then let's find out. Hyrcanus is here."

The numb encased Crusader like armor. It had been a while since he had seen Balaam's liaison officer, but he recognized the look of an espionage agent. The small man didn't simply enter the hotel. He slunk in, his gaze roaming over the nearest people, measuring them. He was a small man, no more than a meter and a half tall. His hair had been cut extremely short, little more than black fuzz across the back half of his scalp. His eyes, wide and brown, shot from side to side as Hyrcanus scanned the room. He wore an earth-brown cloak, much too warm for Eps-Prime's weather.

Crusader held his breath. This would be the trickiest part. If Hyrcanus spotted him, it would all be over.

Hyrcanus moved toward the elevators. No sign of panic or hurry. Good.

Crusader turned to Westin. She stared at him with wide eyes. So fragile. Yet not. She confused him, thoughts of her poking through his protective shell. He couldn't worry about that now. Maybe not ever. He'd learn what abd al Sami wanted. And then he would report to Deacon Siseal. Maybe the Deacon would spare Westin's life. Couldn't worry about that now.

"Let's go."

He pulled the parrot from his jacket pocket and affixed it to his shoulder. He rose from his perch, abandoning his half-finished sketch. More images of Westin. Had plenty of them. She followed. He paused in the entrance, watching as Hyrcanus entered an elevator. A few moments later, the readout indicated it stopped on the third floor. Crusader entered the next elevator and pressed the button for three.

Crusader drew his weapon. Westin's eyes widened even further. He turned to her and extended his hand. "Take it. Just in case."

Her hands trembled but she took it. He nodded in approval. He didn't want her to use it. It was a risk to arm her at all. But the precaution had to be made. He then drew another gun.

Westin laughed. "How many of those do you have?"

"Four."

She choked. "Seriously?"

"Better hope I don't need them all."

The doors opened on the third floor. Crusader edged out, checked the hallway. Clear. He darted down the hall. At least thirty rooms. Which one held Hyrcanus? He couldn't search them all.

He spotted his salvation. Fire alarm. He motioned for Westin to duck into an alcove then took up an opposite position. Quick aim and fire at the alarm.

Red lights erupted through the hall accompanied by a shrieking siren. Doors snapped open and patrons poured into the hallway in various stages of undress. Although they were clearly scared, they obediently filed down the hallway to the stairs. Crusader pressed up against the wall and watched them pass. Within a few seconds, the hallway had cleared out.

"Where is he?" Westin whispered.

Crusader held up a hand. The doors to one room remained closed. That had to be Hyrcanus's room.

He slid down the hall and stopped next to them. "Parrot, access lock and override."

The device chittered quietly and the doors slid open.

"Sir?" Crusader shouted. "Hotel security. We need you to evacuate. Didn't you hear the alarm?"

A red laser flashed through the open door, burning a scorch mark up the far wall. Westin flinched, but Crusader was already moving. He ducked low as he went through the door.

Hyrcanus tried to aim, but Crusader barreled into him and knocked him off his feet.

Hyrcanus looked up at him and the initial panic gave way to true fear. "Crusader, I—"

A quick right cross cut him off. Crusader dragged him out of the room and toward the stairs. Thankfully, the other guests had already cleared out. The lobby was deserted as well. Crusader slipped through the front doors. He hustled away from the hotel just as the emergency vehicles started to arrive.

Half a block away from the hotel, they found Odell returning from his shopping trip empty-handed. Crusader motioned for him to fall in. He started to speak but Westin cut him off with a sharp wave of her hand. Once they had traveled half a kilometer, Crusader ducked into a nearby alleyway. This would have to do. Crusader dumped Hyrcanus onto the cement next to the wall of one of the buildings.

The cool night air must have roused Hyrcanus. He stirred, but when he looked at Crusader again, he tried to scramble to his feet. Crusader clamped his hand over his mouth.

"We need to talk," Crusader said. "You going to cause trouble?"

Hyrcanus whimpered, but he shook his head. Crusader slowly let go of his mouth, but when Hyrcanus tried to get up again, Crusader knocked his legs out from under him.

"Please, I didn't do anything, I didn't," Hyrcanus said.

Crusader leaned in close. "But you helped set me up, didn't you? The Connor Trap?"

Hyrcanus looked up at him, tears staining his cheeks, and he nodded. "Yes! Yes. I did. I'm sorry, but we had our orders. You know how it is."

He did. But that didn't matter now. "What does abd al Sami want?"

"The girl!"

"Why?"

"I don't know! He didn't tell us. Do they ever tell us?"

Crusader slammed Hyrcanus's head against the wall. Lightly, just enough to get his attention. "You know more. Spill it."

"I don't. Honest." He hesitated. "Well . . ."

"What?"

"It's nothing, just something I noticed. Something big's happening. Huge. I don't know what, but Deacon Siseal has us all on the lookout for Praesidium spies. And yet, in the middle of it all, abd al Sami pulls Balaam off task to get Westin. Said to get the girl and bring her to . . . to . . . Crasman's Rift. That's all he said, honest!"

"Crasman's Rift?" Odell asked.

Crusader shot a warning look at Odell, but then noticed Westin wore a similar shocked expression. He frowned at her.

"Now I think I know what abd al Sami wanted." Her voice barely audible over the howl of distant sirens.

"And so do I," a voice said.

A cool metal barrel pressed against Crusader's neck. He raised his hands and slowly turned.

Kolya Krestyanov smirked at him. "He wants you. All of you. And lucky for me, I am the one who now possesses you."

26

Crusader's gaze flicked to Kolya's hand. The man didn't have his finger on the trigger; it rested against the guard. The Praesidium agent wasn't going to fire just yet. "Shouldn't be surprised you're here," Crusader said. "You part of the Praesidium cell?"

Kolya laughed. "The one your friend has been hunting? No, I am not. But that operation has proved quite helpful, the perfect bait to draw him out. And now you, as well. Traps within traps, yes?"

Crusader took a step back. Probably couldn't dodge a shot at this range but might as well try.

Kolya noticed and raised the pistol higher. "Far enough, my friend. Don't think I won't shoot you if I must."

Crusader froze, his arms tensing. No options presented themselves. "So now what?"

"We wait. My team will be here in a matter of moments. Then we will take a little trip."

"To where?" Keep him talking, search for an opening.

"Somewhere safe. At least with you in custody, I know we won't have a repeat of Lanadon."

Crusader nodded. True. He doubted the Ministrix had any agents in place who could mount such an operation. So what would happen now? He had a fairly good idea. Kolya would use them for bartering. He and Westin would be handed over to abd al Sami. Once they realized who Odell was, he'd likely be extradited. And Hyrcanus would be used in an exchange to secure the release of some minor Praesidium agent the Ministrix held. Out of all of them, Hyrcanus would survive. He'd be forced into early retirement, sent to some out-of-the-way system. Odell would be executed for treason.

And Crusader? Abd al Sami had ordered his death. Crusader had no doubt abd al Sami would see that he was executed. He probably wouldn't do it personally, but the moment Crusader crossed the Ministrix's border, he'd be dead.

He looked to Westin. What about her? Once abd al Sami got what he wanted from her, she'd most likely die too. Or be put into a penal colony. Neither idea appealed to Crusader.

He could ask for asylum. No, wouldn't help. He had no real knowledge to offer. He was a tool in the Ministrix's hand, nothing more. A hammer didn't understand the builder's plans. Even if he could convince the Praesidium to keep him, they'd probably execute him for the many operations he'd carried out against them.

Even if they did offer asylum, could he leave the Ministrix?

Ice clawed at his skin. Separating from the Church would guarantee his damnation. There was no salvation unless offered from Christ's Revered Hand. He had hoped that, by revealing abd al Sami's treason, Deacon Siseal would pardon his temporary disobedience. But if he broke all ties with the Ministrix, that forgiveness would never be his.

The void smashed through the numbness, the pieces digging deep into his chest. His arms twitched, a tremor that worked its way down his body and into his legs. They wobbled and he collapsed, his head bouncing off the side of the building. Fire erupted across his brow, chased by warm stickiness. He touched his face and pulled away blood. His stomach lurched and his mind spun. He curled in on himself. The parrot hissed a warning to him. His vital signs were spiking, out of control. He wanted to smash the annoying device onto the pavement.

"Crusader!" Westin's voice was little more than a buzz in his ear, drowned by thunder.

He retched. He'd die at the hands of the Praesidium or those of abd al Sami, and what waited for him afterwards? Pain. Torture. Eternal separation from the Ministrix and from God. What could he do? Nothing. And that knowledge alone wracked him with even more pain.

Feet tramped around him, hands touching him, probing his shoulders and back. Westin and Odell? No, he counted at least five separate touches. One gentle, the caress of wind. Another tentative, unsure. The third, rough.

Kolya. Crusader snared that hand and dragged hard, pulling the Praesidium agent off balance. Kolya tried to pull away. Crusader clamped down harder, ignoring the agony that snaked up his arms. He lurched to his feet and yanked, spinning around to slam Kolya face-first into the wall.

But the gun snapped back to his face. Kolya glared at him. "It'll take more than a bump to the head to stop me, friend."

Westin kicked Kolya's hand. The gun clattered against the far wall. Crusader ducked in, smashing into Kolya's stomach and slamming him into the wall again. Kolya crumpled.

Crusader looked at Westin.

She smirked at him. "That's two you owe me."

Electricity coursed through him. A debt he would be glad to repay, provided they survived long enough.

"Where's Hyrcanus?" Crusader asked.

Westin looked around the alley. Hyrcanus was gone.

"He must have slipped away," she groaned.

"Does that really matter? Once this guy's team gets here, we'll only be caught again. We'd better get out of here," Odell commented.

Crusader nodded. "Definitely. Just give me a moment to—"

The pain slammed shut, the panic dissolved. He closed his eyes, took a deep breath. The numb oozed through every fiber of his being and stilled his raging thoughts. When he opened his eyes again, Odell and Westin were regarding him with puzzled expressions.

"Moment to what?" Odell asked.

"Nothing," Crusader answered. "Let's go."

He scooped up Kolya's weapon as they went. Odell cast an unsure look over his shoulder back at the Praesidium agent.

"We're just going to leave him there like that?"

"You going to kill him?" Crusader asked.

Odell winced and followed, keeping his gaze down.

They exited the alley. Crusader checked down the street. More emergency vehicles clustered around the hotel. Police herded the guests into one group. Probably wondering who had shot the fire sensor. He tucked Kolya's pistol into his belt. He doubted anyone could spot it at such a distance, but caution never hurt.

"This way. Back to the ship. We need to leave."

"No kidding," Odell muttered.

They set out, Crusader leading the way through shadows. No police. No Kolya. Acceptable for now. The sooner the *Purim* was orbital, the better.

"Crasman's Rift." He knew little about it. The Rift was a gravitic buckle in space. Conventional tunneler drives couldn't penetrate it and it disrupted sensors if a ship drew too close. But there were many nooks and crannies within it, bearing planetoids, stray planetary systems—perfect cover for pirates and outlaws. So far as Crusader knew, the Ministrix had no posts near there. Why would abd al Sami want Westin sent to the Rift?

He glanced at her. She wouldn't meet his gaze. She knew about Crasman's Rift. He could read the knowledge in her stiff posture, her hooded expression. She wouldn't share her knowledge easily, not now especially. But later. When they were safe.

Crusader turned back to the street and stopped short. Four men blocked their path. He held out his hands, stopping Westin and Odell behind him. These newcomers tried to appear casual. But they stood too straight, their expressions too alert. These were no locals.

He turned, intending to find a side alley. Instead, a ground car squealed to a halt a mere meters in front of him, blocking his escape route. The side door opened and three men wearing heavy armor jumped out. They immediately trained laser rifles on Crusader. In spite of their tactical helmets, Crusader recognized the man in the middle.

"Amalric."

The commando nodded at him from behind his rifle sights. "I want you to know, I don't want to do this, Crusader. You've been a righteous friend."

"I understand," Crusader's hand crept down toward Kolya's pistol. If he moved carefully enough . . .

A gun barrel pressed against his ear. "I wouldn't, traitor."

Crusader froze. He turned his head. The four men had closed in on them. He should have expected this the moment he'd spotted Amalric. His team was good, no doubt about it.

"So now what?" He didn't need to ask.

"We're taking the girl back to the Ministrix mission." Amalric snapped his fingers and two of his men darted forward, snaring Westin's arms. Westin tried to pull free, but her struggling didn't help.

Crusader stared at her. Something boiled behind the numb. Crimson crept along the corners of his vision, threatening to spill over at any moment. "And what about me?"

Amalric smiled but Crusader saw no joy in it. "Sorry, but our orders are clear."

Crusader relaxed his arms, flexed his fingers. He'd have to move quickly. Best to keep Amalric talking. "So abd al Sami wins."

Amalric's eyes widened and he laughed, a harsh guffaw. "Looks that way, huh?"

Crusader frowned, heat poking through the numbness throughout his body. He clenched his fingers. There had to be an opening soon.

Clattering boots echoed down the street. Crusader turned to see who would be stupid enough to charge a group of Ministrix commandos.

The newcomers wore similar tan fatigues, shining black boots, and packs. And they all carried the same blaster rifles. Local authorities? Doubtful. Eps-Prime security was never very good. They skidded to a halt, their guns snapping into position. Crusader froze. Now what?

Then Kolya Krestyanov stepped through their ranks. He smirked at Crusader. "Surprised to see me? I learned from our last encounter, friend. This time, I made sure to have back-up."

27

Isolda didn't move. Neither did her captors. Even the Praesidium strike force appeared frozen. Isolda didn't want to breathe. If the moment was broken, things would only get worse.

Then the Ministrix commander spun toward the newcomers and opened fire at them. The night erupted in crimson slashes of light.

Something slammed into her and she went down. It was Crusader, covering the sides of her head with his arms.

Their eyes met. She realized his eyes weren't dead. Now she saw, in their crystal depths, the fire. The passion. Isolda gasped. All else fell away, the battle cries, the sirens. There was only

Crusader and her, locked together, staring into each other. His warm breath tickled her cheeks, teasing a blaze within. Her fingers brushed his cheek. His eyes widened.

Then heat sliced her leg. Pain radiated along a narrow line up her thigh. She shrieked.

Crusader yanked her to her feet. "We have to go."

He pulled her away from the fight. Gavin leapt after them, clambering across the street.

Crusader dropped his shoulder and slammed into two Ministrix commandos, bowling them over. Someone shouted behind them and lasers flashed after them. Isolda wanted to offer a quick prayer that both sides would miss, although the only word she was really able to bring to mind was, "Help!"

They barreled around another corner, knocking back a gaggle of passersby. Isolda worried Crusader would rip her arm free at any moment. Then Gavin shouted, pointed down the street. A taxi.

Crusader pulled her to the vehicle. Before the doors had fully opened, she fell inside, propelled by Crusader. Gavin came next, landing on her in a heap. Crusader leapt inside. "Drive!" he shouted.

"Greetings, my friends." The autopilot's tinny voice was a bare buzz. "Thank you for selecting my conveyance this fine evening. I have a wide array of pleasurable destinations from which you may choose."

"Just go!"

The taxi crept forward two centimeters then halted. "I'm sorry. I understand your desire to depart but without a suitable destination, I'm afraid that I am unable to—"

"Main starport," Isolda said.

The autopilot blatted at her. "I'm sorry, but the city is currently experiencing a temporary civil emergency. As a matter of protection, a cordon has been set around the port that we may not enter. Might I suggest—"

"No. Override cordon. This is an emergency also. We must get to our ship." Isolda leaned over the small partition that kept the passengers from the controls. Not that she could have accessed them. A round device enveloped the controls, lights blinking around its perimeter. The autopilot module, if Isolda had to guess.

"I am sorry." The smooth voice took on a harder edge. "Local regulations prohibit taxis from violating an emergency cordon. Due to your repeated insistence that this cab break said cordon, I am now transporting you to the local security station."

The cab pulled out into traffic. Isolda turned to Crusader. "What do we do?"

"Parrot, override autopilot controls," Crusader said.

The parrot blatted at him.

"It is a felony to tamper with the programing of taxi autopilot functions," the autopilot said at the same time. "Your continued illegal activity has been noted."

"The hard way, then." Crusader whipped out his gun and fired over Isolda's shoulder. The entire cab shuddered but kept going. Crusader fired again.

Isolda peeked into the front. The autopilot sparked, two holes scorched in its silver exterior.

Crusader reached forward and yanked it from the controls, tossing it into the front. He snared Gavin and shoved him over the partition. "Drive. Starport."

"I'm a pilot, not a chauffeur," Gavin muttered.

"One less dimension to worry about. You'll be fine. Go." Crusader turned in his seat to stare out the back window.

Gavin reached for the controls, only to pull his hands away. He did that twice.

Isolda leaned over the partition. "What are you waiting for?"

"Hey, I've never driven one of these things before," Gavin said. "Give me a second to familiarize myself—"

Hot glass spattered Isolda's neck. A hole blossomed in the windshield. She spun and spotted a group of men racing after them, all of them armed.

Crusader returned fire. "Long enough for you?" Crusader shouted.

Gavin shouted and mashed his hand over the controls. The cab lurched, sputtered a few times, and launched away, weaving into oncoming traffic. The jerking movement threw Isolda into Crusader. He gently pushed her aside and turned to the back again. She likewise looked back. No sign of any pursuers. That was good.

"Now what?" Isolda asked.

"Get back to the ship. Leave the planet." He turned to face her. "Maybe check out Crasman's Rift."

Isolda chewed the inside of her cheek. "I may know what abd al Sami was up to."

"Isolda, no!" Gavin snapped.

She glanced at Gavin. He looked over his shoulder, a warning in his eyes. "He has a right to know," she said.

"No he doesn't," Gavin countered. "You know better."

Isolda slumped against the seat. He was right. She hated it. Crusader was Ministrix. He couldn't be trusted.

He was touching her leg?

Her head whipped down and she stared as his fingers gently probed along her thigh, down her calf. She tensed, not sure what he thought he was doing. He frowned, leaned in closer.

"Stray shot."

Isolda winced as he touched the laser burn on her leg, which she had gotten in the alley.

He nodded. "Not too deep. Can patch that up on the *Purim*."

She caught his hand before he could withdraw it. His eyes leapt to hers. "Thank you," she whispered.

His mouth worked, forming words he didn't actually speak. She rubbed her fingers against the back of his hand, then leaned forward. She closed her eyes, yearning to feel his lips against hers.

Then the cab swerved and she was thrown off balance. She fell back and her head slammed into the side window. She glared at Gavin.

"Sorry," he said. "Had to dodge some slow moving traffic."

But she could see the tension in the corner of his eyes. She'd have to talk to him later. She turned back to Crusader, but he had turned back to the rear window, scanning the traffic behind them. She sighed and nestled lower in the seat.

Ten minutes later, flashing lights filled the front of the cab.

"We've got a security blockade ahead of us," Gavin said.

"Keep going," Crusader said. "Dodge or ram, your choice."

"Oh, well, if it's up to me then," Gavin grumbled.

The cab jerked as it shot forward. Isolda braced herself, digging her fingers into the seat cushion. Crusader appeared frozen, not even blinking as lights raced by the windows. A number of security vehicles blocking the street loomed larger and larger. Isolda spotted a pair of officers, standing near one vehicle, raising their hands in warning. Gavin shoved the accelerator handle forward. The engine screamed, blending with Isolda's own cry.

And then they were through. Isolda blinked, surprised that there hadn't been a collision. She turned in her seat, looking out the back window. The security vehicles were still standing in their position. Yes, there was a gap between them, but she didn't think it looked wide enough for the cab to slip through, certainly not if it was traveling as fast as it was. The two security officers popped up behind the cars, staring after them with wide eyes.

Crusader grunted. "Good driving."

"Thanks," Gavin said, tension radiating through his voice.

Gavin wove the cab through other cars and then brought it to a jerking halt in front of the city's starport. Crusader kicked open the door and leapt out, gun up and at the ready. Isolda scrambled out after him. No sign of extra security, although from the sound of the rapidly approaching sirens, they'd be there soon.

An Eps-Prime security officer charged out of the door, shouting a warning. Crusader caught the man with a quick jab to the throat, then clocked him with his handgun. The man pitched to the ground and sprawled. Isolda leapt over him, wincing. Hopefully he'd be okay, but she couldn't stop to check.

A few brave individuals poked their heads into the corridor to see what was happening. They retreated when they saw Crusader barreling down the hall, Isolda and Gavin barely keeping up with him.

They arrived at the *Purim*'s dock. Isolda had never been so happy to see a ship in her life. The sooner they could get off this planet, the better.

"Check the exterior," Crusader said, nudging her by the shoulder. "Odell, start the engines. I'll be back in a moment." He turned and strode back to the hall.

Gavin turned to her, a sour look puckering his face. "Boy, he doesn't think he's in charge at all, does he?"

"Just do it, Gav," Isolda replied. "We can argue about this later."

Gavin grumbled something but then jogged to the ship's hatch. Isolda likewise sprinted a circle around the ship, giving it a cursory examination. No visible damage, no issues that would have to be corrected before liftoff. Her engineering instructors would probably chide her for being too shallow, but she doubted Crusader would give her the time to really do a good system check.

When she'd made it around the ship, Crusader returned from the hall.

"What were you doing?" she asked.

"Leaving a present for our friends in case they follow." He crossed past her to the hatch.

She followed, casting a nervous glance over her shoulder. She followed him into the cockpit.

Gavin slammed a hand against the controls and swore. "We've got a problem. The navigational computer is still slaved to Eps-Prime docking control. And with the cordon, they're not releasing it anytime soon."

Isolda sat down in the copilot chair. Sure enough, the computers refused to release them.

Then a rumble worked its way through the deckplates. Isolda looked up. Smoke billowed from the dock's entrance. She turned to Crusader.

His mouth pinched into a fine line. The parrot beeped quietly. "Company's coming. That was the first of my traps." He leaned over Gavin's shoulder. "Why not shut down the shell program?"

Gavin stared at him blankly. "The what now?"

Crusader tapped at the controls, pulling up a sub-routine menu. "Standard issue for Intelligence craft. There's the true computer control and then a dummy around it. Outside systems are given access to the shell, not the core. Shut down the dummy and . . ."

The cabin lights flickered and then blazed even brighter.

"Navigation coming online. Engines, defensive systems." Gavin glanced at Isolda out of the corner of his eye. "We're good to go."

"Lift off then," Crusader said. "Random tunnels like before. Once we're clear of pursuers, I'll give you a course."

"Aye, sir." Gavin said.

Another shudder rocked the deck, this one stronger than the previous. More smoke poured into the dock, followed by men in black suits. Ministrix? Praesidium? Locals? Isolda couldn't tell from here, but they certainly weren't friendly. They each carried weapons they fired at the ship.

"Go!" Crusader said.

The *Purim* shuddered and shot skyward, leaving the port far behind. Red lights exploded across the panels.

"*Logankirk*," a voice said over the speakers. "This is Eps-Prime docking control, you do not have permission to depart. You are hereby ordered to reconnect your navigational computer to our systems and land. Failure to comply will result in your interception and boarding." The automated message repeated itself.

Isolda found the volume control and muted it. No sense in listening.

The roar of the engines faded as the *Purim* slipped free from Eps-Prime's atmosphere. The computer pinged.

Gavin glanced at the readout and sighed. "We've got a customs enforcement ship on an intercept course."

Isolda looked where he was pointing. A silver needle drew closer to them.

"Keep going," Crusader said. "We can tunnel before they get close enough to use a tractor beam."

Gavin nodded, his fingers flying over the controls. The planet spun before them, the *Purim* righting itself to a new heading. Isolda relaxed, leaning back in her chair. They would make it.

Then a nova erupted before them. Harsh red light poured into the cockpit. She screamed, covering her eyes with her forearm.

"Another ship reverting to real space!" Gavin shouted. "Right on top of us too!"

The light faded and Isolda risked a peek. Hanging before them was a massive black shape, boxy and bristling with sensor and communication arrays and what she could only assume were weapons.

"Oh, that's not good," Gavin muttered.

"Why? What is it?"

"That is the *Bared Arm*, flagship of the Ministrix navy," Gavin said. "And it's moving for an intercept course." He turned from the controls. "There's nothing I can do. We're trapped."

28

Crusader stared at the *Bared Arm.* Three boxes connected by large pylons, bristling with weapons: laser bursters, missile launchers, point defense emplacements. This was a ship bred for space and battle. No aesthetics. Only brute force. Like him.

He cleared his throat. "Do we have an escape vector?"

"Weren't you listening?" Odell asked. "We're stuck. Between the planet, the customs ships, and now that monstrosity, we don't have a clear vector."

"You're the best pilot the Ministrix had and you can't escape?" Crusader asked.

"If I had more time, sure, but by the time I find a course, one or both of those ships will have a tractor lock on us."

Crusader's eyes narrowed. There had to be a way out. Always was. Just had to look for it.

"Parrot! Specs on the *Bared Arm*."

The parrot flared, projecting a hologram that filled the cockpit. Data streamed by, explaining the output of the cannons, the yield of the individual missiles. Only one tractor beam emitter.

"How is any of this going to help us?" Odell demanded.

Westin studied the specs. "I'm not sure it will. No way the *Purim* can take this thing on." Her eyes narrowed. "Wait. I've got an idea." She turned to Odell. "Bring us about. Close as you can to the customs ships."

"Are you crazy?"

"Just do it, Gav."

Crusader leaned in to watch Westin's fingers fly across the controls. "What are you planning?"

She flashed him a predatory smile. "Picking a fight."

How could he disapprove of that? He took a step back, watched her work. Odell, to his credit, did as he was told. The ship lurched, spun, and dove for the nearest Eps-Prime custom ships.

"Do they have any weapons emplacements topside?" Westin asked.

"Two laser turrets and a missile launcher," Odell answered.

"Good." She peeked back at Crusader. "Man the fire control station. Target the turrets and fire on my mark."

Crusader frowned. "What about the launcher?"

"We'll need that. Trust me. Gav, sending you coordinates for our run on the ship. When I tell you, open up full throttle, okay?" Westin consulted the sensors. "But for now cut back by ten percent. You're losing the *Bared Arm*."

Odell glared at her. "Isn't that the point?"

"Eventually, yes. But I want to make sure they're too busy to follow."

Odell didn't reply, but from his stiff posture, Crusader could tell he wasn't happy.

Crusader counted ten seconds. Then fifteen. He glanced at the sensors. The *Bared Arm* was getting close. Too close. Another three seconds and they'd be within tractor range. It'd be all over then. One . . . two . . .

"Gav, full throttle. Crusader, fire on the customs ship."

The ship shot forward, picking up enough speed that Crusader almost missed when he fired. But the targeting computer reported hits.

The deck bucked under his feet. He grabbed onto the console and turned. They weren't moving. The engines roared, their pitch climbing into a whine. The sharp tang of metallic smoke clawed up his nose. Circuits overheating. Not good.

"What are you doing?" Odell roared. "Shut off the tractor beam!"

"No," Westin replied. "Keep us shimmying. They've nearly got a missile lock on us."

Odell stared at her before turning back to his controls.

Crusader consulted his screen. Westin had indeed activated the *Purim*'s tractor beam, snaring the Eps-Prime ship as they passed overhead. But the sheer mass of the larger ship had acted as a brake on the *Purim*. Their ship now strained against her own tractor beam, trying to fly forward yet held in place. He supposed that eventually, the *Purim* could overcome the larger ship's inertia, but more likely the tractor beam emitter would fry out first. Or the engines would give out. He winced as the shrieking engines pitched even higher, driving a sharp spike into his ears.

"Careful, Gav, they almost had us there!"

"I don't see what the point—" A panel flared and then died next to Odell, cutting off his words. He managed to restart it and then slammed a fist onto it. "Now the Ministrix ship has us in *their* tractor beam. I'm not crazy about the idea of being the rope in a tug-of-war contest!"

"We won't have to be for long. Keep the engines on full but nudge us over . . . one-point-six degrees."

Odell started to do as he was told but froze. "You realize that'll put us directly in the sights of their missile launcher."

Westin placed a hand on his arm. "Do it."

He hesitated but then stabbed at the controls with a shaking finger. In spite of the cacophony swirling around him, Crusader still heard the tactical computer warn of a possible missile lock. The new tone stuttered. The customs ship hadn't gotten them yet. Then the tone went solid. Any moment now.

"Hang on!" Westin cried and stabbed her finger onto the controls.

The *Purim* lurched forward, the view out the front port swinging wildly. Crusader's stomach flopped and he dug his fingers into the panel. He closed his eyes, trying to bring his breathing and heart rate under control.

When he looked again, the field was clear. The whine of the engines descended, sputtering a bit as they went.

Westin collapsed back in her chair. "Plot a course out of here, Gav. Neither of them will be coming after us any time soon."

Crusader frowned at the confidence in her voice. He called up the tactical sensors and his eyes widened. The *Bared Arm* was trading shots with the Eps-Prime custom ship. How had she done *that?*

He ignored Odell's chatter as he laid in a course. He pulled the sensor data from the past two minutes and fed it into the tactical computer. In a moment, he watched a simulation of what Westin had done.

She had used the *Purim*'s tractor beam to snare the customs ship. That much he knew. Then the *Bared Arm* had locked on their own tractor beam. The *Purim* had drifted into missile lock and the customs ship had fired. Westin must've dropped the *Purim*'s tractor beam and used the *Bared Arm*'s beam to swing them out of the missile's path. Then the *Arm*'s beam had snared the missile and sucked it in, destroying the beam emitter. The captain must have assumed that the Eps-Prime ship had fired on them, and he'd returned fire.

Crusader chuckled, warmth bubbling through him. The perfect distraction the captain of the *Bared Arm* would have never expected.

"Starting up the tunneler drive," Odell reported.

A shudder clattered through the ship but the *Purim* still shot forward.

Westin turned in her chair, her gaze roaming across the cockpit. She frowned. "I don't like the sounds of that. I think we may have done some serious system damage. Hang on. I'll be back in a second."

Crusader laid a hand on her shoulder. "No. It can wait. Get down to the medical bay. We have to check your leg."

She smiled, her face softening to the point that she almost glowed. "I'll be okay. Really. Let me just do a cursory check first, see what's wrong."

Westin slipped past him, touching his hand as she walked. Electricity tickled up his arm and danced through his skull. He turned and watched as she walked down the corridor and disappeared into the engineering bay.

Crusader took a step to leave, but then pain sliced through him. He gasped, trying to catch his breath. He clutched his chest, trying to tear open his shirt to find the source of the agony. But his strength rolled up his limbs and before he knew what had happened, he had collapsed to the deck.

Someone shouted, the voice echoing as if through a metallic tube. Hands touched him, probed his back and shoulder. Soothing, stroking. Westin's voice. Cooing in his ears. He breathed deep, flooded with her scent. Citrus and cinnamon coursed down his jangled nerves, leaving peace in its wake. He clung to her, drawing her arms around him like a blanket. She rocked him gently back and forth, back and forth.

"Gavin, what is wrong with you? Don't just stand there!"

"Are you kidding me?"

Their argument descended into buzzing as Crusader screwed his eyes shut.

Better a good Turk . . .

Palti's voice echoed through his mind. Why think of him now?

He had to regain control. He couldn't give in, not now. Steps. Get up first. Breathe. Then rest. And he knew just the place.

He allowed Westin to help him up. She tried to steer him toward the corridor but he dug in his heels. She looked up at him, her shining eyes questioning him. He stumbled to the navigational panel. He tapped in a set of coordinates and then looked at Odell. "When you're done with the random tunnel jumps, head here."

Odell frowned at the board. "That's in the middle of nowhere. What's there?"

"My oasis."

29

The intercom in the engineering bay chimed. Isolda sighed and pushed the hair out of her eyes. She reached over and flipped the switch for the microphone.

"We're coming up on Crusader's coordinates. Just thought you might be interested."

Isolda sighed again, frustrated at the latent anger in Gavin's voice. She had spent as much time as she could with him during the three day trip, trying to remind him of happier times. But he had remained sullen and quiet, answering her questions with grunts and other noncommittal sounds.

And after a few hours in the medical bay, Crusader had sequestered himself in the cargo hold, keeping the doors sealed from the inside. He emerged only for meals, which he ate in silence.

So Isolda had spent the majority of her waking hours in the engineering bay, coaxing the systems to keep working. As near as she could tell, the only reason they had made it this far was because of her. The damaged inertial sink had almost failed twice. When Isolda had mentioned that to Crusader over lunch the previous day, he had smiled and said they'd be fine.

She put her tools away and left the bay. She froze when she saw Crusader coming up the ladder from the cargo hold. He motioned for her to go first. She did, walking down the corridor, all too aware of his looming presence behind her.

She stepped into the cockpit. Gavin didn't say anything. He didn't even look in her direction. She gritted her teeth. When all of this was over, she'd have to talk to him. They had to get past this.

"Ready for real-space reversion," Gavin reported. He counted down from five. When he reached zero, lights flared outside the cockpit which faded to blackness. And hovering before them . . .

Isolda gasped. A massive metallic structure hung in space. The upper part was shaped vaguely like an octagonal gem, the facets at gentle angles. The lower part tapered into a cluster of squat spikes bristling with antennae. It was a Waystation, a small one. Had it been damaged? It didn't look like it. A few hull plates were missing, but not from a battle. The station appeared abandoned. She turned to Crusader, who bent over a panel and pressed some buttons.

When he straightened, he pointed to the station. Isolda looked and gasped. Lights flared across the surface, illuminating windows and the hull. Then a set of docking doors opened along the side. "That's where you go, Odell," Crusader said. "The automated system will guide you in."

"As ordered."

The *Purim* dove for the docking port.

"Where are we?" Isolda asked.

"No idea," Gavin answered. "Why not ask him?"

If Crusader noticed the venom in Gavin's voice, he didn't react. "Lightning Station."

Isolda frowned. "I've never heard of that one."

"Not surprised." Crusader sat down in the copilot's chair to look over the readings. "Little more than a refueling depot when it was running. Hasn't been officially open for a hundred years."

"Why?"

"Wasn't needed anymore, thanks to improvements in the tunneler drive systems. Ships could go farther on less fuel. There are lots of abandoned stations if you know where to look for them."

"Seems like the perfect staging base for pirates," Gavin said.

"Who do you think I took this from?"

A chill rippled through Isolda. Crusader's matter-of-fact tone left no doubt about his methods.

"So why would an assassin need a Waystation?" Gavin asked.

Crusader shrugged. "The Ministrix gives me downtime between assignments. No family, not many friends. I need a place to go. This is it."

Isolda shivered. The hollowness in Crusader's voice tugged at her. She wanted to wrap her arms around him again. How could one man be so alone?

The *Purim* dropped through the docking port. Much to Isolda's surprise, half a dozen ships of various sizes were lined up on one side of the bay. She pointed to them.

"Leftovers from the pirates," he explained. "I use them as transportation. Gives me a little more independence that way."

The ship shuddered as it touched down on the deck. Gavin flipped a series of switches. "We are secure and docked." He turned to Isolda. "Now what?"

She hesitated, unsure of what to say or do.

"We fix the *Purim*," Crusader interjected. "Plenty of parts here. Rest up too. Get patched up. And after that, the Rift, right?"

Isolda could feel Gavin's eyes boring into her head. But she nodded. "Sounds like a plan."

She just hoped it was a good one.

30

Crusader closed his eyes and took a deep breath as the doors to Lightning Station's command deck closed behind him. It was a round room, with large windows looking out into space. Underneath the windows were control panels. Most were dark since the majority of the station was powered down. In the center was a raised dais, ten meters in diameter. Another bank of controls filled the center of the dais.

Peace cascaded over him. How long had it been? At least nine months, probably more. His bed was shoved into an empty corner, partitioned from the rest of the room by a curtain. He stepped onto the dais and dropped into his chair.

Environmental controls were nominal and could go for another ten years. Sensors were primed to identify anyone who stumbled across the station. He double-checked the exterior defenses. Still good. Communications would warn off any intruders. Weapons would punctuate the message if the intruders ignored it.

Crusader glanced at the internal switch. His finger hovered over it, wondering if he should spy on his guests. Better safe than sorry. A quick flip of the switch brought up internal security. Odell was in his cabin. Not a surprise. That one preferred to sulk. And Westin . . .

A smile tugged at his lips. They had spent the last hour in Lightning Station's medical bay. While she'd undergone a full medical gel treatment for the burn on her leg, he'd run a complete battery of tests on himself to determine why he'd lost consciousness. Unfortunately, the scanners hadn't detected anything out of the ordinary, at least, nothing that explained it. Westin, on the other hand, had responded well to the treatment. She had left the medical bay, saying she wanted to explore the station.

Crusader adjusted the security feed to see where she was. Given her profession, maybe she had gone down to the power plant to look it over. Or maybe she had found one of the living quarters so she could take a shower.

On the screen, Westin approached the main commissary.

Crusader leapt out of his chair and headed for the elevator. No telling what she might think if she went in there alone.

As the elevator car descended through the station, Crusader cursed his stupidity. He should have thought of the murals right away. The car doors opened and he sprinted to the commissary. He rounded the corner into the room and stopped short. Westin was already there.

The commissary was the largest public space on Lightning Station, with enough seating for nine hundred people. The ceiling soared fifteen meters above the floor in an arch formed by two long walls that met overhead. In many ways, the space reminded Crusader of the cathedrals the Ministrix constructed throughout their territory. That's why he'd chosen the commissary for the murals.

Westin stood in the middle of the room, staring at one wall. Towering before her was the Victorious Christ. He stood upon a high cliff. His left arm raised His iron staff above His head. With His right hand, He pointed to a valley that stretched over most of the wall. The valley was filled with shadows, ominous shapes hinted at in the darkness. A claw here. An upraised dagger there.

Yet in the middle of the darkness stood a solitary figure. Tatters clung to his bruised arms and legs, his chest covered with welts and slashes. The man carried a gleaming sword, but the weapon drooped in his hand. His hair, matted down by sweat and grime, barely concealed the man's face. Pain radiated from his eyes. He looked ready to collapse at any moment.

Westin turned to the other wall, probably to see what the man in the mural faced. On the opposite wall towered another imposing figure: a woman reaching out a hand, her fingers straining to touch the man. She wore a form-fitting white jumpsuit, immaculate and almost gleaming. Her eyes were half closed, tears pooling in their corners. Her full lips turned down. Fire ringed her, radiating out to the edges, consuming the wall. Her sorrowful expression seemed to amplify the man's pain.

Crusader stood quietly in the entrance, waiting for Westin's reaction. He knew it wouldn't be good. He had been working on the murals for five years now, whenever he'd come to the station. They were almost complete. There were only a few details to correct, colors to fill in, nuances to add. Long ago he had realized that the man's face was his own.

And the woman's face was the same as Westin's.

No, not exactly. Westin's face was thinner, the woman's body rounder. But the similarities were striking. They had the same blond hair, the same full lips, the same piercing green eyes.

Westin finally turned to him, her eyes wide, her lips trembling. "What is this?"

His mouth went dry and he took a step inside. "Can't explain it. Not really. It's what I do here. When I'm by myself." He nodded toward the mural of the Victorious Christ. "Started that one after I evicted the pirates. Wanted to clean it up. Make it more sanctified."

Westin walked over to the wall. She ran her hand across it, looking up at Christ. "Is that how you see Him?"

His gaze dropped. Christ's eyes were hard, accusing. The void roiled within him. "It's how He is."

"So stern? So angry?"

"Why wouldn't He be? We are sinners, all of us, deserving His righteous wrath." His voice dropped low. "Some more than others."

Westin's face pinched into a frown.

A pang surged up his spine. The strange ache opened in his chest again. He wanted to press her against it, plug it.

"That's true," she said. "But where does God's grace fit in?"

He laughed harshly. "Are we worthy of it?"

She shook her head. "Of course not, but—"

"Then we must become worthy of it. Through what we do. Through who we are."

She smiled sadly, and the void within him grew. She took a step back and placed her hand against the painted swordsman's knee. "And look how well that works."

He looked at the painting of himself. He had never really understood why he'd painted himself the way he did. Three years ago, when he'd worked on that part of the mural, he had stayed up for two days, working feverishly, roughing in the shapes, adding in the fine details. He hadn't even realized that he had been painting himself until he had finished.

"Crusader, this isn't the Jesus that I know. I wouldn't want to know Him, not if He was so stern and disapproving. The Jesus I know would never leave you like this. He wants nothing more than to forgive you and set you free."

Crusader looked between the Victorious Christ and his battered image. He could see why Westin thought the way she did. The painting radiated despair and longing. His breathing heaved in his chest. He tried to calm himself but with little success. He reached out and grabbed a chair and sat down with a thud.

Westin took a step toward him. "Are you okay?"

He held up a hand to stop her. He would be fine. He had to be. This wasn't him. He didn't want to be this weak.

"I'm sorry," she said. "I didn't mean to—"

"I know," Crusader said.

Westin took a step back again and turned to the painting of the woman. Her gaze roamed over the wall.

She looked at him again. "Is this supposed to be me?"

Crusader shrugged. "Don't know. Seems that way, doesn't it? Painted it before I ever met you."

"How is this possible?"

Crusader shook his head.

She laughed, musical sadness. "I wish I were this beautiful."

"You are." The words slipped out of his mouth before he realized he was going to say them.

She froze, her eyes wide. Her lips trembled.

He looked away. "You are that beautiful. More, actually."

Westin took a few hesitant steps forward, then rushed to kneel down before him. She took his hands in hers, pressed her forehead against his. "You'd never hurt me, would you?"

He could feel the weight of the Christ's gaze on him. Too much rode on his next words. He knew how he should answer. He knew what he had to do. He had his orders. Isolda Westin had to die. If he didn't do as he was ordered, the guilt would continue to plague him until it consumed him. Without her death, he would be lost forever to the Almighty.

But he couldn't do it. Even though it would be so easy. Right now. Snap her neck. Smother her. So easy. Yet impossible. He wanted more than that. More from Westin. More from Christ. More than the Ministrix could ever offer. His head came up and he met her gaze. Warmth cascaded over him.

"No," Crusader whispered.

He wrapped his arms around her, drawing her even closer. Her heady scent flooded him, buoying him even higher. Her fingers slipped through his hair. He pulled back, studied her face, and then leaned in.

Their lips brushed and fire blossomed through his face, rushed down his spine. He pulled her in tight, kissing her fiercely. She responded, her hand dropping to his shoulders, raking his back. It felt as though they spun together, orbiting each other around a common point. Crusader thrilled at the sensations coursing through him, relishing the heat and cool, the sheer giddy delight . . .

Only to have it all fade as the numb reasserted itself. He knew he was kissing Isolda. He felt the pressure of her lips still against his. But the joy was gone, walled off in some distant corner, inaccessible. He pulled away.

She searched his face, uncertainty and fear painted across her features.

He sighed. "It's not you. It's me. I—"

Then the commissary was bathed in red light. Crusader's head snapped around to the rotating alarm. He leapt to his feet and sprinted to the nearest control panel, calling up the sensor data. He froze, staring in disbelief.

Isolda's hand touched his shoulder softly, tentatively. "What is it?"

"The *Bared Arm*," he said. "It's found us."

31

How could the *Bared Arm* have found Lightning Station? Crusader had been the *de facto* owner for five years and no one had ever stumbled across it.

The panel blatted. Incoming message. He jabbed the proper button with a trembling finger.

A middle aged man in a crisp blue uniform appeared on the screen, his chin tipped up and his eyes narrowed. A Ministrix ship captain if Crusader ever saw one. "You are hereby ordered to power down all defensive systems. Ready a landing bay. Our boarding team shall dispense the Ministrix's divine justice."

The image disappeared.

"What are we going to do?" Isolda tugged at his elbow.

A bloody haze dropped over his vision. He didn't know. Lightning couldn't withstand the full assault of the *Bared Arm*. The Ministrix ship's superior weaponry would batter down the defenses in minutes. How many troops could the Ministrix flagship hold? More than enough to do the job.

Isolda stepped even closer. Her warmth washed over him. He had to protect her. He closed his eyes, took a deep breath, and let the numbness seep through him again. Steps. Break it down into steps.

The *Bared Arm* could overwhelm Lightning's defenses, but it would take time. Crusader activated the automated defense halo. Resonant thrums rattled the deckplates as the lights dimmed then flared to red. He turned to Isolda. "We don't have much time. Were you able to repair the inertial sink on the *Purim*?"

Her eyes were wide as she shook her head. "Not entirely. It's maybe three quarters done."

Crusader frowned. The other ships in the docking bay were technically functional but none of them would have the *Purim*'s speed or defensive capability. They could use the *Purim*, but with a damaged inertial sink, it would be a rough ride.

Make the decision. No time for hesitation. He took Isolda's hand and dragged her after him to the elevator. "We'll take the *Hyperstar*. Not as fast as the *Purim*, but it's a tough little ship."

Into the elevator. The lights above them flickered, then surged back to life. Probably a hit. Lightning couldn't take too many more. Had to move fast.

"What about Gavin?"

Crusader had forgotten about Odell. He ground his teeth, then turned and flipped open the auxiliary control panel. He thumbed the intercom switch. "Odell, report to the docking bay. We're abandoning the station. You've got two minutes." He glanced at Isolda. She stared at him wide-eyed. He shrugged. "We can't wait forever."

The elevator bucked under their feet. The lights died and with a screech the car came to a halt. The defensive halo must have been breached.

He flipped open another panel, revealing a small hand-crank. A few minutes of quick work wrenched the doors open. He shimmied through the opening and helped Isolda out. He glanced at the nearest directory. H Deck. The docking bays were on T Deck. They'd be able to traverse most of the distance through crawlspaces, but they'd still run the risk of discovery at a few points if enemies got inside the station. Crusader jogged down the corridor and pulled back on an access panel.

Isolda knelt next to him. "An escape route?"

"Something like that."

He reached behind the panel and pulled out two blasters, tucking them into his waistband. He withdrew a dozen throwing knives and a rifle, which he slung over his shoulder. A few more steps brought them to another access hatch. He pulled it open and dropped into the darkness below, then looked up and called. "Come on. We don't have a lot of time."

Isolda joined him in the cramped tunnel, and he led her off into the darkness.

When Crusader touched her hand, Isolda clamped her mouth shut. They froze in the darkness. There. The rhythmic tromp of feet across the decking over their heads. She held her breath, screwing her eyes shut. That was the third patrol they'd heard in the last half hour. Not good. She had no idea how many soldiers were in each group, but there had to be at least a dozen of them on this level alone.

Once the footsteps receded, Crusader withdrew his hand. She wished he hadn't. There was something comforting about his touch in the bleak darkness, an anchoring presence. She bit her lip. Could they actually make it off Lightning Station? Had Gavin been captured? Too many questions.

Crusader moved in front of her and she followed. Eventually, the crawlspace opened into a larger juncture barely lit with pale blue lights. Conduits roamed through the cramped nook, but there was a small computer terminal mounted in one wall. Crusader scooted to it.

"Do they know where we are?" she asked.

Crusader shook his head. "No. That's why they're using patrols. Hoping we make a mistake, reveal ourselves." He tapped at the panel. "*The Bared Hand*'s five hundred kilometers from the station. Stable orbit. Two boarding craft, docked topside and bottom. Internal sensors register fifty troops."

"Is that good?"

He turned to face her, his face washed out by the pale blue light. He almost appeared dead. "Could be worse. I can tip the odds." More work on the panel. "There. Isolated each deck, lockdown procedure. Electrified portions of the deckplates. Should slow them a little."

He started for another tunnel but she placed a hand on his shoulder to stop him. "What are we going to do if we make it clear of the Station?"

Crusader frowned. "Don't know for sure."

She hesitated. "If we make it . . . or if only you make it, head for Crasman's Rift. The Lowside Eddy. Any navigational computer should have the coordinates."

"Why go there?"

Isolda looked down. If Elata found out what she was about to do . . .

She steeled herself. "There's a communication buoy there, a disguised one. When you arrive, activate your communications relay to transmit a five-minute stream in frequency 2520-Omega. The buoy will respond. Transmit the following phrase: 'I seek the horns of the altar.' Then wait."

Crusader's eyes narrowed, his gaze roaming across her face. She flushed. "Why?" he asked.

She managed a weak smile. "Hopefully we can find out together. Let's go."

Crusader nodded and crawled down another tunnel. Isolda followed. As they moved, she offered up a short prayer. *Lord, I don't know if we're going to make it out of this. If we do, thank You in advance. If I won't, let Crusader survive and may he find what he needs without me.*

Isolda wasn't sure how long they crawled through the stifling darkness, dropping down a number of levels using ladders. At least another half hour, she figured. At one point, they had to sneak through a deserted hallway. Thankfully, no Ministrix troops were visible. While that was a relief, Isolda couldn't help but wonder where Gavin was in all of this. Had he found a corner to hide in? Had he been captured? Or would they find him waiting in the docking bay? She'd have to check the *Purim* when they got there. He probably didn't know about the change in ships.

Halfway to the next access hatch, the lights overhead blazed back to life. Crusader froze, then motioned for her to hurry. They dove into the hatch and closed it up behind them.

"Problem?" She already knew the answer but felt she had to ask anyway.

"Could be. Might mean they've accessed the main computer," he said. "That'll make it harder for us to make it to the docking bay undetected."

She pushed at his shoulder. "Then let's keep going."

He smiled and dipped his head in a nod.

Another two ladders took them deeper into the Station, the crawlspaces winding between the decks. They didn't bother stopping when they heard the patrols. Instead, they crept through the tunnels, finally emerging outside the docking bay.

Crusader poked his head around the corner then jumped back, pressing up against the wall. He turned to Isolda. "At least seven in there. All armed. This won't be easy." He unslung the rifle and checked it. "Follow in after me. There are crates to the right. Hunker behind them, stay down until we're clear. Have to move fast."

Isolda shook her head. "I'm heading to the *Purim*. I want to make sure Gav isn't in there."

The barest hint of frustration flickered across Crusader's face but he nodded anyway. "Don't take too long. Remember, *Hyperstar*. Denthian blockade runner, third from the left." He pressed up against the wall, closed his eyes, and dove into the bay. His war cry mingled with the surprised shouts of the Ministrix soldiers. Isolda swallowed the panic clawing up her throat and followed.

She paused in the doorway. Two Ministrix soldiers were down, one clutching his leg and the other curled around a smoking wound in his shoulder. Crusader had abandoned his rifle and was now crouched in a ready stance. A Ministrix soldier charged him, drawing back a fist. Even Isolda could see the blow coming.

Crusader caught the man's fist. The man stumbled forward. Crusader snapped his elbow up into the soldier's throat. The man collapsed, clawing at his neck. Crusader spun, drawing the pistols from his waistband. He fired at the cluster of soldiers crouched behind a set of crates.

He glanced in Isolda's direction and jerked his head toward the *Purim*.

She sprang forward, sprinting across the bay to the ship. She scurried up the ramp and skidded to a halt in the main corridor running from the cockpit to the *Purim*'s aft. "Gav? Gav! Are you here? We're not taking this ship. Come on, we have to go!"

No answer. She didn't know how much longer Crusader could hold off the Ministrix troops, but she didn't want to leave Gavin behind. She rushed to the cockpit. No one. A quick check of the internal sensors revealed no one else on board. She frowned. Where could he be? Captured? She didn't like the idea of leaving Gavin in the hands of the Ministrix, but what other choice did they have at this point?

She dashed out of the ship. Crusader glanced in her direction, and yet he was still able to pick off another soldier. She shook her head. He jerked his head toward the *Hyperstar*. She started for the ship.

Halfway to the smaller ship, fire exploded in her calf. She shrieked and tripped over her own feet, tumbling to the floor. Her hands spasmed as she clutched at her leg. What had happened? She looked down. A scorch ringed a hole in her pants, the same color as the wound in her leg. She had been shot?

She turned to Crusader. His eyes widened and he started after her. But then two crimson bolts slashed through him, shoulder and knee. He fell but rolled through and kept moving. Isolda thought he'd make it. She expected him to pull himself the rest of the way and carry her into the *Hyperstar*.

He didn't make it. Soldiers erupted from their positions and swarmed over them. A screen of bodies cut her off from Crusader. She didn't truly see them, focusing instead on the cloud of weapons that hovered in her face.

Rough hands pulled her up. She winced, biting her lip to keep from crying out. Agony ricocheted through her leg as she hopped along. Two soldiers held her, and a half dozen troops kept Crusader in check. His entire body coiled, ready to strike at any moment. But Isolda could read the uncertainty in his eyes.

"Oh, very good."

A small, wiry man stepped around one of the ships. Isolda stared at him. He wore an immaculate Ministrix uniform, all crimsons and greys. He straightened the front of his shirt and brushed his palms against his legs, even though his hands looked perfectly clean. He smirked at Crusader.

The barest snarl twitched at Crusader's lips. "Inquisitor." He spat the word.

The man's smile grew larger. "Hello, Crusader. It's a shame that it's come to this, my friend. A true shame. I've always had such high hopes that you would be the one to survive. But I see that is not to happen."

Crusader frowned. "Spare me. How long have you known about Lightning Station?"

Inquisitor laughed. "This place? Not until we arrived. Oh, we always knew you had some hidey-hole away from the Ministrix. But we had no idea you had commandeered an entire Waystation. Good for you, friend."

"Then how did you find us?"

Inquisitor's eyes hooded as his smile deepened into a feral snarl. "We had help."

A low-pitched whine sounded behind her. It sounded like a weapon's power pack charging. She managed to crane her neck around to see what it was. Ice clawed at her spine.

Gavin stared at her, his face blank, cradling a sniper rifle in his arms.

32

"Why?" Isolda's anguished shriek tore at the back of Crusader's mind. He studied Odell. Didn't hold the rifle properly. Never been trained on it, most likely. Lucky shots then. Not much comfort. The numbness tamped down the pain, but he couldn't find the strength to stand, let alone fight free from his captors.

Odell dropped the rifle. Inquisitor winced then nodded to one of the soldiers, who darted forward to retrieve it.

"Do you really have to ask that question?" Odell asked. "Look at what we've been reduced to. Sneaking around, taking meager jobs, hiding in decrepit ruins like this."

"He finally saw the light. Or rather, saw it again," Inquisitor added.

Odell froze, casting a glare out of the corner of his eye. "I've had enough. I'm going back to the Ministrix."

"But what about your orders, killing all those people?" Isolda asked.

Odell flicked his hand as if waving away a pesky insect. "A misunderstanding. Besides, given the reward the Ministrix is giving me for your capture, I won't have to ever work again."

Isolda's lower lip trembled. "I thought you were my friend."

"I was." Odell hesitated. "Sometimes you have to make hard choices. Sorry, Isolda. I made mine."

Inquisitor snapped his fingers. "This has gone on long enough, touching though it is. Escort Mr. Liddell and Ms. Westin to the boarding ships. There is but one more thing to deal with."

The lead soldier saluted and most of them marched away, flanking Odell. The traitor tried to walk taller, but he stumbled as he marched with the soldiers back into their landing craft.

Isolda wrenched her arms and twisted, but her escorts wouldn't let her go. Her legs wobbled and she collapsed. The soldiers hoisted her up between them and dragged her back to the landing craft. She looked over her shoulder, tears welling in her eyes. "Crusader!"

He closed his eyes. He couldn't look at her anymore. It would kill him if he did.

"It seems you made quite the impression on her." Inquisitor's voice was a bare hiss near his ear.

Crusader tried to rip his arms free but the soldiers pulled him back. He glared at his former liaison officer.

Inquisitor merely smirked. "So this is how it all ends. A pity. Truly a pity. You led us on a merry chase, but this is the end for you."

"Why? I've been nothing but loyal."

"There is no question of your fealty, my friend. None at all. But our orders were quite clear. Capture Isolda Westin. Return her to New Jerusalem Station for questioning. Kill Crusader. We've accomplished the first. The second will be no problem. Now for the third."

The soldiers slammed him up against a support girder on one side of the docking bay. They wrenched his arms around the metal then chained his wrists together.

Crusader didn't bother to struggle. Instead, he focused on Inquisitor. "So what did I ever do to abd al Sami?"

Inquisitor's eyes went wide and then he laughed, a reedy chuckle. "Oh no, my friend. You have it all wrong."

Crusader frowned. "What do you mean?"

"Do you really think that a lowly sub-deacon could authorize the assassination of a Ministrix operative? Do you think abd al Sami could have requisitioned the *Bared Arm* for this operation on his own?"

"But the Connor Trap—"

"Ah, so you did intercept Balaam's orders. We had wondered, though the Deacon was sure you had." Inquisitor shook his head. "Is it any wonder that he has ascended so high?"

Then it was as if a heavy blow landed in Crusader's stomach. "No."

Inquisitor's grin turned feral. "Oh, yes. Now you realize, don't you?" The liaison officer took a step closer. "The person who set all this in motion was Deacon Siseal himself." Inquisitor turned away, taking a few steps.

Crusader reeled, barely aware of the soldiers pulling his legs back, tying them behind the strut as well. "Why?" Crusader was surprised he was able to muster the breath to say it.

"In truth, I do not know. The Deacon never shared his reasons with me. All he ever said was that Isolda Westin has vital information. You know we never question our superiors. Only obey them. As it should be with the Almighty's children."

"Perhaps that's a mistake."

Inquisitor favored him with a sardonic smile, then pulled a small holo-emitter from his pocket. He set it on the deck a meter from Crusader and nudged it with his toe. A band of light leapt from the disc and hovered above the floor. "Now, my orders were to simply leave you to die. But you and I have history. I would like to think that we are friends. And so I've decided to bend my orders a bit." He met Crusader's gaze. "I leave you with this interface. May it help guide you into whatever reward awaits you."

Crusader laughed. "Not dying."

Inquisitor's smile turned hard. "Not yet."

The smaller man drew a pistol and shot Crusader in the stomach.

Crusader lurched, his eyes bulging. Needles tore through his midsection, nibbling away at the numbness. Inquisitor knelt down in front of him.

"I know this might seem cruel, this lingering death, but it truly is a mercy for you. You now have at least fifteen minutes to prepare yourself for the end. Goodbye, Crusader. Perhaps we will meet again in the Great Beyond."

With that, Inquisitor rose and strode up the ramp into the landing craft. The soldiers followed, keeping their weapons trained on the landing bay. The boarding ramp withdrew into the ship. With a roar, the thrusters fired and the Ministrix landing craft slipped through the landing bay's atmospheric shielding and was gone, taking Isolda away and leaving Crusader alone.

Crusader closed his eyes. Had to focus. Ignore the failing numbness. Get free. Somehow. Medical kits in the *Purim* or the other ships. Could easily stop the bleeding, at least patch things up until he could make it to Lightning's medical bay.

The lights in the bay flared to red, accompanied by a loud alarm. "Self-destruct sequence engaged. Twenty minutes and counting."

Unless, of course, Inquisitor was thorough. Crusader tugged at his bonds experimentally. No good. They were too tight. He had a little give around his left wrist, probably slicked by the blood from his shoulder wound. Not enough, though.

Legs next. He leaned against the column while pulling forward. Not too much give there either. He collapsed. Cold crept through his body.

The holo-emitter buzzed and an image appeared. The Revered Hand stared down at him. "My child, are you ready to face the final justice?"

Crusader glared at him. Last thing he needed right now was an audience, simulated or otherwise. Maybe try to free his arms again?

"I realize you may never have thought of such matters before now, but it is an end we all face, ordained by the Almighty Himself. So now, you must ask yourself: Have you conducted yourself rightly? Has your behavior been in harmony with the teachings of His Most Holy Church, the Ministrix?"

Crusader took a deep breath and pulled against the restraints. He thought he felt the left cuff give a little, but still not enough. He couldn't slip his hand through. Break his thumb? Might help. But try as he might, he couldn't get the right leverage.

The Revered Hand's face contorted into a frown. "Your lack of answer displeases me. I can only assume that you see the truth. You have not lived as you should. Yes?"

Crusader sighed. The void within him snapped and snarled, cutting through him like a razor. The guilt smothered his mind. "Yes."

"That is a shame. Unfortunately, there is nothing more I can say for you. When you face the Almighty, know that whatever happens, it is because you earned it."

The hologram disappeared. Crusader strained again then collapsed. As much as he hated to admit it, the Revered Hand was right. His whole life, he had followed orders. He had done as he was told, every day, every mission, all for divine favor. And where had it left him? Tied up, bleeding out, and soon to be reduced to subatomic particles. Could he expect mercy in the hereafter? Apparently not, especially since he had been condemned by Deacon Siseal.

And yet . . . There had been times, talking with Isolda, when he had felt drawn to her strange heresy. That idea that the Christ wasn't a demanding taskmaster, that what He really wanted was to set Crusader free. So wrong yet so uncomplicated. So easy. He wished he could go back, talk with her some more. Find out more about what she believed.

Darkness swam at the corners of his eyes. He tried to keep alert, awake. But coldness seeped through him and soon the shadows closed in, cutting him off completely.

33

Isolda leaned forward, trying to peer through the bars of her cell. No sign of the guards. Were they monitoring her? Probably. But she had to try.

She had noticed the loose access panel when the guards had tossed her into the cell. She had bided her time until now. How many days had it been? She thought at least one, though the lights in the brig never dimmed. But she kept track of the guards' patrols and, if she had the pattern down, she'd be undisturbed for a few minutes. Hopefully enough time.

She wedged her nails behind the panel and pulled. The plate came away a little at a time until it fell off completely.

Inside was a power conduit, some random wiring. Nothing promising.

Wait. The power conduit met a juncture half a meter into the wall. Although she couldn't be sure, it looked like the connection was loose. If she could wrench it free, get enough play, she could use it as a weapon. She could jab the exposed end into the guards when they came to feed her, hit them with an energy discharge. She smiled grimly. Her time with Crusader had rubbed off on her.

She bit her lip, trying not to cry. She had done enough of that already. She knew he was dead. He had to be by this point. Forget about him for now. There'd be plenty of time to mourn after she escaped. She wrapped her fingers around the conduit and braced herself to pull.

"I wouldn't do that if I were you."

She spun, startled to find Gavin staring down at her. How had he snuck up on her? He crossed his arms over his crisply pressed uniform. The sight of it revolted her. Dark grey pants, a clingy red shirt. No rank insignia to be seen. That figured if he was really going back to the Ministrix as a civilian.

"The power cord isn't real. It's a trap set by the guards." He took a step closer to the bars. "They do that sometimes. They let the prisoners attack them with a fake power conduit. It gives them an excuse to beat them up or . . ." The apologetic expression on his face spoke volumes about what the guards might try with her.

She wanted to vomit. Or scream. Maybe both at the same time. She slumped down against the wall. "How could you do it?"

Gavin closed his eyes. "There was no other way."

"We could have kept going."

"Where could we go? The Ministrix would have stayed after us."

"Maybe." She couldn't believe she was actually going to say this. "But God would have watched out for us."

Gavin laughed. "That would be a first, wouldn't it? Let's face it, Isolda: He's forgotten about us."

"That's not true."

"It is, and you know it. Look at what's happened to us. His people, trapped between a rock and a hard place. We can't live openly anywhere. Heretics to the Ministrix, outlaws in the Praesidium. Where's our safe haven?"

Isolda laughed ruefully. "Were we ever promised one?" His face soured but she pressed on. "Really. Name me one verse that promises His children will have an easy time."

"We deserve better than that. You deserve better than what you got. Your mother, what happened with Elata, now this. Don't you think He owes you better?"

"For what, exactly? Isn't it enough that He saved us? Is He supposed to smooth over all the rough patches too?"

He didn't answer.

She sighed and knocked the back of her head against the bulkhead, a rhythmic pattern that caused a dull ache to grow. She didn't mind. "There's got to be more to this," she said. "It was Crusader, wasn't it?"

"He was no good for you."

She waved at her bandaged leg. "He's not the one who shot me."

He winced. She rolled her eyes.

"Look." Gavin roughed a hand through his hair. "I know you may not believe this, but things could turn out okay. I don't know why Deacon Siseal wants you so badly, but when you see him, just give him Keleman's research, okay? Maybe he'll let you go. Then we can find someplace together, somewhere on the Ministrix fringe."

"You think I'd go anywhere with you now? After—" Her eyes narrowed. "Wait, why Keleman's research? Why not . . . Gavin! You didn't!"

He looked down. "No. They haven't asked about the Catacombs."

"But what if they did? Would you tell them?"

"It's not like I would have a lot of choice. If they want the information, it's not like I can withhold it."

She lunged for the bars, reaching through to grab him. She wasn't sure what she'd do if she caught hold, but she strained. Her fingers brushed the front of his shirt.

He sighed and took a step back. "Face reality, Isolda. This is the best way. It's three weeks before we reach Earth. Maybe you'll see reason before then." Gavin turned and walked up the hall.

She strained, still trying to get a hold on him. But then he was gone. She collapsed to the floor, her head in her hands. Why? How could this happen? Things seemed so right when she was with . . . "Crusader."

His name wrapped around her like a blanket, warming her. But a chill chased the comfort away as quickly as it came. She closed her eyes.

"God, I don't know what happened to him. But let him wind up in a good place."

Sounds. Drifting. Lights swimming through the darkness and teasing his mind. He grunted. Shoulder itched, leg too. Dull heat radiated through his stomach. He rolled, trying to find some comfort. A blanket moved with him. He touched it then allowed his fingers to roam to his stomach. Fresh bandages.

He opened his eyes, unable to see through his fluttering eyelids. Lots of light. Gleaming surfaces all around. The hum of equipment, punctuated by steady pinging. Medical facility? Looked like the one at Lightning Station.

He frowned and tried to push himself up. He couldn't. Strength wasn't there. He collapsed, slamming his eyes shut. How had he gotten here? Had he somehow freed himself? Crawled the whole way? Didn't seem likely, given his injuries.

"Good. You are up."

His eyes snapped open. He knew that voice.

Kolya Krestyanov smiled at him from a nearby chair. "I'm glad to see that my nursing hasn't made you worse."

"How'd you get here?" Crusader tried to inject steel into his voice but couldn't muster more than a murmur.

Krestyanov shrugged. "How does anyone get anywhere?" His smile broadened. "Personal shuttle. My superiors, they thought I was wasting my time. 'There's no way that Crusader wouldn't notice a tracking device on his ship. You're chasing a comet's tail.'"

Crusader moaned. Tracking device. He should have known, should have checked.

"You are welcome, by the way. When I arrived, your little paradise here was about to detonate and you were barely holding on. Nasty wounds, those. Who did the honors?"

"Inquisitor."

"I am afraid I do not know the man. Sloppy work, though. If he'd wanted you dead, you'd think he'd have done a better job."

"Not just dead. Wanted me to repent first."

Krestyanov rolled his eyes. "Of course. How silly of me." He slapped his thighs and rose. He looked over the nearest bank of sensors. "Now to business. I am no medic, but these readings seem to be improving by the hour. I didn't want to risk moving you from the station until you were more stable, but now I would guess you'll be ready to travel in a day or so. Ah, I can hear the accolades now. While I wish I could have captured that Westin to sweeten the deal, I'm sure you'll be more than enough for me to secure the release of Simone Weathers."

Crusader choked on a laugh. "Think they'll trade for me?" He shook his head. "They want me dead. Inquisitor acted on Siseal's orders."

Krestyanov stared at him. "Then you will be good for intelligence. We'll turn you over to the interrogators, see what you know about this mysterious 'Sharp Sickle,' and—"

This time Crusader did laugh. "Don't know anything. Just ran missions. You could try, but everyone would just wind up frustrated."

Red crept through Krestyanov's face, his jaw slack. "You mean I traveled all this way for nothing?" He stumbled back to his chair and collapsed into it.

"Not nothing. You saved me. Thank you."

A long pause. "You're welcome."

Crusader sank back onto the pillow and stared at the ceiling.

"So now what?" Krestyanov asked.

Crusader wondered the same thing. He knew what he wanted to do: rescue Isolda. But that didn't seem possible. The *Bared Arm*, while not the fastest ship, had at least a day's lead. He'd need a tunnel buster to board her, and those were hard to come by. Even if, by some miracle, he could find them, he would never survive an assault. Isolda was gone. He didn't want to admit it, but there was no way he would ever see her again.

So what now? He remembered her instructions. Go to Crasman's Rift. The Eddy. The signal. See what happened.

He pushed himself up and swung his legs over the edge of the bed.

Krestyanov bolted upright in his chair. "Where are you going?"

"Going to take a little trip."

"I do not think so." Krestyanov leapt over to the medical bay entrance. "Do not forget, you are my prisoner."

Crusader narrowed his eyes, allowed a snarl to twitch his lips. "My station. You have no backup. Only one ship. Really think you can stop me?"

To his credit, Krestyanov didn't flinch. Instead the Praesidium agent crossed his arms and cocked his head to one side. "You forget, you are injured."

"So it'll take me an extra minute to take you down."

Krestyanov snorted. "You forget, my friend, I've been monitoring your biosigns for the past several days. At best, you could maybe take down a kitten. A sleepy one, perhaps. No, we are returning to the Praesidium where you will be thoroughly debriefed."

"A waste of time," Crusader said. An idea occurred to him. "I don't know anything useful, but I may have another source."

"Oh?"

Not much interest in Krestyanov's voice. Would have to work on that.

"Got a ship down in the bay. The *Purim*. Used by Balaam. Know him?"

A pause. "I might."

A nibble. Might work after all.

"Been on a lot more missions than me. Not all of them obvious. Terabytes of data, keep your analysts busy for years. Interested?"

"And what is to stop me from just taking it as well as you?" Krestyanov asked.

"The ship is voice-locked to me," Crusader said. "You try to dump the data, it'll wipe the memory banks clean."

It was a lie, but hopefully not an obvious one.

Krestyanov studied Crusader through narrow eyes. "So you'll give me these terabytes of data . . . in exchange for what?"

Crusader turned, met his gaze. Couldn't show any weakness now. "Your help." He ignored Krestyanov's surprised look. "You're good, Krestyanov. You are. Could use an extra set of hands on this one. Outsider's perspective. You help me, the data on the *Purim* is yours. Deal?"

Krestyanov smiled, a generous flash of teeth. "Done! So where are we going?"

34

"And how long are we going to search the Rift for what is obviously not there?"

Crusader's fingers tightened around the edge of the control panel. Krestyanov had done nothing but complain since they'd left Lightning two days earlier. First it had been about the repairs on the *Purim*. Then it had been about the lack of guest quarters. After that he griped about the lack of data in the *Purim*'s files. Thankfully, by the time he realized that, he was curious enough to see where they were going that he didn't press the issue. Now it was boredom. Crusader wanted to lock him in the cargo bay but he needed help. The Rift disrupted the ship's sensors. He needed an extra pair of eyes to keep things running while he looked for Isolda's beacon.

A solitary light popped up in one corner of the controls. There it was. He dialed up the appropriate frequency and broadcast the burst, just as Isolda had told him to do.

Krestyanov leaned over his shoulder. "Is that it? So anticlimactic."

Crusader looked over his shoulder and glared at the Praesidium agent. He stabbed a finger at the copilot chair.

Krestyanov didn't sit. Instead, he frowned and leaned in closer. "How are you feeling? And yes, I know, you're 'numb.' But I fear you haven't taken enough time to recover from your injuries."

"I'm fine," Crusader growled. "Sit down."

Krestyanov sighed. "It is not that I care what happens to you one way or the other, you understand. But given our proximity to the Rift, there is no telling what could happen should I need to pilot this ship without your assistance."

Crusader ground his teeth. "Noted. Sit."

The console pinged. Krestyanov's eyes widened. "A response?"

Crusader jabbed the communications controls with his thumb.

"Who are you?" a gruff voice demanded.

"Depends," Crusader answered. "Who are you?"

"I asked you first, smart guy."

Crusader exchanged a glance with Krestyanov, who only shrugged.

"A friend sent me. Said to broadcast the signal and say, 'I seek the horns of the altar.'"

No response. The silence dragged on long enough that Crusader began to wonder if the other person was simply looking for advice or was getting ready to trigger some sort of weapon system.

Then the guttural voice came back. "Okay, here's the deal. I don't know who your friend was—and no, I don't want to know either—but he or she shouldn't have just sent you in by yourself. You got no *bona fides*, understand? No one to vouch for you. But since they told you to use the passcode, we have to bring you in. So this is how this is going to work. You tie in your navigational controls to this frequency. We'll take control of your ship, plot the course, and bring you in."

"We can't do that!" Krestyanov's voice was a bare hiss. "There's no telling what this person may to do to us."

"Those are the terms. Non-negotiable. And the offer's only good for the next minute, got it? You turn over control right now or nothing."

"A bad idea," Krestyanov whispered. "They could overload our engines, send us hurtling into space. Let us just leave. We'll go back to the Praesidium. Work with me. We can get some vengeance against the Ministrix that wronged you so badly."

Crusader perked up. Revenge? He liked that idea. With Krestyanov's resources, they could take the fight to the Ministrix. He could track Inquisitor down, pay him back for what he tried. He could be a thorn in the Revered Hand's flesh, and no amount of prayer would remove him.

"Thirty seconds."

The blunt announcement snapped him out of his thoughts. Reality crushed in on him. Yes, he could avenge himself against Inquisitor, the Hand, the Ministrix. But none of that would give him who he really wanted. None of that would bring back

Isolda. He could make himself a nuisance. He could cut a bloody swath through Ministrix space. Yet he'd still lose her.

He leaned forward and called up the navigational systems, cross-connecting the programs to the communications array. Krestyanov cried out, but Crusader ignored him, dropping the security software and leaving their entire ship open to the stranger's control.

"Stand by." The disembodied voice fell silent.

Crusader leaned back in his chair, ignoring the heat of Krestyanov's glare boring into the side of his face.

"I hope you know what you're doing."

He smirked at Krestyanov. "No problem."

The lights in the cockpit died. The panels went dark. They were left in the pitch darkness, staring out at the undulating glow of the Rift, but then even that was taken away as the blast shields for the viewport slid shut with a thunderous groan.

"Small problem," Crusader allowed.

"Hello? We seem to have lost our instruments," Krestyanov called.

"That's intentional, friend. Tracking computers, sensors, it's all shut down. Like I said, we'll guide you in. No record, no way to find us afterwards. We'll see you in the Catacombs in four days."

Any annoyance Crusader felt disappeared in an instant. The Catacombs? His eyes widened. Not only were they real, but he was on his way. If he could somehow get this information to Siseal, he could trade it for Isolda's life. His hand darted out to the controls. Sure, the controller had said he'd shut down the circuits, but Crusader was certain he could get them online again.

But his hand froze a mere centimeter from the controls. He couldn't do it. Isolda had given him the Catacombs. He couldn't sully her gift. He wouldn't betray her. He dropped his hand in his lap and glanced at Krestyanov.

The Praesidium agent tapped at the controls, a frown deepening on his face when nothing happened. He glanced at Crusader and froze. "You did not think of trying to restore the sensors?"

"Not at all."

A vibration wormed through the deckplates, followed by a low-pitched whine that steadily built, higher and higher. Then the whole ship shuddered. The *Purim* had engaged its tunnel drive.

Krestyanov fell back into his chair. "I suppose we are in for a wait then. Do you play chess?"

Crusader was about to answer when a wave of dizziness crashed over him. He drooped forward.

Krestyanov was out of his chair immediately, gently pushing him back up. "Your injuries seem to have caught up with you, friend. Let us get you to bed."

Crusader couldn't argue. Krestyanov helped him out of the chair and supported him down the corridor. They stumbled into the main cabin and Crusader collapsed onto the bed. The room spun around him. How could he be expected to sleep?

And yet, as he lay there, a scent stole across the sheets, cloying and soothing. Citrus and cinnamon. Isolda. Her memory wrapped around him and he fell into a dreamless sleep.

He swam in an ocean of her scent, buoyed along and light. His eyes drifted open and he pushed himself up. He looked around the *Purim*'s cabin. Isolda? Was she here?

Of course not.

Instead, Krestyanov lounged in the desk chair, scrolling through lists of data. He glanced at Crusader and smirked. "Not the one you wanted to wake up to, eh?"

"What are you doing here?"

Krestyanov shrugged. "Where else would I be but acting as nurse for you? There is little else to do on this ship. The system displays are mostly shut down. Our paranoid friends even went so far as to shutter the viewports. They left us access to the databanks, and so I have continued my sifting of inconsequential nonsense. And, I figured, if I did so here, I could monitor your recovery as well."

Crusader pressed a hand against his forehead. A dull ache throbbed behind his eyes, slowly dissolving into nothing.

Krestyanov rose from his perch and took a step closer to the bed. He peeked underneath one of Crusader's bandages. "Excellent. You are healing quite nicely. All due to the ministrations of your caregiver, yes?" He hesitated before turning back to the computer terminal. "I have found something for you. Embedded in the files. Very well hidden."

Crusader frowned. Something for him? From Balaam? Unlikely. How would the other Ministrix agent have known that Crusader would appropriate his ship?

"Do not fear, I have not viewed the file." Krestyanov hesitated by the desk, then turned and headed for the door. "I will give you your privacy. Whenever you are ready, it is cued up."

With that, the Praesidium agent left. Crusader scooted across the bed. He tapped in the command to play the message.

The lights in the cabin dimmed and the holoprojector hummed to life.

Isolda appeared above the device.

Crusader gasped. How could he have forgotten how beautiful she was? Her hair was matted, her face stained with grease, and yet Crusader wished he could gather her into his arms, hold her tightly. She looked around furtively, then leaned closer. Crusader matched her movement.

"Crusader . . . I don't know if you'll ever get this. I hope not. I really do. I know I should be down in engineering, monitoring that inertial sink, but I had to . . . I had to come up here and leave you this message. Just in case. I don't know where we're going. I don't know what will happen after we get there. But there's something important I need to talk to you about. Maybe I'll get the chance after we arrive wherever you're taking us. Just in case, though, I need to talk to you about the Ministrix and the Church.

"I know you think that the Ministrix is the one true Church, but let me tell you, it's not. This isn't what God intended for His people to be like, so paranoid, so violent and murderous, so wrapped up in power. If you read the New Testament—and the real one, not the twisted version your 'Revered Hand' uses—you never see Jesus looking for political power. While He was a king, His kingdom was built on truth and love, not political domination. I don't know what happened that made the Ministrix forget this, but this is why so many of us had to go underground. We understood what God's kingdom was and what it wasn't."

She hesitated, her eyes dropping. He reached out to her, his fingers sliding into the image. Part of her face disappeared, blotted out by his hand. He jerked his hand away, allowing the emitter to restore her beauty, just in time for her to look up at him again.

"Sorry. That was a bit arrogant, wasn't it? Gav has told me so much of what it was like in the Ministrix. Striving to earn divine merit, worrying the whole time about falling out of favor. It makes me sick to think that you believe the same things. I just want you to know the truth about grace. I can try to tell you more, but I'm not sure I can explain everything. That's why I'm thinking of bringing you to the Catacombs. They probably won't be happy to see you . . . or me, for that matter. But I have to try."

Her head jerked up and she looked to the side. She leapt forward, and the image disappeared. Crusader frowned. Someone must have interrupted her.

He leaned back, a dull ache settling into his chest. He closed his eyes, wishing for the first time that the numbness would take it all away.

35

"So are you going to move or not?"

Crusader ignored Krestyanov's newest complaint and studied the board. His king was pinned between his opponent's rook and knight. He thought he could get Krestyanov's king in five moves, but he'd need room for his queen to maneuver. Not good. He nudged a pawn forward, blocking Krestyanov's rook's path to his king.

Krestyanov slapped his thighs and crowed in triumph. "A foolish move, my friend, as you will soon see! Finally, finally I shall wrest victory from you."

"Big talk."

Once Crusader had emerged from the cabin, he and Krestyanov had engaged in a seemingly endless series of chess matches. They'd proved evenly matched for the most part. Krestyanov obviously had some formal training while Crusader relied on what he had picked up over the years. Yet Crusader's reckless style and risky moves were enough to counter Krestyanov's careful strategy. Their win/loss record was about even, with many of their matches ending in draws, something that seemed to horrify Krestyanov. He seemed determined to decisively defeat Crusader at least once.

Now it appeared as if he were about to achieve his goal. Crusader flinched inwardly as Krestyanov captured a bishop, tightening the noose around Crusader's king. He didn't see any way to avoid the checkmate. It'd be over in a move, two at the most.

Then the *Purim* lurched beneath them, the pieces spilling across the board.

Krestyanov shrieked in protest. "You did that on purpose!"

Crusader shook his head. "Wasn't me. Might've been the inertial sink."

Krestyanov's overacting died immediately. "Can we be sure?"

"You head for the cockpit. I'll check engineering."

They left the pieces spilled through the galley. Krestyanov headed for the cockpit while Crusader slid down the ladder into engineering. A quick check revealed the worst: The inertial sink had blown out completely. Crusader went to the cockpit, where Krestyanov tapped at the dead controls.

"Inertial sink is gone." Crusader slid into the chair. Hopefully their remote pilot was listening. "Hello? We've got a situation here."

"We are aware." It was the same voice from the relay. "Don't worry."

"Easy for you to say, my friend," Krestyanov said from where he stood. "You're not on board this vessel."

"Easy for me to say because you've arrived. Reverting to real space in three, two, one."

The ship lurched again.

Crusader looked over the controls. Still dead, but the warning light had gone out. "Don't suppose you'd let us see where we are?" he asked.

The voice chuckled. "No harm in that now."

A rumble rose from the viewport and the metal blastshield hissed open, pulling back from the middle into the edges of the window. At first, all Crusader could see was a blanket of stars stretched out before him. Then he spotted it: a dark speck that blotted out the stars behind it. He frowned. Couldn't be a planet. Too dark, so they weren't in a stellar system. A ship? Unlikely. The bulbous form was too ungainly.

Krestyanov gasped. "Do you realize what that is?"

Crusader didn't want to admit to his ignorance, so he kept quiet.

"It's a *Ceres*-class colonizer."

As Crusader studied the object, he realized that the Praesidium agent was right. "I thought they were all scrapped two centuries ago."

Krestyanov waved a hand toward the viewport. "Well, our friends out there found one."

The *Purim* dipped closer, revealing more of the ship's rocky exterior. The *Ceres* colonizers were hollowed out asteroids, fitted with rocket engines for interstellar voyages. They proved excellent sanctuaries for the first colonists to depart Earth to other stars, each capable of carrying close to fifty thousand colonists along with animals, building materials, whatever the passengers might need to start a new colony.

Yet as they approached the ship, he could see numerous modifications. Communications arrays bristled from small craters. Two sets of landing bays had been grafted to the ship's sides. Instead of the original massive engine bells, smaller fusion pulse drivers glowed at the stern. But what caught Crusader's attention most was what appeared to be a large portion where the rocky shell was missing. Metal closed up the gap.

The *Purim* spun, the colonizer disappearing from the viewport and replaced by stars. They must be coming in for a landing. Sure enough, the *Purim* reoriented itself on the nearest docking bay and within a few moments, slid through the immense doors. A thud sounded deep within the ship as it came to rest.

Crusader turned to Krestyanov. "Shall we go?"

Krestyanov bowed, sweeping his arms toward the door. "After you, my friend."

When they arrived at the docking hatch, the inner doors hissed open and the ramp extended, revealing the colonizer's docking bay.

And the two rows of men armed with rifles trained on the entrance.

Crusader stood there, dumbfounded. What kind of welcome was this? Did they treat all incoming ships this way? Or was it because Isolda wasn't with him? Out of the corner of his eye, he saw Krestyanov raise his hands in surrender.

Crusader hesitated. The security team wasn't that much of a threat. He could read the indecision and uncertainty in their eyes. Most had probably never handled a weapon before. One young man, furthest on the right, practically vibrated. Crusader calculated the distance, how fast the boy and the other guards might react. He could cross the distance easily, tear the gun out of the boy's hands.

He stopped himself. He wasn't raiding the ship. He stretched his arms out, palms forward.

"Slowly now," the most confident looking man said. "Come down the ramp."

Crusader and Krestyanov did as they were told. Two of the men darted forward, hastily running their hands across arms, legs, backs. Crusader kept his expression stoic at the clumsy frisking. If he had been armed, these amateurs would never have found his weapons. They did manage to find one pistol on Krestyanov, which they confiscated.

Once the men were safely back with their comrades, the guards' leader spoke again. "Which one of you is Crusader?"

He blinked. How did they know who he was? He hadn't identified himself to the pilot controlling their ship. But lying didn't seem wise. He raised his hand.

The leader stepped forward, producing a pair of handcuffs. "I'm sorry, but you're to remain bound until we figure out what to do with you."

Crusader didn't like it, but what could he do? He stretched out his hands, but before the man could slap the cuffs on, Krestyanov stepped between them.

"I'm sorry, I cannot allow this. This man was severely injured less than a week ago and, while I have tried to minister to him as best as I could, he should be checked for further injuries. Please, before you subject him to anything else, could we at least visit your medical facilities to make sure he is all right?"

"I don't really care," the leader said. "He gets cuffed. I'll do the same to you if you don't shut up right now."

"Jack! What are you doing?"

The piercing voice belonged to a woman dressed in a tan jumpsuit. Although her hair was solid black and her skin unlined, she radiated age. He would have expected to see her likeness carved in stone in a museum, a severe pagan goddess, especially given the withering stare she had fixed on the guards' leader. The guard straightened, his face flushing.

"What are you doing with those weapons?" Her words, though softspoken, thundered through the landing bay.

"We talked about this, Elata."

"Yes, and if I recall correctly, and I am sure that I do, I forbade this, did I not?"

The leader spun to face her, yet he didn't seem able to look up at her. "Yes, you did, but I felt that, given the obvious danger the Catacombs was in—"

"You would countermand my orders and our long-standing tradition regarding newcomers?" By her tone, she made it clear such a sin was near unforgivable.

The guard deflated further, his shoulders slumping and the rifle drooping in his grip. "Well, no, Elata, not exactly. But I thought, given what we've learned about him—" he jerked a thumb toward Crusader—"it would be prudent to change our policy just this once. You know, in case this turned out to be a Ministrix trick."

"Ah, I see." Elata took several steps toward the leader and the guards shied away from him. "Tell me, did the earliest Christians arm themselves when the Emperor Nero trundled them off to the Vatican hippodrome as arsonists? Did the martyrs fight back when taken to their executions? And did our Lord commend St. Peter for striking Malchus?"

He started to answer but she cut him off with an upraised palm.

"No," she said. "'Those who take the sword die by it,' yes? Do you wish what you hold in your hands to be your ultimate fate?" She stood toe to toe with Jack. Even though she was half a head shorter than him, Crusader felt as if she were looking down at him. But then her face softened. She placed her hands on his shoulders. "I am sorry, Jack, to chastise you so severely. But I do because I love you so. Now, might I suggest instead of threatening Crusader, you welcome him? And then tonight, be sure to pray for him and the people he represents. We pray for those who hate us, bless those who persecute."

Jack nodded and handed off his weapon to one of his companions. He then took a few steps toward Crusader and Krestyanov. Crusader could still read the uncertainty, the fear in his eyes. Yet he managed a stiff bow. "Welcome to *The Catacombs*. Please forgive my rudeness. We'll make sure that you get medical attention immediately."

The guards who had barred their way formed an honor guard of sorts and escorted Krestyanov and Crusader out of the landing bay. Before they could cross through the doors, Crusader paused to look over his shoulder at the woman who had scolded Jack. She stared back at him with hard eyes that betrayed only the tiniest flicker of warmth.

36

Crusader would have never guessed he was walking through an asteroid. A dilapidated Waystation maybe. The corridors were run down, open panels exposing wiring and circuitry. He could spot dozens of areas where salvaged metal replaced original paneling, creating a patchwork of dingy tiles. The lights that should have illuminated the hallway didn't work. Small lamps strung along a top corner barely lit their way. And the smell of smoke dogged him every step.

"How long has this ship been in service?" Krestyanov ducked to avoid a metal beam.

"Close to four hundred years. It was originally used to transport colonists to the Beta Hydrii system. We're not entirely sure what happened after that, but somewhere along the way, the Red Nebula pirates used it as a mobile base."

"Kind of like what you're doing now," Crusader observed.

Jack fixed him with a sour look. "I suppose."

"So how did you come into possession of this antique?" Krestyanov asked.

"Elata." Jack chuckled. "From what I understand, she was a freighter captain the Red Nebs took hostage twenty-five years ago. They got more than they bargained for, that's for sure."

"I thought she does not approve of violence," Krestyanov said.

"She doesn't. After spending two weeks with her, half the crew repented and the pirate chief turned the ship over to her direct command. A couple of them are still working as part of the support crew. She was the one who rechristened her *The Catacombs.*"

They rounded a corner into a scene of barely restrained chaos. Half a dozen crewers hunched at various points down the hall, some of them grumbling, but all working on exposed wiring. Jack sighed and led them on a winding path through the crew.

"Why do you not find a new ship? I would think that there would be many suitable candidates to replace this . . ." Krestyanov's voice drifted off when a crew member glared at him.

"That's not exactly an option for us," Jack said once they were free of the hall. "We'd love to, but we can't exactly go visit either the Ministrix or the Praesidium to go shopping. On the one hand, we have the Praesidium with its Toleration Act, which we apparently flagrantly violate just by holding any faith. And then on the other hand . . ." He waved in Crusader's direction.

Krestyanov reddened.

Jack's eyes narrowed and he leaned in closer to him. "You never did say who you were. And Naaman didn't say anything about Crusader having a partner."

"I . . . I am Kolya Krestyanov. I work . . . well, that is to say, I—"

"He's my friend."

Krestyanov and Jack both turned to Crusader with surprised looks on their faces. Krestyanov's expression quickly melted into one of relief. Jack still didn't look happy, but he shrugged and motioned for them to keep following.

They soon entered a medical bay. A woman looked up and smiled. "Hi there, Jack. Who do we have here?"

Jack smiled, his lips tense. "This is Kolya and Crusader."

The woman's eyes widened. "Is this . . . Is he . . ."

"Elata." Jack grimaced.

The woman's eyes widened but she nodded. "I should have known. What can we do for you today?"

"Crusader, he suffered severe injuries a week ago," Krestyanov said. "I have patched him up to the best of my ability but I fear he may require more attention. You are a doctor?"

The woman rose from her desk. "I am. Dr. Grace Smithson, at your service." She motioned to a nearby diagnostic table. "If you would, please?"

Crusader hopped onto the table.

Dr. Smithson produced a sensor packet and ran it over his body. Her eyes widened. "So what exactly are you worried about here?"

Krestyanov frowned. "I do not understand."

"According to my readings, he's got dozens of minor injuries, most of which haven't healed properly. Scar tissue everywhere. Which is the injury you're concerned about today?"

Krestyanov came around Dr. Smithson and looked over her shoulder. His eyes widened. "How is it possible that you can even breathe?" Krestyanov asked.

Crusader shrugged. "Hard to kill. You should know that."

Krestyanov stared at him and then burst out laughing. "True." He frowned and poked at something displayed on the scanner. "What is that?"

A look of annoyance flitted across Dr. Smithson's features, only to be chased away by one of confusion. "I'm not sure. I've never seen anything like that before." She fiddled with the scanner's controls for a few moments. "It's broadcasting a radio signal. Low power."

"What's the message?"

Dr. Smithson squinted at the readout, her frown deepening. "Doesn't make any sense to me. 'Code 34-Omega.'"

Crusader's head snapped up.

Krestyanov glanced at him. "You know what this means?"

"It's a Ministrix code, used in Intelligence. It's the 'eyes off' code. You see that code, you ignore whatever it is. Doesn't exist." He took the scanner from Dr. Smithson's hands. "What's it on?"

Crusader studied the data while Dr. Smithson sputtered. Some sort of implant where his appendix should be. He touched his side, trying to see if he could feel it. Nothing. What did it do? Didn't look like anything he'd ever seen. Explosives? Not likely. If it was, Siseal would have tripped it to eliminate him. What then? It looked like the device was tied into his bloodstream through the abdominal aorta. Fine tendrils snaked out from the small object, winding through his circulatory system. A filter?

The doctor pulled the scanner from his hands. "Let me get some more readings and maybe we'll be able to figure this out."

"There will be no need for that, Dr. Smithson."

Crusader turned. Elata had stepped into the medical bay, still as imperious as before. She met Crusader's gaze and he flinched, looking down at his feet. Even though he was bigger and stronger than her, she radiated strength and authority. This must have been what standing in the Revered Hand's presence was like, only more intimidating.

"Do you know what this is?" Dr. Smithson asked.

Elata nodded, stepping around the table, still staring at Crusader. "I do, thanks to Naaman. The large data file on this gentleman we received was most enlightening. Tell me, sir, are you aware of what the 'Crusader Project' is?"

A whole project named after him? He shook his head.

"I thought not. If this is what I suspect it is, then it explains much."

"What is it?" Krestyanov asked.

Elata hesitated. "I will answer in due time. But first. Do you know who Aaron Sloan is?"

Crusader frowned. "Never heard of him."

"Interesting." Elata paused again, her lips pulling into a tight line. "Then I wonder, have you ever heard of his wife, Victoria Sloan?"

The void shattered. A tight band wound around his chest and he choked. Images of fire flashed before his eyes and he smelled smoke. A woman's voice, husky, echoed in his ears.

"Stay asleep, baby." He fell back, catching himself with his hands. Dr. Smithson leapt forward to steady him.

Elata nodded. "Even more interesting." She released a long breath through her nose. "Perhaps you should join me on the command deck, sir. We can go over Naaman's data there."

"Not quite yet," Dr. Smithson said. "I need to finish his exam first, make sure he's okay."

Elata nodded. "Very well. When you are ready to discuss it, you know where to find me." She turned and stalked out of the medical bay.

Krestyanov shuddered. "Carved from cometary ice, isn't she?"

Crusader smiled. "I don't know. Kind of like her."

Within the hour, Dr. Smithson had finished her examination and pronounced Crusader fit to leave. She seemed concerned about the extent of his injuries and urged him to stay in the medical bay for observation. Crusader declined. He had to find out what Elata knew.

Jack was waiting for him outside the medical bay, speaking to Krestyanov in low tones. They glanced at him when he emerged.

"Jack here has graciously offered to escort us to the command deck," Krestyanov explained.

And keep them from sneaking off into sensitive areas, no doubt. Crusader motioned for him to lead the way.

They again wound their way through the corridors of *The Catacombs*. At one point, the hall gave way to a large bank of windows overlooking a darkened interior. Crusader paused and looked out at the shadowy interior.

Carved into the center of the asteroid was a large chamber, honeycombed with rows of doors. If Crusader remembered correctly, they led to living quarters for the colonists. Why were they all so dark?

Come to think of it, he hadn't seen that many people as they'd walked through *The Catacombs*. Maybe two or three dozen at the most. The rumors that he and his colleagues at Ministrix Intelligence had heard suggested that there were thousands, even tens of thousands, of people hiding in here, more than enough to repel anything but the staunchest attack. Where were the people? Where were all the heretics?

"Something wrong?" Jack asked.

"Just wondering why that part of the ship is unused."

Jack looked through the windows. "Mostly because we don't have the power to maintain life support. Fuel for this ship is hard to come by, especially in quantities large enough to maintain all of our systems. Besides, we don't really need all that space. All told, we only ever have about six hundred people here at a time. The support crew quarters can house that many while we leave the main bay powered down."

"Six hundred?" Krestyanov asked as they started walking again. "I thought this was the great refuge of the faithful, the one place guaranteed to harbor those oppressed by both Ministrix and Praesidium."

Jack smiled. "Not exactly. We're more a port in the storm, not a final destination."

Krestyanov frowned. "I do not understand."

"Well, it's really not my place to explain it."

"But I did ask you," Krestyanov said with a smile.

Jack sighed and ran a hand through his hair. "When someone converts, we try to have them sent here. That's not always possible, you know. But when it is, they come for intensive training and teaching. Then, after about two or three years, we send them out again."

They started walking again. "Why not have them stay here?" Crusader asked.

"You know part of the reason why," Jack said. "We just don't have enough resources. And even if we did, it wouldn't be right."

"I do not understand," Krestyanov said.

"Things are bad for us right now, no doubt, but that doesn't give us an excuse to hide. We're to be a city on a hill, a light in a dark room. That's hard to do if all of us are here."

"That makes no sense!" Krestyanov insisted. "You seek death?"

"No, of course not," Jack replied. "But if that's what comes, that's what comes. We don't seek trouble, but if it should find us, we accept it. Jesus did say, 'If they persecuted me, they will also persecute you.' This is just a fulfillment of that promise, that's all."

"So why let anyone come here then?" Crusader asked.

"Training," Jack said. "How many people do you think understand what it means to be a Christ-imitator right away? Not that many. Here they receive intensive catechesis . . . er, training. We try to explain what it means to be a Christ-imitator and then send them back, some to their old life, some not. It depends on who they were."

They entered an elevator.

"I still do not understand," Krestyanov murmured.

"Think I do," Crusader said, meeting Jack's gaze. "That why you sent Isolda Westin out?"

Jack hesitated. "No, but that really isn't my place to explain. You'd better ask Elata."

They continued their ride in silence. Then the doors to the elevator opened, depositing them onto the command deck. Crusader looked around. Much to his surprise, he found the spacious room filled with more modern controls. He had expected to see the original panels and screens.

Elata stood in the middle of the room, watching the half dozen crewers go about their work. She turned. "Welcome to the command deck," she said. "Are you ready to hear what we know?"

Crusader nodded.

She motioned toward a door on the opposite end of the room. "Then let's go into the conference room. I suspect this will require some privacy."

The new room was dimly lit, hewn out of the asteroid's rock. The walls were mottled browns and greys, rough and seemingly damp. A large painting of Earth filled one wall, looming over an oblong steel table surrounded by high-backed chairs. Elata sat at one and motioned for Crusader and Krestyanov to take others. When they did, Elata pressed a button on a nearby control panel. A holo-emitter descended from the ceiling. The lights further dimmed and an image sprang to life over the table. Much to Crusader's surprise, it was of him. Or rather, a much younger him. He looked to be no more than twenty.

"Tell me, Crusader, what is your earliest memory?" Elata asked.

He shrugged. "Can't say for sure, really."

"Try."

He frowned. He could remember his training, all of his instructors. Images of previous missions spilled through his mind. That was about it. He said as much.

Elata nodded. "That makes sense, given what Naaman has told us. Allow me to fill in some of the blanks." She nodded toward the image. "This is obviously you. It was taken when you were twenty-two years old, shortly before you became Crusader. Your name was—is—Aaron Sloan."

She fiddled with the controls again. The image dimmed and then flared to life, this time revealing a young woman.

Crusader gasped, the iron bands wrapping around his chest again. Isolda! No, wait. While this woman shared many of Isolda's features, they were softer. Her cheekbones were a bit higher, her curves more defined. Her eyes were darker green. This was definitely not Isolda, so who was it? With a trembling hand, he reached out and traced the surprisingly familiar features. He knew this woman. He had been trying to draw her for years.

"Who is she?" he whispered.

"Victoria Sloan," Elata answered. "Your wife."

37

Crusader snapped around as if punched, his mind reeling. "Wife? Don't have one."

Elata steepled her fingers and nodded. "That is true. But you did. According to Naaman, there is much you are not aware of concerning yourself and your past. Do you wish to know what that is?"

Crusader stared at the hologram of the woman. An odd paradox rippled through him. On the one hand, he didn't know this "Victoria." Not really. And yet, she felt as familiar to him as breathing. He both wanted and loathed whatever he could learn. He needed to know whatever Elata had. He wanted to rip the holo-emitter from the ceiling and throw it out into the vacuum of space. He looked to Krestyanov, but his Praesidium opposite had nothing for him but wide eyes.

He turned back to the image of Victoria. Even though he knew she was only a facsimile, it seemed as if her eyes bored into him. Heat flushed through him, only to descend into the numb. He owed it to her somehow. No matter how unpleasant, he had to learn the truth. He met Elata's gaze and nodded.

"Start with her." Crusader jabbed a finger at Victoria's image. "With my . . ." He couldn't bring himself to say the word.

"Please do." Krestyanov leaned over the table to get a better look at the hologram. "She bears a remarkable resemblance to Isolda, no?"

"We have noticed that as well," Elata said. "Truth be told, we're not entirely sure why that is. We've been sifting through her biographical data, but it's a bit sparse. Both her parents have died. She has an older sister and two younger brothers. She grew up on a planet called Mishael."

Crusader's head snapped back. "Mishael?"

"You've heard of it?" Elata said. "From what I understand, it's not a well known system."

"Isolda said she had relatives from Mishael. A . . . cousin, about her age," Crusader whispered. His words came out as a question, even though he wasn't really asking one.

Elata hunched over the table and adjusted the controls. Victoria's image shrunk and shifted to one side. A similar-sized picture of Isolda appeared next to her. Side-by-side, the resemblance was extraordinary. Beneath their images, their individual biographical data fled by until both information streams came to a halt. Sections of each flashed red.

Elata looked up. "You are correct. Isolda and Victoria's mothers were sisters."

"That would certainly explain the similarities," Krestyanov said.

Crusader leaned back in his chair. He didn't know what to say, couldn't even begin to form the words.

Elata touched a control on the table. The images disappeared. "Now that we've answered that, let's move on. Have either of you heard of the Crusader Project?"

Crusader shook his head. Much to his surprise, Krestyanov raised his hand a bit, just above the level of the table. "My colleagues and I, we have heard some rumblings about this. We could not decipher its meaning and finally decided it must be some sort of organizational subheading to refer to all of Crusader's . . ."

His voice trailed off as Elata's gaze zeroed in on Krestyanov.

"You are not another Ministrix officer?" Elata asked. "Who, then, are you?"

Krestyanov reddened, then straightened up in his chair. "My name is Kolya Krestyanov. Praesidium Intelligence."

Elata's face betrayed nothing. Her lip twitched, that was all. She nodded. "This complicates things. No matter." She turned back to Crusader. "As it turns out, sir, you are not the first 'Crusader' to work for the Ministrix. You are the sixth."

Crusader frowned. "I don't understand."

Elata manipulated the controls and a new hologram appeared over the table, this time a series of figures and images that Crusader didn't understand. He thought he saw a technical schematic of what looked like the device implanted inside him, but he couldn't be sure.

Elata nodded to the swirling information. "According to Naaman, the Ministrix began the Crusader Program twenty years ago. They wanted to create a superior agent, a living sword who could destroy any opposition. It was their belief that the best way to accomplish this was to deaden the subject's emotions and pain receptors. That is what the device in your abdomen does. It floods your bloodstream with chemicals to make you numb."

Crusader's shoulders sagged. All this time, he had believed his numbness to be a divine gift. But it was just a trick of science.

"Why?" Krestyanov asked.

"They believed that, in a combat situation, pain and emotions were a distraction," Elata said. "Too much fear or a bad injury, and the agent stops what he or she is doing. Deaden the emotions, stop the pain, and they keep going no matter what."

Krestyanov glanced in Crusader's direction. "No argument that it can work. It just seems a bit . . . inhumane."

"Any more so than what happens in Praesidium research labs?" Elata asked. "We have heard the rumors even here about what your scientists do in the name of 'progress.'"

Krestyanov reddened.

"Please, keep going," Crusader said.

Elata nodded. "As you wish. The first two iterations were successful, by and large. The implant succeeded in doing what it was designed to. The agents, however, developed severe psychological problems. They showed a complete disregard for human life, not only on their assignments but also outside of their missions. One even went so far as to murder his liaison officer in cold blood.

"The Ministrix scientists decided the best way to deal with these problems was with a bit of creative brainwashing. They engineered mental blocks in the subjects' minds, giving them a form of amnesia. They wouldn't remember their lives before the procedure. Instead, they would believe that their numbness was a divine gift."

It felt as though the room spun around Crusader as Elata kept talking, discussing the technical details of the implant and the psychological manipulation. Only one thing she said registered: The implant couldn't be removed or it would kill him. He finally came back to himself when Elata shifted subjects.

"According to the files, you were by far the most successful of the Crusaders," she said. "Whereas most of them only lasted a year or two, you have managed a ten year career."

"Then why did Deacon Siseal order Balaam to kill me?" Crusader asked.

"Naaman believes it has something to do with the circumstances under which you volunteered."

Krestyanov laughed, a sharp bark punctuated by him slapping the table. "Volunteered? Why would anyone wish to undergo this procedure?"

"To escape." Crusader surprised himself when he spoke. The void pressed against his mind, shadowy images, muted sirens, smoke and blood. He frowned and closed his eyes. Victoria Sloan appeared before him again, laughing and leaping away from his groping hands. She blew a kiss to him as she skipped away, turning to give him a coy look over her shoulder.

He jolted, looking up at Elata. She locked her gaze with his. Silence hung between them before she nodded slowly.

Elata pressed a few more buttons and a new image appeared over the table. An official report from the Ministrix, detailing an accident aboard an asteroid penal colony. Crusader skimmed it. A small group of prisoners, some of them Praesidium, some "heretics," had tried to break out by cutting the power conduit to their cell. The attempt had resulted in a freak plasma fire that had sparked a riot. Thirty hours of chaos later, the crew brought the blaze under control. Two dozen injured. Three dead, one a security guard: Victoria Sloan.

"Aaron Sloan approached the Ministrix military after the accident, wishing to enlist," Elata said. "His psychological evaluation caught the eye of Intelligence, who recommended him for the Crusader Program. And so you signed up for ten years."

Crusader closed his eyes. Of course. Both Palti and Siseal had promised to help him ease the guilt, that doing so would be easy. How much easier than by killing him? No guilt when a person is dead. Intelligence had probably expected him to die on a mission. When that didn't happen, Siseal had to finish the job himself. Or assign it to a subordinate.

"Do the files explain why Siseal wants Isolda?" Crusader asked.

Elata shook her head. "No. Naaman has no idea why your deacon wants her so badly."

"The Catacombs?" Crusader suggested.

"Unlikely. While it is true that Isolda spent many years here, she never knew our location. We use the same remote piloting procedure that brought you here when people come or go. Only a handful of individuals know where *The Catacombs* is at any given time."

"Then it must be Dr. Keleman's research," Krestyanov said. "We in the Praesidium have wished to gain access to that as well. He was showing quite impressive results before he went into hiding, results that our own scientists have been unable to reproduce."

Elata laughed. "I doubt very highly that Deacon Siseal wishes to acquire Dr. Keleman's research." She pressed another few buttons and the accident report was replaced with a new set of data.

Crusader looked it over. Nothing but equations and charts, none of which he could decipher. A logo toward the bottom of the hologram denoted it as coming from Ministrix Intelligence, specifically the Research and Development branch.

"The Ministrix recently proved that Dr. Keleman's theories are in error," Elata explained.

Krestyanov frowned at the data. "When did they determine this?"

Elata glanced at the image as well. "Two and a half years ago."

Krestyanov shook his head. "There will be many in the Praesidium who are disappointed. Our researchers believed that Keleman's theories would lead to a revolution in space travel."

"None more so than Fredek himself—until he learned of this," Elata murmured. "Now all he does is mope in his lab."

Krestyanov froze. "You mean . . . you mean that Dr. Fredek Keleman is here? On this very ship?"

Elata's face soured.

Krestyanov's expression lit up. He leaned forward. "Please, may I meet him?"

Elata sighed. "I suppose that would be permissible." She rose from her chair. "Follow me, gentlemen."

Crusader and Krestyanov fell into step behind her. As they walked, Crusader mulled over what Isolda had told him about the reclusive scientist.

"There is something you wish to ask me, yes?" Elata asked.

Her question snapped him out of his reverie. "Yes, there is."

"Why Isolda left *The Catacombs*?"

Crusader nodded.

"You will understand when we reach Fredek's lab."

38

Crusader slouched in a corner of the elevator. Krestyanov and Elata exchanged small talk. He tuned them out. His mind drifted back to the conference room, back to the hologram of . . . what should he call her? Victoria? His wife? His mind couldn't classify what he'd learned. He couldn't remember her. Not really. Maybe snatches. The smell of burnt flesh. The crackle of the emergency sirens. The feel of her weight in his arms, pulling him down toward the grimy deck.

Heat stabbed through his chest and he crumpled, hugging himself. The conversation died.

"Aaron?" Elata touched his shoulder. "Aaron, are you okay?"

He almost didn't realize she was speaking to him. Crusader took a deep breath, ignoring the needles that radiated through him. "Not my name. Call me Crusader."

"What can we do?"

He shrugged. "Couldn't tell you. Having problems with . . . with . . . memories."

Elata frowned, not unkindly, and took a step closer. "I thought you said you did not remember Victoria."

"Don't. Not really. Lately, been having dreams. About her."

Elata blew out a breath through her nose. "Then their concerns were true."

Crusader frowned at her. Now what?

"They could not be sure how permanent their mind wiping technique truly was. None of the previous Crusaders survived long enough to find out, but based on preliminary data, they suspected it would not last forever. It is entirely possible the amnesia is beginning to fade. Your true identity could reassert itself."

"How is that possible?" Krestyanov asked.

"The human mind is very versatile. The Ministrix researchers warned their superiors this could happen. It might help further explain why Siseal wants to eliminate you. You have outlived your usefulness." She hesitated. "Tell me . . . is the numbness fading as well?"

Crusader's head snapped up. "Not fading. Cutting in and out."

She nodded. "They posited that might happen as well. The implant can't last for the rest of your life either."

Crusader frowned, hugging himself tighter. He wasn't sure he wanted his memories back. He wasn't this Aaron Sloan anymore. He was Crusader. Without the blocks, without the numb, who would he be? Who could he be without either Victoria or Isolda? He didn't want to know.

"So what do we do now?" he asked.

"We trust in God, son," Elata said gently, placing a hand on his shoulder. "We may not understand what's happening, but He does and He has it all under control."

Warmth coursed through Crusader's chest, soothing the aches and bringing his frayed mind under control. He had heard his superiors spout such platitudes before, but coming from Elata, the words sounded sincere. Real. He relaxed, straightening up.

The elevator thudded to a halt and opened, depositing them in another dingy hallway. This one was largely deserted and darkened.

Krestyanov looked around, a frown pinching his face. "What happened down here?" he asked, nodding toward a wall panel.

Crusader looked as well, noticing the scorch marks that lined several panels, some of which had cracked. Circuitry hummed behind them. The lights flickered unevenly along the corridor.

Elata led them out. "Fredek 'happened,' with Isolda's help. Watch your step, gentlemen. The grav plating has been uneven since the accident."

Crusader inched forward, probing with his feet to check for irregularities. Even though he did that, he was still surprised when he stumbled into a section of hallway with only a quarter of the gravity. His stomach lurched as one of his steps nearly sent him into the ceiling. Then they were through the corridor and gravity returned to normal. They stood before large doors, bordered with yellow and black striping and splashed with an X of red paint down the middle.

"Friendly, no?" Krestyanov asked.

Elata tapped at the keypad next to the doors and they ground open, slowly retracting into the walls along a geared track. They parted, revealing a large laboratory, filled with rows of equipment Crusader couldn't identify. Unlike the corridor, this room was pristine and well-lit. The sharp tang of disinfectants assaulted him.

Elata held up a hand to keep them from entering. She leaned forward, ducking her head into the room. "Fredek? It's Elata. Are you down here?"

Something from within the lab crashed. "Of course, my dear, of course. Do come in, won't you?"

"Not until you power down whatever it is you're working on."

"I have told you, have I not, that my experiments are perfectly safe? How you go on!"

Elata sighed. "So you say, but I do not wish them to run while you are distracted. I have visitors for you to meet."

There was a long pause. "Oh, very well. Be with you in a moment."

A few moments later, a squat man waddled around one of the rows, wiping his hands on a towel tucked into his belt. He couldn't be more than five feet tall, a considerable gut bulging at the fabric of his white coveralls. His hair was mostly gone, a speckling of white and black across a blotchy scalp. Much to Crusader's surprise, the man wore glasses, an archaic fashion statement if he'd ever seen one. The thick lenses magnified the man's rheumy eyes as he squinted through them. "And who are these fine young men?"

Krestyanov moved first, extending his hand. "Kolya Krestyanov at your service, Dr. Keleman. This is my colleague, Crusader."

Crusader nodded at the scientist, who looked between him and Krestyanov. He then turned to Elata, his face lit up and eager. "Assistants? Finally?"

Elata shook her head. "No, I'm afraid not."

Keleman frowned. "I don't know how you expect me to make any progress on my work if you won't allow me a proper staff."

"That is the point," Elata said. "You know what happened the last time you had an assistant."

Keleman dismissed her words with a quick wave of his hand. "An accident, I tell you. A mere miscalculation that wasn't even her fault. I suspected the device wasn't ready yet but I proceeded anyway."

"Because she insisted! If you hadn't been so crushed when we told you what the Ministrix had discovered, she wouldn't have insisted you go ahead."

"Bah! You were too quick to judge her, and now look at what's happened. She left, and now she's out there, working as an engineer." He frowned. "Or was it a steward? I can never remember . . ."

"Isolda?" Crusader asked. "She was your assistant, right? What happened to her here?"

Keleman brightened. "You know her? How is she? Poor dear, she felt so guilty after what happened that she left me here, all by myself."

Elata sighed. "It was her idea, Fredek. She could have stayed. We are not going to have this discussion again."

Crusader held up his hands. "What happened?"

Keleman turned and headed around a bank of instruments. "Well, that could take some time to explain. How familiar are you with spatial displacement theory? Fifth dimensional folding?"

He may as well been making animal noises so far as Crusader could follow what he was asking.

Krestyanov nodded. "I've seen a bit of your work, Doctor. It is simply fascinating."

Keleman beamed at him but kept walking. "It all has to do with space travel, m'boy. Back in the late twenty-first century, our ancestors left Earth using fusion engines. Steady acceleration out of the solar system, using ships like these, gradually going faster and faster until they hit, oh, half light-speed or so. Tedious process, fuel intensive, took forever. And the problems! Time dilation, communications lag, the possibility of interstellar radiation. Each ship was an exercise in poorly placed hope.

"Then two hundred years ago, we had the tunneler revolution. Inertial sinks, grav plating, it all came from scientific discoveries that allowed us to tunnel under normal space. Gone were the pesky Einsteinian relativity problems. It used only a fraction of the fuel, no need for rocky radiation shielding. The Ministrix—" he paused to spit—"and the Praesidium—" another gob—"were built upon the foundation of that technological breakthrough." Keleman turned to Crusader, who could only stare at him. Keleman sighed. "You're not understanding any of this, are you?"

Crusader shook his head.

Keleman sighed again and looked around. He snatched up a piece of paper and crumpled it. He then spread it out again and held it out. "Let's pretend this is the fabric of space/time. I know, space/time is really four dimensions, not just this paper's two, but it's the best I can do." He produced a pen and placed two dots on either end of the paper. "Let's say that we want to get from point A to point B. A traditional propulsion system, the kind that *The Catacombs* and its sisters originally used, push them over the paper's surface, up and down the wrinkles, which are gravitic irregularities, spatial displacement, that sort of thing. Modern tunneler systems allow the ship to bypass most of the wrinkles by 'tunneling' through them. It's a crude analogy, but it's the best I can do on short notice. With me so far?"

Crusader ignored the condescension in the doctor's voice and nodded.

"What I propose is a new revolution. Suppose, instead of going up and down the wrinkles, instead of tunneling through them, we were to bend space itself." He pushed the two dots together, the paper sagging in the middle. "Instantaneous travel. You're in one place. The next, you're at your destination."

Krestyanov gasped. "And you can do this?"

Keleman said, "Yes."

At the same time, Elata interjected, "No."

"So it is like traveling through a wormhole, yes?" Krestyanov asked.

Keleman shook his head. "Not exactly, no. The end result is the same. The process is entirely different. To open a wormhole, you'd need some sort of singularity to punch through time and space to your destination. Very problematic. With my method, you simply coax space and time into bending temporarily."

Elata snorted and rolled her eyes. "'Coax space and time to bend.' Can you understand why very few take his theories seriously?"

Keleman reddened. "They lack vision, Elata. As do you, I might add."

"It's not vision I lack, Fredek. I simply do not share your disregard for the crew's safety."

Keleman shook his head.

"I do not understand." Krestyanov said. "What happened?"

"Do you wish to tell them or shall I?" Elata asked. When Keleman didn't answer, she continued. "Two and a half years ago, we received word that Sub-Deacon Altair abd al Sami's research team had refuted Fredek's theories. Bending time and space the way he suggests is impossible—"

"Einstein believed breaching the speed of light to be impossible too, but tunneler drives proved him wrong!"

Elata tensed at Keleman's outburst. She unclenched her fists and went on. "As I was saying, the Ministrix proved Fredek's theories wouldn't work. Fredek took it badly, but it was his research assistant who was bound and determined to prove Fredek right. She set up an experiment—"

"And she was right to do so! Abd al Sami and his goons don't know the difference between a quark and a quasar! How can they possibly hope to grasp what I'm doing here?"

Elata waited to see if Keleman was done with his rant. When he fell silent, she continued. "The experiment was a failure. Worse, it caused a hull breach that injured four emergency crewmen." She looked at Keleman.

The scientist hung his head. "That was regrettable. I should have supervised her better."

"You should have dissuaded her, you mean."

Keleman shook his head. "No. Isolda had the right idea."

Crusader turned to Elata. "That's why the hull is patched? That's why you sent her from *The Catacombs?*"

"We did not send her from anywhere," Elata said. "Isolda felt guilty over what happened. The crew was very forgiving, if a bit wary. But Isolda chose to leave of her own accord. Perhaps I should have done more to persuade her to stay, but that would have been dangerous too. After all, she might have tried the experiment again."

"Yes, exactly. She would have. *We* would have. Oh, I know, she didn't get it exactly right. But she was so close. If we had been allowed to try again, we would have achieved so much. Let me show you."

Elata paled. "Show us what?"

Keleman smiled impishly. "What do you think I've been working on down here for so long, Elata? Do you really believe I'd give up that easily? I've done it, I tell you. I have succeeded."

He led them around a bank of instruments and through a rocky arch into a larger cavern. When Crusader stepped through, he stopped short so quickly that Krestyanov collided with him.

Hanging from the ceiling was a machine, an inverted cone crisscrossed with conduits, flashing lights, wires trailing down to various displays. Set beneath it was a large boulder half Crusader's height. Keleman scurried over to a control panel and started thumbing the switches. Lights came on across the device.

Elata stepped through the opening and gaped at the machine. "I thought we decommissioned this death trap. Didn't you take this apart after the accident?"

Keleman smirked over his shoulder at her. "Not exactly. I hid the cave's entrance from your engineers and gave them scrap parts. They never knew the difference."

Elata's eyes narrowed.

Keleman's smile disappeared. "I had to, Elata. I can't stop now, not when I'm so close!"

She crossed her arms and glared at him. He turned back to the controls.

"So this will work?" Krestyanov asked, stepping closer to the boulder.

"Yes," Keleman said, holding up a hand to signal Krestyanov to stop. "Watch the rock."

Keleman touched another button and a low whine filled the chamber, ramping up in volume and pitch. Soon it rattled the teeth in Crusader's skull. Sparks erupted from the device. He took a step back.

"That's normal!" Keleman called over the noise.

"Fredek," Elata shouted, "stop this right now, or I shall—"

Keleman ignored her. "Bending in three . . . two . . . one . . ."

Elata rushed at the machine, but Keleman intercepted her and pulled her back. Crusader braced himself. He didn't quite know why. He expected some sort of sensation, maybe a churning stomach, maybe the hairs standing up on the back of his neck. But aside from the growing storm of needles in his head from the annoying noise, nothing happened.

And then the rock was gone.

Crusader blinked. What had happened? One minute, it had sat before him. The next, it wasn't there anymore.

Keleman's face split in a wide smile as the squeal faded to silence. "Go through the door again," he said.

Crusader turned and stopped short. He could see the rock in the middle of Keleman's lab, sitting in the midst of swirling papers, some of which were scorched.

Keleman brushed past him into the lab, nodding. "Yes, you see, not everything is fine tuned yet. There are still some energy leakage issues that can result in unfortunate events. Last week, I accidentally started a fire in my kitchen—"

"You said that was from cooking!" Elata said. "And how did you know that rock wasn't going to materialize in the middle of our bodies or blow another hole through the hull?"

Keleman ignored her. "But as you can see, gentleman, the theory is solid. It's practical. Moving this stone took a fraction of the energy it would have to strap thrusters to it to overcome its inertia. Imagine what we could do if we could apply this principle to space travel."

Krestyanov stepped out of the cavern, his face pale. "Waystations would become obsolete overnight. You could move an entire fleet behind enemy lines with little or no notice. If either the Praesidium or the Ministrix acquired this technology . . ."

Crusader didn't need him to complete the thought. Whoever got this to work first would win the cold war between the two interstellar governments. Much to Crusader's surprise, he didn't really care who got it. But he knew how he wanted to use this technology now. "Have you tried to make this more practical? For a ship?"

Keleman's smile grew broader. "As a matter of fact, I have. Actually, Isolda did. Her basic design was good but needed some tweaking. I've gone back to it when I could to refine the design. In theory, I have it worked out." The scientist stepped to a panel and called up some schematics.

Crusader quickly crossed to the display and looked it over. "How long would it take to build a prototype?"

Keleman's smile vanished. "A prototype? Unwise, my friend, unwise. We need more small-scale testing, make sure the principle is sound. I suppose we could cobble this together in ten days, maybe fifteen. But to do so would be so risky . . ."

A hand dropped on Crusader's shoulder. He glanced over it at Elata.

"What are you thinking, my son?"

The *Bared Arm* might have arrived at Earth already, but there was no telling what Siseal would do with Isolda. If they started building the prototype now . . .

"I'm thinking of rescuing Isolda."

39

Isolda sat up in her bunk. The low thrumming in the deck-plates had faded just enough to catch her attention. Had they already arrived at Earth? It didn't seem likely.

She sighed and lay back, resuming her inspection of the ceiling. There was little else for her to do. Gavin hadn't visited since their argument. Her only human interaction had been with the guards. While she didn't know why the ship had stopped, at least the change had broken the monotony.

Within what she guessed was a half hour, the vibrations intensified, the sound building through the deck before breaking into the usual hum of a ship in tunnel space. Isolda rolled over and stared at the empty corridor. By her calculations, the next patrol should pass by the bars at any time. At least it would change the scenery.

The patrol never came. She frowned. The Ministrix guards were very precise in their timing. Something big must have happened for them to be this late. She sat up, leaning toward the entrance. What could it be?

Crusader! Her heart raced. Maybe. If anyone could force a ship out of tunnel space on his own, it'd be him. He could be storming through the ship even now, on his way to rescue her. She almost stood but caught herself. She laughed. Ridiculous thought. Crusader was most likely dead. And even if he wasn't, there was no way he'd be able to stop the *Bared Arm*. A silly dream, that's all that was.

And yet . . . She settled against the wall, closing her eyes. A pleasant fantasy, and she really didn't have anything better to do. Her mind drifted, envisioning Crusader, his shirt torn and his hair mussed, bursting through the doors to the ship's brig. He'd dispatch the guards quickly and efficiently, then run down the corridors shouting her name. She would rush to the bars, calling for him, then fall into his arms, and they would kiss . . .

Someone cleared his throat from outside the cell.

Isolda's eyes snapped open. A man in Ministrix robes gazed through the bars. He was tall, broad in the shoulders, his skin bronze and his hair black with a peppering of grey. Standing beside him was a shorter woman, her red hair pulled back into a severe bun. She wore a loose skirt that fell just below her knees as well as a loose top.

"I hope I'm not interrupting anything important," the man said.

"Who are you?" Isolda asked.

"My name is Sub-Deacon Altair abd al Sami."

Any irritation at the intrusion vanished. Isolda's eyes widened. Abd al Sami, here? This was perfect! She had been hoping she could meet him at some point but she had never dreamed he would actually come to the *Bared Arm* before they reached New Jerusalem Station. This explained the sudden stop. He and his assistant must have just boarded. Now she could find out why he wanted Balaam to bring her to Crasman's Rift. If he was really Naaman, the Christian mole in Ministrix Intelligence, he'd be able to help her!

She tamped down on her enthusiasm as another thought occurred to her: She had no way of knowing if he was really Naaman. She'd have to be sure before she asked him for help.

"I've heard quite a bit about you," Isolda said.

Altair's eyes widened. He turned to the woman. "Would you excuse us please?"

The woman favored him with a scowl that surprised Isolda. She wouldn't think an assistant would be so openly disrespectful to a superior. But the woman complied anyway, stalking down the hall.

Once she was gone, Altair pulled a small device from his robes and activated it. A series of green lights flashed around the box's perimeter. "This should block any monitoring equipment in the cell," he explained. "We can talk freely."

Isolda wanted to start right in, but still those doubts nagged at her. Could she trust Altair? There was only one way to find out, as risky as it was. "*Su ei ho erpxumenos ay allon prosdokomen?*"

Altair frowned.

Dread settled in Isolda's stomach. She shouldn't have done it. Risking a call sign in the presence of a Ministrix sub-deacon? What was she thinking?

"*Poiaysate oun karpon axion tays metanoias.*"

Relief surged through her. But she had to finish or he might panic. She could already read the worry on his face. "*Qol qoray bamdebar panu derek YHWH yashru ba'aravah m'sileh laylohaynu.*"

Altair smiled and sighed deeply. "Sorry it took me a while. I have only recently learned the triptychs."

Isolda leapt from her bunk and crossed to the bars. "Can you get me out of here?"

Altair shook his head. "Would that I could, but I can't. The captain has strict orders from Deacon Siseal himself to make the best possible time to New Jerusalem. The only reason I was able to board at all was because Siseal dispatched his assistant, Charis, to make sure you arrived unharmed."

"So what? Say you want to question me 'privately.' Add as much insinuation as you can and that'll at least get me out of the cell. Then maybe you can claim infatuation with me when we get to Earth and—"

Altair, who had reddened with each passing moment, held up a hand to cut her off. "Creative but futile. The Ministrix demands chastity of its leadership. No, we must be more careful than that."

Isolda groaned and pulled her legs up under her chin. "So can you at least tell me what Siseal wants me for? Is it *The Catacombs*? Dr. Keleman's research?"

"I don't know, unfortunately. Believe me, I've been sifting the data hoping to uncover his interest. I've found nothing." A grim smile tugged at his lips. "But I doubt it's for the Catacombs or Keleman's ideas. While Siseal would kill to learn about the former, he's got his own people working on tracking it down. As for the latter . . ."

She waved for him to continue.

He grimaced. "I'm sorry, but I can't explain. It'd take too long. If I don't deactivate this jammer soon, someone will come looking." He stepped closer to the bars. "Just stay calm for now. If I see a way to get you out of here, I will. But you might want to prepare yourself for whatever's coming. I'll see you again soon if I can." He turned off the device and tucked it back into his robe. Then, with one more curt nod, he left.

Isolda groaned and tipped her head back until it hit the wall. She tried to hang on to a small bit of hope: She at least had a friend on board now who would try to help her. And yet, as the minutes dragged into hours, she realized that even that small hope wasn't enough. Crushing depression hovered around her for the rest of the day and finally struck as she tried to sleep. She wound up crying and praying until exhaustion took her.

40

Crusader looked around the conference room. His jaw tensed. Not enough people had joined him. Krestyanov. Keleman. A few engineers. He had hoped for more. The news had spread through the ship fast enough: The Ministrix agent was going to invade New Jerusalem Station, the heart of the Ministrix itself. He needed help in planning. And yet only half a dozen people had volunteered. Elata's doing? She hadn't seemed too pleased with Crusader's declaration the day before.

Didn't matter. Had to be done.

He turned to Keleman. "So is this do-able? You can build the prototype?"

Keleman nodded. "I have consulted with these helpful young men and women—" He nodded at the engineers seated across the table— "and they are confident that they can have the engine ready in two weeks." His bushy eyebrows drooped behind his glasses. "More problematic is the astrogational software. The standard tunneler drive guidance systems simply will not be sufficient. We need to program it from the ground up, and that is beyond my capabilities. Or those of these helpful engineers."

Crusader leaned back in his chair. "Is there anyone on board who could do it?"

Keleman nodded. "There are. And I have approached them about this problem. But they are unwilling."

"Give me names later. I'll talk to them."

"You?" Krestyanov asked.

Crusader's lip twitched. "I can be persuasive."

Krestyanov held up his hands in surrender. "I do not doubt it, my friend, but perhaps a more delicate touch is needed. Allow me to speak with these reluctant programmers."

Crusader shook his head. "No. Need your help with the exit strategy. Need fake Ministrix identities. Three of them. Can you do it?"

Krestyanov stroked his chin then nodded. "I believe so. The fabrication facilities here are quite impressive."

That had been one of the biggest surprises. Jack had shown them a bank of computers he said were dedicated to producing false identities. "Sometimes people need a fresh start away from who they were," he had explained.

"Good," Crusader said. "We'll meet again in two days to report on our progress. Agreed?"

The doors behind him hissed open. "I am not intruding, am I?"

Crusader sat up straighter and swivelled in the chair to face Elata. "I thought you didn't approve of this."

"I do not. That is why I am here."

Elata sat at the end of the table. The participants shifted to face her. Crusader frowned. He felt as though he were seated at the foot now. He had lost control. Not good.

"I cannot allow you to proceed." She folded her hands on the table.

Crusader stared at her, unsure he heard her correctly. He glanced at Krestyanov, who rubbed at a spot on the gleaming table. Keleman gathered up his data cards and looked ready to bolt. Fire crept up Crusader's neck. He couldn't buckle.

He sat up straighter, stuck his chin out. "We can do this."

"It is not a question of 'can' but 'should.'"

"Fine. We should do this. You know what will happen to her on New Jerusalem?"

Elata's right eyebrow tugged upward. "Interrogation. Beatings. Torture. Perhaps more. I am aware of how the Ministrix treats its prisoners, especially we 'heretics.' While we do not seek such treatment, we accept it. We are called to carry our cross no matter where that path leads. We do not respond to violence with more violence."

Crusader's fingers dug into the palms of his hand. "'Those who live by the sword'?"

The corners of Elata's mouth turned up a fraction. "Yes, precisely that. Those who live by the sword die by it."

"You forget: I was the Ministrix's sword."

"True. And perhaps a select few would deserve whatever would happen if you were to come home to roost, so to speak.

Deacon Siseal. The Revered Hand. But is it your place to mete out God's justice instead of Him?" She leaned forward. "And what of the security guards who would be in your way?"

Crusader's mouth pressed shut. He couldn't call them collateral damage. Elata wouldn't accept that answer. Worse, he knew she was right. He closed his eyes, took a deep breath, then another. His eyes watered. He didn't want to let Isolda go. But without Keleman's drive, there was no way he could rescue her in time.

"However . . ."

Crusader opened his eyes.

Elata's gaze had dropped to her folded hands. She pursed her lips, then looked up. "There may be a compromise. Jack?"

The doors hissed open and Jack stepped inside. Crusader froze. He carried a massive rifle, snapped it up to his shoulder. A high-pitched whine sliced the air. Before Crusader could move, Jack fired three shots. Something hissed past Crusader's ear. Then the squeal dropped in pitch, Jack adjusted his aim and fired again. Crusader turned to his right. Three darts had sprouted from the chair next to him. He swivelled only to find three more projectiles embedded in the metal bulkhead behind him.

"Jack, would you care to explain?" Elata asked.

Jack set the rifle on the table. "We call it a zap-dropper."

"Zap-dropper?" Krestyanov asked, the barest hint of a giggle in his voice.

Jack fixed the Praesidium agent with a sour look. "We're working on a better name. The projectiles are a combination mini-tazer and syringe. When it impacts a target, the dart stuns the person and then injects a sedative."

"Hence the name?" Krestyanov asked.

"It's a work in progress," Jack said.

Crusader picked up the rifle and raised it to his shoulder, looked down the sights. Bigger than a standard laser rifle. Heavier too. Balance was a bit off. He ejected the magazine. The weapon's power source was grafted into the magazine. "How many rounds does each magazine hold?"

"Twenty-five," Jack answered.

Crusader grunted. A decent number, but might be too few in a true firefight. "How does it work?"

"It's a mini-rail gun. Magnetic coils accelerate the projectiles out the barrel." He took the rifle and pointed to a switch on the grip. "It has two settings: normal and armor piercing. The latter uses more coils for greater penetration. We haven't tested them against ballistic armor, but as you can see—" he pointed to the wall over Crusader's shoulder—"they should do the job. This light turns red when it's set for armor piercing, blue for normal. Make sure you have it in the right setting when you use it."

As if Crusader would. A laser rifle could get off more shots with a standard power pack. If the magnetic coils on this "zap-dropper" went out of alignment, the whole weapon could jam. Add in poor balance and the extra weight? He'd stick with lasers.

"If you want to go after Isolda, you will use the zap-droppers in your assault," Elata said.

Crusader's head snapped back as if punched. "Rather not."

"That is not open to negotiation." Ice crept into Elata's voice. "We have already removed all standard weapons from your ship and impounded them. If you wish to attempt this rescue, and unless you wish to leave here and undertake the journey back to Crasman's Rift before procuring new weapons and starting your voyage to New Jerusalem Station—all without Dr. Keleman's technology, of course—you will use Jack's zap-droppers. They will ensure no one needlessly dies. By their very nature, zap-droppers are non-lethal."

"Maybe. Have these been battle tested?"

Jack looked away and fiddled with a switch on the zap-dropper. All the answer Crusader needed.

"I'll be careful. Aim to injure, not kill. I promise."

Elata's lips twitched into a hard smile but her eyes remained cold. "I have no doubt that you would try. But that is not good enough."

Crusader ground his teeth together.

"You must understand," Elata said, "I do not believe any rescue attempt is wise. I fear for you and Isolda should you fail, and I fear the ramifications should you succeed. The way of Christ is never that of the sword. Yet many of *The Catacombs'* crew quietly support such a venture. So I find myself in a tenuous position. Either I forbid this entirely and risk fomenting bitterness, perhaps even mutiny, or I allow you to proceed, which might result in the death of dozens of people and set a precedent of violence incompatible with true faith. So I have sought a middle way. Now I invite you to walk it with me. If you wish to rescue Isolda, you will use the zap-droppers."

Crusader stared at the ungainly weapon in Jack's hands. He didn't like it. Not at all. But if it was the only way . . .

"Deal."

Elata sat back, her face blank. Was that disappointment in her eyes? Crusader couldn't tell for sure.

"We'll get started on making the projectiles," Jack said. "How many will you need?"

Crusader considered. "One hundred fifty magazines. Four zap-droppers total. Do-able?"

Jack's eyes widened and he choked. "You really think you'll need that many?"

Crusader shrugged. "Better safe than sorry."

Jack nodded, a bare twitch of his head. "We'll get things started immediately." He turned and stumbled out of the room.

Elata followed him without casting another glance in his direction.

Crusader looked at the others. "Let's go. We've got a lot of work to do."

The others sprang from their seats and headed for the exits. Crusader glanced over his shoulder at the darts. Maybe not the way he wanted to operate, but he'd adapt. He had to. Isolda's life depended on it.

He only hoped he'd make it in time.

41

Something slammed against the bars of her cell. Isolda jolted upright and whirled. A pair of guards sneered at her.

"Better get yourself ready, girl," the one on the right said. "We're almost there."

Isolda froze. Already? Had it been three weeks?

"Get up!" the other guard said.

She sprang to her feet without really wanting to.

The guard on the right trained his weapon on her through the bars while the other tapped in the lock code. The door popped open and the man stepped through. He grabbed her arm, squeezing too tight. She winced and tried to pull back.

"No trouble from you," he said, the threat rumbling in his voice.

They half led, half dragged her out of the brig and through the brightly lit corridors of the warship. No one met her gaze as they went, the crew diving out of the way and pressing up against the walls. They probably worried they'd somehow catch whatever it was that had made her a prisoner. She wanted to groan but knew the guards might react badly. These poor people, so lost and afraid. Their fear slipped into her pores, suffocated her from within.

She stumbled as they approached an elevator. Pain exploded across the back of her head. She clutched it and choked back a sob, glaring at the guard who had hit her.

"None of that. You can't buy any time, so don't even bother trying."

They tried to drag her forward but she shook off their hands. She marched under her own power into the waiting elevator. No more weakness.

They rode in silence but Isolda could feel their gaze burrowing into the back of her head, their leers like poison. She kept her face forward, her gaze locked on the line between the doors. She wouldn't buckle.

The doors whooshed open and she stepped through before the guards could tell her to. She smiled at her small victory as they rushed to keep up with her. She tried to keep leading the way, but when they came to a split and she tried to go left, one of the guards hip-checked her into going right. She stumbled but, much to her surprise, they didn't hit her again.

A massive set of doors slid open before them and she found herself walking into an observation deck. Large windows stretched across one wall, the swirling lights of tunnel space dancing on the other side. Small knots of people clustered in the room, talking quietly. A few glanced in her direction when she entered. She didn't recognize anyone, but the room was too dark to know for sure.

Then someone stepped away from one of the groups and strode over to her. She recognized Altair as he drew near. He fixed her with a withering look, then turned it to the guards. "Thank you, gentlemen. You are dismissed."

They exchanged uncertain glances. "Sir, our orders were to escort her to this observation deck—"

"Which you have done admirably."

"—and then guard her here."

Altair laughed. "Do you think her a threat? Look at her! She can harm no one. And if she were to run, where would she go? I relieve you of your duty and I take full responsibility for her. Dismissed."

The guards hesitated but complied, tromping out of the observation room. Isolda turned to watch them exit. She stared at the doors. Could she make it if she started running now? She could find a place to hide, hunker down. Support systems, find a crawlspace, maybe near the main reactor to confuse internal sensors.

"Don't even think it." Altair's murmured words startled her. "They haven't gone far. My guess is that they're stationed outside the doors, in case you try something stupid."

She glared at him. He turned and started walking toward the windows. Was she supposed to follow him? She doubted that any of the other groups would want to talk to her, so she fell into step with him.

"So have you figured out a way to free me yet?" she whispered.

Tightness tugged at his eyes. "No. I haven't. I'm not sure what we can do."

She closed her eyes and groaned.

"Don't give up hope yet. Deacon Siseal wants you alive and unharmed. If you can stall him, I might be able to work something out. I've got contacts in the New Jerusalem support staff, good men and women who would help."

"Are they . . ." She wasn't sure how to ask in case anyone was listening.

He must have understood, because he shook his head. "No. But we can trust them until we find a way out."

She forced herself to keep looking out the window although she wanted to snap her head around and stare at him. "'We'?"

He nodded. "I've been looking for a reason to leave ever since . . . Well, ever since."

She took a step closer to him, started to reach for his shoulder.

He jumped back and glared at her. "Do not."

Before she could respond, a small tremor ran through the deck. Isolda braced herself but there was no lurch. Instead, the swirling colors beyond the window vanished, replaced by a blue-green orb. She turned and gasped.

Earth. She had never been here. It was too dangerous to come, with the Ministrix in charge. But here was where humanity had started, where they'd taken their first steps into space and then beyond. She wished she could touch down, explore the planet of her ancestors. But that wasn't to be. The planet grew larger and larger and then disappeared beneath them as they passed it by.

Their destination appeared, a cube set on one corner, a space station slowly rotating in the night. It gleamed golden in the sun, casting beams of light that blinded her. She winced, throwing up a hand to block the reflection.

"It is glorious, is it not?" Altair's voice was breathy, barely more than a whisper. "I only wish such beauty could be held by better hands."

Isolda squinted, trying to make out the details of the station but couldn't. The glare was simply too bright to distinguish viewports, docking bays, anything. She closed her eyes, a glowing blob dancing in the darkness. Hopefully she wouldn't go blind from the approach.

When she opened them again, a massive wall of light filled her vision, but relief was coming. She spotted a small patch of darkness that grew ever larger. She realized it was a massive docking port, large enough to swallow the *Bared Arm* whole. She gasped. New Jerusalem Station had to be huge.

Soon the ship slipped into the seeming darkness of the bay. It took a moment for Isolda's eyes to adjust but when they did, she could see support gantries and docking stations scattered throughout the bay. She realized that the bay couldn't hold just the *Bared Arm*. It could also hold two more ships the same size.

The doors behind her opened and the guards tromped in again. They took up positions on either side of her.

"We're to escort the prisoner from here to Deacon Siseal's chambers," one explained.

Altair nodded. "As well you should." He turned to Isolda, tipping his nose upward slightly. "Let's go, Ms. Westin. The Deacon awaits."

Altair led the way and Isolda didn't even consider trying to show him up. She doubted the guards would be as forgiving

JOHN W. OTTE

as they were before. They paraded through the ship corridors until they came to the main airlock.

Standing near the thick doors was Gavin. He didn't meet her gaze. She glared at him, trying to set him on fire with just her eyes. No luck with that. He hadn't even had the courtesy to check on her for the rest of the trip. She could have died in her cell and he would have never known.

"Good to see you again, Mr. Liddel," Altair said coolly. "I trust your journey was pleasant?"

Gavin mumbled something under his breath that Isolda couldn't quite hear. He peeked at her and looked away immediately. She straightened, trying to intensify her gaze. Maybe she couldn't set him on fire, but she wouldn't be surprised if she could make him lose control of his bodily functions. That'd be just as good.

A guard shoved her from behind. "Get moving."

The airlock doors had opened and she hadn't even noticed. She was just as surprised to realize that Charis, the wraith-like assistant, had joined their group as well. Charis flicked a disapproving gaze between Isolda and Gavin. Isolda almost told her not to lump the two of them together but she figured that wouldn't help.

A quick prod to her back from one of the guards sent her lurching forward. She quickly regained her stride and walked into the New Jerusalem station. Cool prickles erupted across her skin as she crossed the threshold. Her mind ricocheted from thought to thought. How did they power such an immense structure? Why did Siseal want her? Was Crusader still alive and if not, what had happened to him?

She winced at the last one. She took a deep breath, trying to find a calm center for herself. Breathe. Calm. Be ready to give the answer for your hope. You will be dragged before kings and emperors and . . . how did the rest of that go? Did Deacons of Intelligence count?

A short walk through the airlock brought them to an elevator. Isolda and her escorts crowded into one elevator and within moments, her stomach dropped as it rocketed upward. She closed her eyes. Breathe. Be ready to answer. Be ready to be dragged. What would Siseal do to her? What would he ask? Could she stall like Altair wanted? What was he thinking? Were his contacts nearby? How long until he could plan something?

The doors in front of her opened and she was once again shoved forward. Did being shoved count the same as being dragged? She didn't have time to consider it as her eyes adjusted to the scene spread out before her.

She had emerged within a garden. Lush tropical plants bordered a stone walkway that wove through gently sloping hills. A waterfall rumbled in the distance. Birds called to each other. A sweet, almost honey-like scent hovered in the air. Isolda turned and looked around. Large windows showed the inky darkness of space around them.

Something rustled in a tree overhead. She glanced up in time to see something black and hairy dart up a branch. She tried to track the creature and finally spotted it peeking down at her. A lemur! A robot? No, it moved too smoothly to be artificial. She could hardly believe it. Someone had recreated a small section of tropical paradise on the station.

"I see you like our Eden Restored," Altair said.

She glanced at him. Was she the only one who heard a hint of sarcasm in his voice? No one else seemed to notice. Gavin gawked at everything. The guards too, although they did their best to hide it. The only one seemingly unaffected by the beauty around her was Charis. She stabbed a finger down the walkway and they kept going. Isolda drank in as much of it as she could.

The trail wound through the trees and shrubbery. They passed by several station workers, all so absorbed in their work that they barely noticed their passing. At least, that's what Isolda thought at first. But then she caught one of them peeking out of the corner of his eye at her and she understood: They were afraid. They didn't want to be noticed by Altair and Charis. She could hardly blame them, especially about the latter.

At one point, they passed a frail old man perched on a small boulder. His shoulders sagged beneath his heavy crimson robes, an iron staff resting in the crook of his arms. Isolda slowed to study his drooping face, his liver-stained hands.

The man must have noticed her attention. He looked up at her and their gazes locked. Isolda wanted nothing more than to offer him some comfort. There was no reason for him to be so sad, so lost. Was this what the Ministrix offered? Fear and sadness? Why would anyone stay?

But then steel appeared in the man's eyes. His features hardened. Using his iron staff as a lever, he hoisted himself to his feet and strode forward. Although he leaned heavily on his staff, his gait was powerful and strong and his eyes continued to flash with fire. "Sub-Deacon abd al Sami, greetings."

Altair turned at the man's approach. His eyes grew wide and he dropped to one knee. The guards, Charis, and Gavin all followed suit, bowing low. Isolda considered running, but she found herself transfixed under the older man's stern gaze.

"Your Eminence," Altair murmured. "You honor us with your attention."

The man waved away Altair's words. He strode up to Isolda and leaned in close enough that she could smell his breath, which was sour and almost overwhelming. "Who do we have here?"

"Her name is Isolda Westin, Your Eminence. I am bringing her to Deacon Siseal."

"Ah, so she has important secrets, does she?" The man sounded like a snake slithering around its prey. "A pity that one so young and lovely has been caught in Siseal's web. Carry on, Sub-Deacon."

"At once, Your Eminence."

The man strode away from them, his staff thumping against the deckplates. Isolda watched him go. Everyone who spotted him dropped to the floor, bowing their heads. One person even fell prostrate, pressing her body against the floor and quivering while he passed.

Altair rose and cast a cautious look behind them. "Let's go."

"Who was that?" Isolda asked.

"The Revered Hand."

Isolda's mouth dropped open. *That* was the Revered Hand, the most feared individual in the Ministrix? But she didn't have long to consider it. Her guards kept her moving.

Then they broke into a clearing where yet another elevator waited. Once again, they crowded into it. This time, though, Isolda noticed the faintest odor of sweat. She glanced around. From Gavin maybe? Or the guards? Was it from the heat of the garden? Or fear?

A short ride deposited them in a long hallway. The walls were made of mahogany paneling, and lush, deep carpet lined the floors. If Isolda hadn't known better, she would have thought she was at some high-scale planetary hotel. Someone had obviously splurged to develop this part of the station. Of course, after having walked through a miniature jungle, it shouldn't have surprised her.

They marched her down the hall and into an antechamber.

Charis kept going, passing through massive wooden doors. She returned only a moment later, wrenching them open. She turned to the group with a tiny smirk. "The Deacon will see you now," she said.

Isolda couldn't move. Her arms and legs locked. She stared at the doors, at the wicked gleam in Charis's eyes, and she knew she couldn't go through the door. The guards had to grab her by the arms and drag her.

That brought her back to herself. She was being dragged after all. At least that conundrum had resolved itself.

The office beyond was huge. Not as big as the jungle, but in Isolda's mind, it was pretty close. A large wooden desk sat near an immense viewport overlooking the Earth. Off in one corner was a stone fireplace, complete with a real fire burning in a stone hearth. She stared at it in surprise. What did they do with the smoke? Recycled it, probably. She wondered where the chimney led.

Then the high-back chair behind the desk turned and a man rose from it. He wore a wheat-colored robe with a royal blue stole over it. Charis moved to his side. He towered over her. Although the wrinkles around his eyes betrayed his age, he still had remarkably blond hair. Steely eyes perched over an aquiline nose. He smiled when he saw her, but it did little to calm her churning stomach.

"Ah, my dear Ms. Westin. I am Deacon Horatio Siseal. So glad you could finally join us here at New Jerusalem Station." He whirled toward Altair. "It certainly took longer than you promised, Altair."

The sub-deacon straightened. "Hardly my fault, sir. Crusader proved to be less than cooperative."

Siseal smiled. "Ah, yes. Poor boy."

Isolda's breath caught in her throat. Did that mean Crusader was dead? No, that couldn't be possible. He was coming for her. She knew he had to be.

Siseal strolled around the desk, his hands tucked behind his back. Isolda stiffened as he drew near, but at the last second, he veered off, heading toward a large wooden cabinet along one wall. "May I offer you some refreshment? The journey was long and I suspect you have gone without basic human comforts for the past three weeks." He opened the cabinet, revealing a row of pale green glasses. "I can offer you no alcohol—the divine rules of the Ministrix, you understand—but I do keep a variety of juices, waters, and teas on hand."

Isolda didn't answer. She stared ahead. Would that count as stalling? When would Altair get out of here and start working on her escape?

"No?" He clucked his tongue as he poured himself a glass of water. "A pity your mother never taught you proper manners. But no matter. To business then."

Isolda tensed. Here it came. She glanced around. No torture devices in the office, but then, she doubted Siseal would be so bold with it.

He chuckled. "Oh, no. Not your business. Not yet. There are other issues that have arisen that must be dealt with. For example, Mr. Liddel."

Gavin's eyes widened and he snapped to attention.

Siseal crossed over to him, a fatherly smile on his face. "I know you have had your doubts, but I am glad to see you are over them." He clapped Gavin on the shoulder and kept walking. "Perhaps the Almighty One will take that into account when you answer for what you've done."

Gavin frowned. "Sir?"

"Perhaps you should have asked us to detail the terms of your pardon, Mr. Liddel," Siseal continued. "You see, you were only forgiven by the Revered Hand for disobeying orders. Not for desertion. Not for lapsing into apostasy. Not for fleeing from the fold. Those are crimes for which you must still pay."

A dagger appeared in Siseal's hands. Where had he hidden that? Gavin blanched. A tremble worked down his body and into his hands.

Siseal smiled. "I'm sure you know what the penalty is for such crimes." He took a step closer, spinning the dagger lazily in his hand. "I could mete out the justice here, if I so choose. But luckily for you, I won't stain my floor with blood as unworthy as yours."

Charis clapped her hands and two guards appeared in the room. They clamped onto Gavin's arms and dragged him from the office. Halfway to the door, Gavin snapped out of his shock and tried to pull free, shouting apologies and pleading for forgiveness the whole way. Isolda wasn't sure if he was talking to her or to Siseal.

"A sorry business, that," Siseal said once Gavin was gone. "He held such promise. A shame he threw it all away. And now Altair."

Altair snapped to attention as well. To Isolda's surprise, he didn't even look at the dagger.

"You did well, my friend. I wish you had been a bit more efficient. But Isolda Westin does stand before me, as I ordered. And you even brought in Gabriel Liddel. Very well done indeed."

"Thank you, sir."

Siseal circled around Altair. Ice crawled through Isolda's stomach. The Deacon's smile was gone. Instead, Siseal measured Altair with his eyes, like a predator sizing up its prey. "But you should know that the irregularities have not gone unnoticed."

"Sir?"

"Such as your orders for Balaam to bring Ms. Westin to Crasman's Rift. Or the fact that you tried to have a private conversation with her in the *Bared Arm*'s brig. I know what you said to her . . . and what it means."

Altair stiffened, his mouth popping open. He sputtered and then pain slashed across his face. He dropped to his knees and pitched forward, the dagger embedded in his back.

"Your blood is not so common as Liddel's. And I take particular pride in the fact that I was able to purge the Revered Hand's ranks of yet another heretic." Siseal stood over Altair's dying body then frowned at Charis.

She jolted and clapped her hands. Two more guards appeared and without hesitation grabbed Altair by the arms and legs and dragged him out of the office.

Siseal turned his attention to Isolda now. She took a step back, only to run into one of her guards.

"Oh, don't worry, dear one. You will not share the same fate. Not yet. But I believe we have much to discuss. These men will show you to your accommodations. I look forward to our next encounter. Very, very much."

42

Crusader stared out over the landing bay where engineers crawled over the *Purim*. He leaned against the glass and drummed his fingers. They were behind schedule by a full day. There had been some miscommunication about what mechanical systems Keleman's propulsion unit would need. The engineers had started to remove the tunneler drive's coolant system, only to learn it was still needed. The chief engineer insisted that they would make up the time but Crusader still worried. The *Bared Arm* might have already reached Earth. Siseal might be done with Isolda already.

He considered going down to the bay and asking for another status update, but it was unlikely to have changed in the hour since he'd last asked. He pushed away from the window and resumed pacing. This was the hardest part of the mission prep. He couldn't help overhaul the *Purim*. He had already mapped out the mission. Jack reported they were ahead of schedule in manufacturing the zap-dropper projectiles. Krestyanov was almost done with the false identities, although he wouldn't stop asking Crusader why he needed them.

So what else was there for him to do? Nothing. Five more days of waiting, five more days of worrying, five more days to wear a rut in the deckplates beneath his feet. Not a good use of his time, but he didn't know what else to do.

The doors to the observation room hissed open. He glanced toward them as Elata breezed in.

She watched him for a second before smiling. "You'll only tire yourself out if you continue at that pace."

He grunted. They hadn't spoken since the planning meeting, not directly. She had sent messages urging him to relax, to spend some time with her or the other religious leaders on *The Catacombs*. He had refused. He didn't need any additional distractions. Getting to Isolda would be enough.

"How have you been feeling?" she asked.

"Fine."

Her eyes narrowed and he wondered if she could see the lie festering within him. In truth, since learning where his numbness came from and how it could kill him, it had been cutting out more and more often. Emotional storms broke over him at random, overwhelming him along with aches and minor pains that descended on him and then vanished as the numb reasserted itself. He ground his teeth as a throbbing heat built at the base of his skull.

"Sit. Right now."

His head snapped up, only to find his gaze locked with Elata's fiery eyes. Her arm, rigid as steel, jabbed at a nearby couch. Before he really knew what he was doing, he dropped into the cushions. He never even considered ignoring her. Elata took another chair. Much to Crusader's surprise, she didn't sink. Instead, she remained ramrod straight, as if perched on a board. Her eyes softened, but only slightly.

"You cannot simply keep pushing yourself. There is a time for everything, and now is the time to rest, to recuperate, and to trust my crews to do their work. We all know our jobs and our tasks. Yours, now, is to let us do what we must, and to prepare yourself for what is to come."

He nodded.

She hesitated and then leaned forward. "Tell me, have you given any thought as to what you will do should you succeed?"

A smirk tugged at his lips. She had said "should," not "when." He appreciated the reality of her words. "Go to ground. I know the location of another abandoned station. No pirates there. Figured I'd claim it and hide out until the dust settled."

"I see." She pursed her lips, then smiled. "Might I make a suggestion? Find your way back here. Dr. Smithson is reviewing your medical files and she believes she can remove the implant without killing you. She is also relatively certain she can undo the memory blocks. You may not be Aaron Sloan right now, but you could be once again."

He looked down and away. Elata had given him Naaman's files on Aaron Sloan but he hadn't read any of them. Didn't need the distraction. "We'll have to see." He forced his voice to stay even.

Her face melted into a smile. "I understand. I envy you. Even if the numbness isn't constant, it will serve you well. A wonderful gift."

Heat flared up his spine and his hands spasmed into fists. "Gift? This is no gift. This is the Ministrix's curse."

"True. But God is all about redemption: of people, of situations, even of 'curses.' Your superiors may have intended your numbness for evil, but God can and will use it for good. Emotions can be such fickle things. Such as the guilt you carry with you."

"How did you—"

"It was in your file. The Ministrix knew your guilt weighed you down and could be used to shackle you even more closely to their will. And it worked."

"They promised me the guilt would go away."

"Did it?" Her quiet question sliced through him.

"No. Not yet."

"Of course not. They lied to you, said that by obeying them, your guilt would ease. Pile on the 'holy' works. Do what they say is right. No wonder your chains are as heavy as before. They sent you in the wrong direction. Instead of bringing you to the One who could remove your guilt entirely, they drove you further from His arms."

"Why would He ever want me? It's my fault Victoria died."

"Oh? And how do you figure that?"

He closed his eyes tight. He still couldn't remember it all, but he had pieced together enough. From the Ministrix records. From his fractured dreams. "When the fire started, they paged me to go down to the cell block, oversee the evacuation. But I had been up late the night before—can't remember why—and so she went instead. To let me sleep. If I had done my job instead of leaving it to her . . ."

"And you believe this is a sin?"

"The Ministrix would say it is."

Elata snorted. "The Ministrix. They have invented more sins than the devil ever thought possible. They haven't just heaped guilt on you but on all their subjects. But here is the incredible thing. God's grace is wide enough to even swallow the made-up sins with which we torture ourselves."

"What do you mean?"

"People deal with guilt in so many foolish ways. Some, like you, slather on obedient works, hoping to somehow tip the scales in their favor. Others will do their best to hide their indiscretions, hoping that if no one else knows about them, they will somehow forget as well. The only true cure for guilt, any guilt, is found at the foot of the Cross."

He still couldn't look at her. This God she spoke of was completely unfamiliar to the one the Revered Hand spoke of. He suddenly understood why this heresy was so appealing. Austere but approachable. Almighty but alluring. He wished he could step out from behind the numbness and experience His warmth in its entirety.

"It pains me to see how badly the Ministrix twists this. That's why I hope you will come back to us after all this is over. But I understand you may not want to."

He looked up and nearly leapt out of the chair. Elata had silently crossed over to him and knelt before him. "Whatever you choose, know that He will redeem it for His glory."

When had she moved? "Even if I remain numb?"

Elata's smile radiated warmth. "You would be surprised at how large a family He has and how He finds room for everyone, no matter what their disposition. Not everyone is warm. Not everyone is emotional. Do you suppose I experience many 'warm fuzzy' moments with God? But that doesn't matter. Our relationship with God isn't a matter of how we feel toward Him but how He feels toward us. He has the same love for us when we're happy, sad, angry, or even numb." Her hands fell on his shoulders, pulled him closer. "Trust in His love. Trust in His will. And you will be fine."

They remained that way, faces hovering mere centimeters apart. He felt as if her strength flowed through her hands and into his heart, easing his pain and rebuilding the numb—only now, it wasn't a curse. It was safe. It bound him up. He could do this. He would do it.

Elata rose from her crouching position and glided toward the bay windows. "I know you are loath to talk about your future plans right now, but I'm still curious. Suppose you were to come back to us? What would your next stop be?"

Crusader frowned after her. "I wouldn't be allowed to stay?"

"We would have to discuss that, but *The Catacombs* is rarely the end of a person's journey. It is simply one stop along the way. We train here. We teach those who come to us how to live out their faith in the real world. The true Church is never called to hide in any sort of catacombs but to be among God's many people, no matter what the situation. So I ask you again, where would you want to go? Would you want to return to the Ministrix? Or would you prefer the Praesidium?"

Crusader flinched at the choice. Hard to say. If he survived this rescue attempt, he doubted he'd find any safety within the Ministrix. Siseal would hunt him for the rest of his life. He doubted the Praesidium would be much better. Given his many missions within Praesidium space, he was likely a wanted man. But maybe he could work out some sort of deal with Krestyanov.

"If I can't reclaim that station I mentioned? Probably the Praesidium. Someplace quiet."

Elata laughed. "Better a good Turk."

Crusader rose from his perch. "What does that mean? Deacon Palti said it before . . ."

Elata turned to him with a sad smile. "It is a quote from Martin Luther. This is something of a paraphrase, but he said, 'Better a good Turk' —or more appropriately, Muslim— 'than a bad Christian.' I think it means that he considered it better to live under a leader who is a good non-Christian than under a Christian who doesn't live out his or her faith. Many of the people who come through *The Catacombs* wind up agreeing with that sentiment. In many ways, the Praesidium is not much better than the Minsitrix due to the Toleration Act. But at this time, in this place, the Praesidium is the better Turk to the Ministrix's bad pseudo-Christian."

Crusader mulled that over. He could see her point. The conversation with her had helped more than she might realize. He felt stronger, surer, more so than he had in a long time. But there was one detail that refused to be silenced. "What about Isolda? Would she be welcome here with me?"

Elata smiled. "Of course."

A communications panel near Elata buzzed. She stepped over to it and thumbed the switch. "Yes?"

"I'm sorry to disturb you, ma'am." Jack's voice. "We have a situation. Someone is trying to access the communication relays. We think it's Krestyanov."

Elata spun to Crusader, her eyes wide.

He was up and moving for the door immediately. Perhaps the Praesidium couldn't be trusted after all.

He tore through the corridors, diving into a nearby elevator. Elata barely made it inside the car before the doors slid shut. She seethed next to him, her fury palpable as the car dropped into the depths of *The Catacombs*.

They finally emerged deep within the support structure. They were met by Jack, who jogged along beside them, a gun drawn and ready. Not a zap-dropper. This time, Elata didn't protest. Crusader suspected that she was half wishing to be armed as well.

They rounded a corner into a room filled with computer banks. Krestyanov sat hunched over one of them. He slapped the machine's side. Jack stepped behind him and pressed the gun to the back of his neck.

Krestyanov froze, then raised his hands. He turned, a false smile on his lips. "Is there a problem?"

"Did you really think we wouldn't find out about you hacking into our communications system?" Jack asked, his voice a bare growl.

"In truth, yes." Krestyanov shook his head. "Perhaps I have become too sloppy."

"You have abused our trust, Mr. Krestyanov," Elata's tone could have flash frozen a star. "I can only assume you were trying to bring in your associates and betray the location of this safe haven. I have half a mind to let Jack do what he wants with you. Do you have a reason why I shouldn't?"

Krestyanov's eyes widened. He turned to Crusader.

"I was not trying to contact the Praesidium," he said. "Well, not exactly. I gave my word that I would not betray *The*

Catacombs, and I do not intend to. I merely wanted to access my personal files back at my office."

"Not what I asked you to do," Crusader said. "Wanted you to make fake IDs."

"And I have them done! No, this had more to do with why your Deacon Siseal wants Isolda. I think I have the answer! But I needed some additional data to verify my thoughts. I was going to merely tap into my private files, retrieve said data, and shut down the connection."

Crusader frowned. "Why not ask for help?"

"Two reasons. I suspected this would be the reaction if I asked. Second, I do not wish for anyone to look over my shoulder while I bypass Praesidium security protocols. You know that just isn't done."

He had a point.

Krestyanov turned to Elata. "Madam, I do apologize for not coming to you with this first. But I really do believe that I may have the answer. May I please proceed?"

Elata's eyes narrowed and Crusader fully expected her to order Jack to fire. Instead, she turned to Crusader. "I leave this in your hands."

Crusader narrowed his eyes at Krestyanov. He finally nodded. "Let's see what you have."

Krestyanov beamed. He turned back to the computer, weaving a bit to avoid Jack's aim. He sat down and started to work. "The idea occurred to me while I was fabricating dear Isolda's false identity," he said, calling up some data on the computer. "I kept looking at her image and I kept thinking she looked familiar."

"Similar to Victoria." Crusader winced at the sharp stab to his stomach.

Krestyanov shook his head. "No, I do not mean her. The more I thought about it, the more I realized that I might be onto something. Once the fabrication process was done— Oh, and about those: Are you ever going to tell me why you want these false documents?"

Crusader shook his head.

"Well, I found I could not ignore my hunch, so I hacked into the medical records here to pull up Isolda's data." Krestyanov leaned in to the computer and his fingers flew over the controls. Crusader tried to follow what he was doing, but the screens shifted so rapidly he couldn't keep up. Within moments, Krestyanov leaned back with a triumphant smile and stabbed a finger at the data that now filled the screen. "I was right. Take a look at this."

Crusader leaned over. Two columns of data spilled past him. One was Isolda's. The other's was . . .

His eyes widened.

Elata touched his shoulder. "Does this change things for you?" she asked quietly.

Crusader closed his eyes. "No. If anything, it means I have to succeed."

"Ah, my dear, so good of you to join me."

Isolda didn't look at Deacon Siseal as he came around his desk. Her eyes remained fixed on the dark stain marking the spot where Altair had died. Wouldn't Siseal have cleaned that up by now? It had been a week already! She half-expected to find Altair's head mounted over the fireplace.

Siseal glided across the room, taking her arm in a gentle but firm grip. He steered her from the door and shoved her toward a large chair. "I hope that your week alone has made you more cooperative. Please, have a seat. There's much we have to discuss."

"I'm not going to tell you anything," she said.

Siseal smiled. He resembled a piranha. "They all say that. You'd think I'd tire of hearing it but no, it just entices me. I hope you prove to be a challenge." The smile hardened. "Sit down."

She fell into the chair. He stared at her with burning eyes for a few moments before going to the cabinet at one end of the office.

Isolda looked over at the door to the office. It was only a few meters away—a quick sprint and she'd be through. Siseal's assistant was just outside at her station, but Isolda was pretty sure she could make it past her.

"I don't suppose I could interest you in a drink now? I've heard our jailers are not the most hospitable individuals."

No, she wouldn't make it far if she tried to escape. She didn't know the layout of New Jerusalem Station. With her luck, she'd flee right into the arms of security. But she had to do something. Her gaze fell on a black poker resting near the fireplace less than two meters away.

"But then, we're not running a luxury resort either. Even so, for the time being, you are my guest here. Provided you are cooperative, I can make things much more enjoyable."

Isolda slid out of the chair. Could she do it? She wasn't sure. She glanced at Siseal. Ice clattered in a glass. She had to try.

Two silent bounds to the fireplace. She scooped up the poker and pivoted. He kept prattling, spouting nonsense about her cooperating. Right. She'd show him how cooperative she could be. She leapt forward, raising the poker high over her head. It sailed down, the iron cutting the air.

Only to stop as her wrist was caught in a steel grasp.

Siseal's eyes bored into hers. His features drooped into mock sorrow. "A shame you have decided not to help of your own free will." He wrenched her around, twisting her arm behind her back. The poker fell from dead fingers and he marched her back to the chair, shoved her in it. He walked to the desk and leaned against its edge. "A pity, that. If you had been forthcoming, I might have even considered releasing you. I suppose your parents must be worried sick about you right now."

Isolda clamped her mouth shut, blinking back the stinging tears. How dare this monster bring up those memories? She didn't need the reminder of how alone she was. First she'd lost her mother, then she'd had to leave *The Catacombs*. Gavin had betrayed her, and now Crusader was dead.

No. She wasn't alone. Not even now. The gentle thought rustled through her panic like wind through dry leaves. She relaxed, sat up straighter. "They'll be okay," she said, surprised at how confident she sounded.

Siseal's face soured. "Not for long, they won't." He pushed himself from the desk and started pacing a looping circuit around her chair. He clasped his hands behind his straightened back. "I suppose you're wondering why I brought you up here."

"Interrogation. Torture. That sort of thing."

He looked down at her, the corner of his mouth pulled up in a wry smile. "I hope it doesn't come to that. I truly do. I'm hoping you might come to see things my way, to understand what I hope to accomplish. And then you will tell me what I need to know."

Isolda glared at him. She kept her mouth screwed shut.

Siseal wandered from the chair to look out his window at the Earth. "I often wonder if the Almighty is ashamed of His people."

"That's a good bet," Isolda muttered. "Some more than others."

Siseal glanced over his shoulder, the same wry smile in place. "Oh, yes, I know how you heretics view the Ministrix. Barbarians. Violent oppressors. It's how the weak often view the strong. You fail to realize that we are simply fulfilling our Master's command." He pressed his hands against the glass. "'Go and make disciples of all nations.'"

Isolda laughed again, a bitter chuckle. "You're crazy."

He whirled on her. "Am I? Notice the phrasing. 'Go and make.' Imperatives both. This isn't a matter left to debate or opinion. We are to go and *make* disciples. Not invite. Not coax. Make. We are doing just that. If they do not wish to come into the Kingdom willingly, we will bring them in by any means necessary. And so I shall." He stepped away from the window and turned to his desk. "Tell me, child, are you familiar with the Paulson Compromise?"

Isolda frowned. She knew it had something to do with the military, a limit of some kind. But she didn't know the particulars. "No."

"I envy you. Would that I were so ignorant. The Compromise is a shackle on the hands of the Ministrix. It keeps us from fulfilling that divine mandate. It is an obstacle that must be overcome." He smiled. "And overcome it I shall."

He stabbed a finger onto the controls of the desk. The lights dimmed. Even the flames in the fireplace dropped lower. A massive hologram sprang to life over Isolda's head. She gasped.

Warships. A hundred at least, all in orbit of a gas giant.

"I call it the Sharp Sickle, the fulfillment of our Lord's mandate. Once it is complete, it will burst from its hidden womb and sweep the galaxy clean. It will overwhelm the heathen Praesidium and bring all under our Lord's feet."

"If the Praesidium finds out about this . . ." Isolda whispered.

Siseal laughed. "Oh, they have tried. But they're looking in the wrong place. They sent a spy to Jupiter, thinking I would be foolish enough to use our official shipyards. No, I am more subtle than that. Hidden shipyards, far from the Praesidium's border. They still don't understand what we're doing. They won't until it's too late."

Isolda stammered. "It'll never work. The Praesidium would know you're coming, and—"

"There are ways around that."

Panic twisted in her gut. No wonder Siseal wanted her. Gavin had been right: He wanted Dr. Keleman's research! In spite of what Altair thought he had discovered, in spite of how the theory had apparently been disproved, Siseal somehow knew it worked. If the Ministrix were able to harness his ideas, the Sharp Sickle could appear anywhere, overwhelm the Praesidium in one fell swoop. She stared up at the ships, trying hard not to imagine them popping into existence over other worlds. But the images wouldn't stop pouring through her mind.

Siseal knelt down next to her. He stared up at the hologram, his face awash with giddy delight. "I know. Magnificent. It has taken me years to fulfill this vision. So many obstacles. So many opponents." He rose from his crouch. "Did you know the Revered Hand opposed this plan when I first suggested it? He was more concerned about you heretics bringing down the Ministrix from within. He feared the Praesidium military, how much we could lose if we fought head-to-head." He clucked his tongue. "A shame about him. Truly."

Isolda tore her eyes from the ships and looked at Siseal. "Why?"

"Didn't you see him in the Garden? I hear he likes to spend his time there lately, ever since he became so sick."

"What's wrong with him?"

"No one knows for certain," Siseal said. And yet his tone implied he knew better than anyone. "I suppose I would benefit most if he died. I am next in line to be the Revered Hand, you know. And if that were to happen, what I envision for the glory of our Lord would come to pass. The Sharp Sickle would go out. All would be brought to heel. It is for their own good."

Isolda couldn't take her eyes off him. "But that's not what Jesus wants."

"Isn't it? Our Lord came to this world to found a kingdom."

"But a kingdom of servants, one built on grace and forgiveness."

"Such weak foundations—"

"—which have lasted for over two and a half millennia now, no thanks to people like you who want to mix the Gospel with political ambition."

Siseal leaned forward. "Such brave words, but I see the fear lurking within you. I know. I understand. You worry that your family and friends would be cut down by the Sickle. But I am gracious. I would be willing to make a trade."

What? "What kind of trade?"

"I will offer you Rahab's clemency. Like the Israelites at Jericho, I will allow you to save five people from the coming wrath. Just five. Tell me who they are, where they are, and we will make sure to spare them. All you have to do is give me what I want."

Isolda shrank back in the chair. She wanted to wrap her arms around herself, to rock back and forth. This was insane!

"You have the power now, Isolda Westin. Save your mother. Your friends. Save whomever you can. Just agree to tell me what you know and we will find them and make sure they are safe."

Isolda closed her eyes to stem the tears. She wanted to laugh. Power? What power? She had no one. No one but God. Even if she gave him what he wanted, who knew if he would keep his promises? She met his gaze. "I won't tell you anything."

A flicker of regret passed over his features. "We'll see."

44

Crusader drummed his fingers against the control console of the *Purim*. He looked around the cockpit, ignoring Krestyanov's groan.

"My friend, please settle down. We shall be ready when we are ready," the Praesidium agent said.

"The *Bared Arm* has surely made it to Earth by now," Crusader countered.

"And if we do not perform these final checks, there is a great chance that we will not."

"She could be dead!"

"But if she yet lives, can we help her if *we* are dead?"

Crusader closed his eyes, took a deep breath, let it out. Steps. Go over the steps. Completed ones first. The *Purim* was now fitted with Keleman's experimental drive. *The Catacomb*'s top programmers, with Keleman's guidance, had cobbled together an astrogation program that would target their insertion point. Crusader had bypassed one of Keleman's steps, a quick test run with the new drive system. Crusader had vetoed the idea, both in case the engines could work only once and because he didn't know what he would do if it failed.

He shook himself out of the reverie. He mentally reviewed their equipment. The fake identifications Krestyanov had crafted. The zap-droppers and their ammunition. Explosives. Computer bypasses. He and Krestyanov had spent a full day reviewing what Crusader knew about New Jerusalem and its layout. The station was huge, and security would likely lock it down the minute they realized what was happening. But Crusader was confident he could find his way even under the circumstances.

Next came Krestyanov's personal computer. Krestyanov had insisted that he come along and, if he had the time, tap into the Ministrix's secure mainframe. Crusader knew he'd need the help so he had agreed on the condition that Krestyanov plant a copy of what he had discovered about Isolda. He still had a hard time believing it, but the facts were plain. That kind of information had to be shared.

He glanced at Krestyanov. If the Praesidium spy master was nervous, he didn't show it. He ran down the pre-flight checklist with *The Catacomb*'s main controller, ticking off each item verbally. At one point, though, he paused and glanced at Crusader.

"Problem?"

Crusader shook his head. "Wanted to thank you. Didn't need to come with me."

"Oh, yes, I did," Krestyanov said. "When else will I get the chance to tap the Ministrix's central mainframe?"

"We may not have long to do that."

"I understand, but I must try anyway."

"*Purim*, are you ready?" The voice of the controller sounded strained. Crusader couldn't imagine why. He wasn't the one about to rely on an untested, experimental method of space travel that might wind up killing him.

"When you are," he replied. He closed his eyes. Breathe. In. Out. Ready.

"You may proceed."

"God's blessings on your errand, gentlemen." Elata's voice was a surprise, yet her calm tone braced Crusader.

"Thank you, ma'am. See you soon." Crusader turned to Krestyanov. "Set?"

"Let us see what happens. Firing Kelemen's system in three . . . two . . . one . . ." Krestynov reached out with a trembling finger and stabbed a button on the controls. "Now."

A screech ripped through the *Purim*, tearing through Crusader's ears and into his brain. He slammed his eyes shut and gritted his teeth.

And then it was gone. When Crusader opened his eyes, so was *The Catacombs*.

Hanging before them was New Jerusalem Station.

Crusader couldn't believe it. The engines had worked. They had arrived, having instantly crossed hundreds of light years. Hope surged through him, quelling the lingering guilt, poking through the numb. He almost giggled.

Almost.

"Any sign they've spotted us?" Crusader asked.

Krestyanov's gaze flew over the panels. "None." He flashed a toothy grin at Crusader. "We may pull this off yet!"

"Don't get cocky," Crusader responded. "Status of Keleman's drive?"

Krestyanov winced. "Fried. Completely."

"Too bad." Crusader flipped a series of switches. "Proceed as planned. Activating costuming."

A low rumble worked its way through the ship. Crusader checked the screens. The cargo doors had opened, dumping debris in their wake. The lights around him flickered. He glanced at Krestyanov. His friend nodded grimly.

Crusader took one last deep breath. Then he activated the communications relay.

"New Jerusalem, New Jerusalem, this is a priority one distress call. Repeat. Priority one distress call." He hoped he was injecting enough panic into his voice. Hard to tell for sure. "We have suffered a major system failure. Explosion in our engineering bay. We are losing power and life support rapidly. Say again, we are losing power and life support."

He paused and glanced at Krestyanov, who nodded and gave him a thumbs up. The fake transponder, labeling them as a freighter from an asteroid mining consortium, was in place.

The relay crackled. "Identify yourself."

"This is the *Holy Calling*, based out of Fides colony. Headed for the Perth Stardock when we had this emergency. We won't make it!"

Another pause. "*Holy Calling*, we don't see you on our incoming manifest. Please explain."

Krestyanov jumped in. "Look, buddy, we met our quota early and our foreman sent us in. We can talk about this more after we're safe. Or you can have our deaths on your conscience. Your choice."

Crusader gripped the edge of the panel. They weren't going for it. They'd have to use Plan B, namely ramming through the nearest docking bay doors. He doubted the *Purim* could take such an impact, but if he had to do it, he would.

"*Holy Calling*, you are cleared to land in docking bay eighteen. Please slave your navigational controls to us and we will guide you in."

"Roger that, New Jerusalem." Crusader leaned back and waited.

"*Holy Calling*, please turn over navigational control."

"We did. Aren't you receiving our telemetry?"

"Negative."

"We must be worse off than we thought," Krestyanov said.

"Very well. We are clearing the landing bay. Bring her in and try to land her as gently as you can."

"Will do," Crusader said, although he intended to do no such thing. Instead, he opened up the engines, propelling the ship forward at ever increasing speeds. He locked in the navigational computer, targeting it on docking bay eighteen.

The docking bay loomed larger and larger as the *Purim* dove for it. The New Jerusalem controller screamed for them to throttle back, reverse thrust, brake somehow. Crusader ignored him and closed his eyes.

The world exploded around him in a roar of screeching metal. He was thrown into the seat's straps, which cut into his chest and stomach. He curled around himself even tighter as the ship skidded to a halt.

When he opened his eyes, he saw emergency crews boiling out of a nearby hatch, swarming over the wreckage left by the *Purim*'s sudden entrance.

"Here we go," Krestyanov murmured as he released his straps.

They both pressed up on either side of the cockpit entrance and waited. A moment later, the docking hatch toward the rear of the *Purim* banged open and Crusader could hear several people working their way into the ship.

"Hello!" a voice shouted. "Is anyone in here? Are you okay?"

They had to be in the main hallway, approaching the bridge. He pressed farther up against the wall, closing his eyes in concentration. He counted two people. The one who had shouted was in the lead. Someone behind him relayed messages out. Anyone else? Didn't sound like it.

He opened his eyes. Krestyanov held up two fingers. He must have come to the same conclusion. Crusader nodded.

With a groan of protest, the doors to the cockpit wrenched open. An emergency technician popped his head inside and looked around. "Hello?"

Crusader snared him by the neck and dragged him inside. Krestyanov struck next, reaching through the open door to pull the man's partner inside. Crusader clamped a hand over his victim's mouth and waited. No other shouts. No alarm. Good.

"Keep quiet if you want to live," Crusader whispered. "And get out of your uniforms."

Neither set of clothing really fit but Crusader did his best with what he had. He and Krestyanov dragged the two men, whom they had rendered unconscious, closer to the hatch. They paused to grab two bags and sling them over their shoulders. Crusader paused and looked up and down the ruined hallway.

"Feeling sentimental?" Krestyanov asked.

"No."

His partner laughed. "I suppose that was a foolish question. Will you do the honors?"

Crusader reached over and ripped open a panel in the wall, exposing a large switch. He wrenched it down and then pressed a series of three buttons. Red warning lights erupted along the hallway.

Then the two of them dove out of the hatch, dragging their unconscious victims with them.

"Reactor overload!" Crusader shouted.

"We've only got two minutes!" Krestyanov added.

Panic exploded within the bay. The advancing techs turned and fled, slamming past the security guards. Crusader and Krestyanov followed in their wake, doing their best to get lost in the shuffle.

They made it out of the docking bay and kept running up the corridor with everyone else. Then the entire station rocked. Lights flickered overhead, then snapped to red. While some of the emergency crews stopped, Crusader and Krestyanov dropped their victims in the hall and pressed on.

Crusader smiled grimly. Now to find Isolda.

45

Barely restrained chaos reigned through New Jerusalem. Workers shoved past Crusader and Krestyanov, most without acknowledging them. That was fine with Crusader. If no one noticed them, they could move freely through the Station. Crusader kept an ear open to passing conversation. So far as he could tell, Station Command had evacuated the sections surrounding the docking bay. No deaths, only a few minor injuries. Elata would be pleased.

A short elevator ride deposited them in the detention center, where they were stopped by an officer, short and thin with a wispy mustache.

"What are you two doing down here?" he demanded. "The emergency is up on the docking bay level."

Crusader flicked a glance at the man's identification tag. Lieutenant Gordon Smithers. Crusader's eyes narrowed. The man tried to present himself as important: straight posture, precise pronunciation. Yet Crusader could read the tension around the man's eyes. Smither's voice wavered. Fear lurked under his cool mask. Wouldn't take much to push him to break.

"Look, Lieutenant, I know that. You know it. But our supervisor—what's his name, the new guy?—he said we had to come down here. Something about a resonance feedback in the main power conduit." Crusader pointed over the man's shoulder toward the massive pillar that ran from ceiling to floor, banded with red and yellow. "Said we should make sure it doesn't breach."

The color drained from the man's face. "B-breach? Here?" His wide eyes turned to the conduit. "Is it safe for us to be down here?"

Krestyanov shrugged. "Who can say under the circumstances? Personally, I would not remain here unless I had to, but that is me. You may be braver than I."

Crusader motioned for Krestyanov to follow him. He pulled his lockpicker from his pocket and ran it along the conduit, frowning at it. "Uh oh."

Smithers gasped. "What? What is it?"

"Nothing to worry about." Crusader pocketed the device. "Unless you haven't lived a full, rich life."

Smithers's knees wobbled and he looked ready to collapse. Another nudge should do it.

"Look, Lieutenant," Crusader said. "We're paid to take this risk. You guys aren't. Why not get out of here? Give us a half hour. We'll handle it."

Relief spread across Smithers's face. He bolted for the door, calling for his men to follow. He paused in the door and turned back to Crusader. "But what about the prisoners? There aren't many but we are supposed to guard them."

Crusader shrugged. "Not going anywhere. And if the conduit breaches, well, they'll face judgment a little sooner."

Smithers lurked in the door and then nodded. "Sounds good to me. The Almighty protect you both." He left and the door hissed shut.

Krestyanov leapt for the main security terminal, sliding into place behind it. "According to this, the lovely Miss Westin is assigned cell one-one-three-eight. I'll get to work here. With any luck, we shall be done in short order."

Crusader headed down the hall, checking the numbers by the cells as he went. Smithers was right. Not many prisoners, and they didn't seem to notice him as he passed, huddled on bunks or in corners, eyes downcast. Crusader ground his teeth. He wished there was a way to release them all. But it couldn't work. No way to get them off the Station.

Cold puddled in his feet with each step. He paused and closed his eyes. Images of Victoria danced through the darkness. The coy smile. The bright eyes. She had died in a Ministrix prison like this one. The guilt surged, surrounded him. It should have been him, not her. How could he have failed her like that? "I'm sorry," he whispered. "God, please, I'm sorry."

Then warmth coursed through him. The guilt slackened, as if slithering from his limbs. Renewed strength coursed through him. He had failed Victoria. He wouldn't fail Isolda. He took a step forward. Then another.

There. One-one-three-eight. He rushed to the door and looked through the bars.

Empty.

He stared at the bunk, not sure what to do. Could Krestyanov track her through the internal security sensors? Doubtful. No way to distinguish her from the other people on the station, and Smithers could come back. He turned, looking at the nearest cells. Unoccupied? Better to double check. Right side, empty. Left side.

He stared at Gavin Odell, a flash of anger rising in his chest.

Gavin leapt from the bunk and rushed to the bars. "Thank goodness you're here. You have to get me out of here."

Crusader took a step back, willing the numb to swallow the inferno building inside him. "Why?"

Odell blinked. "Why? What kind of question is that? Do you know what they're going to do to me here?"

"Only what you deserve."

Odell tried to say something, but his mouth snapped shut. He scuffed at the floor. "I know, I know." He closed his eyes. "You're right, of course. I betrayed you. I betrayed Isolda. I grew tired. I don't suppose you understand that, do you?"

Crusader hesitated. "More than you know."

Odell's eyes snapped open, new determination in them. "Then take me with you! Look, I know I don't deserve a second chance. But if you leave me here, it'd be like you killing me yourself."

Crusader crossed his arms over his chest. "Where's Isolda?"

Odell winced. "She's probably up in Siseal's office. At least, that's where I think they said they were taking her."

Not good. Siseal's office was higher up in the station. They'd have to take multiple elevators, run a kilometer of corridors at least, filled with security. And the confusion from their entry wouldn't last forever.

But he had to try.

The lockpicker made short work of the cell door. It popped open and Odell rushed out.

Crusader snared him by the arm. "Head to the locker room and find a uniform that fits," he ordered. "Then meet me in the main lobby. Go."

Odell sprinted away and Crusader stalked back down the hall.

Krestyanov looked up from the terminal, a frown creasing his brow. "Where is Miss Westin?"

"Have to go get her," Crusader answered.

Krestyanov leaned back in his chair, slapping the terminal. "Just as well. I cannot breach the security measures here. I hope we can find unguarded access elsewhere."

Crusader smirked. "We can arrange that."

———

Crusader's hand dropped behind his back, his fingers inching toward the bag carrying the zap-dropper. He did his best to keep his face neutral. They had almost made it to Siseal's office and no one had questioned them. But now they approached a security checkpoint, the threshold to the highest echelons of the Ministrix hierarchy. No one could make it through without a thorough screening. No weapons were allowed into the area where the Deacons worked and the Revered Hand lived. Would the sensors detect their weapons? Probably. One way to find out.

Krestyanov, Odell, and Crusader stood in line with those trying to get through. The hall narrowed at the checkpoint so only one person could pass at a time, stepping through a door whose edges shimmered with green light. A scanner, probably strong enough to count the air molecules in a person's lungs. Crusader narrowed his eyes and looked over the guards. Credible threats, every one. The best the Ministrix had to offer. In spite of the continuing emergency, they went about their business deliberately, stopping each person, inspecting their identification badges, frisking each person even after they'd stepped through the scanner. None wore armor but Crusader wondered if they'd even need it in a fight.

Nothing ventured.

Crusader glanced at Krestyanov. He nodded. He checked Odell. The smaller man, now in the uniform of a Ministrix guard, practically vibrated. Crusader winced. They had been over this. Odell had to act confident, like he belonged where he was. Authority. Had to project authority.

No sense in waiting, letting him get any more nervous. "Let's go." He turned to the people in front of them. "Make a hole! Emergency!"

The Ministrix personnel in line, so used to obeying orders, parted, allowing Crusader and his companions to sprint up to the checkpoint. Crusader nudged Odell forward.

"Uh, excuse me, Major," Odell said, "but we have an emergency in Deacon Siseal's office. Er . . . maintenance says that there's a harmonic feedback building in the conduit near here that could breach to space, and these men have to check it out immediately."

The major pointed to the shimmering door. "They go through the scanner like everyone else."

"They . . . they really don't have time for that, sir."

Crusader clenched his teeth as Odell's voice broke. Not good.

The major looked up, fixing a penetrating glare on Odell, then Krestyanov, and finally Crusader. Was that a hint of recognition? Crusader didn't know if he'd ever met this man, but it was possible. "Everyone has time for this," the major said, his voice a growl. "I have standing orders to search everyone who wishes to enter this sanctuary. Even if St. Peter himself showed up, he'd have to go through."

Crusader glanced at Krestyanov.

The Praesidium spy master shrugged. "Plan B?"

Crusader nodded. Then he lashed out and smashed the major with a right cross.

To their credit, the other guards didn't hesitate when their leader went down. They drew their weapons, but they weren't fast enough. Two of them went rigid as darts slammed into their knee and shoulder, then fell to the ground unconscious. Crusader swung the zap-dropper around, sighted, fired. The projectiles hissed through the air, catching another guard in the arm. Crusader glanced at Krestyanov. His friend slammed a new magazine into his weapon, then met his eyes.

Odell? Crusader glanced. He'd found cover. Better for everyone. He'd be out of the way.

Crusader ducked as a stray bolt flashed past him. Pain lanced through his shoulder. He cried out, almost dropping his gun. He managed to snap off another shot, taking down the man who had injured him.

Another shot came too close. Time to finish it. He looked around. The guards had clustered behind the checkpoint. Most of the bystanders had fled, but a few hid in nearby alcoves and offices. He winced. Couldn't be helped.

He unslung his pack, reached inside, and flipped a switch. Then he slid it into the checkpoint door, the scanners screaming in warning as the bag skidded to a halt. Crusader dove for the closest cover.

Thunder. Stabbing light. Smoke. Piercing screams. It all washed over him in a moment. Hot debris rained down on him, some of the fire slicing into his back. He winced but the numb mercifully returned, taking the pain with it.

He lifted his head. The fire had subsided, moans and groans began to carry over the ringing in his ears. He checked. Krestyanov emerged, mostly unscathed, though soot and some blood stained his face. Odell . . .

Crusader dropped to his side. He lay, eyes closed, arms and legs splayed. Crusader checked his pulse. Still there. A hand under Odell's nose. Still breathing. Fainted? Maybe. Crusader shook his head.

He rose and turned to Krestyanov. "Shall we?"

"I thought you'd never ask."

They picked their way across the rubble. A few of the guards tried to stop them, but their injuries prevented them from doing much more than taking a few feeble swipes at them. Deaths? Didn't appear to be any. Good. He'd hate to think of how Elata would have reacted to this.

There were more guards waiting beyond the rubble but he and Krestyanov dispatched them quickly. Crusader led the way through the winding corridors, finally arriving at the doors to Siseal's office. He checked his weapon. Five darts left in his current magazine. He glanced at Krestyanov, who had settled in at the desk outside of Siseal's office, and nodded. Then he kicked open the doors.

The room beyond was in darkness, illuminated only by flickering firelight. He inched in, gun at the ready. Crusader scanned the room. No immediate threats, although a solitary chair faced the fireplace. He crossed around it. Isolda! She slumped, her wrists manacled to the arms, apparently asleep. Crusader knelt down next to her and shook her shoulder gently.

She stirred and her eyes fluttered open. She looked at him and she gasped. "What are you doing here?"

"I came to get you." He wanted nothing more than to rip the manacles from the chair, but Isolda was obviously bait. He scanned the surrounding shadows for some hint as to where the attack would come from. No sign. Still, he couldn't leave Isolda here. He looked over the manacles. A computer controlled lock. Remote access? Possibly. He didn't see a keypad or any other sort of interface.

"Why? You have to get out of here! He knows—"

The lights blazed on. Crusader whirled, his gun at the ready.

Deacon Siseal already had a weapon trained on him. "Ah, Crusader. So good of you to join us. I see now that our party is complete."

"Siseal." Crusader rose from his crouching position.

"Stop. I don't wish to kill you."

"Lying doesn't become you, sir."

Siseal paused for a brief moment, then his smile widened. "Ah, so you know."

Crusader nodded. "More than that. I know why you wanted Isolda so badly."

The Deacon chuckled. "Do you now?"

Crusader nodded. "At first I thought it was because of Deacon Palti, like you said. But Isolda says she never spoke to him."

"Too true. We knew that already."

"Then I thought it might be *The Catacombs* or Dr. Keleman's research."

"Both admirable goals, to be sure, even if Keleman's research has proven to be false."

"Not exactly. How do you think we got here?"

Siseal's eyes widened and he laughed. "I'll add it to my list of topics to discuss with dear Isolda. Perhaps Dr. Keleman has a place in my plans after all."

"If that's not the reason he wanted me, what is?" Isolda asked.

"He wanted to talk to you because he wants to know what happened to your mother."

Siseal froze, his face frozen in surprise.

"My mother? Why would he care?" she asked.

"Because Deacon Siseal is your father."

46

Isolda's head spun and greyness crept into the corners of her vision. Her father? That ridiculous man, holding a gun on Crusader? It had to be a joke. Crusader was playing for time, coming up with a nonsensical story to stall for whatever the next part of his plan was.

Only Crusader didn't look like he was lying.

And Siseal wasn't denying it either. The deacon's face purpled, the color creeping up his neck and spilling over into his cheeks. "How did you find out?" Siseal asked.

"We pieced it together by comparing Isolda's DNA and yours. Praesidium had it on file," Crusader said.

"How is this possible?" she whispered.

Siseal didn't answer. Instead, he leveled his gun on Crusader.

"Why would he want to track me down?" Isolda asked. "Why hunt me, bring me here like this? I don't understand!"

"Probably to save his own hide," Crusader said.

"Shut up!" Siseal roared.

"You said your dad took off before you were born. My guess is, Siseal and your mom had an affair that resulted in you. Small problem: Their relationship was sinful. Not only was it out of wedlock, Siseal had yoked himself to an 'unbeliever.' What do you suppose the Revered Hand would do to him if anyone learned about you or your mother?"

It looked as if Siseal was about to explode. "Shut up, Crusader!"

"You don't think she has a right to know?" Crusader took a step forward. "Especially about what you did to her mother?"

Isolda stared at Crusader. What? Did Siseal have something to do with it? Crusader's tone suggested he did, but how was that possible? It had been an accident, a horrendous, awful . . .

"Isolda told me her mother died on the *Vaettir*. We both know the Ministrix did that. And Isolda said that her mother was scared beforehand. Almost like she knew someone was after her. But what did she fear?" Crusader paused. "Maybe her former lover's wrath? Over the fact that there was now tangible proof of their affair, namely a daughter whose DNA could prove he had sinned?"

Siseal fired. Crusader had already moved, rolling out of the way and diving for cover. Siseal roared in frustration and fired again. "You think it didn't kill me? I had no choice! If anyone found out what I had done, they would destroy me. I had to . . . I had to . . ."

"You had to kill her. And now me." Isolda was surprised her voice had the strength it did.

Siseal froze. He looked at her, sorrow stitching across his face. But then he turned and fired into the shadows again.

Apparently he missed. "You thought you got them both, didn't you?" Crusader said. "Isolda was supposed to be on the *Vaettir* as well. Then Palti went heretic. You probably saw Isolda's name on the crew roster of that Praesidium ship. Wondered if she was your daughter. Better take care of her, just in case. And that got you thinking. She'd survived the 'accident,' maybe her mom had too. Only one way to find out."

Isolda winced as Siseal fired. He had to have hit Crusader this time.

Nope. "Connor trap. Get Isolda, kill me. Two birds with one stone. You'd interrogate Isolda to find out if Mom was dead, you'd have the only proof of your indiscretion, and your position would be safe."

"Yes! All right? That's exactly how it is! If my beloved brethren learned about what I did, it would all be over. The Sharp Sickle. My carefully laid work. All of it gone! She had to die. They both did."

"You had no right!" Isolda screamed. "How could you do that? How could you do that to me?"

Siseal glanced in her direction and then he was gone, tumbling into the darkness.

⚊⚊◖═▸

Siseal tried to get free. Crusader wouldn't let him escape. The older man tried to punch him, tried to push him away. Wouldn't help. This ended now.

Crusader smashed a fist across Siseal's jaw and the man fell still. Crusader looked down at the fallen man. Fire and ice chased through his limbs, deep into his heart.

Siseal had started this. He had set Crusader after Isolda—ordered the murder of his own daughter. He had given Balaam his orders. All to save his miserable life.

Shame it didn't work.

He nudged Siseal with his toe, rolling the man onto his stomach. He unslung the zap-dropper and checked it. The indicator light still shone blue. Normal setting. But Siseal deserved more than just to be knocked out.

He thumbed the selector switch on the grip and the tone pitched higher, the light shifting to a harsh red. He lined up the barrel with the back of Siseal's skull. A little pressure on the trigger and the dart would be driven through his head and into the decking below. No way bone could stop it.

Just a little pressure.

"Crusader?"

His finger tightened on the trigger but froze.

Siseal deserved this. He wanted to live by the sword. He had unleashed it countless times. Now he could die by it.

His finger refused to squeeze.

He frowned. Siseal had tried to kill him. He would have killed Isolda once he'd learned what he wanted. Only fair. Eye for an eye. That was the way the Ministrix did things.

But is it the way He would do things?

The voice sliced through the angry thoughts roiling through his mind. The barrel drooped away from its target.

The void exploded in his mind, snarling and thrashing, demanding Siseal's blood. He had sins to answer for.

"Crusader? What are you doing?" Isolda asked.

He closed his eyes. Siseal deserved to die. He had no doubt of that. But Crusader also knew that if he did the killing, the void would only grow worse. This was the Ministrix's way. It was his no longer.

He switched back to the nonlethal setting and aimed a bit lower and shot Siseal in the rear. The older man twitched and then relaxed. Now for Isolda. It was time to do what he had to do no matter how much it would hurt.

Crusader appeared out of the darkness and knelt down next to her. "You all right?"

She laughed, bitterness bubbling through her. All right? How could she ever be all right? She'd learned that the "accident" that had claimed her mother's life had actually been a murder, that her father was the monster who had done it. That he had ordered her own assassination. Her entire life had tipped and scattered and . . .

He leaned in closer, his eyes wide and searching. "Are you okay?"

The fear subsided. It vanished in a warm haze that wrapped her in a cocoon. He touched her arm, caressed her cheek. She closed her eyes, leaned into it. She wanted to wrap her arms around him, hold him close, thank him for coming after her, even if they'd never make it off the station.

Her hands moved of their own accord, clutching at his shoulders, twining around his neck.

Wait. What had happened to the manacles?

"You found the controls?" Crusader asked, but not of her.

"I apologize that it took me so long," a man's voice said. "I found much to occupy my attention, as you might well imagine."

Isolda's eyes snapped open. Kolya Krestyanov stood behind Crusader. She gasped.

Krestyanov smiled. "A pleasure to see you again as well, Ms. Westin. Shall we leave?"

Crusader helped her out of the chair. "Long story."

She looked between them. "I imagine so."

They started for the door. As they went, Isolda looked at Siseal's crumpled form, a dart of some kind poking out of his robes. "What about him?"

Crusader glanced in Krestyanov's direction. "Taken care of. Right?"

The Praesidium agent nodded. "I submitted a report to the Revered Hand, detailing your parentage. I believe he shall find it quite illuminating. Of course, I also helped myself to whatever data I could find. As you originally promised, Crusader, I finally have enough for Praesidium analysts to sift for years. That is, if we can escape."

"You two don't have a plan?" Isolda asked.

"He does," Krestyanov said. "But he has yet to share it with me."

Isolda glanced at Crusader. His face remained calm as they strode out of the office and into a hallway heavy with smoke.

She stumbled to a halt. "Gav!" She rushed to her friend's side. She whirled to Crusader. "What happened to him?"

"Fainted," Crusader said. "Would've thought he'd have recovered by now."

"So now what?" Krestyanov asked.

"You inserted the fabricated identities into the database?" Crusader asked.

"I did. And I cleared the shuttle like you asked along with setting up the core overload to start in half an hour."

Isolda froze, ice spiking through her spine. "Overload?"

Crusader smiled, his eyes hooded. "All part of the plan."

"Are you ever going to share it with us?" Krestyanov demanded.

Crusader nodded. "But you have to do one more thing for me."

"What's that?" she asked.

"Forgive me." Crusader's arm snapped up and he fired. A dart hissed through the air and slammed into Krestyanov's back. The Praesidium agent stiffened and then crumpled to the floor.

Isolda gasped. What was Crusader doing? Had he lost his mind? Why had he attacked Krestyanov?

And why was he looking at her like that? She backed up, stumbling over loose debris.

Crusader turned, his features slack. He raised his gun again. Her eyes locked with it. Would he really shoot her? He aimed. "I have to do this."

"Please . . . no . . ."

He fired. A prick in her thigh. Then fire coursed through her body as every muscle contracted. She screamed. Then the inferno subsided and warmth rushed through her veins and darkness swam in her vision. She tried to speak, tried to move, but the blackness crushed her down . . . down . . . down . . .

Crusader waited as Isolda fell into unconsciousness. He removed an identity chit and tucked it into Isolda's pocket. He fixed another chit to Krestyanov's collar. He glanced at Odell. He pulled out the third chit, the one he had intended to destroy. He knelt down and affixed it to Odell's collar.

"You're welcome," he whispered.

Standard operating procedure. What were three more bodies in the aftermath of a rogue attack? No one would realize they had been part of the raid. And when the station's core threatened to overload, probably because of damage incurred from the *Purim*'s collision, the emergency personnel would evacuate all three from the station. If the identities held, they might be able to disappear, lie low, get to safety. Maybe back to *The Catacombs*. Who knew? Best chance they had.

Only one problem: Security would have to find someone, fight someone. If they didn't, everyone would be suspect. Isolda, Krestyanov, Odell, they'd be caught.

Crusader squared his shoulders. He'd planned this from the beginning. He'd be the decoy. Lead them away. Escape if he could. Sacrifice himself if he couldn't. He smoothed back Isolda's hair. "I'm sorry for so much. But not for meeting you." He kissed her forehead. Then he started running. Had to put as much distance between the checkpoint and himself as possible.

The security teams caught up with him two levels down. Three squads, thirty men. The young man at the fore hesitated, pausing to shout that he'd found the intruder. Crusader didn't hesitate, opening fire. The boy went down screaming. Crusader ran, lasers flashing past him. He turned and returned fire. He winged one, hit another, couldn't be sure. More boiled out of side hallways. He emptied the weapon's magazines as quickly as he could, discarding the depleted cases as he went. The final guard went down in a heap. Crusader glanced around. He'd made it to the bay.

The doors ground open, revealing a tiny, one man shuttle. Crusader started forward. He'd have to skip the pre-flight checklist. He'd warm up the engines, blow the doors to the bay if he had to, and lead whatever ships waited on a chase. He slipped into the pilot's seat and started the engine's pre-flight warm-up. Nothing would stop him . . .

Except for the cool metal of a gun pressed against the back of his neck. He turned slowly and found himself face to face with Charis, Deacon Siseal's personal assistant.

"I think that's far enough, don't you?" she asked.

47

"**Did you hear what just happened?**"

Whose voice was that? Isolda tried to focus. Did she know this person?

"No, what?"

And who was that? What had happened to her? Why was she on the floor?

"You know how they're saying some intruder got into the station? Well, I heard he stole a shuttle."

"How'd he manage that?"

"Don't you know who it was? It was Crusader, Siseal's top guy."

Crusader? Isolda's eyes snapped open.

Two medics in clean white uniforms knelt down by her. One ran a scanner over her while the other sorted through a bag of supplies. What was going on? How had she gotten here? Wherever *here* was.

"Oh, come on. Why would he attack New Jerusalem?"

"Scuttlebutt is, he went rogue. Flaked out on a mission and everything. I've got a friend in Intelligence and he said that they've been searching for him for weeks."

"Wow. Must be true if he attacked us here."

"He got what he deserved. Like I said, he stole a shuttle, piloted it out of here. And an entire wing of fighters destroyed him."

No! Isolda moaned and tried to sit up.

That got the medics' attention. One gently pushed her back down. "Careful, ma'am. You're pretty banged up. You must have gotten caught in the crossfire, huh? Don't worry, we're going to take very good care of you."

"And once you're feeling stronger, you'll have to tell us your version of what happened. I'm dying to hear all about Crusader."

Isolda doubted he'd really want to hear what she thought of Crusader, the Ministrix, or this stupid medic. She groaned and tipped her head to one side. There was Krestyanov. A medic looked him over as well. He met her gaze. She bit her lip. How could this happen?

An alarm klaxon ripped down the hall. The medics' heads snapped up and they looked around.

A security guard rushed into the hallway. "Okay, everyone, evacuate! Core breach in progress. Engineers are trying to lock it down, but they want all non-essential personnel off the station in case they can't. Let's go."

The medics helped her onto a gurney. And then they were off, the overhead lights whizzing past her. She tried to look around. Were Krestyanov and Gav with her? Would they be separated?

They reached an elevator and she was wheeled in.

"Sorry, ma'am. I guess it'll be a bit of a squeeze, huh?" one of the medics said.

Isolda popped her head up. She was still with Krestyanov and Gav. Good. But standing in one corner of the car . . .

Charis stared back at her, recognition flashing through her eyes. Isolda dropped to the gurney, cursing herself. If she hadn't looked up . . .

"Hold it." Charis's voice cut through the medic's chatter. "These three patients. I was coming to look for them. I want you to take them to Deacon Siseal's personal shuttlecraft. He will see to their care."

"Ma'am?"

"You heard me! Or do you wish to contact the Deacon of Intelligence so you can question his orders to his face?"

"No, ma'am!"

The doors to the elevator opened a short while later and the overhead lights whizzed past. Isolda reached around, trying to feel for what kept her on the gurney. Maybe she could roll off, run. She might not make it far, but she should at least try.

It was too late. More doors opened and Isolda could smell fuel. A docking bay. The gurney tipped as it went up a ramp and then Isolda found herself staring at the ceiling of a shuttle craft, two conduits running the length of the cabin.

"Thank you, gentlemen," Charis said. "You may leave us."

"But uh, ma'am? Don't you think you'll need some help? I mean, there are three of them, and—"

"I said you may leave us. Or shall I get the Deacon to reiterate my orders?"

The medics left in a scurry of feet. Isolda tensed, trying to hold back the tears. It wasn't fair. Siseal might get what was coming to him, but it wouldn't matter. Crusader was dead and soon she would be too.

Charis appeared over her, looking her over. "Can you sit up? I'd like to move you to a seat before we depart."

Isolda glared at her. Charis smiled, an impish twist of her lips. "I am sorry, Isolda. Shall I assume that I've let the king of Aram lean too heavily on my arm in the house of Rimmon?"

What did that mean? Aram? Rimmon? The names were familiar. Where had she heard them before?

Her eyes widened. Could it be? Was Charis really . . . "Naaman?"

Charis nodded, pulling her up. "Don't worry. You're safe. Siseal is still in his office. I believe he's trying to expunge a report submitted to the Revered Hand. I don't think he's having a lot of luck."

Isolda stared at her. "I thought . . . I thought Altair was . . ."

"One of us? He was. Too impetuous and too quick to take risks," Charis turned to Krestyanov and helped him sit up. "I should confiscate whatever it is you stole, but seeing as I've recently resigned my position, I'm not all that worried about it."

Krestyanov bowed, dipping his head a bit. "I thank you, madam. And for the rescue."

Charis moved on to Gavin.

"Now what?" Isolda asked.

Charis glanced back at her. "Now we get out of here. The shuttle will bring us to Earth. I have some contacts with the underground church in Bolivia. We'll land there, lay low. We can arrange for transport off Earth in a few days."

Isolda nodded. It would be good to put this behind her. But with that thought came the crushing realization that Crusader was gone. She crumpled, hugging herself, finally letting the tears come.

Charis was at her side in an instant. "What's wrong?"

"Crusader . . . he . . . the medics said that he . . ."

"That I what?"

She whirled.

Crusader stepped into the cabin. Isolda gasped and tried run to him but her leg buckled beneath her. He covered the distance and caught her. "I'm so sorry," he whispered. "I didn't want to hurt you but I wanted it to look as realistic as possible."

She cried, ignoring what he was saying. She just held on to him, glad to have him there. She looked at Charis.

"They said he died. In a shuttle he stole."

"That was the plan," Crusader said.

Charis nodded. "But I caught him and brought him here. Autopilot handled the rest. Now come on, take a seat. We'll need to enter Earth's atmosphere soon."

Isolda did. Crusader sat next to her. She laced her fingers through his. "You won't leave me again?"

He shook his head. "No. Count on it."

EPILOGUE

"How is he doing?"

Isolda looked up as Kolya sat down next to her.

"I don't know," she answered. "Dr. Smithson hasn't come to see me yet. It's been six hours. What's happening in there?"

He shrugged. "It is a delicate procedure, yes?" He placed a hand on her shoulder, gave her a squeeze. "Relax. He is strong. He'll be fine."

Isolda closed her eyes and offered up a silent prayer that it'd be true.

The trip back to *The Catacombs* had gone better than she'd ever expected. Charis had arranged for a private yacht, an expensive one, to take them back to Crasman's Rift. Then

Siseal's former assistant had disappeared into the crowd at a Waystation, leaving a cryptic note about spending some time in the wilderness.

Gavin had left at the next Waystation. Isolda had tried to convince him to stay, but her friend had refused. "I have a lot of soul searching to do," he had said. "Don't worry. I may show up at *The Catacombs*. Apparently I have a lot more learning to do too."

That left Krestyanov, Crusader, and Isolda together. She had hoped the Praesidium spy master would leave at some point, but he'd refused. He'd insisted on escorting them the rest of the way.

But he had given them their privacy. He'd spent most of his time in his quarters, beginning a preliminary analysis of the intelligence he had stolen from New Jerusalem's mainframe. When Isolda had asked Crusader what he thought of that, the former Ministrix assassin had simply shrugged and said, "Better a good Praesidium agent." Whatever that meant.

They had spent their time together discussing what Crusader had learned about her family. Accepting that Deacon Siseal was her father was hard enough. Learning that Crusader had once been married, and to her cousin . . . she could barely wrap her mind around it. It seemed so incredible, and yet, flying back to *The Catacombs*, she couldn't deny that God had brought good from this bizarre situation.

Much to Isolda's relief, Elata had welcomed them back with open arms. She'd never mentioned the accident. And Dr. Keleman had been ecstatic, demanding to debrief Crusader and Krestyanov on their experience on board the *Purim* immediately.

Crusader had refused. He'd scheduled surgery with Dr. Smithson. And so, earlier that morning, he had gone in, leaving Isolda to pace in the waiting room.

She glanced at Kolya. "So what are you going to do now?"

"Well, there is the matter of this 'Sharp Sickle.' Nasty business, that. But we have people who can deal with it. And even official channels for diplomatic protests if my methods fail." He shrugged. "For now, I was hoping to convince your man to come back with me. Not as an agent, mind you. As a consultant. I think my colleagues would find that he would have insight into how the Ministrix operates, yes? He—and yes, you too—would live quite comfortably."

"What about the Toleration Act? You'd have to report us, wouldn't you?"

Krestyanov's wide smile faltered. "Technically, yes. I would. But perhaps . . . well, perhaps I would have to overlook the . . . the eccentricities of my friends. From what Elata tells me, Ministrix Intelligence isn't the only one to have a Naaman. Apparently we have a similar infestation. I may just have to find those people."

Isolda met his gaze. There was something about his tone, something plaintive. "Why?"

He smiled. "Much of what I do, much of what my government does, it is in reaction to the Ministrix. The Toleration Act, for example. It was believed that any form of faith led to powermongering and hate. But after spending so much time with you 'heretics' here in *The Catacombs*, I wonder if maybe we have gone too far." He slapped his thighs and rose. "But listen to me. Too sentimental. Let me know when he's able to talk. At the very least, I wish to say goodbye to him." And with that, Kolya left.

Isolda sat back. The Praesidium? Maybe. As good of a place as any for God's people to work.

———

Steps. Break it down to steps.

Breathing first. In. Out. He could breathe. Good sign.

Next, the light, stabbing through his eyelids. He groaned and shifted. A dull ache radiated through his abdomen. Dr. Smithson had said that there might be some postoperative irritation. He hadn't expected it to be so bad.

Wait. He had an ache. He had pain. It had stayed with him. No numbness.

Giddy twinges danced through him. He opened his eyes.

Dr. Smithson smiled down at him. "Glad to see you're awake."

"The operation?" His voice was little more than a croak.

"A complete success. The implant's out. We're working on a procedure for the mental blocks, but we have some leads and can probably get to work on that soon if you want. In the meantime, you have a visitor."

Crusader let his head loll toward the door. Isolda stood before him, more radiant than he ever remembered her. She looked down at him, her lower lip trembling. How he wanted nothing more than to sit up, take her into his arms, and hold her. To let her know it was okay. To say to her how much he thanked God—the real one, not the copy the Ministrix had invented—that he had met her.

"How do you feel?" she asked.

He smiled, and the sheer joy of her swept through him, making his smile the most real experience he could remember.

"I feel great."

ACKNOWLEDGMENTS

This one has been a long time coming. I actually wrote *Numb* a long time before I started writing Failstate's adventures. A lot of people helped me along the way. If I have forgotten anyone here, please know that it's due to faulty memory on my part, not because your contribution wasn't appreciated.

Thanks go, first and foremost, to my wonderful wife, Jill, who continually spurs me on to pursue my dreams. Superheroes and space assassins are nothing compared to the adventure of being married to you, and that's a good thing! I also want to thank my boys, who inspire me to greatness, because I know that they're both destined for greatness themselves.

I also want to thank Ronie Kendig, Sharon Hinck, and Jill Williamson, all who looked over different drafts of this story. Their insight and enthusiasm were invaluable.

The folks at American Christian Fiction Writers are a literal Godsend, a valuable resource that cannot be discounted. I can honestly say I wouldn't be where I am now if it wasn't for ACFW.

I am continually in awe that I'm represented by the fantastic Amanda Luedeke. She is a great partner and a great friend and I appreciate everything she does for me.

The same can be said for Jeff Gerke. I am so proud to say that I'm a Marcher Lord and I appreciate the fantastic way that Jeff supports, encourages, and teaches me.

Most of all, I want to thank and praise my Creator, Redeemer, and Sanctifier, for the way His grace upholds, strengthens, and inspires me. May all I do be for His glory!

CPSIA information can be obtained at www.ICGtesting.com
Printed in the USA
LVOW06s1636160915

454435LV00007B/959/P